VALE
OF
STARS

By
Sean O'Brien

JournalStone
San Francisco

JournalStone books may be ordered through booksellers or by contacting:

JournalStone
199 State Street
San Mateo, CA 94401
www.journalstone.com

The views expressed in this work are solely those of the authors and do not necessarily reflect the views of the publisher, and the publisher hereby disclaims any responsibility for them.

ISBN: 978-1-936564-61-3   (sc)
ISBN: 978-1-936564-62-0   (ebook)

Library of Congress Control Number: 2012949587

Printed in the United States of America
JournalStone rev. date: December 14, 2012

Cover Art and Design: Jeff Miller

Edited By: Dr. Michael R. Collings and Elizabeth Reuter

ACKNOWLEDGEMENTS

I am grateful for Christopher Payne at JournalStone for believing in this novel, and to his staff for their hard work on it.

I want to thank my mother, Gina, and my father, Jim, who fostered in me a love of reading and of telling stories.

I also want to thank my brother, Jeff, for allowing me to test my childhood theories of propulsion on our Radio Flyer wagon. With him in it.

Lastly, my gratitude to my family knows no bounds. My beautiful wife, Sue, and our children, Katie and James, have been an unending source of support. I love you all.

DEDICATION

To my mother, Gina; my wife, Sue; and my daughter, Katie.

BOOK ONE
SHIP

CHAPTER
1

The ball arced through the air, curving gently in the slight Coriolis effect. Jene Halfner, watching her daughter catch it, wondered if either of them could ever really adjust to planet-bound life.

"Here you go, Mommy," Kuarta said, tossing the ball high into the air. The rays of the sunrod caught the ball in flight. Jene tracked the ball as it sailed over her head, but was momentarily distracted by the sight of New Omaha above her. The ball landed on the street where the two were playing, the rows of six-story apartments on either side of the narrow lane.

"Mommy!" Kuarta said, laughing.

"Sorry, hon. I think it's time to go in. Daddy will have dinner ready by now."

"Well, okay," Kuarta said, and skipped lightly into the tiny building that contained their apartment along with the apartments of thirty-five other families.

Jene shielded her eyes from the sunrod and tried to make out the horses in New Omaha. She thought she could see a few Neoclydes grazing above her, but at this distance the tiny specks could easily have been people. Even though the Omaha orchard was almost as far away from their apartment as anything could be in Ship, they were still close. Maybe she would take Kuarta and Renold for a picnic there tomorrow, if she could clear some time from her schedule and if no broken bones came into the hospital. Perhaps the three of them could even take a world-walk. Kuarta had only been on two before, and both times had been greatly amused. "Mommy," she had said, "how did we do that? We walked the same direction and came back to where we started!" Jene smiled as she remembered watching Renold roll up a piece of paper into a tube to explain the nature of their world. Yes, she thought, the orchard for tomorrow.

She had always liked the orchard, and not because it was an island of openness amid a sea of crowded humanity. Jene did not mind the crowds; in fact, she enjoyed the closeness of human contact. The orchard was attractive because it was the only place in Ship where Kuarta could dig as deep as she wanted and not run into the cold deck-plate. Jene remembered the first time Kuarta had done that about a year and a half ago in one of the tiny greenbelts that dotted the Residential Four complex. A careless hull worker had not bothered to properly replace the surface soil to its proper depth of one-point-six meters, and Kuarta had found herself, and her toy shovel, up against a dull grey barrier. There had been no tears from the little girl, just gentle amusement at the sight of the metal.

"You okay, Jene?"

Jene spun around, her mind snapping back into the present. Franklin Mussard stared at her good-naturedly from under the brim of his old-fashioned straw hat. He was standing in the entryway of his ground-floor apartment, below Jene's family's apartment on the sixth floor. All he needed to complete the picture of the fabled Terrestrial farmer was a strand of hay clamped loosely in his teeth. And, of course, blue sky behind him.

"Oh, sure, Frank. Just thinking of taking the family to the orchard tomorrow."

Frank nodded his approval. "Sounds good. We haven't been there in…hell, five months, I think. So damn busy. I should take Nancy and Wendy. But the work is…."

"I know what you mean. Things are starting to get hectic for me, too."

"How's the panimmunity going?"

"Pretty good. I'd say we've got about seventy, seventy-five percent of Ship done. We'll be ready." Jene stopped to smile and wave a silent greeting at another shipmate leaving the building.

Frank nodded again, then was silent for a moment. When he spoke again, it was in a husky voice, an expectant voice. "You think we'll be able to make it?"

Jene knew what he meant. He was not asking now about the Panimmunity Project but about the future in general. The question was on every adult's mind, if not their tongues. To have lived thirty-plus years, from birth to middle adulthood, on board Ship—Ship, which was the whole world—knowing the day would come when the journey that your great-great-grandmothers and -grandfathers had started over one hundred years before would come to a close in your lifetime was not easily dealt with. The inhabitants of Ship did so by tending to their work, preparing the great Ship for the final leg of its voyage, but not thinking too precisely on the event. Only the eighteen-member Flight Crew ever looked out at Epsilon Eridani, around which their future home orbited. Jene and the rest of the eight thousand-plus complement of colonists worked on their tasks, almost able to keep their thoughts inside Ship.

"We have to, Frank. Not for us, though. For the next generation."

Frank nodded, but his eyes frowned. "That's what everyone says. I wonder, though...." He stopped as the Delacruz family of four approached. Frank and Jene exchanged greetings and a few pleasantries with the Delacruz family before the latter entered the apartment complex. Jene waited until they were out of earshot to prompt Frank again.

"You wonder what?"

Frank looked away. "You've seen things," he said vaguely.

Jene scowled at him. This had been brought up before, but now, Jene was determined to make him say what he was implying. "What things?"

Frank snorted. "You know. The effects of the trip." He paused, as though gathering strength for the word that was to come. "Radiation." The taboo word hung in the air for a moment before Frank spoke again. "Hell, Jene." Now he turned to her, aggressively, daring her to refute him, hoping she could. "We're the fourth generation. Your kid and my kid are in the fifth. That's a helluva lot of cosmic rays they've soaked up. I've heard what's come out of the hospital. Cancer. Leukemia. Downs Syndrome. Congenital brain defects. That's the next generation, Jene. Is that really what we are working for? Because...." he stopped.

"What, Frank? Because what?" Jene felt her anger rising. "Say it, dammit! Because we should just start over?"

Frank quickly looked around for others who might have heard the outburst. There were, of course, several people nearby, working on this or that or simply enjoying themselves in the rays of sunrod. There were always people around—it was an accepted aspect of Ship life. Politeness and courtesy were very important social constructs in Ship; Jene's exclamation, though relatively mild, was nevertheless powerful.

Frank did not meet her gaze but looked away, giving no answer.

Jene pressed her point. "I've heard that before. Gen Five has got some problems. So what? You ready to take little Bobby and throw him into the fusion converter?"

"Damn it, that's not what I mean, and you know it," Frank said, taking his hat off and slapping it against his leg. He did not bother to look about him this time.

Jene saw she had gone too far. The image of little, blind, microcephalic Bobby Yancy, smiling up in her direction as she sponge bathed him, swam in front of her mind's eye. Just as most of Gen Five had come to represent the collective dream of the colonists, Bobby was their reminder of their nightmare.

"Yeah," Jene whispered. "I'm sorry." The tension and despair was almost palpable between them. Both shuffled uncomfortably in their stances, but Jene was reluctant to leave the conversation on a note of dread, and she suspected Frank was as well.

She spoke first, her voice bright. "Why don't you and Nancy and Wendy come along with us to the orchard? I'm sure your work crew can spare you for a day. Don't you have some vacation coming up?"

"Not really. You medical doctors have it easy—us spin doctors do the real work," he said, smiling.

Jene smiled back. Frank returned to his usual banter about the merits of propulsion reorientation work, or "spin doctoring" as he and some of the others called it. Since the solar sail had been redeployed a few weeks ago for deceleration, angular acceleration of the drum had combined with deceleration effects to produce slight g forces in inconvenient corners of Ship. Frank and many other workers were busily reconfiguring the more essential elements of Ship for the remaining few months of the journey so those inside could continue to function.

"I keep telling you, all you have to do is build one of those science-fiction anti-gravity machines," Jene said as seriously as she could.

Frank slapped his forehead in an exaggerated motion. "Of course! Anti-gravity! And after that, we'll make a teleporter so we can just"— he snapped his fingers—"over to E.E. three. No more spin, no more complicated calculations, no more radiation...." He stopped again. The word had snuck up on him, and both knew instantly that their conversation and the issue they had raised would not be so easily dismissed by a trip to the orchard.

"Yeah," Jene said. "Anyway, Frank, come with us, okay? It'll do both of us good."

"Yeah. I'll see what I can do."

"G'bye, Frank."

"Bye."

* * *

Jene looked over the dinner plates at Renold. He was fussing with the garnish—a sure sign he wanted to talk but would wait until she was ready.

"I invited Frank and his family to go with us to the Orchard tomorrow for a picnic," Jene said carefully.

"Oh, that'll be good," Renold murmured absently. "You can arrange for time off from the hospital?"

"Sure. I'm owed some back time."

Renold nodded. "I'll have to take my finder, of course."

"I know." He was always on call, never on duty. As Ship's most trusted and competent psychotherapist, he dealt with only the most serious cases: ones that threatened Ship itself or some vital part of the mission. He had had more contact with the eighteen members of the Flight Crew than any other colonist. He never talked about them. Jene had stopped asking years ago.

"Kuarta, dear, you have homework to do, yes?" Renold said.

Kuarta nodded.

"Well, go on to your room and start on it, please, dear. I'll be in shortly to help you if you need it. You can use computer, but no games until you're done, all right?" He spoke calmly, as if to an adult, as he always did to his daughter. There was very little difference in Renold's tone no matter the audience.

"Okay, Renold," she said, addressing him as she always did. It was "Mommy" and "Renold," even though he was her biological father. Long ago, the discrepancy had bothered Jene, but Renold, as usual, had been able to soothe her. It was of no consequence, he said often, but Jene couldn't help but wonder if there was even the smallest bit of regret behind his words.

Kuarta disappeared into her section of the tiny apartment. Fewer than sixty square meters of space were allotted per person in Ship. It was claustrophobic, even if one had lived their entire life on board, as all Gens had since Gen One. The human need for open spaces could not be entirely bred out or conditioned away. It was why Renold and his lesser colleagues were so valuable—technicians kept the machinery operational, but Renold kept the technicians themselves operational.

"Why the orchard, dear?" Renold said, clearing the table.

"Oh, I don't know. I just thought...."

"Since we'll be landing in four months, you want to get Kuarta used to openness?"

"I guess that's it."

"I see," he said, then fell silent, like he always did. He would wait her out.

"It's not going to work, is it?" Jene said finally.

"What? Trying to acclimate Gen Five to life planet-bound? Or the mission itself?"

"I wonder if those aren't the same thing."

"Hmm. Good point."

Jene handed her husband the rest of the tableware. "Frank talked about radiation today."

Renold stopped wiping down the dishes. "Oh?"

"Don't you ever wonder why Kuarta came out the way she did?"

"We've talked about this before, dear. You cannot feel guilty about this. You're genetically pure, and so am I. You've told me time and time again that we escaped radiation damage through chance."

"Is that why you married me?" As soon as she uttered the words, she looked away. "I'm sorry, I...."

"Do you think that?" Calmly. Jene knew he would not allow himself to grow angry at the accusation.

It was useless trying to lie. "Sometimes."

"Well, it isn't true. I married you because I fell in love with you and I wanted to create a family with you." He spoke matter-of-factly, as if he were discussing the meal they had just eaten. "Frank bothers you, doesn't he?"

"Well, yes. Wendy is Gen Five too. I think he's angry at us."

"I thought Wendy only has minor, inconsequential mutations."

"Doesn't matter. You've seen the way Frank watches Wendy and Kuarta play together. You're an analyst—don't tell me you can't read him."

"Yes, I can."

"Frank wants to know why his kid isn't perfect like ours, doesn't he. And there's no goddamn answer!" Jene slammed her fist down on the small counter. One of the dessert plates clattered to the floor, the unbreakable plastic bouncing noisily off the tile.

"The orchard tomorrow, then," Renold said evenly, picking up the plate and wiping it down.

Jene looked at him for a long moment, wanting to speak, or more accurately, wanting him to do something, feel something. He was infuriatingly cold as he continued the chores. Jene knew it wasn't his fault—it was a combination of his personality and his training. She just wished—fruitlessly, she knew—that with her, at least, he could abandon control.

* * *

The orchard was beautiful. Frank, his wife, Lena, and their daughter, Wendy, had traveled there with the Halfners on the bicycles that the inhabitants of Ship used for nearly all long-range personal transportation. There were, of course, ground vehicles for emergencies and freight platforms for bulk cargo, but when people needed to travel even long distances, they walked or rode bicycles.

Gil Tannassarian, who ran the orchard, was a kindly Gen Three well-known to Jene. He smiled at her and her five companions as they dismounted and parked the bicycles in their racks in front of the orchard. Gil was leaning his elbows on a simulated wood-beam fence that surrounded the acreage of the orchard and beaming at his visitors.

"Jene! How are you, my girl?" Gil had promised he would never forget the life-saving procedure Jene had performed on his Gen Five granddaughter Millicent, who had had severe heart defects. Millicent had pulled through despite all predictions and was now about Kuarta's age.

"I'm good, Gil." She smiled back. She knew the rumors: that the old Gen Three had been a candidate for Flight Crew in his youth but had been rejected during his final psych tests. People said (out of his hearing, of course) that something had happened to him up there on the Flight Deck that he had never talked about. He had not been the same since and had started working at the orchard shortly thereafter. He became the custodian of the orchard a few years after that when the previous caretaker had died. Renold, though never directly addressing the rumors, had dismissed them as impossible and irresponsible. No one, he had said, was assigned to Flight Crew. He would not elaborate on this cryptic remark, and over the years Jene had almost stopped wondering about it.

Gil had met the Mussards before as well, and after a few pleasantries with them, turned back to Jene.

"I've checked your recreation ration status, Doctor," he said with a touch of formality tinged with embarrassment, "and you have more than enough accrued for a whole day here. The Mussards, though...." He did not look at them. Such rationing was necessary in Ship—recreational resources such as the orchard were doled out by the Council in a strict regimen. The Halfners, as important medical personnel, received a greater allowance than Frank and his family. It was an arrangement that Jene had never liked.

Jene kept her eyes away from Frank as she muttered to Gil, "Take it out of ours, Gil."

Had Gil Tanassarian followed procedure, he would have had to refuse Jene's offer. Ration sharing was not allowed for any reason. The Council had decided such activity would result in class warfare. But Gil was a man of compassion. He looked down at the dirt and kicked it to and fro a bit.

"Sure, Jene. I'll make it work somehow." He looked up at the Mussards and found Wendy's wide eyes. Gil smiled down at her and swung the gate open. "You folks have a good time."

Kuarta and Wendy had thanked him hurriedly and dashed off down the path into the woods. Kuarta stopped on her way to the nearest tree and looked back at the adults quizzically, as if she suspected something had happened back at the gate that she did not understand. For a moment, she appeared to be preparing to speak, but the moment passed and she hurried to join her friend in the sunrod-dappled fields of the orchard.

The adults strolled behind them, talking pointedly of nothing in particular. There was an almost tangible feeling of tension, a curtain that could be felt but not seen, separating the two families. There was no money in Ship, but ration privileges served the same purpose. There were no aristocrats, but there was a Council that had grown increasingly aloof. Ship society had been carefully engineered to near-perfect socialism, but recently, Jene had noticed a subtle stratification. She could not help but realize that her place was uncomfortably high in the almost-invisible hierarchy of Ship's social classes.

The pair of children, with their attendant parents in tow, soon arrived at a clearing, where the adults spread out their picnic supplies and settled down for a leisurely meal.

"Frank tells me you think you'll be ready with the immunizations soon," Lena said when the families had finished eating.

"Yes, I think so," Jene answered. "It's going very smoothly."

"Who's still left?" Frank asked, and Jene thought she could detect tension in the question.

"Just some people who had some unusual blood chemistry. The vaccines have to be individually tailored, you know."

"Any Flight Crew?"

Jene stared at him before answering. "No, they refused to be immunized."

"What?" Frank and Lena asked almost simultaneously.

"We asked for their blood chemistry when we began the project. At first, they refused to send us anything, then they told us that immunization was not necessary for them."

"Did they say why?" Frank leaned forward.

"Nothing. But we're not going to force it on them. They've always been able to take care of themselves"—she cast an involuntary glance at Renold, who sat impassively nearby—"and we assume they will do so in this case as well."

There was considerable silence before Lena found her voice. For generations, Flight Crew had been a forgotten element of Ship life—now, four months from their destination and with Ship beginning its deceleration, the Flight Crew had become the most important group in Ship. Their welfare was immutably wedded to the welfare of every inhabitant of Ship.

"What about the Council?" Lena asked.

"We did them first," Jene answered, not bothering to hide the venom in her voice.

"Why?" Frank asked.

"It was at their request."

Lene snorted. "Their order, you mean. They got the first shots? Do they think they are better than we are down here in Ship?"

Jene shrugged. She did not trust herself to speak; she had thought the same thing months ago when the directive from Council had come down. If she started talking about it, she would undoubtedly lose control of her bitterness, and she did not want Kuarta to see that. Kuarta did not need to see her mother openly challenge the supreme authority in Ship.

"What if we run out of time or vaccine?" Lena asked, the beginnings of panic entering her voice. "What if you have to hurry and you miss someone?"

Jene tried to smile reassuringly. "We're not going to miss anyone. Everyone gets immunized. Panimmunity for all—everyone immunized against everything we know of and lots that we don't."

"Everyone?" Frank asked.

"Yes."

"Even Bobby Yancey?"

Jene gasped quietly and felt her eyes widen. Lena looked away. Renold swiveled his head to stare thoughtfully at Frank. Jene could almost feel her husband's intellect enter the conversation and begin to analyze. But he would stay on the edges.

"Yes, even Bobby. Are you suggesting—?"

"Yes!" Lena stood up suddenly. "Oh, Jene, you know us. We're not bad folks. But suppose there's a shortage of panimmunity vaccine. Are you saying that the Council wasn't treated first just in case we ran out? And are you saying that Bobby should be considered as important as...well, us?"

Jene stared at Lena in cold horror. Yes, she had known Frank and Lena for years—they had housed together for four years, ever since both families had grown to three persons each. Although she knew Frank and Lena did not share all her ideological views on life, she had never thought the two families were this different. The Council had hinted that perhaps the immunization schedule should prefer the genetically strong first, but their reasoning had been that those without unusual defects would be easier to immunize in any case and could be taken care of quickly, leaving more time to deal with the unusual cases. Jene had been skeptical as to the sincerity of the Council's motives, but as there had been no sign of trouble with the vaccination program, she had agreed to treat the Council first. She had not anticipated the effects of the decision on other inhabitants of Ship—the Council had not kept their request secret. Jene scowled as a thought occurred to her.

"Do you think our family is more important than yours, Lena?" Renold's calm, cold, calculating voice drifted across the blanket.

Lena's eyes darted at Renold, then to Jene, then to the ground. Frank looked away. Jene knew what her husband was analyzing now— their body language and posture answered for them. Conversations over the years replayed themselves in Jene's head—talks with Frank about

Wendy, Lena's eyes focusing intently on Kuarta whenever the two were together—and Jene knew what her husband was concluding. Frank and Lena considered themselves in a lower caste from the Halfners.

"I think that it doesn't matter what we think," Frank said, his eyes locked on the remnants of his lunch before him. "We all know what's going to happen when we make planet-fall."

Jene glanced at Renold. He seemed to be deep in thought. She knew that he would not debate with Frank. She turned to Frank again, but found she had nothing to say.

Frank continued. "We may not like what the Council is doing now. Hell, I know I don't. But how much worse is it going to be in four months? Could we really expect total equality? Would that even be fair?"

Jene snorted. "Total equality isn't fair, Frank?"

"You know what I mean," he said. He brought his eyes up and started at her for a long moment.

Jene did know what he meant. Frank was not stupid; he could sense what was coming and what it might mean for his daughter. He was perfectly willing to support the notion of a social hierarchy that placed the Council at the peak and others in descending order determined by their genetic health. Such a scheme would not put his family at the top, but it would put Wendy, with her minor genetic defects, closer to the apex than the base. If some arbitrary line were to be drawn, separating society into those who would live and those who would not, Frank intended his family to be on the correct side.

Jene fought the impulse to argue with him. She liked Frank and tolerated his wife. There was no need to prove to them that no line needed to be drawn at all. They would come to that conclusion on their own, as would the Council and the rest of Ship.

"Well, we've all got busy days tomorrow. I think we'd better get back," Jene finally said with false enthusiasm that none of the others cared to question. The families packed up, called their children, and headed back to their home the way they had come. Jene felt a twinge of regret that Kuarta would not be going on a world-walk after all.

The trip back was a silent one. When the two families parted to their separate floors, the Halfners above their friends, Jene wanted to speak but did not know the words. She was sure her husband did.

Later that night, when the sunrod had dimmed and the lights from the settlements above twinkled vaguely like stars she had seen in Ship's record vids, Jene was tucking Kuarta in to bed. Her daughter looked up at her thoughtfully and asked, "Mommy? Why does Uncle Frank not like me?"

"Why do you say that, sweetie?"

"He looks at me and frowns."

"Oh, dear, that doesn't mean he doesn't like you. He's just worried."

"How come?"

"Well, it's his work. Sometimes his work worries him."

"Oh." Kuarta digested this, and Jene kissed her.

"Now sweet dreams, little one. I'll see you in the morning."

"Okay. Mommy?"

"Yes?"

"Maybe we can give Uncle Frank a present tomorrow so he will not be worried."

Jene smiled to cover up her real feelings. "Sure, honey. Now go to sleep."

CHAPTER
2

"Push one more time, Ute," Jene said. "I see her head. One more push and she'll be out."

Ute bore down again, her face contorted, and delivered her daughter.

Jene was a professional. She had delivered dozens of babies and treated hundreds of patients. Furthermore, she had known from numerous prenatal exams that Ute's daughter would have gross anatomical malformations and major genetic disorders. Jene had performed four in vitro surgeries on the developing fetus and had gotten a good look at what it would become. Even so, Jene could not totally suppress a slight shudder—a tremor that shook her shoulders and one which she hoped the loose-fitting scrubs hid—when she saw the end product of nine months of gestation.

Jene expertly cut the umbilical and passed the baby to Tym, her assistant, who suctioned out the child's mouth and malformed nasal passages. Jene forced herself to watch for a moment, then turned away, though not before she caught sight of the baby's sole many-fingered hand reaching up towards Tym. She concentrated on the afterbirth instead. She harvested it carefully and passed it to another assistant from Ecological Engineering. The placenta would be put to good use in Ship's botanical store.

"How is she?" Ute asked weakly. Her partner, Howard, stood near her, holding her hand, looking balefully at Jene.

Jene glanced at Tym. He gave a slight shake of his head.

"We'll put her in neonatal intensive care immediately," Jene said. "She's got an excellent chance."

"But how is she?" Howard asked. Jene knew what he meant. The question could have annoyed her. They had known for months that the baby was going to have severe malformations. Their previous son, Howard, Jr., had been a hemophiliac with practically no immune system. He had been in and out of Children's Crèche all his young life.

But it was not in Jene to be angry at them for something not their fault. The cosmos had conspired against these people, inflicting upon them, their parents, and their grandparents untold numbers of neutrons that sabotaged the reproductive process. And Ute and Harold had chosen to try to defy the cosmos. Their baby was the result. Ship had thick shielding, but one hundred years at one-tenth the speed of light meant cosmic radiation. Those genetic defects had increased despite careful outbreeding programs.

Tym stopped briefly on his way out with the baby in the newborn support tank so Ute and Harold could see her. One look and they both paled. Ute buried her head in her partner's chest and sobbed.

Jene nodded to Tym, and he continued out. Jene followed him with her eyes and was startled to see one of the white-suited members of the Governance Council in the doorway. It was Ernst Sorensen—one of the Council's lackeys.

Tym had to push the tank past him, and the Councilman got a good glimpse of what was inside. Sorensen did not hide his disgust at the sight of the baby.

"Excuse me, Mr. Sorensen," Jene said testily, "but this is a private room. If you'll wait outside, we'll be—"

"When you're finished," Sorensen said, and left. Jene had dealt with the man often enough to understand his meaning. She did not hurry to complete Ute's exam.

"As soon as she's settled, I'll come back to tell you how she's doing. You can see her then," Jene said, and gently stroked Ute's sweat-soaked hair once, twice. She lingered with the family for a moment, then left to meet with Sorensen.

He was leaning against a wall in the small waiting room, arms crossed in front of him. He straightened when he saw Jene.

"What do you want?" Jene asked, suddenly tired. She was in no mood to deal with the Council—especially not their sleek attack dog.

"The Council meets today. Special session. Wants to talk to you."

"Me? What for?"

"Not the inoculation progress."

"Then what?"

Sorensen smiled. "They'll let you know. Council Chambers at seven," he said, and started past her.

"The Council can't just order me to appear before them at their convenience."

"Not an order."

"Look, Sorensen, enough guessing games. What is the meeting about and why should I go?"

"Make sure you take care of that...*baby*...first. Seven tonight in chambers." And he strode away. Jene started to call after him again, but stopped herself. Sorensen was clearly not going to tell her any more, and she did not feel inclined to talk to him. She had not missed his pointed emphasis on the word "baby" and she seethed at it.

* * *

"How'd it go?" Doctor Werner asked when Jene joined him at one of the tables in the hospital cafeteria.

"The procedure was fine."

Werner looked up from his meal. "Something the matter?"

Jene did not answer for a moment, then glanced guiltily at him. "Sorry, Oskar. Yes, something's wrong. Ernst Sorensen came to tell me the Council wants to see me tonight."

"Up in the core?"

"Yes."

Werner shook his head. "Your muscles are going to turn to goo. The core will 'sap your strength and vigor required to forge a new home for your children.'" His voice deepened as he quoted Ilene Shapiro's famous speech of seventy-four years before when Ship had been debating building recreation areas in the null-g center of the great cylinder. Shapiro's viewpoint had won out—the central core now contained only the computer mainframe, the power plant, the Council Chambers (with its attendant police department) and the Flight Deck. This latter facility comprised the vast majority of the core, where the seldom-discussed and never-seen Flight Crew carried out their duties alone.

Werner speared a triangular piece of his yeast patty. "What's it about?"

"I can only guess." Jene stared at her peas, pushing them around aimlessly with her fork.

"I told you," Werner said, his voice muffled momentarily as he finished chewing his yeast patty, "you shouldn't be so free with your criticism of the Council."

Jene looked up at him. "Why not?"

Werner stared gravely at her before drawing his knife slowly across his throat in the age-old gesture of sudden death. He noisily scraped his tongue along the sides of his mouth as he did so to complete the metaphor.

Jene laughed.

Werner stopped mid-sound. He turned the knife towards Jene and stabbed the air as he said, "You mark my words, young Doctor Halfner: you're going to end up in the hydroponics vats someday."

"Aren't we all, Oskar?"

Werner blinked in surprise. "Yes, I suppose that's true. Comforting to know that we'll still be useful even after our deaths. Even if we weren't useful in life."

Jene's smile faded. "What is that supposed to mean?"

Oskar's eyes widened at the sudden anger in her voice. "Huh? I meant that—"

"You asked me about Ute's daughter. You knew the baby was going to be deformed. Are you trying to tell me she should be recycled? Now? Maybe we should both go to neonatal care and shuttle her up to the vats immediately."

Werner grimaced. "Stop it, Doctor. You know that's not what I meant. I think we should treat the Class D's for as long as we're able."

"Don't call them that."

"What?"

"Class D's." She had argued against the terminology when it was first put forward a few years ago to describe and categorize newborn genetic status. Class D was the highest level of deformity. "It's a baby, not a label," she added, then glared at him.

Werner did not look at her as he put his silverware back on his tray with a loud rattle. "I have to go. I've got a procedure soon." He stood up.

Jene knew she had caused a major breach of etiquette by insulting him, but she could not bring herself to utter an apology. She was not sorry, and all Ship's unspoken rules of politeness could not make her say she was.

* * *

The shuttle trip to the central core was uneventful and brief. She knew that the Council Chambers were located behind the sunrod on one end of the core, though she did not know if it was the front or the back of Ship. She also knew that the Panoptikon was located in the core. The thought took her back to the last time she had visited the core fourteen years ago. She had gone to listen to her grandfather argue, one last time, for the Council to return to the ground-level and govern from there.

"You have operated in this chamber for a year now," she remembered him saying, "and in that time, you have moved the constabulary up here and increased its staff from three officers to thirty-one. Why?"

Jene had not listened to the Council's answer—she had been only twelve years old and had venerated her grandfather. The argument soon left her behind as her grandfather and the Council argued esoteric points she could not follow. Only one thing had struck her. Towards the end, when it was clear the Council was not going to move, her grandfather had said, "This Council and its Panoptikon will begin the end of the happy egalitarian paradise we have enjoyed for nearly ninety years. I am glad I will not be alive to suffer through what you have done."

He had died a few weeks later. Jene had looked up the word "Panoptikon" – the all-seeing watchtower – and had taken to using it as a tribute to her grandfather whenever she referred to the constabulary. The word had taken root and was now the common term for the police facility.

Jene wiped her eyes as the shuttle entered the tiny port within the sunrod's housing. The craft's polarized windows cleared instantly when the shuttle passed the outer ring of the sunrod and was, effectively, behind the sun. It was early evening, and although the sunrod was dim, at such close range the mammoth banks of light would still blind.

The queer sensation of weightlessness had not suited her fourteen years ago, nor did it now. She debarked from the shuttle and entered the Council antechamber in ill humor, to find Sorensen there, waiting for her. His oyster-white uniform blended in almost completely with the white simulated-marble interior. For a split second, Jene imagined him as a disembodied face floating in the room.

"On time," he mumbled.

"Let's get this started so I can get back home."

Sorensen shrugged and pushed off the wall where he had been hovering. Jene followed, clumsily. Sorensen opened an arising door and entered a larger room. Jene collided with the wall near the door and had to scrape her way towards the opening. She fumbled her way into the Council Chamber and gasped.

Almost the entire chamber was glass: she could see the expanse of Ship from her vantage point. The mere turning of her head was enough to survey her entire world. She could easily make out people, livestock, machinery, everything.

"Breathtaking, is it not?" one of the Councilmen said pleasantly, swimming gracefully over to her. "I find myself looking down all the time."

Jene knew the voice. It was Benj Arnson, de facto head of the Council. His had been the hand behind the changes in Ship. He was a Gen Three, and a young one at that—only some twenty years older than Jene. He floated next to her, to all appearances completely at ease in the weightless environment.

He wore the same jumpsuit-uniform as the others, but something about his bearing gave his suit a military appearance.

"I imagine so." Jene tore her eyes from the ground below and looked at Arnson. "Perhaps you should visit us down there, Councilman."

It was a credit to the man that he managed to smile disarmingly at the barb. He spent most of his time in the central core now, as did many of the Council. "Well. I am glad you decided to visit *us*, Doctor. But I am sure you would like to know why we have invited you here. If you'd like to start, please," he indicated the rest of the Council, and began introductions. They weren't necessary—Jene knew all five Councilmembers, as did the entire Ship. But Arnson was nothing if not smooth.

"Councilmembers, this is Doctor Jene Halfner, director of medicine at Balgeti Hospital. You may recall her grandfather, Orson Halfner, who worked with Ship's Council until his death some years ago."

Jene started at the comment. Her grandfather had not worked with the Council—he had opposed virtually every new program they had put forward. It was a desecration of his memory to remark on a collaboration that had never existed. Jene suddenly felt ashamed she had accepted the invitation to come here.

Arnson addressed the rest of the Council, who were hovering near what must have been their personal stations. Jene saw electronic clipboards floating near the Councilmembers. "No doubt Doctor Halfner wishes us to conduct our business with her quickly, so let us begin. Doctor Halfner," Arnson said, pivoting in air to face her, "I understand there was a birth today."

"Yes. Ute and Howard. They had a daughter."

"Ah. Good. Always a pleasure to introduce a new life into Ship." He paused just long enough for his comment to hang in air, then continued with mock casualness, "How was she?"

"What do you mean?"

"The infant. How was she?"

"I'm not allowed to divulge medical data, Councilman Arnson."

"Please, you can refer to me—all of us, in fact—informally. As to the child, Ernst happened to see her as she was being sent to infant intensive care." Arnson nodded toward Sorensen. "He's not a doctor, but he seemed to think the girl was in distress. I hope everything is all right with her."

Jene frowned. Arnson must have known that the baby was severely malformed: why was he doing this? "She'll be all right. We'll take care of her."

"Oh, of course," Arnson said quickly, waving his hands gently in front of him, as if trying to drive away any implication to the contrary. "We know that you and your staff will commit all the necessary resources to the welfare of the child. And yet...."

"What?"

"Well, I hate to be the one who must say it, Doctor, but as you seem unwilling to face the unpleasant truth, allow me to remind you and the Council that no Class D has survived without intense, round-the-clock medical care."

Jene fought to control her anger. Three times in one week she was having this discussion—and in both cases, she found herself the only advocate for the unlucky children of radiation's curse. "Even if you're right, what of it? The girl will receive the necessary care. Bobby Yancey has been with us for six years, and he's doing fine."

"Yes, the Yancey child. I've met him. The Yanceys live near me, you know."

Jene grunted.

"I've no doubt you are right about your conclusions, Doctor, but you are aware we are within half a year of planet-fall?"

"So?"

"At which time, resources will be slim indeed. You and the medical staff have all you need on Ship, but when we disembark and begin the colonization process, you will no longer be able to practice the kind of medicine you have become accustomed to. You will have to adapt to rather harsh conditions. I believe the term you doctors use is 'frontier medicine.'" Arnson chuckled once, then grew serious again. He looked away, focusing neither on Jene nor the Councilmembers. "It will be at least two years before Ship is fully dismantled and shuttled down to the surface. What do you plan to do with Yancey and the other Class D's during this process?"

Jene clenched her fists. "You are proposing—"

"I propose nothing, Doctor. I simply asked a question. What will you do with the Class D's?"

Jene stared at him for a moment, then her gaze found the other Councilmembers. They were all awaiting her answer. They seemed quite content to let Arnson do their talking for them—no doubt his views were the views of the Council. Jene wondered how many other colonists shared the Council's attitude.

"The medical staff will handle the children." She said it evenly, as close to emotionlessly as she could.

"How?"

"That's not a concern of yours."

"I should think it is a concern of all aboard. If you don't have a plan, it is up to the Council to formulate one and execute it."

Jene's voice raised on its own. "This Council you've formed is simply, by your own admission, an oversight committee. You have no power to enact legislation. Ship has been a direct democracy for one hundred and eight years and all your comic-opera meetings won't change that."

Arnson matched her fury with coolness. "You are quite right, Doctor. The Council has no power. No formal power, at least. I simply asked you, from one shipmate to another, what is going to be done. Surely, the medical personnel aren't keeping their plans a secret?"

Jene saw a slight shifting in the positions of the other Councilmembers. They had heard the implication in the last remark. She also heard Arnson use the term "shipmate," a recent innovation of the Council.

"You know there's no secret agenda among the medical staff."

Arnson paused a fraction of a second and allowed a smile to spread across his orderly face. "If you say so, Doctor. And yet, you still have not answered my question. I am concerned for the safety and well-being of Ship and all in her. Why will you not answer?"

Jene glared at him. She knew he was not asking out of genuine human concern for the unfortunate mutants under constant care; he was playing rhetorical games with her. She thought of storming out of the Council Chambers, but the urge to resist authority, to "fight the good fight," as her grandfather used to say, made her answer.

"All colonists will continue to receive care at the highest level we can provide them."

"And if that means choosing between a Double-A and a D for medical resources?"

"I can't make a blanket answer. Such developments must be dealt with on a case-by-case basis."

Arnson sighed—the first real sign of annoyance he had displayed. If he was tiring of the game, good. Jene wanted to leave, but her grandfather's memory would not let her depart until she had won some sort of victory, however small.

"Surely, Doctor, you are familiar with the procedures of triage? Producing a treatment hierarchy when medical resources are overmatched by medical emergencies?"

"Of course. If you know what triage is, you know that under triage procedure, the most severe cases receive immediate care while the less critical patients wait. The strong help carry the weak. Such a system has always been in place in Ship and it has worked. I see no reason to abandon it once we begin planet-fall." There! Jene smiled at him smugly. Let him chew on that.

"Yes, yes. Your description of triage is accurate, as far as it goes. But tell me this, Doctor—is it not true that in following triage procedure, the terminal cases are abandoned so as not to waste resources that might be going to patients who have a chance at survival?"

Jene's smile faded. He had trumped her.

He continued. "I agree with your description of Ship's history. We have until now existed in a communal socialism that has worked well." There was something in his voice, Jene noted, that hinted at bitterness. Arnson swept on. "But we are fast approaching a crisis the likes of which we have not seen in the entire history of Ship. It will be two years before Ship is completely stripped and shuttled to the surface. In those two years, resources planet-side will be extremely thin."

"We can't just let them die," Jene whispered, anticipating his conclusion.

"The strong must carry the weak, Doctor, but should they also carry the dying?"

Jene had no answer for that. She had been manipulated adroitly by the Councilman, and although she knew, at a level deeper than logic, that she was right, she could not match his rhetoric. She simply looked at him, then at the other Councilmembers. Her eye rested briefly on the sole woman among the five-member council, Luise Ryu.

"We want you on our side, Doctor," Ryu said, breaking the silence.

"Your side?" Jene scowled at her.

"Councilwoman Ryu tends to see things in terms of us and them," Arnson said, flashing a wolfish smile at Ryu. "She means that we are quickly approaching a pivotal moment in our mission, and Ship will no doubt be split between those who see what must regrettably be done and those whose reason is clouded with emotion. At the moment, Doctor, I must say that you belong to the latter category. It is my hope, indeed, the hope of the entire Council, that you see that we are right." He pushed off the wall and floated slowly towards her. "Doctor, we are not animals. We do not wish to see any of our children hurt or deprived. But we cannot continue our present policy of total care for all. Surely, you must see that."

Jene kept her voice under control. "All I see is that you are willing to sacrifice human lives for the sake of other human lives."

Arnson blinked. "Yes. Rather than lose the entire colony, I would. Wouldn't you?"

"I would not."

"You would rather all of us die than some of us?"

"I would rather die than make the decision of who will live and who will not."

Arnson stared at her. "I deeply regret this, Doctor. You realize that the Council will, despite your opposition, attempt to convince Ship of our position?"

"And I will stop you."

Arnson nodded. "Such is your right to try. I suppose you may go." He swam away from her and indicated the portal.

Jene made her way awkwardly to the door, but before she exited, Arnson called after her.

"Doctor, one last question."

She turned.

"What if the choice was between saving a Class D and saving your daughter?"

Jene swallowed with a dry throat. She opened her mouth to speak, but nothing came out. She could not answer.

Arnson raised his eyebrows. "I see. Goodbye, Doctor."

Jene left the chamber, worried for Ship, its future, and, inexplicably, for her own family.

CHAPTER 3

"The question was not intended to be a rational one, dear. It was purely a rhetorical device designed to elicit an emotional response from you." Renold spoke softly, at his wife, infuriating her. "Arnson knows full well that—"

"But I still couldn't answer it!" Jene shouted back, hardly aware of her own shrill voice against Renold's soft one. She gained a level of control over herself before continuing, more quietly. "Don't you see, Ren? What would I do if it were my own daughter who had to do without medical attention because someone else was getting it instead?"

"There is no meaningful answer to that. That's why we have laws in the first place—so people do not make decisions from an emotionally charged state."

Renold was resorting to his hyper-rational mind again to try to soothe her fears. He always tried the same approach, and Jene hadn't had the heart to tell him it rarely worked. She did not want to be given answers, like a child; she wanted simply to be heard.

She sighed in frustration. Renold spoke again. "Dear, his question was similar to asking the surviving husband of his wife's brutal rape and torturous murder what he thinks should be done with the perpetrator. The husband will almost undoubtedly want a brutal death sentence carried out on the criminal, but the husband is not the one who should be making the decision. Of all the people in Ship, he is the least qualified at that time to make a rational choice. Arnson's hypothetical question is similar. Should Kuarta need medical help at the same time a different child needs it, and only one can be treated, Kuarta's mother should not be the one deciding."

Jene imagined she felt pressure building in her head. Renold's speech was only making her angrier. "And if I am the only one who can decide? I'm a medical doctor, Ren, and an administrator. The decision falls to me. So what do I do? And how do I make a similar decision with two children who are not mine by blood?"

Renold hesitated. "It's not a valid question. The—"

"Dammit, Ren, it is valid!" she shouted. "It's more than valid—it's likely to happen. Why do you insist on shoving it aside and dismissing it as hypothetical? I ask again: what would I do if it came down to a choice between Kuarta and a...D?" She loathed herself for saying it—her own words echoed in her mind. *It's a baby, not a label.*

Renold did not answer. His normal mask of composure was gone and a look of uncertainty plastered across his strong, chiseled face. She had never seen him like that. It unnerved her at the same time it exhilarated her.

It was a long time before either spoke again. When Jene did, it was to change the subject.

Jene talked with Renold about inconsequential matters, knowing that he was unable to see that she needed an "emotional episode"—what he called any show of anger, joy, guilt, or the like. He wanted to explain away her frustration, while she wanted to scream it out. They went to sleep that night without revisiting the issue.

* * *

She compromised the next morning. Before her shift at the hospital, she visited the Ship-wide broadcasting station. The station was run by a small but dedicated collection of young men and women who provided Ship with news, entertainment, and occasionally, opinions. It was this latter function Jene wished to employ. Some years ago, the Council had expressed their desire to restrict public access to the channels, but Jene's grandfather and others had fought them. The Council had, however, managed to arrange matters so that those who wished to use the communications web had to visit the station in person—computer uploads were not allowed. The Council had argued that no one's rights were being taken away—the slight commitment required of visiting the center would reduce the number of pranks, hoaxes, and junk on the web. They had been right.

"Doctor Halfner?" The station administrator squeaked in surprise. She was a tiny, birdlike woman wearing tight clothing in defiance of the current fashion towards looseness.

It was not surprising the woman knew Jene. Ship was not so populous that the community did not know itself well—and an influential personage such as Jene would be known to nearly all on board.

The station administrator, however, was one of the few women unknown to Jene. "Yes, that's right. I'm sorry, but I don't know who you are."

"Oh, that's all right. I only just changed over to fem. You probably knew me when I was…"—the woman hesitated, as if in distaste—"…male. My name is Yale now. How can we help you?"

Jene looked at Yale, admiring the work. Jene hadn't done her conversion, but one of her colleagues must have. It looked like a good job.

"I need some band time. On your opinion channel."

Yale nodded. "Sure. Let me just check the transmission schedule, all right?" She looked away for a moment, obviously accessing the biocomp implant all colonists wore. Jene had never liked her own and rarely used it. Yale looked back at Jene and said, "We can put it on opinion channel ninety immediately. Does that suit you?"

"Is there any way to get me on the news channel instead of opinion?" At Yale's hesitation, Jene quickly added, "You could call it a medical services update."

Yale sucked air through her teeth. "Sorry, Doctor. To do that we need Council permission."

Jene blinked. "The Council oversees the news channel?"

"Well, yes," Yale said, chagrined. "But we have over one hundred opinion and free access channels."

Jene started to argue that Ship's official news channel was the only one that mattered but thought better of it. Yale and her compatriots were doing the best they could, and Jene appreciated it. She nodded at Yale. "Channel ninety will be fine."

"Great. Did you want to record your opinion now?"

"I would, but I would like to do it text/speech only. No e-photo." Jene knew she was in no state for emotional photography—in her anger, she would drown the image in hate-filled reds and violets, and her rational message would be lost.

"Certainly. Go on ahead to the recording booths, then, and follow the instructions," Yale said, pointing. "If you need any help, just ask."

"Thanks. Oh, Yale?"

"Yes?"

"I'm curious—who did your conversion?"

"Oh, Doctor U'Ulanee."

Jene nodded.

"I thought I'd better get it done now, before planet-fall, you know. No chance then." Yale said brightly.

"What do you mean?"

Yale blinked at her. "Why, medical services will be on a needs-only basis then, right?"

Jene nodded slowly. "I suppose so."

"So, anyway, I got it now while I still can. I certainly wouldn't want to take away doctors' time with such a...well, frivolous procedure after planet-fall. There are plenty of kids who will need attention more than I will."

Jene smiled. "I agree. I think you made the right choice."

Yale smiled back. "Thanks. Anyway, just through there." She pointed again and accessed her biocomp, looking into nothingness.

Jene entered the tiny recording booth and read the instructions on the screen. Essentially, she was to just talk into the screen and the studio techs would edit out any area she wished in post-production. It couldn't be simpler for a layperson such as herself.

Jene took a deep breath and started her prepared speech. "My name is Doctor Jene Halfner, and I have grave news to report." She paused, then continued.

"As you all know, we are nearing our destination and will arrive within four months. Preparations have been in progress for the better part of a year, and I am happy to report that all medical procedures are proceeding well ahead of schedule and without a glitch. We in the medical field have served our Ship well so far and will continue to do so once we achieve planet-fall. There are those, however, who doubt that the medical community of Ship will be equal to the task of maintaining quality care for all of us when we transfer to Epsilon Eridani Three.

"You should be told the truth. We will all have to accept the fact that there will be changes in medical services. I anticipate it will take two years to return to our current level of medical availability.

"I cannot deny that there will be a significant alteration in medical priorities. Still, it is my firm belief that no one who needs medical attention should be turned away. It is true, however, that high-maintenance individuals will demand and receive more attention than those seeking less critical care. In some cases, it may happen that minor inconveniences will be temporarily ignored while more critical, life-threatening conditions are treated to the best of our ability. Ask yourself: are you willing to tolerate your arthritis for a bit so that a child with a defective heart receives a synthetic one and therefore lives to become a productive member of our new colony? Can you self-treat your diabetes for a little while so a young girl can replace her bone marrow to defeat hemophilia? I do not think any of the healthy members of this Ship would begrudge care to the unfortunate sick ones.

"Your Council disagrees. It is the view of the Council that the upcoming debarkation will prove too difficult and that we must take steps now to abandon our care of the infirm. Your Council feels that it is not the responsibility of the strong to help the weak. Look up at the sunrod. Behind it lies the Council Chamber, where the government floats in null-g and proposes we abandon the social structure of communal living in favor of a hierarchy. You make your own guess who will occupy the highest places in the hierarchy.

"We are nearing the end of a one-hundred-year-long journey. Those who put this voyage in motion sacrificed much to get us here. Generations One and Two knew they would live and die on board Ship, never seeing either the planet they came from or the one they were going to. They paid a price higher than what I am asking all of us to pay in the future. We have a difficult road to travel, shipmates, but we can walk it together. And we must carry those who cannot walk so they may bask in the warm glow of a new sun with us. I believe in all of you, and I know we will do the right thing. Thank you and good bye."

She pressed the panel marked "end recording" with a flourish. She regretted not using e-photography; her rage had dissolved and the thrill of public speaking had replaced it. She exited the booth and waved to Yale in the outer offices. "Thank you again, Yale."

"Oh, you're welcome, Doctor."

Jene nodded and went to work, pleased with herself.

* * *

Jene was walking through the cafeteria the next day, intending to grab a quick bite of something before returning to the mountain of paperwork she had to deal with, when she heard her name mentioned in conversation. She turned automatically to see three students, two of whom she did not recognize, sitting at a table nearby. All three looked pointedly in different directions, but not quite fast enough—Jene saw that they had been looking at her.

She hesitated, then approached the trio. One of the three was Sander Calderon, a promising young Gen Four medical student whom Jene had had in class the previous semester.

"Did you need something, Sander?" Jene asked the young man.

"Oh, uh, no, ma'am," he said. Jene saw the other two students glaring at him, prompting him with their eyes. Sander swallowed and added, "We were just talking about the, uh, posting you made yesterday."

Pleased, Jene asked, "May I sit down?"

The three students hurriedly made room for her and she slid into the fourth chair.

Sander looked at his companions, then turned to Jene and said, "We were just saying that we agreed with you."

"You do?" Jene nodded. "Why is that? You're not in my class, Sander. There's no need to keep me buttered up."

Sander laughed nervously. "No, ma'am. It's just that...well...." He looked desperately at one of the other students, who broke in forcefully.

"Doctor Halfner, we want you to know that we have been thinking along the same lines recently. But we wanted to ask you—do you really think the Council will go so far as to propose, well, *euthanasia*?" The student whispered the last word.

Jene leaned in and asked, "What's your name?"

The student hesitated a fraction of a second, then answered, "Delores."

"Well, Delores, if by that you mean they will systematically go door to door killing people, then of course not. But what they propose is essentially the same thing." Jene turned to look at Sander and the other student. "You have a different opinion?"

The other female student said, "Well, I don't want to criticize, Doctor...."

"Please do. Your name is?"

"Aunda. I mean, first of all, how do we really know the Council will do what you say? I'm not saying you're lying to us, Doctor," Aunda said quickly, "but I have never heard them say anything like that."

Jene nodded. "I can see why you would want to believe the best of your Council. But be assured that I know what I am talking about." Jene looked around the table, hoping her position in the hospital's informal hierarchy would lend weight to her words.

Aunda did not look convinced. "Well, all right. But that raises another point. Even if they propose what you say they will, is that so bad? I mean, why shouldn't we take a look at the way we do things and—"

"You're not serious," Sander said, rounding on Aunda. "You mean you agree with them?"

"I didn't say that, necessarily. It's just that—"

"You think we should judge if a person lives based on how lucky they were to escape genetic damage?" Delores said angrily. Jene saw Aunda's eyes dart from left to right. She was sitting between the two other students. Despite the geography of the table and the double-team she was being subjected to, she held her ground.

"I just think we should examine the Council's position. Maybe they have something."

Jene stood up. "Well, I think you three have enough to talk about. I'll leave you to it."

They murmured goodbyes. As Jene walked away, she heard the argument start up again. Sander and Delores spoke in indignant tones at their companion. Jene had a momentary feeling of unease at leaving the third student, Aunda, to her certain defeat—it didn't seem fair to her. But the feeling passed, and Jene continued on her way to the vending machines.

The next few days at the hospital were unusually hectic. A string of nagging injuries and minor complaints kept Jene busy, working well past her normal hours every night. There were always such injuries, as some of the younger set engaged in dangerous sports and other distractions quietly encouraged by the Council. Pseudo-gladiatorial games involving real person-to-person combat were broadcast weekly across the Ship comweb. Jene didn't watch them, but she saw the results every now and then as a combatant was rushed to her hospital.

She understood the Council's official position on the games: people need conflict, and in the absence of natural conflicts they would create their own. Ship could not afford to have even the smallest of internal skirmishes, so the Council created artificial ones. It all sounded perfectly rational, but Jene couldn't help feeling it was like Imperial Rome in its brutality and crass disdain for the plebeians for whom the Games existed. Still, Jene would not begrudge care to any of the Gen Four and even Five patients that came into her hospital, no matter how or why they came to her. She simply healed.

"So, did you at least win?" Jene asked the young Gen Four sportsman who fought to keep his face stoic despite the pain of his dislocated shoulder. His cuirass and helmet lay on the ground next to him, but he still wore his leggings.

"No," he said. "Lost in the last few seconds."

"Oh, well. You'll get them next time. Now, hold still. This is going to hurt a bit." Jene nodded to her assistant, who held the young man down while she pulled steadily on his arm. The young man gasped but kept his composure, and Jene felt and heard his shoulder pop back into place.

"All better. We'll get another scan before I talk to you about rehab. You'll be playing again in no time."

"This was the last game," he said, looking at her with faint distaste.

"Oh? Well, next season, then."

"No, this was the last game. Ever. We won't play anymore after we get to the planet."

"Why not?"

The young man stared at her for a moment, then said with poorly concealed anger, "Because our league director saw your posting on channel ninety. He says that we have to make up new sports so we don't get hurt."

"Oh," Jene said. "Well, I'm sure you can think of some new games to play."

"Maybe," he grumbled. Jene made a few notes on his chart, then started to leave. The youngster called out, "Hey, Doctor, can I ask you something?"

Jene nodded.

"Is it true that if I get sick on the planet you won't help me because I'm not...one of those kids? The ones with the special problems?"

"No, that's not true at all. Who's been telling you that?" Jene said, her eyes narrowing.

"No one. My friends and me were talking, that's all. And my dad. I saw two kids in my school get in a fight about it." He grinned at the memory.

"Really?"

"Oh, yeah. That's all we talk about at school now." He paused, then said in a bright voice, "Hey! Can I get out of school with this arm?"

Jene smiled. "No, sir. You can still go to school." She patted his good arm and left as he swore under his breath. She walked the short distance to her office and found herself thinking about the young man's words. Only three days had passed since her posting, and it sounded like a growing number of people were interested in what she had to say. Jene entered her office in good humor and sat down to work. She had only been there a short time when she heard footsteps approaching.

"Doctor Halfner. Need to talk." Sorensen said, sauntering in.

She looked up and focused her eyes on him. "Oh, go away, Sorensen. I don't have time."

"Quite a stir you've created," he said, surveying the surroundings.

Jene shrugged. "So?"

"New game plan, Doctor. You stay out of politics."

Jene snorted. "Yeah? And why should I do that?"

"Consider it a request from the Council."

"Yes? Well, you know what you can do with your request."

Sorensen didn't reply immediately. When he finally did, his voice had lowered almost to a whisper. "You do not fully understand the…resolve of the Council in this matter, Doctor. I urge you, with all possible force, to remain out of Ship politics henceforth."

Jene was taken aback. She didn't know why she was unsettled by Sorensen's answer. It was one of the only times she had heard him speak in complete sentences. Still, she found the courage to challenge him.

"Or what?"

"Good day, Doctor," he said, turned, and left.

Jene was still staring at the space where he had been when one of her assistants entered her office with a report for her to initial.

"Everything okay?" The young man asked.

"What? Oh, yes. Fine." Jene looked at the report, her mind still on the encounter. The young intern had to tap the spot where Jene was to initial before she saw it herself.

"Thanks, Doctor Halfner. Oh, by the way, your partner called. He said it's nothing serious, but he'd like to talk to you at your earliest convenience."

"Thanks." Jene waited until the intern had left, then called Renold on his biocomp.

"Yes?"

"It's Jene. What's the matter?"

"I had a call today on my biocomp. From the Council. They wanted me to talk to you and try to keep you out of their business, as they put it." Renold's voice was calm as always—and that angered Jene almost as much as the Council's actions.

"Did they threaten you?"

"Not directly."

"How, then?"

"They made it clear that if you were to continue in your public opposition to the Council, they would not be able to guarantee your safety from fringe elements."

"Fringe elements?"

"Their term, not mine."

"There aren't any fringe elements in Ship. Not any, at least, that would get involved in this kind of thing." Jene thought briefly of the Society of Life, which advocated that E.E. not be tampered with or terraformed in any way, but she could not see how such a group would cause her harm personally. Besides, they only numbered in the twenties and were largely harmless.

"I agree. As I said, the Council made their meaning clear enough," Renold said evenly.

"This is because of the posting I made." Jene had an impulse to ask, "Kuarta still at school?" She felt her pulse quicken.

"Yes."

Again, a surge of rage at her partner's stoicism threatened to burst out of her. Their daughter might be in danger, and he was just—

"I'll go to the school and retrieve her," Renold said. Jene let out a breath she hadn't realized she'd been holding.

"No, I will. I love you," she said, surprising herself.

"And I, you. I will talk to you soon." He disconnected.

Jene stared at the dead comm panel for a moment, then turned to go. As she did, a thought struck her. She couldn't tell if the thought was merely a product of her growing concern for her family, and therefore ultimately groundless, or if it represented a real possibility:

What if the comm line had been tapped?

She had to admit, it sounded silly. Like one of the thrillers Gerd Taylur published on the Ship library every few months. But she also had to admit that the current Council was capable of such a feat—both from an engineering standpoint and an ethical one.

As if in a dream, she told her scheduling computer she would be off for the rest of the day. She had accumulated sufficient favors from other workers and from the computer itself to call some of them in now. With a growing sense of urgency bordering on panic, Jene left the hospital and, still in her uniform, grabbed one of the public bicycles.

The ride to Kuarta's school was claustrophobic. Jene had never had an attack of the dreaded condition, but she had seen the effects on those unfortunates Renold had treated. He and his crew were far more worried about the condition of agoraphobia once Ship arrived and its colonists debarked. Jene was aware of the walls of Ship for the first time in a long while. She was aware of walls inside the hull of Ship—social walls constructed by the Council that were closing in on her and her family.

* * *

Her heart leapt into her throat when she arrived at the school to find three white-uniformed constables addressing the assembled student body on the outer lawn. In some corner of her mind, Jene realized it was some kind of presentation by the constables—nothing to do with Kuarta. But that was only a corner of her mind. Jene leapt off the bike before she had stopped. One of the constables looked behind him at the sound of the crashing frame. Jene hurried towards the assembly, slowing when she heard the presentation.

"...Why you must always obey a constable. So, one more time, children. Who are your friends?" Jene jumped when the assembled children, perhaps one hundred strong, shouted in unison, "The constables!"

"That's right. And who is looking out for you?"

"The Council!" The treble voices of the school children were somehow more chilling than the presence of the law officers.

Jene saw the constable who was eyeing her smirk. "Can I help you, Doctor Halfner?"

"I came for my daughter."

"Kuarta? Sure. She's in the front row." The constable turned and called to her. "Kuarta Halfner?" He said in a commanding voice. The entire assembly hushed. The constable hesitated just long enough so Jene was sure the worry was building up in Kuarta's child brain.

"Your mother is here." He moved aside to reveal Kuarta's anxious face. She got up and ran to her mother.

"Mommy? What is it?"

"Nothing, dear. Just come with me." Jene shot a glance at the constables. "And you...keep away from her."

"Doctor?" the constable who had been presenting to the students said with mock confusion. "Have we done something wrong?" He and his two companions were snickering but had turned so that neither students nor teachers could see. Jene saw Tigh Penelost, Kuarta's teacher, approaching her and the constables, concern on his face.

"Just leave us alone. Tell the Council to stay away from my daughter."

"Why, Doctor Halfner," came the affected response, "we were just connecting with the students here. Reminding them about the importance of civic obedience, respect for authority, that sort of thing. Children need to follow the rules that their elders set. Surely you agree?"

Penelost interrupted from behind, his soft voice breaking in. "Is there a problem, Jene?" Tigh's kind face was wrinkled with concern.

"No, Tigh. I'm just going to take Kuarta for the rest of the day. I'm sorry. Can you arrange that?"

"Of course. Call me if you need anything." Tigh looked fondly at Kuarta and shot an unreadable glance at the three constables. "Are you done here?" he asked somewhat coldly.

"Are we, Doctor?" one of the constables said.

Without another word, Jene took Kuarta by the hand and together they started the walk home.

CHAPTER
4

"Greetings, shipmates. Our grand quest is nearly complete—the journey approaches its end. One hundred and one years ago our ancestors began the quest we will complete in four months. All of you have been working nobly to complete the massive task set before you—preparation of Ship for planet-fall. We in the Council want you to know that *you* are Ship—you are the future of the human race. Your children and grandchildren will tame the first new planet humans have ever set foot upon outside our own Solar System. Many of your children and grandchildren will be born there. It is imperative we make every effort to strengthen and empower our children to survive what will inevitably be a pioneer existence. To that end we have developed a plan to ensure the well-being of the future."

Jene snorted at that. She sat alone in her office at the hospital, watching Arnson's smiling image pour forth its sickening bonhomie. When Arson made the comment that the Council's views were not hidden, the information border around his face flashed the message, "Reference Council Directive 11.123.3."

Arnson went on, "Our plan ensures the safety, health, and vitality of our new colony and all who live in it. Our vision for the future is bright and full of promise." He paused, and Jene sensed a subtle change in the tenor of his comments was to come. "There have been objections to our plan, and while our home here in Ship has always been a polite one, recently these objections have caused turmoil to our once-stable community.

"Shipmates, I urge you to refrain from violence in this matter. Those few who oppose the majority view have the right to do so. I urge the rest of us to try to reason, peacefully, with those who do not yet see what must be done."

Jene resisted the impulse to turn around and make sure there was no one else in her office and instead concentrated on the rest of Arnson's message.

"Shipmates, the future is ours. There will be difficult choices to be made in the very near future, but we in the Council fervently believe we all have the strength to make them. Thank you for your attention."

Arnson's image disappeared from the comweb screen and was replaced with all manner of reference codes where viewers might follow up on the story. Jene noted without surprise that her own piece was not one of the cross-references.

She leaned back in her chair and thought. There was a hidden message in his words—one only she could hear. His appeal to Ship to "try to reason" with her sounded peaceful, but she saw through it. Politely, gently, and with great dignity, Arnson had declared her an enemy of the state and had enlisted the aid of the entire community to neutralize her.

Jene closed down her office and hurried home. Even on the darkened, empty streets, she felt eyes on her. The crowded conditions on board Ship had always been a source of comfort to her, but now, for the first time in her life, she wondered if she was completely safe.

When she finally reached her apartment, she sighed and entered the bedroom. Renold looked up from his book and nodded. "Hello, Jene. Everything all right?"

Jene told him what had transpired at the hospital and the school.

Renold leaned back in his chair in the couple's tiny private room and hummed to himself. Jene looked at him expectantly.

"I think you are right," Renold said softly. He had just finished watching Arnson's broadcast and had listened to Jene analyze it. He hummed for a few more seconds, then said suddenly, "You're sure the constables were at the school to scare you?"

Jene sighed. "No, I'm not. They could've been there as part of some routine field trip, of course, but...I don't know," she said, burying her head in her hands. She knew how she must look to her husband, but at that moment she couldn't help herself. The walls of Ship, real and social, were still pressing in on her.

Jene started when she felt Renold's hand caressing her shoulders. "I understand," he said softly. "I feel the same way." Jene was reminded of why she had chosen Renold as a partner and why she would stay with him. She reached over her shoulder and touched his hand. It was warm.

"Something's going to happen soon," she said quietly, almost calmly. "I can feel it. The Council...us...Ship. I hope...." She never finished her thought. Renold's arms encircled her. He continued to hold her for a long time.

In the morning, she awoke to find Renold gone already. She sat up in bed, all traces of sleep gone, and found the notepad blinking with a message. She pressed the play button and listened to Renold's soft voice.

"Dear, I was called on my finder in the middle of the night. There was fracas at Palmatier Square—several dozen people, I understand. They need my staff and me to counsel the combatants. I'll call you when I can. I love you."

Jene took a deep breath. She would be needed at the hospital. She started to pull on clothes, then stopped with one leg halfway in her pants. She checked the time on the message: Renold had recorded it three hours ago. If there was a major fight in Ship with dozens of injuries, she should have been called for emergency duty at the hospital.

Jene thought for a moment, then reached over and called the hospital. She wove her way through layers of secretaries until she got the chief of staff.

"Jene?"

"Yeah, Jyudi, what's going on? I heard about the fight. Why didn't you call me in?"

Jyudi hesitated, then said, "I've got enough staff here now. No need to bother you at home."

"Bother me? Since when have you worried about that?"

"Well, I...."

Jene cocked her head slightly. Jyudi was not being as forthcoming as he could. "What's going on?"

"I thought it would be better if you didn't come in."

"Why?" As soon as she asked it, Jene suspected she knew the answer.

"Your presence here might...make things worse, if you know what I mean. The fight started because of a disagreement involving medical policy. Kids, mostly. Nothing too serious. We can handle it."

"I'm coming in anyway."

"There's no need for that."

"Jyudi, you've got a near-crisis on your hands. I promise, I won't make trouble. Anyway, I've got the heart procedure today."

Jyudi took a long time before he answered. His voice was faint as he said, "All right. But don't walk through the trauma center when you arrive. Use the surgery entrance, all right?"

"All right. Bye."

Jene took a deep breath and continued to dress. She would have to hurry to get Kuarta to school and leave her with Tigh.

* * *

"Doctor!" Jene looked up from the microscope, through which she had been performing a delicate procedure to repair a heart. Hoverd, one of her assistants, was at the door of the operating room, struggling to keep a white-clad figure out of the sterile environment. A constable. Jene's eyes widened when she saw that the officer was holding a child in his arms—Kuarta was holding a blood-soaked bandage to her forehead and crying.

Jene started to rise but sank back into the saddle before the microscope, torn in an agony of indecision. "Damn!" she said. She glanced back into the microscope display. The procedure was in a critical phase. She had perhaps an hour, hour and a half left before the heart she was repairing had to resume its work. The patient, a Class C child born not two weeks ago, could last on the artificial pump (which Jene herself had helped design) but the young heart itself needed to be returned to its normal work as soon as Jene finished the procedure.

"Doctor Halfner!" the constable shouted over Hoverd's repeated commands to step back, "your daughter was hurt."

"What happened?" Jene asked, glancing quickly at Kuarta but forcing herself to remain in the microscope saddle.

"Some kids at school threw rocks at me," Kuarta sniffled.

"One of them hit her on the head. Lucky I was there to stop them," the constable said.

"But…but you didn't stop them!" Kuarta said.

The constable looked at Kuarta with menace but said sweetly, "Of course I did."

"No, you watched them throw the first two rocks. You only stopped them when they hit me."

"Quiet, now," the constable said.

"I *saw* you. You were standing there. You didn't do *anything!*"

Jene listened with mounting anger, her eyes locked to the microscope eyepiece. "Kuarta, dear, do you feel dizzy? Sick?"

"A little dizzy. Not sick."

"Do you know who I am?"

"You're my mommy." Through the sniffling, Kuarta managed to convey surprise.

"Do you know where you are?"

"In the hospital."

Jene nodded. Kuarta most likely did not have a concussion. "Honey, how big was the rock?"

Kuarta opened her palm halfway.

"She's bleeding pretty badly," the constable said.

"Scalp wounds do that," Jene said quietly. She felt herself beginning to slip into rage. She closed her eyes for a moment and thought away her emotions. "Take her to the trauma center. Someone will look at her there." She opened her eyes and forced herself to look at the heart before her.

"Mommy! It hurts! I want *you* to fix it!" Kuarta wailed piteously.

"I know, honey. I can't…one of my friends will help you, okay?"

"You aren't going to help her yourself?" the constable asked, his voice pitched high, unbelieving.

Kuarta, who had begun to calm down upon seeing her mother, started to cry again at this.

"Damn it! Get her to the trauma center! Now! Hoverd, help me."

Hoverd took Kuarta from the constable and hurried out of the room.

Jene grasped the laser scalpel she had been using. Through the microscope, she saw the guide beam shaking in her grip. She could not continue in this state. Jene withdrew from the microscope and leaned towards the hospital intercom. She pressed the all-call and said, "Doctor Werner to operating room nine. Stat. Doctor Warner to operating room nine, stat."

The constable nodded. "Going to the trauma center, then?"

"Why did you bring her here?"

The constable looked at her with affected blankness. "To the hospital?"

"No, to me. Here."

"I thought you'd want to look at your own kid. Give her the best treatment, you know."

Jene flexed her fingers and returned to the microscope. The heart was still safe, for now. She looked at the constable. "I have this child to take care of," she said, indicating the silent figure in the sterile field before her.

The constable looked at the child. He did not try to conceal his disgust. "If her heart is so bad that you have to cut it with a microlaser, she's not going to make it long on EE3. You're just prolonging her life a little bit. I hate to say it, but she might be better off dead, don't you think?"

"No, I don't." Jene again had to close her eyes and remain calm. If Werner didn't show up soon, she'd have to resume the operation. Werner was the only other doctor on site today who was fully capable in cardiac microsurgery.

The constable shrugged. "Anyway, your kid is wrong. I didn't even see them throw the other rocks at her."

"Yes, you did. You might even have encouraged them." Jene said with certainty.

"Doctor, how can you think that? I'm not the kind of person who would hurt a little girl. I'm sorry she's hurt, but I did all I could do."

"Why were you there at all?"

"We've received orders to watch out for her. And you and your partner. Good thing, too."

Jene was prevented from answering by Werner's arrival. He pushed past the constable and looked inquiringly at Jene.

"Oskar, I need you to take over. You prepped?" She got up from the saddle. Werner slid into it and immediately pressed his eyes against the eyepieces. "All set. What's the story?"

"The heart has been stopped for..."—she looked at the wall timer—"...ninety-one minutes. I've begun the valve replacement and aortal weave, but I still have to—"

"I see it. Whew. This is going to take some doing. I'll need an assistant."

"Hoverd will be back soon."

"Where'd he go?" Werner was already at work on the heart.

"He had to take Kuarta to the trauma center."

"Serious?"

"No." Jene turned on the constable. "When the rock hit Kuarta, did you contact Arnson for instructions?"

The man hesitated, apparently considering his answer. Jene did not let him speak. "You did. You son of a bitch, you called your goddam superiors first!"

Werner said, his eyes never leaving his work, "Calm down, Jene. Or take it elsewhere. I'm sort of busy here."

The constable smiled reassuringly. "Doctor, listen to your friend here." His hand moved slowly to his belt and rested on his paralyzer.

The movement was not lost on Jene. She glanced at his weapon, then fixed him with a cold stare. "You were waiting for something like this to happen! And when it did, Arnson capitalized on it."

"Stop right there, Doctor," the constable said, drawing his paralyzer and leveling it at Jene.

Out of the corner of her eye, Jene saw Werner jerk his head up from the microscope. He raised both his hands and said, "Officer, don't shoot in here. You might hit the patient. In her state, it would probably be fatal."

The constable kept his eyes on Jene, but said to Werner, "So? Less baggage for the rest of us when we reach EE3."

Jene acted without thinking. She snatched the laser scalpel from Werner's raised hand and, in one smooth motion, twisted it to its widest possible setting. As she turned on the constable, a small part of her mind wondered why she hadn't been gunned down by a paralyzer bolt in the second she had acted. Jene did not hesitate as she fanned the scalpel at the constable's face. The high-powered beam found his eyes. The man dropped his paralyzer and pressed both hands to his eyes as he screamed in agony.

Jene dashed around the operating table, heading for the constable's weapon. She did not know how long the peace officer would remain dazzled by the low-powered laser; the device was meant for short-range surgical work, not for offensive purposes. Jene reached the constable's gun an instant before his searching hand closed over hers on the weapon. She wrenched her hand out from under his and sent bolt after bolt of synapse-disrupting electricity into him, knowing full well that the so-called "stun gun" was indeed painful and potentially harmful, especially at such close range. At that moment, however, she did not care. The constable slumped to the floor at the first charge, jerking spasmodically as Jene continued to shoot.

"Jene!" Werner seized her arm after the fourth bolt and thrust it upward, sending a wayward blast into the ceiling. A rain of sparks descended on the two, which brought Jene back to her senses.

She looked down at the constable and threw the weapon aside. He was still alive, and she knew the damage to his eyes was temporary and superficial. He would recover his eyesight as soon as he awoke in a few hours. The stun burns would heal, as well. Jene found herself automatically running through the treatment procedure in her head.

Werner lifted her gently from the fallen officer. "I'll handle it, Jene. You'd better go."

Jene stared at Werner for several seconds, noting for some reason the almost perfectly flat contours of his hair. She whispered "thank you" and darted out of the operating room. She had never pegged the conservative Gen Three doctor as one of her supporters, especially after their conversation a few days ago, but mentally revised her opinion of the man as she ran out of the operating room.

Sooner or later, she knew, someone in the hospital would report the disturbance to the Panoptikon. She had many friends in the facility, but she could not expect a wall of silence about her attack to last for long. She walked briskly towards the trauma center and was almost there when she heard shouts down the corridor. Two other constables were charging towards her, drawing their p-guns as they came. Jene turned to leap through the doorway to the trauma center as the stiffening pain of a paralyzer bolt shot through her body. As every major muscle instantly tightened in agony, she realized she had not counted on the constable bringing back-up to his mission. She crashed to the floor and lost consciousness, but not before she saw the white-clad legs and feet of the two constables stand over her. As she slipped away, she heard one of them mutter, "Now let's get her kid and partner."

Again, the Council Chamber. Jene woke up unexpectedly sharply, her eyes snapping open and then squinting in the light. She had for a moment the terrifying sensation of falling, then her scrambled mind realized it was the null-g environment of the chamber that had triggered her vertigo. Her eyes focused on the smiling figure of Benj Arnson floating a few meters away.

"How are you feeling?" he said, and for a split second, Jene thought his concern was genuine. Arson's ability to project false sincerity was well-honed. The illusion only lasted a moment, however, and she soon saw through his carefully constructed countenance of worry. Dimly, she could make out not only the other Councilmembers, but three constables as well, floating in the chamber.

"Damn you," she croaked. "Where are Kuarta and Renold?" She fought back the mild nausea brought on by the aftereffects of the p-bolt.

Arnson blinked in surprise, but recovered quickly. "They are safe," he said. "For the moment. I will not lie to you, Doctor Halfner; they are indeed in our custody. Furthermore, they are under the protection of the constabulary should any shipmates wish to do them harm."

"Harm? That's a damn lie, Arnson. No one wants to hurt my family. No one down there, at least," she nodded towards the huge windows through which she could see her world.

"The incident at Kuarta's school with the rock would seem to indicate otherwise."

"The rock? That was your doing, Arnson. You set that whole thing up."

Arnson leaned in close to her. "Do you think that I would do that? What kind of a monster do you think I am? I assigned constables to your daughter to protect her. You and I may disagree with each other, but I am a civilized, moral man."

Jene hesitated before answering. His forcefulness was compelling — for an instant, she found herself doubting her own convictions. The moment soon passed, however. "The constable called you after Kuarta got hit. Why else but to ask for orders?"

"Yes, he did. And I ordered him to immediately get the child to Belgathi Hospital. The constable's presence might have saved Kuarta from serious harm."

"She says the constable didn't stop the kids from throwing rocks at her until one of them hit her."

Arnson spread his hands helplessly. "Perhaps he was not watching as carefully as he should have been. I wasn't there, Doctor. But why do you persist in thinking I want to harm your family?"

"You had three constables at the hospital when Kuarta was brought in."

"I suppose there is little chance of vigilantism against your family, but we do not wish to take even a small risk. In the meantime, suppose we talk."

"Not until you release them."

Arnson sighed mightily. "Doctor, they are not prisoners, except in the sense that we all are. And in four short months, none of us will be prisoners any longer. But for the time being, let us leave your family where it is and discuss—"

She spat at him. It was an animal's reaction, not unlike her sudden outburst of violence against the constable—as was the torrent of nearly incomprehensible anger that flooded out at him, at his ideology, at his casual arrogance and power. "You bloodsucker! You're a despot who thinks he is in command of a whole world, sitting above everything, not wanting to dirty his hands in honest labor! You've done nothing but take away from Ship, Arnson. You and your petty Council exist only to further your own ends. You're scared that once we reach E.E. we'll realize that we have no need of you: that we never had a need for people like you!"

Arnson absorbed the diatribe calmly and carefully wiped away what little saliva had hit him while she shouted. She paused for breath and for sense, eyeing the constables, who had started to swim over to her.

They stopped when Arnson raised his hand and waved them off. "Doctor, I understand your anger, and I can easily forgive your impolite outburst." He paused, then said, "Use your reason. What could I possibly do to your family? Kill them? You seem to think me capable of such an atrocity, so let us consider the logistics of the act alone. How could I possibly get away with that? I cannot hide nor shirk responsibility for the death of two persons under my care. By placing them in the constabulary, I have made any scenario involving treachery on my part impossible. If I really intended harm upon them, I would have let them stay below. Now, may we begin our discussion in a civil manner?"

Jene's grandfather mumbled inside her head for her to stay stubborn, not to let Arnson win. But the more rational part of her mind overrode him, reluctantly. There was no point in resisting Arnson in the matter of her family. He had them in custody, and it was clear he would not release them until he had had his say. So Jene nodded tightly and waited, her eyes focused on the curving wall of the chamber.

"You have been causing quite a disturbance in Ship of late, Doctor. Attempting to stir the masses with your proletarian rhetoric over the comweb. I wish your cause was one I could follow—your passion is commendable." He smiled patronizingly. Jene remained silent, not trusting herself to speak.

"But you are hopelessly misguided. I will not speculate on the reasons—perhaps you place too great an emphasis on the influence of your grandfather, perhaps there is some latent guilt at your offspring's having escaped genetic harm—"

At that, Jene snapped her head up to stare at him. She opened her mouth to speak but found she had nothing to say.

Arnson smiled. "Ah, the Achilles' heel of the people's revolutionary. Aristocratic blood in her veins, yes? But I should not mock you, Doctor. There remains a…proposal for you to consider."

"What proposal?" Jene croaked.

"Flight Crew informs me that Ship is four months out from EE 3. As you may or may not be aware, telemetry from our first planet-fall probe has been coming in for days now. The probe has done its job superbly—it managed to reach EE 3 with its automated systems intact and has started collecting all manner of planetary samples."

For a moment, Jene forgot about her predicament and her family. This news had not been released to the public. All Ship knew the probe had been launched some months ago, but no one, except apparently the Flight Crew and the Council, knew it had landed. Jene and the medical staff had been waiting for the answers to hundreds of questions that now burned in Jene's brain. She could barely ask them fast enough.

"What microbes have been found? Any macroscopic animal life that our telescopes missed? Trace gases in the atmosphere?" Long-range spectroscopy and laser interferometry had answered many of the questions about EE 3 long ago, but there were still so many other questions. The answers would dictate medical preparedness policy and could help incredibly with the panimmunity project. Jene felt her anger rise again at the Council's decision to withhold the data. She changed her questions into angry accusations. "And how could you keep this a secret? We need to know these answers immediately!"

Arnson had listened patiently to Jene's barrage of questions without visible reaction. Now, into the charged air left behind after Jene's outburst he dropped his words carefully. "All medical and planetology departments will receive the appropriate data soon. I will, however, answer some of your questions now. EE3 is not as hospitable a place as we would have liked. The temperature is somewhat lower than our long-range scans and atmosphere models would have indicated. I am told that the probe estimates average equatorial temperature to be only eighteen degrees centigrade at midday, accounting for thermal lag. Nighttime temperatures are significantly colder— into the single-digit negatives."

"That's all? So it's cold. We can adapt to that."

"That is not all. The atmosphere contains a rather high degree of chlorine—high enough to be lethal in one or two dozen lungfulls, I am led to believe."

Jene wasn't disappointed. The odds had been long against a breathable atmosphere in any case—the mission had been prepared for unbreathable atmospheric conditions on EE3. "What about pressure?"

"As we predicted—somewhat lower than sea-level earth, but—"

"Microbes? Organic materials? We know there's plant life, but what else have—"

Arnson chuckled. "Doctor, you are forgetting what I said earlier. All departments will receive detailed reports very soon. I have a proposal for you."

Jene's mind snapped back to the more immediate problem. She looked at Arnson with fresh eyes. For a while, when she was asking him about the probe data, she had forgotten all the injustices the Council was no doubt preparing to inflict upon her world. During the brief interval when the probe data had consumed her, Arnson had truly been another colonist. Now he was once again the enemy.

Arnson read her expression. "The probe gives us no reason to expect that the first two years on EE3 will be easy. As we predicted, life will be tough, harsh, and unforgiving. The strong will survive and the weak will, regrettably, perish. Supplies will be stretched to the breaking point—food and water will not be a problem, as the hydroponics section will be assembled quickly, and the probe has found many pockets of free-standing ground water that should be simple to purify—but other supplies, especially medical ones, will have to be rationed. We've been predicting this, and the probe data now confirms what we have been saying."

"What's your proposal?"

"I propose that essential personnel receive first priority for all medical services until such time we can provide all colonists with full access. I need not mention that the upper echelons of medical staff, such as yourself, will be considered 'essential personnel.' As will their families."

"You're bribing me." It was a statement, not a question.

"I am removing from your shoulders what would have been a difficult, perhaps even impossible, decision. Your...altruism would not have permitted you to privilege your own progeny, even when such privilege is clearly warranted."

"Why must there be privilege at all? Why can't we treat everyone as if they were vital members of society?"

"Because this is not a vague, hypothetical exercise in social engineering, Doctor. For EE3 to be a viable colony we must have a sound genetic base. We must therefore preserve those Gen Five children who are genetically superior over their unfortunate, flawed brethren." He stared at her, and for a moment, she thought she saw through the politician's mask to the human beneath. When he spoke again, his voice had lost some of its orator's smoothness and had grown almost husky. "Don't think I like this idea. I've been wrestling with the problem for years. I wanted the probe to send back data telling me we had found another Earth so this step would not be necessary. The thought of abandoning children to fend for themselves is...disgusting." He straightened slightly, then said, "But it has to be done." And his mask was back in place. He was a Councilmember once more.

Despite herself, Jene felt a portion of her mind agreeing with Arnson. It was that cold place in her mind that she did not care to examine closely — the place that cried out in terror of the dark and clawed with animal ferocity for a larger share of food than was rightfully hers. That part of her mind realized she could take Arnson's offer and protect herself, Renold, and Kuarta forever.

Her mind suppressed the cold place. Civilization could not be run solely by the dictates of animal desires and base needs of humanity. Jene felt the cold place dim but not vanish. It was still there, lurking, as it always was, waiting for the civilized, transcendent part of every human being's mind to weaken.

A thought occurred to her—Arnson had not completed his proposal. When she spoke, her voice sounded alien. "Why do you need me to agree? Aren't you going to push this through with or without my help?"

Arnson stayed pleasant but the wolf was in his eyes. "You have stirred up more trouble than I think you realize, Doctor. A significant portion of Ship has been led astray by your...misguided views. It would be far more convenient, not just for the Council but for the mission as a whole, if you were to recant your position and convince your...followers to acquiesce to the Council's wishes."

For the first time in the conversation, it was Jene's turn to smile. "A significant portion, you say? How many? Ten? A hundred? A thousand?"

Arnson shook his head slightly. "No point in revealing a figure—"

Jene felt jubilation. There were more than one thousand! Could she have convinced a majority of Ship? She searched Arnson's face for the answer. He was scared—hell, he was terrified! There must be close to two, perhaps even three thousand who were firmly on her side, with another thousand or so who were undecided. The Council no longer had a mandate. Possibly as many as three out of five people agreed with Jene and thus were against the Council.

"You don't have popular support, do you? It isn't going to be just inconvenient to try and enforce your policy—it is going to be impossible. I've convinced the people to defy you. You have lost, Arnson."

Arnson was curiously unperturbed. "An ancient Earth philosopher once said, 'With the proper lever, one can move the Earth.' I have such a lever on you, Doctor. You have indeed convinced the people, as you put it, that your views are worth listening to. But now, I think, you will convince them otherwise. Please, do not make me vocalize the nature of the hold I have on you. It is ugly enough that you have forced me into this regrettable act."

A picture of Kuarta's face swam in front of her eyes. She was digging in the dirt, that day she had discovered the true nature of the only world she had ever known. Mild surprise on her face, but no tears, of course. Strange that Renold did not come to her mind—no, that was not true. His intellect, his calm rationality was in her mind. It suddenly occurred to Jene that although Renold was a creature of reason without emotion, he believed in the same things she did. Unconsciously, she needed him to confirm her beliefs. The irony of the timing of the realization did not escape her. Arnson held her family hostage in return for her cooperation. She knew that her poor, intellectual husband would not be able to solve this dilemma with reason.

Arnson seemed to know precisely when Jene would fully understand the nature of his leverage. "The Ship-wide band has been reserved for your speech. I do not expect you to speak extemporaneously—I have a prepared statement, written in your own style, of course."

Jene interrupted him with a sigh. "No. I want to speak now. After I do what you want, I presume my family will be released?"

Arnson permitted himself a small smile. "I believe after you speak to Ship what little danger your family is in will vanish and they can be released from protective custody, yes."

"Then let's go. I want to see my daughter."

"Of course, Doctor. This way."

Jene, Arnson, and two constables swam out of the Council Chambers and entered the tiny comweb station elsewhere in the Panoptikon. The room had one broadcast station and a chair with a restraining strap for use in free fall. A technician floated behind a glass partition in the control room beyond. Jene saw a clipboard near the microphone; presumably, her prepared speech was already waiting for her.

Jene felt the gentle but firm pressure of one of the constables behind her. She floated into the transmission booth and settled into the chair.

"Very well. Doctor, Ship is waiting." Arnson glanced at the technician in the control room and nodded. The man adjusted some dials and gave a thumbs-up. Arnson and the two constables stayed outside the small transmission booth, but their almost palpable menace pressed upon Jene as she sat and stared into the camera pickup. The technician rapped on the glass to get her attention, then showed her five fingers, then four, three, two, and one. Then he pointed at her.

Jene took a deep breath and silently asked for forgiveness from the people she was about to betray. She had spent her whole life with them, and now she was about to condemn them to a fate she could not begin to imagine. She glanced at the clipboard.

"Shipmates, this is Jene Halfner." Her voice boomed out to the entire expanse of Ship simultaneously. The Panoptikon broadcaster had been used only twice in her lifetime. She knew that below her, virtually all eight thousand people who made up Ship's population were listening.

"I am speaking to you from the Panoptikon, high above you. If I were to look down from the Council Chambers I imagine I could see all of Ship, all of our works and achievements. We are about to enter into the most exciting and challenging phase of our mission to date—our arrival at EE3. As you know, I have been in disagreement with the plans of the Council regarding medical treatment of our children once we begin planet-fall. I have counseled nonviolent resistance to their plan to prioritize resources toward genetically superior stock. I am now prepared to change my views."

She resisted the urge to glance at Arnson, but she was sure he was smiling smugly just outside the transmission booth. Jene took another deep breath and willed her eyes to remain dry. *Forgive me.*

"Shipmates, I recommend full and total resistance to the Council! Armed insurrection may be the only hope for our children and our colony!" Jene saw Arnson bolt into the control room and she knew she had only seconds more before she was cut off. As she spoke, she watched Arnson frantically shouting at the technician.

"The Council has taken my family hostage in order to pressure me to speak against my views. In a few moments, they will stop this transmission. They can silence me, but they cannot silence all of Ship if you rise up against them!" Jene saw Arnson look at her from the other side of the glass. He was no longer shouting, but looking icily at her. She stopped talking and folded her hands in her lap, waiting patiently for him to enter.

Arnson left the control room and came around to the transmission booth. "That was unwise, Doctor."

"You should have made me record my speech first," Jene said softly.

Arnson smiled without mirth. "I see that. I had hoped your love for your family would have been enough."

Jene fought to keep her composure at the remark.

Arnson continued coolly, "Surely you must know that my security force can quell any uprising your transmission may have initiated. I am afraid that I cannot let you go now—you must agree that your inflammatory statements cannot be considered protected speech. You are hereby under arrest and will be confined to the Panoptikon. Constable, restrain her inside the observation deck then report to your precinct for riot control." He looked back at Jene. "You'll be able to see your petty revolution put down from up here."

The constable grabbed Jene, none too gently, and shoved her ahead of him towards the observation deck. Arnson went the other way, toward the Council Chamber.

"Don't give me any trouble, Doctor," The constable said in a low rumble. "I know what you did to Jaq."

Jene stared at him until she realized what he meant: Jaq must be the constable she had shocked in the hospital. "How is he?" she asked with genuine concern. The guilt from that incident had been hovering in her mind for hours but had been deferred until now. This constable guiding her roughly to her jail had brought it to the surface.

"He'll be fine. Burns here and there." He looked accusingly at her. "He's a good man. He didn't want to hit the girl."

"What?"

"That's why he didn't shoot you. That other doctor said if he missed and hit the girl being operated on, she might have died. I talked to him about it."

Jene swallowed. "I...I'm sorry. Can I...can you tell him that for me?"

The constable shook his head. "He's probably not in the hospital any more. He's not supposed to be on active duty, but after what you just did, I expect they'll call him up."

Jene did not answer. She knew very well what must be happening below her. Shipmates who had supported her views and who were already inclined to hate the Council and its authority would unleash their hatred on the few constables who were on the surface first, then the pro-Council shipmates would try to stop the protests, and all would escalate. There would be assaults, some with fists, some with makeshift weapons. There would certainly be injuries, possibly deaths.

But the lives she was most concerned about were those of her partner and child.

"Look, Constable," she said, stopping her progress just short of the observation room doorway by grabbing onto a guide rail, "I am truly sorry for what I had to do. I don't want violence but Councilman Arnson left me no choice. I'm sorry your friend is out there in danger, but I put my friends and family in greater danger. Can you tell me where my partner and daughter are?"

He hesitated, and Jene took the opportunity to press him. "I just want to make sure they're safe. If I knew where they were, I'd feel much better."

"I...can't tell you that. But I will tell you that we have received no orders to hurt them. They really are in protective custody, you know. Councilman Arnson doesn't want to hurt them, or you, or anyone."

Jene couldn't help but smile slightly. Under other circumstances, the constable's almost blind loyalty would be admirable. He truly believed Arnson's lies. Jene could not find it within her to hate or even dislike the lawman. On the contrary—she found herself warming to his simple-minded obedience and gentle manner. Perhaps she could appeal to him directly.

"What's your name, Constable?"

"Rik," he said automatically, then nodded with compensatory gruffness towards the observation room door, indicating Jene was to enter. She turned but kept talking as she floated through the doorway.

"Okay, Rik, can I ask you for a favor?" She said, turning to face him once she had entered the Observation room.

"Look, Doctor, you know I can't let you see your family. Councilman Arnson—"

"No, no, Rik. I don't need to, if you will agree to something for me."

"What?" He seized her shoulders and spun her around. Jene felt the adhesive of restraint tape on her wrists.

She twisted her head around so she could look at him. What she had to say needed to be said with the eyes as well as the voice. "Tell me you will make sure they stay safe."

Rik finished tying her wrists together, somewhat less tightly than doctrine dictated, then gently spun her back around to face him. He looked at her, the beginnings of admiration in his eyes at the question and the implicit trust behind it.

"I will see to it," he said.

Jene smiled a little and sighed—a deep, soul-cleansing sigh. "Thank you, Rik. I won't cause any more trouble for you."

Rik nodded grimly, already thinking about where he was about to go—into the heart of a riot that spanned his entire world. Jene could see the man's loyalty to appointed (or self-appointed) authority battling with his proletarian ideology. Before he closed the door completely on her, Jene added, "I trust you, Rik. You will do the right thing. I know it."

And he closed the door, gently.

CHAPTER
5

Jene could not make out the identities of individual figures below her, but she could see the battle unfold. It was difficult to think of the scurrying specks below her as people—far, far easier on the conscience to imagine they were indeed the ants they resembled from her position. The surreal, soundless images of warfare—no other word would suffice—continued for hours. Jene forgot the aching hunger in her belly and the pressure of her bladder as she floated, hands still bound behind her back, above her world as it tore itself apart.

She could see the hospital in flames. Most of the fighting seemed to be concentrated there. As she watched, she saw a portion of the building collapse on itself, dozens of tiny people fleeing the area. She looked away when she thought she saw some of them on fire.

Wherever she looked, however, she saw the war. The university, a tight group of six buildings on the opposite side of Ship from the hospital, was another source of heavy fighting. A shapeless mob of people clashed in the quadrangle, their affiliations unknown to Jene. She had no way of telling which of the combatants were on her side and which were trying to reassert Council authority. Most of the people who were not fighting hand-to-hand in the quadrangle were clustered around one of the buildings near a ground floor corner. Many of the people were carrying rectangular shields—or were they placards? Jene could only barely make out small objects being thrown at the building—rocks, or possibly bricks. As she watched, a fulisade of tiny sparks shot from the building and the group dispersed suddenly. When the crowd was gone, Jene could see dozens of individuals lying motionless on the ground where they had either been shot by the sparks or trampled by their own compatriots.

Jene closed her eyes and tried to shut out the horror below. She could not, however, ignore the pain in her soul; it was she who had plunged her world into violent chaos.

She must have slept at some point, for she woke with a start at the sound of a loud metallic banging on the door to the observation room. She heard sounds of shouting and fighting beyond the door. A quick scan of Ship below did not help her orient herself in time—the sunrod was still burning, but that meant nothing. If Arnson wanted to, he could keep the sunrod on indefinitely. No doubt he would if it offered his forces a tactical advantage.

There was a sickening, meaty sound of metal on flesh from beyond the door—Jene saw the door buckle inwards. Jene heard a ragged cheer from the other side of the door and forced herself to full wakefulness. The pain in her shoulders would have to wait.

The door burst open and a body came hurtling through the doorway. Behind it was a mob, cheering and brandishing all manner of weapons. The body, in the uniform of a constable, cartwheeled through the air in the telltale starfish pose of the dead or unconscious. The constable's body bumped into a wall and rebounded towards Jene. With a sick feeling she recognized Rik's bloody face. She swam awkwardly towards his gently spinning body and tried to orient herself in the microgravity to examine him. She was hampered by her inability to maneuver in free fall and by her bound wrists.

She heard her name from the doorway. Three of the mob wormed their way through the doorway and floated inexpertly to her. They cut through the adhesive tape, asking her if she was all right. Jene turned to the crowd and shrank away at the excitement and lust for battle in the faces of the mob. She knew what they must be thinking—they had rescued their leader! The fact that the mob was in the Panoptikon meant the revolution must have been carried through successfully. She did not stop to ask the men and women of the crowd what had happened. Instead, she continued her examination of Rik's body and took his pulse. He had several gaping holes in his torso that were oozing globules of blood. Jene withdrew her hand from his neck. He had no pulse, a fact Jene realized she should have inferred from the man's wounds. Had he been alive, blood would have been coming out of his body more forcefully.

His heart had stopped, but he was still warm. He must have been shot defending the observation room. Dragging Rik with her, Jene started moving slowly and awkwardly through the air towards a wall so she could begin CPR, but by now the observation room was thick with revolutionaries.

"Get away, dammit! This man is dying! I've got to save him!" She tried to push her way past the thronging crowd, but it was no use. There were simply too many bodies in free fall around her. "We've got to get him down to the surface and get him to the hospital!"

"Why?" The cry came from an unidentified voice in the crowd. Jene could hear murmurs of approval ripple through the multitude. She continued to the nearest wall and bumped into it. She spent what seemed an eternity in maneuvering Rik's body, flattening it as best she could against the wall. Her ears heard the indistinct sounds of disapproval around her but her brain refused to process the words.

She started chest compressions on Rik and found that the slight rebound from his sternum caused her to float away slowly. She could not get purchase for more than a few thrusts at a time.

"You there! Hold my feet!" She shouted at a nearby revolutionary. He stared at her and looked at her feet.

"What for?"

"So that I can...." Jene realized the fault in her thinking. If the man held her without being himself anchored, she would gain nothing. It would take many people to form some kind of chain so that she could continue compressions.

And what then? Jene felt tears running down her cheeks. She had not even realized she had been crying. The futility of trying to save Rik in the microgravity was too much for her. She rounded on the young man nearest her and shouted, "You want to kill? Is that what this was all about?" The mob grew quiet at her words. "We've come all this way, five generations of humanity, over one hundred years, to tear ourselves apart even as we reach the conclusion of the journey?"

"This is what you wanted!" said another voice.

"I never wanted *this*!" She threw Rik's body angrily into the mob. She herself tumbled away from the body, the crowd becoming a nauseating whirl of faces as she spun crazily about. She felt arms steady her and right her.

"What have I done?" she whispered.

Another voice, this time from the doorway, rang out. "We've got control of the Council Chamber and the Council itself! Ship is ours!"

A deafening cheer went up from the mob in the observation room. Men and women exchanged embraces and private moments of exhilaration all around Jene, who worked her way slowly towards the door.

The bright-faced youngster guarding the door took a moment before recognizing her. "Doctor Halfner!"

Jene said urgently, "There were two prisoners of the Council before this all started. A Gen Four male and a Gen Five girl, about five years old."

The teenager shook his head. "I haven't seen anyone like that up here, but it's pretty crazy right now."

Jene pushed past him and entered the long corridor of the Panoptikon proper.

It was a madhouse. Scores of jubilant revolutionaries floated everywhere, the occasional bound and helpless constable floating among them like a slow-motion volleyball. There was no organization whatsoever. Jene spent hours floating among the mob, asking anyone who could hear her if they had seen Kuarta and Renold. She was well-recognized in the crowd, and as she passed, many of the revolutionaries shook her hand or embraced her.

"Doctor Halfner!"

She whirled at the sound and saw Delores, the medical student who had agreed with her at the cafeteria table, waving frantically in the air. She had a red scarf tied to her upper arm.

Jene pushed aside three floating revolutionaries and made her way to Delores.

"Have you seen my husband and daughter?" Jene had to shout to make herself heard over the noise of celebration.

Delores' smile faded slightly. "No. Are they up here?"

"I think so." Jene turned away, ready to continue to search.

"Doctor, I wanted to tell you...." Delores started. Jene turned to face her.

"What?" Jene looked at the young woman tiredly. Her scarf was in Jene's field of vision, and what she had taken as an emblem or identifying mark was in fact a bandage, soaked through with blood. "Were you at the hospital?"

Delores nodded.

"What happened?"

"The constables showed up and tried to take control. They got inside and got a lot of help from the staff, but some of us fought back." Grim triumph filled her eyes. "We were pushing them out when the fire started. I think some of the deputies did it."

"Deputies?"

Delores nodded. "The constabulary deputized about eight hundred men and women early in the fighting. I think they started the fire."

Jene shuddered as she remembered the scene. "How many were killed?"

"I don't know. Twenty, maybe. Mostly patients."

Delores relayed the datum with such coldness that Jene did not trust herself to speak. The macabre irony in the story seemed to be lost on Delores. The very people the war was meant to save had been killed in the fighting.

"Any staff?" Jene asked finally.

"Doctor Werner."

Jene stared at Delores, searching for any sign of emotion and found none.

Jene did not feel like fighting again. She simply placed her hand on Delores' shoulder and said, "Thanks." She turned away before she lost control of her mask of composure and revealed the disgust beneath.

Then, suddenly, she saw Kuarta. She was being carried by a man Jene recognized from the hospital—Bobby Yancey's father.

"Kuarta!" Jene shouted above the din. She shoved her way through the crowd towards her.

"Mommy!"

The two collided awkwardly, both trying to embrace the other. Jene held Kuarta for a long time before she noticed her daughter was crying hysterically.

"It's okay, sweet. I'm here. Where's—" But before she could complete the question, she could see the answer in her daughter's eyes.

Kuarta stammered, "The constables took him away and then brought him back. Then he was...not moving and he was bleeding, Mommy! He said 'I love you, Kuarta,' then...he closed his eyes and...and he stayed that way." Kuarta buried her head in her mother's breast and burrowed into her. Jene felt her daughter trying to find a place within her where everything was understandable and where her father was alive. Jene tried with all her might to make that place exist inside her but could not. Their world had been forever darkened.

Bobby Yancey's father floated a few feet away, unmoving and silent. Jene finally found his eyes and mouthed a silent "thank you" to him.

He answered in kind. "Thank you, for Bobby."

Jene nodded, just a little, but something in Mr. Yancey's eyes stopped her.

"He's dead," Mr. Yancey said.

Jene closed her eyes like she had in the observation room. This time, it didn't help.

* * *

Jene woke up some time later in her own bed, her arm draped awkwardly across...Renold? No. She realized, despite her attempts at self-deception, that it was Kuarta's sleeping form nestled against her. She did not remember boarding a shuttle to the surface, nor did she remember crawling into bed with her daughter.

She could not completely label the mélange of emotion she felt as she became acutely awake, but that did not stop her from feeling it. Mostly, she had a sense of foreboding. She did not yet miss Renold—her sorrow was for the future when she would. Looking at Kuarta sleeping beside her, she realized that her own pain would not equal her daughter's. The thought that she would have to help her daughter overcome the loss helped to mitigate her own selfish pain. She tried to mourn Renold, but she found it was too easy to pretend that he was simply elsewhere in Ship, busy at work trying to calm emotions after the fighting. She could accept the revolution far easier than she could fully accept Renold's death. She had seen the same inability to face truth in the few colonists who had lost loved ones through accidents—she had respected the survivors' reactions without fully understanding them. Now she did. Her brain could accept Renold's death, but her heart could not.

A muted chime sounded in the apartment. Jene blinked and had to focus her mind to identify the sound as her door announcer. Jene gently eased out of the bed, watching Kuarta carefully as she did so. The girl stirred slightly but otherwise did not wake.

Jene found a robe and, pulling it on, strode to the door announcer.

"Who is it?"

"Doctor Halfner? It's Wynd Perralt."

Jene knew the name. She was a Gen Four journalist who lived in New Omaha. Jene had a vague memory of Perralt's column in one of the newses; she was at least as much a left-wing radical as Jene.

"What do you want?" Jene found herself in no mood for ordinary pleasantries.

"Please, Doctor. I need to talk to you. I'm alone."

Jene sighed. Her impulse was to send the woman away. But her sense of dread for the future when the emotional reality of Renold's death would hit her overrode her impulse. If talking to Perralt would push that future farther away, she would speak to her.

Jene opened the door and let the woman in. Perralt was older than Jene, and considerably shorter. Her eyes were strikingly blue-gray, and she carried herself with the unmistakable air of competent authority natural leaders have about them.

"Thank you. I know you don't want to talk or listen to anyone right now, so I'll leave if you ask me to."

Jene nodded, then motioned to a chair in the living room. When the two were seated, Jene noticed Perralt looking her over.

"What are you looking for, Ms. Perralt?"

Perralt started guiltily. "Oh. I'm afraid that's an old habit from my reporter days. I always size people up when I'm about to interview them."

"I'm not in the mood for interviews."

"Oh, no, Doctor. That's not why I'm here. I'm not a reporter anymore." She snorted quietly and looked away. "I'm not sure what I am now." She looked back at Jene quickly. "Sorry, Doctor. I'm wasting your time. I'll get right to it."

"You can call me Jene." Despite the situation, Jene found herself liking Perralt's frank manner.

Perrault nodded. "We've got to set up some kind of government. We can't go on in anarchy for four months."

"Don't ask me to be the new Czar, or whatever you are planning. I tell you now, I will refuse."

Perralt nodded. "I thought you would say that. Truthfully, I am a little glad to hear it."

In spite of her earlier refusal to take the mantle, Jene was affronted. "Why?"

Perralt shifted in her seat and said, "I mean no disrespect, but how much experience do you have governing people? You galvanized all of Ship to overthrow the Council, but can you preside over them now? I am a little bit of a student of history, Jene. Revolutionaries make poor statesmen."

"Then who is to lead us?"

Perralt sighed. "For the moment, there are about thirty of us who are looking past the immediate effects of the revolution. I won't say we are calling ourselves governors, but we will have some policy proposals to give Ship in a few hours. There may be more groups around Ship, but I don't see how any of them can be any more organized or well-versed in governance as we are. We did not mean to intentionally leave you out, Jene," Perralt added hastily, "but we did think you would not want to be bothered right now. You've done a great deal for all of us."

"But my work is done?"

Perralt looked away. "Not quite. That's what I'm really here for." She got up in a display of nervous energy she had hitherto kept hidden. "The group of people working on the problems of government has been...contacted."

"By whom?"

"The Flight Crew. They want to speak to you."

"Me?"

"They asked for you by name. The governing group feels it would be unwise to go any further until we hear what it is they want to tell you."

"Why do they want me? And why now?" Jene realized the question was rhetorical only after she had voiced it.

Perralt tried to answer it. "I think they want you now because of the upheaval. And why they want you...."

Jene got up from her chair and stared at Perralt. "Why?"

"They said they would have spoken to only one other person in Ship."

"Really? Then get that person. Because I have a daughter to care for."

"It was Renold."

Jene stepped back, as if the force of the revelation had tangible effects on her. Renold had been one of the only people to make even sporadic contact with the Flight Crew. Jene had asked him about them in the early years of their marriage, but Renold had made it plain, politely but with resolute firmness, that he could not speak of his dealings with them. Eventually, Jene had stopped asking and had even stopped wondering.

And now the Flight Crew needed to talk to him. Could they be having some kind of crisis only a trained psychiatrist could defuse? No, for if that were so, they would not call for Jene.

Jene wanted nothing more than to stay with Kuarta and help her live through the loss of a father. She wanted to hold her for four months until the Ship arrived at Epsilon Eridani and the two could pretend to start anew on the surface. But she knew she could not begin the process of healing, for herself, until she completed this last task. She felt she owed it to Renold, if not to her entire world. By taking on a task that would have been his, Jene knew she would be stepping closer to the moment when his death would fall heavily upon her. Perralt's visit had not postponed that moment after all.

"I'll go," Jene said.

Jene and Kuarta were alone in the shuttle as it climbed back up towards the foremost section of the Panoptikon structure where the seldom-visited Crew quarters were. The eighteen members of the Flight Crew had, for all intents and purposes, become a cabal that few outsiders ever saw. For the majority of the voyage, virtually no one on Ship had even thought about them. What little speculation there was regarding the crew involved their backgrounds—it was generally assumed that most of the eighteen current crewmembers were directly related to those who had been aboard when Ship had been launched, either through inbreeding or forced-growth cloning. There was always speculation that a colonist could join the Flight Crew, though no one knew of anyone who had done so. Jene had lived with those casual assumptions for too long to easily question them now. If there was a holy pantheon in Ship, then it was populated by the Flight Crew.

"Mommy?"

"Yes?"

"What do the Flight Crew people look like?"

"Well, I suppose they look like us," Jene said, smiling as best she could at Kuarta. Renold had been killed a scant eighteen hours ago—Kuarta was still unreadable. Her question about the Flight Crew had been asked in a monotone, without any real regard for the answer. Jene had insisted upon taking her along, and Perralt had offered only halfhearted resistance to the idea. Jene had wanted to keep her daughter with her. Now Jene wondered if her instinct had been correct. Kuarta's question was more chilling than she could have realized, for she did not know what she would find when she met the Flight Crew. Was it a good idea to subject Kuarta to another possible shock? Jene shook her head slightly and tried to concentrate on the looming image of the Panoptikon in the shuttle's forward window.

The shuttle stopped a few meters from the control room hatch, hovering in the microgravity that existed that close to Ship's axis. Jene took Kuarta by the hand and the two floated slowly towards the hatch. The hatch was as clean and well-maintained as any other part of Ship—the automated maintenance robots did not discriminate or feel the fear of myth—but Jene still sensed an intangible air of disuse around the hatch. There was a small intercom grille next to the controls, and Jene had just reached out a hand to activate the communicator when the hatch opened of its own accord.

Jene stopped herself at the jamb, peering into the dimly-lit flight deck corridor. No one was in sight. The flight crew, Jene surmised, had been monitoring her approach and had evidently decided to admit her. She had no particular reason to fear these eighteen people—certainly, Renold had never given her cause to fear them—but she was apprehensive just the same.

She pulled herself and Kuarta into the corridor and heard the hatch close behind her. When it did, the lights in the corridor brightened significantly and a lone figure floated effortlessly towards her from the far end. Jene resisted a sudden impulse to gasp. The figure wasn't an angel or a demon, but just a human like herself. He came closer, and one of the corridor sconces bathed him in cool light.

He was an old man, probably a Gen Three, who wore an old-style steel-gray uniform that Jene had seen in some of the history vids of Ship's original launch. The uniform was odd in ways Jene could not immediately place—a hint of epaulets at the shoulders, a bit of gold braid here, an unidentified bird design on the shoulder. The man was unusually tall—perhaps over two meters—and remarkably spindly. He had a kindly face that broke into a smile as he said, "Doctor Halfner. I am glad to meet you." His voice was a pleasant, if somewhat scratchy, baritone. "Welcome to the flight deck. My name is Eduard Costellan, and I am what you might call the Captain of Ship." He thrust out a hand in greeting. Every action he had made betrayed his familiarity with his surroundings: he had none of the characteristic clumsiness or uncertainty Jene knew she displayed in microgravity. It also, no doubt, accounted for his height and relative lack of musculature. Jene had never heard of a medical tech coming up to the flight deck, and now that she thought about it, she wondered if indeed anyone here required medical attention at all.

The man's name was vaguely familiar for some reason. Jene tried to place it but could not. She filed the mystery away for later and took his proffered hand. "I suppose you know what has been happening...outside," she said.

Costellan's smile vanished and his face suddenly looked much older than it had a moment before. Could he actually be a Gen Two? There were some hundreds of them left alive in Ship, but their average age was approaching eighty. Jene knew that even with intensive brain rewiring, such individuals had lost a significant portion of their mental clarity. She was uncomfortable with the notion that such a man was guiding Ship to its final destination.

"Yes, we are. We are always watching Ship." He looked down at Kuarta and smiled widely. "Hello, Kuarta."

"How do you know my name?" Kuarta asked, a hint of interest in her voice.

"I have watched you for a long time." Costellan straightened and looked at Jene. "Both of you." He paused a beat, then made a quick gesture with two of his fingers. Another crewmember appeared from behind him. "Kuarta, this is one of my friends. She will take you to a place where you can see all of Ship. Would you like that?"

Jene answered for her. "No. She stays with me."

Costellan hesitated a fraction of a second, then said, "All right." He dismissed the crewmember with a wave of his hand and turned back to Jene. "Come into the control room, Doctor. I think you'll like it." He gestured with a bony hand to the room at the far end of the corridor and launched himself expertly towards it. Jene followed, awkwardly, noting that she had been staring at his hands—Costellan's hands were always in motion.

The control room, a smallish sphere at the end of the corridor, was frighteningly devoid of machinery. There were four computing stations ranged around the room, staffed by two men and two women. They wheeled in mid-air to face Jene when she and Costellan entered. All four of them were as tall and as underdeveloped as he was, although they were somewhat younger in appearance.

Jene stared at the arrangement wordlessly. Kuarta squirmed out of Jene's grasp and tried to swim towards the nearest workstation. Costellan smiled slightly, then gently pushed her towards her goal. The crewmember on duty at the station smiled indulgently and let the little girl see what he was doing.

Costellan said softly, "We watch you all the time, Doctor. Not just you, of course, but all of Ship. Sometimes we laugh with you, sometimes we cry when we realize we cannot ever join you. But we are content to guide you. It is what we have been bred for."

The man's naked emotion came so suddenly that Jene was not certain how to react. She glanced at the four technicians. Each one had Kuarta's dead-eyed stare. In an instant, she understood what Costellan was saying. None of the flight crew could possibly leave the flight deck and survive the angular acceleration that served as gravity for the eight thousand shipmates below. Worse, the flight crew could never leave Ship when it arrived at EE3 without constant intensive care. Of all the colonists who required medical care, the Flight Crew would be the most demanding.

Jene turned to Costellan. "You say you have seen what has happened below. Why have you asked to see me?"

"We would have preferred your husband...forgive me. I do not mean to bring up painful memories. He had visited us many times to talk. Now, though, Ship does not have any government, but the few who do see the need for some kind of organized system look to you to lead them. It is therefore to you that we must report."

"I've already told Perralt I'm not their leader. You don't need to report to me. I don't want you to report to me."

Costellan looked at the technicians. "They've been here their whole lives. Their sole duty is to monitor and guide Ship to its destination. All of us—we know that in four months, our usefulness to the mission will be at its final end. Renold helped us to overcome feelings of...hopelessness. Despair. Ennui. Call it what you want. Many of our number would have killed themselves, or have been killed by other Crew, if Renold had not intervened. More than you or anyone else realizes, Ship owes Renold a great deal."

"But I don't see why you need me."

"Everyone in Ship has tasks to perform. We have ours. Renold performed his, although it made him a quasi-outcast himself. And now you have one. But you refuse to take it. Ship still needs you."

"Perralt says otherwise."

"Wynd Perralt is a good woman," Costellan said, "but you will note that she did not spark this revolution. You did. You must lead Ship."

Jene slumped her shoulders slightly, as if even in microgravity a weight had suddenly dropped upon her. "I'm not a leader. I'm just...a cranky woman who wanted things her way."

"What else is a leader?"

Jene looked at him for a long moment. "You are the Captain of Ship. Why don't you lead?"

"Flight Crew turns its eyes outward. I have been Captain for a long time, and in all that time, we have not intervened in internal affairs."

Jene had never considered there could be any other kind of 'affairs' with regard to Ship. But his statement reminded her of the question of his age. She looked at Costellan quizzically. "How old are you? Are you a Gen Two?"

Costellan smiled again. "No, Jene. I am much older than that. I thank you, however, for the compliment."

Jene reeled. He was a Gen One? To her knowledge, he was the only one left alive—Old Deborah Waugh had died seven years ago at the age of ninety-six, having been born in year five of the voyage. This man could be the oldest man in the entire mission! Jene was suddenly flooded with questions about the history of the mission—here was a man who had been alive for the vast majority of the voyage.

"You're a Gen One? Sir, I—"

"No, Doctor. I said I was much older than that. I am what you call Gen Zero. I am one of the original launch crew."

Jene did not have any more mental room for amazement. One question, though, was answered: the mysterious familiarity of his name. She suddenly remembered a holograph of the launch crew from her history lessons. Eduard Costellan had been a junior officer then.

"Are you the only one left, sir?" She asked, automatically adding the honorific.

"I am. The workers you see about me are all Gen One." Jene glanced at the hovering technicians. "I suppose as a medical doctor you'd be interested in our antiagathic process?" He chuckled. "Nine-tenths of the process is simple—live your entire life in free-fall. My descendants will live even longer than I, though such a long life, under these conditions, is not the blessing it would at first glance seem."

"How have you kept yourselves from disease? Do you have a doctor?"

"We have a Flight Surgeon, but her talents have not been necessary for many years. We sometimes succumb to degenerative diseases—I myself am in the beginning stages of osteoporosis."

"Microgravity."

"Exactly. But our doctor tells me that if I continue to exercise and take the calcium treatments, I should live another twenty years."

Jene did not answer. She was beyond answering.

"But I did not call you here for that, Doctor. There is a more pressing matter to discuss. As per flight doctrine, we launched a telemetry probe some time ago to begin collecting data on Epsilon Eridani 3. I released our findings weeks ago to Councilman Arnson as the civil authority in Ship. I wish to give them to you now."

Jene found that she did not want to object. She nodded slightly.

Costellan collected himself and said, in a tone that reminded Jene of a resident at the hospital giving a formal report, "Eighty-six days ago, we launched one of our six planetary probes towards EE3 to begin surveying conditions there. We have since discovered far more than I believe Arnson has made public."

"He told me departments would get the data soon," Jene said, anger rising in her. Medical needed that data to prepare for landing. If Arnson had withheld vital data, the medical teams would have to work overtime to provide the necessary panimmunity vaccines. The anger was almost instantly replaced with shame—shame that she could feel more anger towards Arnson for withholding data when the man had killed her husband.

"I do not believe he would have ever released this data. I will allow you to hear the transmission yourself." Costellan floated to one of the technicians and spoke briefly to him.

Jene frowned. What did he mean, transmission? As she wondered at his choice of words, the answer came to her through a static-laced sound that echoed through the control room.

"...to Colony Ship *Odyssey*, this is the New Earth colony on Epsilon Eridani 3. We have picked up your probe on radar. We have been expecting you. You'll be glad to know that we have reserved a sizeable portion of our colony for your use upon your arrival, and we stand ready to assist you in any way we can. We will send you transmission details so you can respond with what we're sure will be a stream of questions. But for now, welcome to New Earth, brothers and sisters!"

Jene stared at Costellan as the voice of the com operator sounded in the room. Costellan glanced at his technician and the voice ceased.

"How?" Jene croaked.

"We've been in contact with them for a while now. It seems that Earth developed a method of space travel that beat our cruising speed of point one c—that's one tenth the speed of light—by a factor of five. Twenty-one years after our departure, the Colony Ship *Argo* was launched. It achieved a velocity nearly half the speed of light and arrived at Epsilon Eridani in just over twenty years. Because of the difference in launch dates and relative velocities, there was no practical way for the *Argo* to contact us even if they knew our position, and as you know, our contact with Earth was terminated fourteen years into the mission due to power demands. We calculate that the *Argo* overtook us about eighty-one years ago. They have established a thriving colony that has been in existence on EE3, which they call New Earth, for sixty years and which has a population of about fifty-five thousand."

Jene felt the room drop away from under her. She was suddenly quite terrified of the constant falling sensation on the Flight Deck and vomited unceremoniously, trying vainly to cover her mouth and spare the surfaces of the room.

The four technicians swam to mop up the offending matter as Costellan quickly hugged her to him. "It's all right, Doctor. The Commissar-General of New Earth is a very likeable woman. I think you'll like it there."

Costellan went on in soothing tones about the nature of New Earth—the planet had been partially terraformed, though the colony was still living in pressure domes. Ample living space had been prepared for the newcomers aboard Ship and the inhabitants of New Earth stood ready to accept their brothers and sisters with open arms.

But Jene knew why she was crying. It was not because suddenly, in a single, ironic stroke of cruelty on the part of the universe, the pioneers of Ship had been reduced to refugees and immigrants, nor was it because of relief that none of the surviving Class D children would have to suffer because of inadequate medical care during planet-fall—it was because she had set in motion a war that had killed her husband and her daughter's father; a war that had killed dozens of people, including Bobby Yancey: a war that had not been necessary. Now the grief of Renold's death came flooding into her, but it was not alone.

BOOK TWO
COLONY

CHAPTER
6

With detached interest, Kuarta watched her daughter play with the small museum's native stone and mineral collection. It was a boon to have such a collection inside the Dome where children could handle some of the harmless specimens of Epsilon Eridani's geology. Yallia had only recently turned five years old by Ship reckoning, but had yet to reach her fourth New Earth year. She was not yet old enough to venture outside, even under strict supervision. There were just too many risks.

"Ma, when is Gramma coming?" Yallia asked, her hands turning over a bleached-green Epsilon stone.

"She had some work to do. I'm sure she'll be here soon."

Kuarta smiled despite herself as she thought of the feisty old woman. Her mother was still as formidable a force as ever—in the familial as well as political arenas. It had been she who had spearheaded the Genetic Integration laws seven Ship years ago—no, eight, Kuarta remembered. It had taken Kuarta and her partner Dolen four years to conceive Yallia. Kuarta remembered her mother's apprehension at Dolen's presence in her life. He was one of the *Argonaut*-descendants, genetically superior to even the purest of the Ship immigrants. Tall, handsome, possessed of a keen intelligence and a remarkably efficient and healthy body, as well as unusual charm and grace, Dolen had nevertheless unnerved Jene. She liked the young professor, certainly; it was the inevitable social friction that worried her. Argies did not marry Shippies.

"I think you should wait, that's all I'm saying," Kuarta remembered her mother telling her those four years ago. "The ink isn't even dry on the legislation, and you want to go and be a test case. Isn't it enough that your mother wrote the damn laws?"

"It's been three years, Ma," Kuarta had said with a grin. "You know very well that by now there have been half a dozen unions between argies and us, some of them with children. No one will take notice of me."

"The hell they won't. Look, Kuarta, for better or for worse, you get the runoff from the attention people splash on me. A Commissar's offspring is always under suspicion, but you're the daughter of one of only two Ship Commissars."

Kuarta had become angry at that comment. "*Ship* Commissar? There's no such thing, Ma. You're a Commissar just like the other fourteen. You've got the same responsibility and authority as the rest of them."

Jene had smiled indulgently at her daughter's charming naiveté. "I'd like to believe that, dear, but it's just not so. Perralt and I have no illusions as to our true stature in the Assembly. Twenty Ship years is a long time but not long enough to erase deeply held prejudices. She and I are only two voices, from different Domes at that. Two voices against thirteen don't get a lot done."

"You passed the G.I. laws," Kuarta countered. "You convinced enough argie Commissars to vote for it. That took some doing." Despite herself, Kuarta referred to the other Commissars by their heritage.

Jene nodded slightly at that. "Yes, it did. More than I think you realize." She sighed. "It some ways, it was easier when we first landed. I remember the immunizations—we had been so wrong, Kuarta." The bitter edge in her voice Kuarta had become so accustomed to faded, as it always did when she remembered the past, especially the past before Renold's death. "We thought we had prepared ourselves on Ship with our so-called panimmunity. But the argies had an immunization program ready for us. We were in quarantine less than a week, and it was not at all unpleasant. After that, for years, we were welcome guests, given the best linens, so to speak. I remember when we first offered to put our colony equipment—and Ship itself—at the disposal of the government here." Jene chuckled. "We had colonization equipment that was at least sixty years out of date! I remember the laughter at that," she said, her eyes looking into the past. "Still, they made room for us, even though we had nothing to offer. Built an entire Dome just for us. Yes, we were welcome here, and we thanked the argies every time we saw one of them."

"Then things changed," Kuarta said. "I remember, too. I was ten…or six, I mean, when it really started."

"Oh, well, it didn't really start like turning on a switch, dear. It had been building up. How could it not? Shippies began to think of the colony as their home, and argies noticed we weren't thanking them as much for the very air around us. Resentment on both sides. It was bound to happen, dear."

"You say that like there was no other way," Kuarta had said. "But then you fought and fought until you made them appoint you and Perralt

Commissars. Why did you do that, if you thought there was nothing that could be done?"

Jene smiled wolfishly. "All right," she growled, "you caught me. I was younger then, Kuarta, and I thought I could make a difference."

"Oh, Mother, you're still young. And you can still make a difference. You just keep fighting for us in the Assembly. I'll make a difference in other ways. Like with Dolen."

Jene snorted. "Got me back to the subject at hand, I see."

Kuarta remembered her mother's sigh—a sigh that had indicated that not only was her mother willing to let her have her way in this, but that said she had never seriously objected to her daughter's union with the young argie.

"Go ahead and unify with your partner," she had said. "You two shouldn't have to suffer because some Earth scientist built a faster starship engine a hundred years ago."

Kuarta remembered her mother's almost hidden pride on the day of their union ("marriage," Jene had insisted upon calling it) and her grudging acceptance of Kuarta's choice of partners.

That night, before going to bed together for the first time, Kuarta had taken Dolen outside the Dome, both clad in their Epsilon suits to ward off the toxic chlorine atmosphere, to her father's grave. Dolen listened for an hour as Kuarta had told him what she knew of Renold Halfner, both from dim memories and from her mother's stories.

Kuarta was jerked back into the present by the crying of her daughter at the E-stone display. She was sitting on the ground bawling, Epsilon stones scattered around her, while three physically impressive young boys— obviously *Argonaut*-descended—hovered thuggishly nearby.

"What happened?" Kuarta said, scooping her daughter up in her arms and examining her for bumps or cuts.

"The boy hit me," Yallia said amid sobs, pointing at one of the three.

Kuarta glared at the trio accusingly. "I'm sure he didn't mean to," she said, cradling her child in her arms.

"Stupid shippie can't even stand up on her own," the boy mumbled, quietly but loudly enough for Kuarta to hear. He and his friends looked to be about ten years old, which meant they were six in New Earth years.

"Come on, Yalli, let's go see some of the other things here," Kuarta said, anxious to leave the area. She could see heads beginning to turn her way—*Argonaut*-descended stares could not be far behind.

"Why don't you go outside and play?" the same boy said, this time making no effort to lower his voice. The other two laughed.

That comment had caused a bit of a stir in the immediate area. Several people, their stature and characteristic jet-black hair identifying them immediately as also *Argonaut*-descended, stopped to watch Kuarta's reaction to the boy's comment.

She knew what he had meant—it was commonplace to refer to the *outside* whenever one wished to symbolically consign something to oblivion. Although the terraforming process had been going for almost eighty years, the chlorine-tainted atmosphere was still almost instantly fatal to unprotected humans. A glance at the expectant faces around her told Kuarta that the boy's sentiments were echoed, albeit silently, by the adults around her.

One face in the crowd caught her eye, a young adult argie woman's. The expression on her face was a mixture of emotions—sympathy for Yallia and Kuarta, hatred for the behavior of her fellow argies, and fear for herself. She looked up at Kuarta and made a tiny gesture with her shoulders, as if to say 'I am not one of these people. I do not share their attitudes toward you and your child. But I cannot speak out.'

Kuarta nodded slightly at the sympathizer and turned back to Yallia.

"Let's go see the science experiments," she said to her daughter, as brightly as she could. She put Yallia down and, gripping her hand tightly, started to walk out of the loose circle that had begun to form around her.

She made every effort to avoid eye contact with the boys, but as she passed, she could not resist a quick glance in their direction. The spokesman was staring at her, feet rooted firmly in place as if to claim the land itself, while his compatriots whispered to each other. Kuarta caught the word "Halfner" from their conversation.

"Hey," The lead boy said suddenly. Kuarta hesitated for a fraction of a second, then continued to move on.

"You're Kuarta Halfner," the boy said, a note of hostile accusation in his voice. "Your mother brought all you here."

Kuarta needed to respond to that. Something about the way the boy spoke her name indicated that he was pointedly ignoring her new surname: Verdafner, a fusion of Dolen's original Verdu and her Halfner, as was the custom. "We came here—" she started, then thought better of it. The boy did not want an explanation, nor did the dozen or so people who had by now gathered around her. She had to change tactics. "Where are your parents, young man?"

"Right here," came the instant answer from behind her, alarmingly close. A burly man with thick black eyebrows looked down on her. "Why don't you get out of here, shippie, and stop making trouble?"

While the context of his words indicated the museum itself, Kuarta knew the man's thinly-veiled meaning was for her and her kind to leave the planet altogether. The slight nods and murmurs of agreement from the rest of the crowd confirmed the sentiment.

"All right, let's just move on, okay?" said yet another voice from beyond the throng. A blue-shirted museum worker wormed her way into the thick of the crowd and, through gestures and encouraging words, dispersed the twenty people around Kuarta. Soon, the area was all but deserted.

"Everything okay here?" she asked Kuarta with a smile. The woman was perhaps sixty-five, her raven hair only slightly less vibrant than that of those around her, her face only beginning to show wrinkles. The longevity of the *Argonaut*-descended was yet another difference that marked them as separate from, and superior to, the immigrants from Ship.

"It is now. Thank you so much," Kuarta said, genuine relief flowing from her. Yallia looked up at the worker.

"Good. Hello there, little one," the woman said to Yallia. "Do you like our museum here?"

"Yes. It's fun."

"Oh, good." She smiled down at the girl and said to Kuarta, "I know you people love the museum. I'm just sorry that had to happen to you."

Kuarta's smile faded slightly. *You people.* "That's all right," Kuarta said automatically. "We still have you to thank." Kuarta let go of Yallia, who wandered the few short feet back to the mineral display.

"Oh, don't mention it. Our colony is your colony. We have to make you folks feel at home here and try to help you integrate into our society. How old is she?"

Kuarta hesitated only a moment to convert Ship age into New Earth age. "She's—three and a half."

"Oh, she's so darling. It's so good to see little ones enjoying the museum." She watched Yallia for a moment, then added conversationally, "It's funny, but she looks almost argie."

The museum worker stared at Yallia, and Kuarta imagined the woman was wondering just how the resemblance to the superior elite had been achieved.

"Her father is *Argonaut*-descended," Kuarta said softly.

"Oh," the woman said, her voice betraying the strain of forced nonchalance. Immediately, the woman shifted her weight to the foot away from Kuarta and seemed to withdraw into herself. She gave Kuarta the courtesy of watching Yallia for a few more seconds before saying, with too much enthusiasm, "Well, I'd better be going back to work. The museum won't run itself. Nice to have met you."

Kuarta watched her retreat to another part of the museum before she gathered her daughter and left the place altogether.

* * *

Botanical Section Nine (more commonly referred to as "the forest of Arden" both because it was the section that housed most of the deciduous trees in New Chicago Dome and because it was the favored retreat of young lovers) was empty the next morning when Kuarta and Dolen took one of the strolls they arranged whenever their work schedules allowed. They lived as close to Arden as was possible, given the topography of New Chicago, the official name for Dome Six. Fully half of the nine-thousand occupants lived in the sixteen towering buildings in the center of New Chicago where the Dome ceiling was ninety meters high, while the rest lived in shorter buildings that formed a series of concentric rings around the metropolitan area. Next came forests, such as Botanical Section Nine, and beyond them, towards the edges of the Dome, were the various industries that kept New Chicago a working, functioning part of the massive Dome Complex, of which it was one of six. New Chicago was home to many shippie families: by now, twenty years after planet-fall, shippies had spread beyond their New Frankfurt Dome and were beginning to live in others. The distinction between shippie and argie was made all the more overtly to compensate, it seemed.

But now, Dolen and Kuarta were merely two people out for a walk in the trees.

"There was more trouble yesterday with Yallia," Kuarta said softly after the pair had been walking in silence for a time.

"What kind of trouble?" Dolen's oval, somber face turned to meet hers. He listened attentively as Kuarta relayed the story of the encounter in the museum, stopping her for brief moments to ask clarifying questions. She could almost feel his anger rising, even while he displayed no sign of distress. He was like that—able to mask virtually any emotion or feeling he wished from almost anyone; Kuarta, however, had learned to read his moods despite his almost perfect inscrutability.

When she had finished, Dolen said, "I suppose we will have to talk to Yallia. No sense in bringing it up with Jene."

"You're saying we shouldn't tell my mother?"

Dolen sighed. "If we tell her, she'll have to try to balance her own feelings against her position as Commissar. I know Jene—she's a fine politician, but no one should be placed in such a delicate situation. She'd get into trouble, politically as well as morally."

Kuarta knew he was right. In the near-perfect socialism the colony had organized, the mere hint of favoritism in the political circles could bring down the most capable of legislators. If Jene acted to protect her family, she would soon find herself facing the Board of Inquiry.

Dolen added, "Plus, if we do anything, the incidents of harassment will only get worse." He hesitated. Kuarta knew he was holding back something.

"What else?" she asked, stopping in the middle of the path.

He turned away and looked abstractedly at the nearest tree. "I've heard...talk. At the University." At his partner's expectant silence, he continued. "It was nothing I was supposed to hear, I know. I was coming back to my office during one of my classes a few days ago—I'd forgotten the holo of those old Earth scenes, the ones from the mid-twentieth century United States, all about immigration. You remember those? With the ships and Ellis Island and all that?"

Kuarta smiled despite the gravity of the situation. Dolen had a habit of trailing off into side issues and completely forgetting his main point. His students could frequently miss an entire class-worth of instruction if they managed to get him talking about Earth history's more interesting moments.

"Yes, dear. I remember. You were talking about something you overheard?"

"Oh, right. Well, I was going back to my office in the middle of class, as I said, and there were two, no, three young student-professors in the history office, which is the one right past mine. But you know that, don't you? You've been there before. In any case, I was going to go straight into my office and get the holocube, then go back to the class, when I heard my name from the history office. 'Professor Verdafner must have it bad for shippie tail,' I heard."

Kuarta's smile vanished. She knew that there had been similar accusations leveled at her, but in reverse, of course. Still, she bristled at the thought that she was just some kind of vessel for an argie's lust.

Dolen continued his story, apparently unaware of the effects it was having on Kuarta. "It was just student-profs griping about us oldsters, you know. Happens all the time. Still, this had gone too far. As you can imagine, I stopped then and there and was ready to go into the history office to have a word or two with those inside, when another comment floated outside into the hallway where I was standing. And that comment made me pause."

He stopped. Kuarta did not prompt him—she knew he would speak when he was ready.

"Someone in the office said, 'Those damn shippies think they're entitled to everything' and someone else replied, 'I wonder how they'd do outside?' and the whole bunch of them laughed."

Kuarta nodded. "Dolen, dear, that's no different than what we have been hearing for a while now."

"Yes, but to joke about genocide? That's...." He could not find the words.

Kuarta smiled at her partner. His depth of knowledge about certain subjects, ancient history, for instance, was matched only by his incredible ignorance about the darker side of his society. He could see evil in history books, perpetrated by human beings one on another, but he sincerely seemed to believe the human race had evolved beyond such institutions as racism and prejudice. He was not capable of seeing it all around him, even when he himself was the target. Kuarta could not bear to shatter her husband's innocence by telling him the students were not joking.

Kuarta patted his arm soothingly. "I know, dear. Let's talk about something else. Have you noticed the leaves are starting to turn?"

* * *

Yallia was an unusually bright girl for her age. Even among the already naturally intelligent argies (who, after all, possessed not only a genetic advantage over their immigrant brethren but had the intangible environment of the colony itself to support them) she stood out. It was for this reason she had been placed in the four-year old (New Earth years) class. There, she could work with others of her ability and receive appropriate instruction. There was no denying, however, the active resentment the other children and their parents felt at the presence of this precocious shippie child, the granddaughter of a Commissar.

Helena Murgat's parents were perhaps the most resentful. They had elected to withdraw their daughter from Cassiopeia School, the school that Yallia and four hundred other children attended in New Chicago, and move to another Dome entirely rather than have to associate with filthy shippies. For their daughter, it meant, of course, abandoning friendships that Helena was just beginning to form and becoming the "new girl" in a different school in a different Dome.

All of which was in the back of young Helena's mind as she prepared the concoction for the cause of all her troubles. Yallia Verdafner would pay for what she had done. Helena scooped another handful of the foul-smelling soil into the bowl. There had been little difficulty in opening her father's soil sample case—as Helena had never showed the slightest interests in her father's work as a xenobotanist, he had never thought to keep the samples of Epsilon Eridani III topsoil under tight security. A bit of observation and a stepstool later, and Helena was mixing the potion that would make Yalli as physically sick as Helena felt inside at the impending move.

Helena smiled a crooked half smile as she saw tiny native worms wriggling in the mixture of dirt, milk, and beer.

The school day went by uneventfully until first recess. Helena had already contacted her confederates through carefully scrawled notes passed during the day—when the children were released for recess, Helena's crew went into action.

"Hey, Yallia," Helena called with false bonhomie. "Come on over here. I've got a present for you."

Yallia was under no illusions as to her status with her class. She was well-hated by all, and there were none that hated her with more fire than Helena. She looked across the playground warily and shook her head.

"Come on, Yallia. I want to be your friend," Helen wheedled.

The ruse worked. Yallia, smart as she was, could not resist entirely the possibility that Helena might be undergoing a change of heart. Yallia came over but stopped some distance away.

"You don't like me," she called out. She waited for an explanation.

"Yeah, well, since I'm leaving soon, I want to tell you something. I'm sorry for everything I did to you."

Yallia scanned the faces of the three girls standing nearby. They radiated malice even as Helena spoke. Something was not right.

"You are?" Yallia kept her eyes on the three girls.

"Yeah." Helena got up from the bench on which she had been sitting and approached Yallia. Her flankers moved with her. "Can I give you a hug?"

Yallia did not answer immediately. Her inexperienced intellect told her not to trust this situation (and her suspicious Halfner genes did as well), but the overriding need for acceptance trumped all her rationality. She nodded slightly.

Helena moved in to hug her. That was the signal. Helena and her three associates tackled Yallia and expertly pinned her to the ground. Yallia found her arms held fast, a girl sitting on each. The third toady sat on her legs while Helena produced a small bag of brown, muddy liquid.

"You smelly shippie. You have to eat all of this before we let you go. Here," she said, stuffing a pungent handful into Yallia's mouth.

Yallia's shrieks of terror quickly became muffled gags as she fruitlessly fought against Helena's hands. Helena managed to force three handfuls down Yallia's throat before Ms. Fletcher's startled cries ended the torture.

Ms. Fletcher had fought off her disgust at Yallia's initial arrival and continued presence in her class with professionalism—she was a teacher and took her job quite seriously. Still, when she arrived on the scene, a tiny part of her applauded Helena's efforts. Outwardly, she radiated concern and disapproval toward the perpetrators, but she could not, despite her attempts to suppress the sadistic corner of her mind, entirely pity the coughing, retching shippie girl who lay at her feet.

Yallia vomited copiously onto the sand of the playground. A sudden, sharp, aggressive odor of chlorine drove the onlookers back and away—they had been trained from birth that the smell spelled death to them.

Ms. Fletcher was not an expert in any particular field, being a primary school teacher, but was reasonably well versed in practically every branch of knowledge. She knew what must be happening to Yallia—Helena must have forced some native plant or animal matter down her throat, which was now dissolving in the girl's stomach acids. The combination of free chlorine in the biomatter was reacting with the hydrochloric acid in Yallia's stomach and producing toxic chlorine gas.

"Children! Run to my classroom and stay there! Get away from her," Ms. Fletcher shouted at the assembled youngsters. They needed no additional prodding. The smell of chlorine was enough to send them running in panic. Helena and her cohorts were among the last to leave. Helena herself showed no sign of remorse at the convulsing result of her anger but retreated with dignity back to the classroom.

Ms. Fletcher herself trembled with indecision. She knew she should help Yallia vomit up as much of the substance she had ingested, but her conditioned fear of chlorine and her disdain for the girl's lineage threatened to override her natural instincts to help those in need. She remained, watching Yallia from perhaps ten meters' distance and advancing in tiny, shuffling steps, as the girl slowly lost consciousness.

The medical personnel arrived soon after the school's administrator placed the call. Yallia had been unconscious for no more than thirty minutes when the paramedics, in oxygen masks, attended to her. Kuarta and Dolen had been called as well and arrived only minutes behind the paramedics.

"What happened?" Kuarta asked of the assembled people around her daughter, her voice showing no sign of the emotions she was feeling. She could smell the chlorine in the air, but the clinical part of her had taken over, and she was prepared to solve the problem, whatever it turned out to be. Dolen spotted Ms. Fletcher, standing with other adults still about ten meters away from Yallia, and guided his partner toward her.

"What happened?" Kuarta repeated, her eyes still on the paramedics' backs.

"Well, your daughter swallowed some native plants, I think." Ms. Fletcher said.

"You *think*?"

"There were some girls, they were just playing," Ms. Fletcher said, her voice already defensive, "and I think they stuffed some plants down her."

"Where are they now?" Dolen barked.

"I don't think this is the time to punish the girls, Mr. Verdafner. They will be dealt with in—"

"I'm not going to punish them, dammit! Have you asked them what they made her eat?" Dolen's voice carried uncharacteristic violence.

"Well, I was more worried about getting them inside," Ms. Fletcher said, then shrank under Dolen's withering stare.

Kuarta broke away from the woman and approached Yallia. Two of the other teachers in the area moved quickly to intercept her. "No, no, stay out of this. Let the paramedics work," one of them said.

Kuarta shook them off. "Let me go, damn you! I just want to see!"

"Kuarta, we'll see her at the hospital. Let them work, dear," Dolen said softly, his hands on her shoulders. Kuarta relented. She knew he was right, and she could hear the paramedics' muffled voices through their masks.

"She's stable. Let's get her up and to N.C.G.," one of them said.

Kuarta turned to Ms. Fletcher. "They're taking her to New Chicago General. Ask the girls who did this what they made her eat and bring the data to the hospital." She barked the commands without rancor—there would be plenty of time for incrimination later. Now she had to secure her daughter's life.

Kuarta and Dolen were allowed to ride in the ambulance as it screamed its way to N.C.G. Public transportation would have been agonizingly slow and there was plenty of room in the little truck. The hospital was located in almost the exact center of the Dome, along with other municipal services. This meant it was no more than two and a half kilometers from the edge of the Dome in all directions, and considerably closer to the more heavily populated sections.

Kuarta rode in the back with one of the paramedics and held Yallia's hand. The girl was still unconscious and masked. The truck's air scrubbers were on maximum but could still not completely erase the chlorine smell.

"What are her vitals?" Kuarta asked, craning her neck to look at the monitor.

"B.P. looks good: one-ten over sixty-four. Pulse stable at seventy-three. Respiration good," the paramedic said.

"What about blood gas?"

The medic looked, then squinted and looked again. "Uh, blood gas is...normal?" He looked at Yallia again, then back at the monitor. "Yeah, it's normal."

As if on cue, Yallia opened her eyes.

"Yallia! It's Mommy, sweetheart. I'm right here."

"Mommy?" Yallia said, then coughed copiously.

"Yes, darling, here I am. Can you see me?"

Yallia nodded and moved her hand up to the oxygen mask.

"No, no, dear, keep that on. That's helping you breathe. Does it hurt to breathe?"

Yallia nodded again.

The paramedic leaned in. "Yallia, My name is Marq. Does it taste funny to breathe?"

Yallia nodded.

Marq looked at Kuarta. "That's the chlorine gas," he said.

"No, like plastic," Yallia said.

"What, dear?" Kuarta asked.

"It tastes like plastic, not chlorine."

Kuarta frowned and glanced at the monitor. "You said her pulse ox is normal?"

The medic checked again. "Yes. Normal and holding. In fact, all her stats are perfect. I don't get it," he mused. "Yallia, honey, I want you to take a deep breath. Can you do that for me?"

Yallia nodded and breathed in, her little chest expanding. She coughed once, a short, sharp sound, but otherwise breathed normally.

"Did that hurt?" he asked.

Yallia shook her head.

"Damned if I know," Marq mumbled. "Okay, that's good, sweetie. Now just lie back and relax." He looked at Kuarta quizzically. "She have any unusual blood chemistry you know of?"

"Nothing I'm aware of. Her natal work was all normal."

Marq shrugged. "She's looking real good now. They'll do more detailed work at NCG. Blood gas, cellular scan, and so on."

The rest of the ride only took five minutes, and Kuarta spent it looking at her daughter and watching the monitor. When they arrived at the hospital, Yallia was rushed to the total exam room where she was placed in the Complete Body Scanner. Kuarta herself had helped design the device—a short tunnel that combined all the possible passive and active scans and lab services a doctor could want. It was fully automated and very quick, gave a detailed analysis of the scans it performed, and otherwise acted as an invaluable diagnostic tool. Doctors still verified the results and prescribed treatment, but their role had been vastly simplified by the machinery. The machines were somewhat expensive and cranky of maintenance, and as a result, every hospital housed only two. Hospitals were always clamoring for more CB units, but they knew full well that no Dome would get another scanner until all did. That was the price of a neosocialist society, but it also meant no colonist would be denied medical care because a more influential citizen took precedence. Even with the obviously prejudicial environment that placed shippies at the bottom of a supposedly nonexistent social ladder, the medical community was still almost entirely egalitarian.

Yallia came out of the scanner a scant ten minutes after being put in, and Kuarta crowded near the read-out screen that was normally reserved for doctors. Her standing in the medical community gave her access others might not have had. When the numbers flashed on the screen, the emergency doctor furrowed his brow and said, "You're sure she ingested chlorine?"

Kuarta could not answer for a moment. The blood work and tissue samples showed no sign of chlorine at all.

"Mommy, can I get up now?" Yallia asked from the exam table.

Kuarta ignored her. Dolen put his hands on his partner's shoulders again, seeing the numbers but not understanding their significance. "What is it?"

"There's no chlorine in her," the emergency doctor said.

"Could the scanner be wrong?" Dolen asked.

"No. Not like this," Kuarta said decisively.

"We've had no problems with it," the doctor confirmed.

"Then why—" Dolen began, but Kuarta interrupted him.

"It was chlorine," she said to herself out loud. "We all smelled it. Has the school called yet?" she asked the doctor.

"Yes. A Ms. Fletcher called it in, and a sample of the material is on its way. We'll know more then. Right now, let's get her to a bed while we wait."

Kuarta, Dolen, and Yallia were escorted to a room in the emergency ward. When they were alone, Kuarta asked her daughter, "Tell me what happened, dear. Did you eat anything?"

Yallia started to tear up again as she remembered the incident. "She— she made me, Mommy! She said she wanted to be fuh-friends, but when I gave her a hug, she—she put it in my mouth!"

Kuarta hugged her close and patted her hair. "Shhh, shhh. That's okay, dear. Now, what did she put in your mouth?"

"Dirt and stuff. Worms," came the muffled answer.

Dolen tried to make light of the experience. "Ewww! Worms, huh? I'll bet they tasted really bad."

"Uh-huh. In the beginning."

"What do you mean, dear?" Kuarta stopped the hug and looked at her daughter's tear-streaked face.

"After a while it didn't taste too bad. It tasted like...that stupid oatmeal Daddy makes." Yallia managed a weak smile at her father.

Dolen thought for a moment, then said, "Irish oatmeal? The kind I cook on the stove and make with water?"

Yallia nodded and wrinkled her nose.

"But that doesn't taste like anything, dear."

"I know," Yallia said.

Dolen and Kuarta looked at each other, confused. Kuarta spread her hands slightly in an "I-don't-know-either" gesture, then held Yallia again. The three sat in silence for a few minutes until the emergency doctor came into their room. "Hi there," he said with too much enthusiasm. "How are you feeling, soldier?"

"Okay. Sort of tired," Yallia said.

"Not hurting?"

"Nope."

"Great. I'm going to talk to your mommy now," he said, silently signaling Kuarta with his eyes, "and then we'll be right back." He held the door open for Kuarta and followed her out.

"We've analyzed the stuff she ate," he said when the door had closed behind him. "Lots of animal matter, soil, microorganisms, you name it. Really bad."

Kuarta took a deep breath. "So what do we do?"

"Well, that's the thing. All the scans show that she's fine. Not a trace of chlorine in her system."

Kuarta thought. "She couldn't have vomited it all up. Some of it got into her. It had to. Her stomach acids must have broken down the chlorine and made chlorine gas. She should be in bad shape."

"Right. And not just from the chlorine. The microorganisms in the soil and the biomatter should be fighting with her immune system—she had panimmunity, right?" It was almost an unnecessary question, as all colonists received the vaccine at birth.

"Of course."

"But still, that much native biomatter should really be hitting her hard. I have to admit, Doctor Verdafner, I'm baffled."

"Maybe she didn't really eat any," Dolen said weakly.

Kuarta shook her head slowly. "I think she's telling the truth."

"The scan did show a small amount of soil in her stomach, and she did throw up recently," the doctor added.

Kuarta nodded absently. She, too, was bringing her considerable medical knowledge to bear on the situation and was coming up short.

"We should keep her here for tests, but...." The doctor shrugged.

"You're not sure why," Kuarta finished his thought for him. She thought for a few more seconds, then turned to the doctor. She seemed to see him for the first time—a vaguely Slavic man, an argie, with a youthful face and what appeared to be perpetual stubble on his chin. She liked him somehow—perhaps it was his unabashedly earnest approach to her daughter's case. She felt the urge to agree with him and keep Yallia here for more observation, but something felt wrong. Perhaps it was the conversation she had had with Dolen earlier, perhaps it was her suspicious Halfner personality, or more likely a combination of both, that made her say, "Well, I guess we'll take her home. Thanks for everything, Doctor...?"

"Wajanowitz."

"Thank you. I would like to invoke my privacy rights, though. No offense," she said.

"Oh, none at all, Doctor. I understand." By invoking the Right to Medical Privacy, Doctor Wajanowitz could not submit any of the particulars of Yallia's identity to anyone, including the medical database. He could, of course, submit a case study in such a way as to preserve the anonymity of the subject by withholding data that was not pertinent (in this case, that would most likely include gender, physical description, and certainly name), but such a study would be restricted to medical research purposes. It was a minor hindrance to research, one which Kuarta herself had run up against many times in her own work, but was essential to preserving the society at large. Genetic and medical prejudice in the social realm could easily wreck a colony such as theirs if measures were not taken to preserve medical and genetic privacy.

Kuarta shook his hand and smiled. He left them and began the discharge process. A few authorizations later and the Verdafners were on their way home. Dolen and Kuarta could not help stealing glances at their daughter as they rode the wirebus, wondering just what had happened to her that day.

CHAPTER
7

"You realize, of course, the impossibility of your request," Commissar-General Jalen Newfield said softly. He gazed out the window of his twentieth-story office, watching the activity below in Valhalla Dome. His office was set on the highest floor of the tallest building in the Dome, which itself was located (as all Domes were) twelve-hundred meters above sea level.

The man who stood on the other side of the Commissar-General's desk was small and mousy and did not fit the argie stereotype at all. Carll Tann was only thirty-one years old (calculated in N.E. years, the only way Carll Tann measured time), the same age as Jene Halfner, but had been showing the signs of baldness in his retreating hairline for at least five years. He could easily have corrected the minor aesthetic fault if he had wished, but he had found the distraction of such an obvious genetic weakness useful in misdirecting his political opponents.

"I know it is...unusual, Commissar-General, but I think it is a necessary application of your emergency powers. The genedata must be turned over to us so that we may begin to analyze just what has happened. Unchecked, this could lead to an epidemic that could wipe out the whole colony."

Newfield smiled, his back still towards his advisor. "Save the alarmist rhetoric for your memoirs, Carll. We don't have all the facts yet."

Tann lowered his voice. "Sir, it is possible that the immunization program set up twelve years ago when the *Odyssey* arrived is beginning to show flaws with the first generation of Ship-descended children." That was a lie, he knew, but it was a lie that had the dual advantages of being plausible and ominous.

Now Newfield turned around. He took pains to keep his good looks unobtrusive, just as Tann shoved his ugliness to the fore. Newfield was boyishly handsome; his broad, dark face softened easily when he wasn't angry, as he was now. "But everyone receives the immunization series. Why should this generation of *Odyssey* children be any different from their parents?"

"I do not fully understand it myself, sir, but I am told that the vaccines we use do have an effect on the genes of the recipient. It is possible that the shippie, excuse me, *Odyssey*-descended children were born...affected by the immunity series."

"This girl...Yallia Verdafner, right? She's a hybrid child, isn't she? Her father's argie."

"I...believe so, sir," Tann said with mock uncertainty. He knew more about Yallia Verdafner than he cared to admit to the Commissar-General.

Newfield considered this for a moment. "You think the vaccinations compounded what may have been a preexisting genetic condition?"

Tann shrugged and spread his hands. "Possibly. We don't really know what has happened. We are operating in the dark. It is for that reason, sir, that I advise you unseal the genedata on the girl."

Newfield hesitated a long time before he responded. When he did, his voice came from far down in his throat. "Genedata is private information. The Commissar-General can't just pry into a citizen's medical records at will. No." Newfield shook his head, but he averted his gaze from that of his advisor. Tann knew his eyes unnerved Newfield.

"I know how you feel, Jalen," Tann said, softly, ingratiatingly, moving a half-step closer to the leader of the planet, "and believe me, no one takes personal genetic privacy to heart more than I. I know that had my genedata been released prior to my birth...well, who knows," he said, smiling away the tension. Both knew what he meant. Among argies, physical beauty was more than a pleasant side effect of wellness—it represented genetic strength. Had his parents been able to peer into Tann's own embryonic DNA thirty-one years ago and presage the ugliness of face and body to come, it was not beyond comprehension that Carll Tann would never have existed.

Newfield turned to look at Tann, interest and sympathy plain on his face. Naturally a warm-hearted man, Newfield was sensitive to the pain of others. Tann gleefully noted the softening of the Commissar-General's face. He knew Newfield's weakness for pathos and pressed his advantage. "This is a special circumstance. We have a genetic anomaly to deal with—something we have always feared would happen but which has until now remained only in the realm of speculation. The child deserves, even demands, scrutiny. You cannot discount the significance of the occurrence at her school in New Chicago."

Despite his sympathy, Newfield was still holding his own. "Can't I? A secondhand report from a schoolteacher. The medical records were sealed by Kuarta Verdafner—we have no idea what went on at the hospital."

"No, we don't. But ask yourself this: why would Dr. Verdafner seal the records if there was nothing unusual in them? Surely, her invoking of the personal genetic privacy laws, drafted by her mother, is suspicious. It deserves our attention." Tann fought to keep his voice level.

"Sounds familiar", Newfield mumbled.

"Familiar? How?"

Newfield sighed. "Back on old Earth, oh, about four hundred years ago—that's O.E. years, of course—there was a man who used the same arguments you are using now. He was something of a demagogue."

Tann shrugged it off. "I doubt the circumstances were the same. Jalen, you know Dr. Onizaka is loyal. She won't leak this data. If there is nothing to it, then we drop the whole thing and no one has to know. There will be no harm done. But what if there is something? Can we ignore the possibility that we have a mutant in our midst, perhaps the first of many? Citizens have an individual right to privacy, of course, but does that right extend to the potential ruin of the entire colony?"

"The right to privacy, to medical privacy especially, is paramount in a society such as ours. The laws were written to protect the individual. They are wise laws." Newfield said quietly. He appeared unmoved, but Tann knew better. The Commissar-General was weakening.

"Sir, I agree. The privacy laws are paramount. But I must say that the safety of the whole colony comes first. When your predecessors drew up the privacy laws, they could not have predicted such a development as the Verdafner child. Laws are meant to change in order to best suit the times. The founders of this colony could not have predicted what you are facing now. But you are here, now, and you can see what must be done."

Tann watched the effect of his words on Newfield and considered the Commissar-General. Jalen Newfield was generally thought to be a good man. He had served the colony as Commissar-General for six years, having been appointed from his six-year position as Commissar of Valhalla Dome. He had been made a Commissar because of his fair-minded approach to government and his soft-spoken manner. But Carll Tann had learned, over the course of those twelve years, where the man's strings were and how to pull them. It took skill and persistence, and Newfield rarely succumbed to his influence easily or quickly, but there was little doubt that when Tann wanted something, he could get it done or could get Newfield to do it for him.

"You're sure Onizaka is aware of the delicacy of the situation?" Newfield asked, and with the question, Tann knew he had won.

"Perfectly. She will maintain complete confidentiality."

"All right. Do it. But Tann—"

"Yes?"

"Don't ever ask me for anything like this again," Newfield said, and Carll Tann allowed a look of somber respect to cross his face before he left.

Carll Tann strode through the outer offices of the Commissar-General and noted the looks of barely disguised loathing the three clerks working there tried to hide. He knew how he was seen in the eyes of the rest of the colony—a genetic throwback that had little to offer the future. He was small, more than ten centimeters shorter than average argie height, and he was slight. Moreover, his facial features had been unfortunately arranged. No single aspect was particularly ugly, or even unhandsome, but the overall effect was one that elicited mild disgust in all who saw him.

His physical appearance, as unattractive as it was, was not the true issue, however. The colony knew he had not produced offspring. Of the many achievements a man or woman could count as their own, Tann thought bitterly, nothing was more important to the public good than siring or bearing children. Many of them. Those who elected not to have children and who furthermore did not release their gametes to the public bank were held in low esteem, no matter their other works for the colony. They were almost pariahs, reviled and disregarded, persons for whom the future held no promise. "Tann made sure others knew he was a homosexual, and while that did not excuse him from donating his gametes, his perceived lack of procreative drive mitigated slightly the loathing others felt for him. In an odd way, it confused the other colonists—something he relished."

Tann smiled grimly. He could handle loathing. Despite his lack of a genetic investment in the future, he knew he was more concerned with the colony's future than any other living man or woman. Difficult choices needed to be made, and he had not spent the last fifteen years idly.

* * *

Doctor Karin Onizaka was staring at a holo display of genetic material when Tann entered her office, a characteristic stylus in her mouth. She glanced at Tann and said absently, "Be with you in a minute." It was a widely told joke that Dr. Onizaka could recognize a friend quicker by his or her DNA sequence than his or her face.

Tann glanced at the holo. He was by no means a genetics expert, but he had worked with Onizaka for long enough to recognize some basic structures. She was examining a sample of one of the gengineered chlorine-breathers so vital to the terraforming project. The process was a slow one, of course, but over the last fifteen years Karin Onizaka had developed literally dozens of microscopic organisms capable of metabolizing the toxic chlorine in the atmosphere of Epsilon Eridani III and producing either carbon dioxide or oxygen.

The men and women of the terraforming project had spread these organisms carefully across the globe and monitored their progress. Within one-hundred and twenty years, Onizaka had estimated, the atmosphere on Epsilon Eridani III would contain a low enough percentage of chlorine in its upper elevations as to be breathable by humans indefinitely. She had become the undisputed authority on gengineering as it pertained to terraforming and had even made more sophisticated animals, including mammals, though they were still little more than curiosities, even after fifteen years. Not only was their DNA far more complicated than that of a eukaryote or prokaryote, but they could simply not terraform the planet anywhere near as fast as the short-lived and fecund organisms already doing so. Still, Onizaka bred her lines of chlorine-breathing lambs and pigs and studied them, and no one dreamed of questioning her motives.

It took considerably less than a minute for Onizaka to turn from the holo display suddenly, snapping her head around to look at Tann. She seemed to truly see him for the first time. "Carll! Did you—?"

"I did. You have your authorization, Doctor."

Onizaka made no attempt to hide her elation. "Good! Very good! I'll get to work as soon as we secure the data," she said, already reaching for her intercom switch.

Tann raised a hand. "Before you begin, I must tell you that this is all confidential. No one must know."

"Of course," she said, blinking with surprise. "Did you think I'd—?"

"I was obliged to remind you. Commissar-General Newfield is less than enthusiastic about this course of action."

Onizaka sighed. "I still don't understand that, Carll. You've told him of the potential importance of the data? What we can do with it? Why else set the experiment in motion all those years ago? Surely, he—"

"He does not share your...expertise, doctor, nor my...ah, decisiveness, perhaps."

"I still think that if I explained it to him, he'd agree wholeheartedly. You really ought to have let me do that when we first started this back in thirty-six. He doesn't need to be worried."

"You forget, Doctor, that Jalen Newfield was not the Commissar-General in thirty-six. Well, no matter. He has consented." But Tann was concerned. Onizaka was a brilliant scientist—there were none better in the field of gengineering in the entire colony—but she was woefully ignorant of the intricacies of politics. Tann would have it no other way, but at times, it led to inconveniences. He lowered his voice and leaned in to his confederate. "And, Doctor, there is, of course, no need to tell him of what really transpired twelve years ago. As far as he knows, all the government did was to immunize the incoming *Odyssey* immigrants. There is nothing to be gained by admission of your more...invasive involvement."

Onizaka looked away from Tann and turned to the holo display of the chlorine-eater. She whispered, "Do you really think it has happened, Carll?"

Tann smiled. "That's for you to tell me, Doctor. I shall leave you to your work. You will, of course, inform me when you have anything to report."

"Of course. Thank you, Carll," Onizaka activated her intercom and said to the waiting computer switchboard, "New Chicago Dome, Central Genebank."

Tann left Onizaka's office and strode down the halls to his own residence. For the first time in a long while, he did not notice the stares of loathing from all he passed.

* * *

"Doctor Verdafner?" said Auel Wasif-Mosaka, one of Kuarta's promising young lab assistants. She waited patiently as Kuarta completed the delicate splicing work under the veescope. Wasif-Mosaka was herself Ship-descended and as such held Kuarta in a sort of semi-awe. Before Kuarta had put a stop to it, Wasif-Mosaka referred to herself as a "Gen Six" instead of a colonist. There was a considerable, but shrinking, number of shippies who had rekindled the old Ship designation against the advice of their elders.

"Okay, seal that one off and hold," Kuarta said to the computer-assisted DNA splicing machine and turned to Wasif-Mosaka. "What's up, Auel?"

The young woman hesitated, then said, "I have a friend who works as a clerk in the Central Genebank and he sent me...well, why don't you take a look at it?" Wasif-Mosaka handed over the sheet of paper she had been holding nervously in her hand.

Auel, it read, *I got a weird bit of news for you. My argie boss actually executed a computer search on his own today instead of telling me or Bhoetin to do it and then watching over our shoulders, looking like he just farted oxygen. I watched him (in secret—he didn't see me) do it because I thought he'd screw it up and I wanted to have a cool story to tell you. He did, a little, but he found what he wanted—genedata on Yallia Verdafner. And then he unlocked it! He actually overrode the privacy codes and sent the whole thing to Karin Onizaka over in Valhalla!*

Kuarta fought to keep her anger in check. She forced herself to finish the note.

I wanted to tell you this because you work with Kuarta, at least you did the last time I spoke with you. You gotta write me back and tell me what's going on! Oops! Ol' Blackeyes is looking over at me. Gotta run. I'll see you later this week, I hope.

Kuarta looked up from the paper to see Wasif-Mosaka studying her reverently.

"Is there anything I can do, Doctor?"

Kuarta forced herself to smile. "Oh, no. We just had a bit of a scare the other day at school. Nothing really. I'm sure the genebank is just sending data to the appropriate medical personnel."

Wasif-Mosaka frowned. "I—I'm sorry I got involved, Doctor. I should know better than to get wrapped up in gossip. If you—"

"Oh, no, Auel. No problem," Kuarta said soothingly. "Thanks so much for showing me the note. I do have to follow up on it. Say, why don't you take over on the chimera for me? You've been studying the sequence long enough. I think it's time you took a shot at some splicing yourself."

Wasif-Mosaka brightened immediately. She thanked Kuarta, then moved to the veescope and carefully began the work Kuarta had abandoned.

Kuarta turned her face towards her young assistant, but her mind was elsewhere. Despite the privacy injunction, Onizaka had overridden the law and had pulled her daughter's records.

The implications were no less than staggering. No one was supposed to have access to a child's genedata, including the parents. In cases where medical information was needed, doctors could call up answers to specific questions from the computer files, but even such referencing was rare. Most medical problems could be addressed without resorting to genetic analysis. Could Onizaka, on her own authority, ask for and receive data on anyone she wished?

Jene would know. Kuarta looked at Wasif-Mosaka, bent over the veescope, and said, "Auel, I'm going to step out for a moment. You look like you've got that under control. Just keep it up and make sure it stays in vee until I take a look at it, all right?"

"All right, Doctor. I'll be fine."

Kuarta left the lab and headed for her office where she could speak in private. Once there, she holoed her mother.

Jene was in session right now, the answering service informed her. Kuarta hesitated just a moment, then swiped her finger through the word "URGENT" that was hanging in air just below the answering service message. The text instantly disappeared to be replaced by the words "Your call has been routed to Commissar Halfner's headphone. One moment."

There was an agonizing three-minute wait before Jene's voice sounded in the room. "Kuarta? What's wrong?"

"I need to talk to you in person, Ma."

Jene answered after a pause. "I can duck this session in a few minutes. Can you meet me in Valhalla next to the Assembly Hall?"

Kuarta would have rather met in her mother's home, but she did not want to place too many demands on her. Kuarta was already taking her away from the Assembly floor during a session; she might have to go back soon after meeting with her daughter.

"Sure. I'll leave now." Kuarta terminated the connection and absently noted the deduction from her personal allotment of time. She swiped her fingers through the glowing numbers and they vanished. Kuarta took a moment to decide not to tell Dolen just yet what had happened, then left the lab and took a wirebus to the Dome exit.

The trip was perhaps twenty minutes long. Valhalla Dome was not in the same hexagonal Dome complex as New Chicago, so it meant a transfer not only of Domes but also of entire Dome Complexes. The tube that joined the two complexes was made out of the same transparent material as the Domes themselves, allowing the natural sunlight of Epsilon Eridani to filter in. The chlorine content of the atmosphere cast a bilious yellow-green glow through the tube, far more pronounced than in the Domes, that always made Kuarta slightly nauseous. Today, with her growing sense of dread, she could feel the saliva in her mouth and fought to keep herself from becoming sick.

The wirebus was an open-air trolley that ran above tracks in the ground, powered by magnetic levitation. Once it had exited New Chicago, it was no longer under municipal speed controls and quickly reached its cruising speed of one hundred k.p.h.

Kuarta hardly noticed the increase. Ordinarily, she watched out the transparent canopy, looking at the green-tinted countryside in an attempt to distract herself from the nausea, marveling at the accomplishment that had put her where she was. Now, though, her thoughts were focused on her daughter. After the incident, she had had a brief moment when she thought she might secure a genetic sample from Yallia herself and run tests using the lab's equipment, but the thought died almost as soon as it was born. Such a breach of privacy was unthinkable, and the use of colony equipment for personal gain was almost equally abhorrent to her. She had not told Dolen of her idea.

The wirebus slowed as it entered Valhalla, the first Dome the argies had built upon their arrival in 1 NE (although some of the die-hard shippies, like Wasif-Mosaka, privately put the year at 42 SY) and which was almost entirely populated by descendants of the *Argo*. There was no mistaking the symbolism present in the fact that the center of government was in Valhalla, that the Commissar-General lived there, and that vanishingly few shippies made their homes there. There was, of course, no official law or statute that forbade shippies from entering, as long as a resident family (invariably an argie one) left. And that happened so infrequently that the composition of Valhalla Dome was likely to remain argie for the foreseeable future.

The wirebus made three stops before arriving at the center of Valhalla Dome where the planetary government made its seat. There, Kuarta disembarked and walked the short distance to the Assembly Hall, noticing but not reacting to the subtle glances of interest a few passing argie officials threw in her direction. She had kept out of her mother's business for the most part during her tenure in the Assembly, and so Kuarta was not well known as the Commissar's daughter. She was simply a shippie woman walking in the public thoroughfare. But that was enough.

Kuarta was glad to reach her mother's offices, even if it did mean announcing her presence to a suspicious argie sentry who guarded the Commissars' chambers. The man seemed resentful that Kuarta had indeed been authorized to pass through and waved her in with a sour look.

Jene's office was on the far side of the hall, and Kuarta had to pass many others on her way there. She kept her eyes forward and strode purposefully toward her goal. No one challenged her directly, but she could feel the eyes on her as she walked. Jene waited inside with her door halfway open.

"Ma?" Kuarta said softly. Jene was at her desk, dictating to a holophone.

"...Disagree with the majority opinion," Jene was saying. She slashed her hand toward the text of her speech floating in air before her and said, "Save and fade to point one." The words dimmed to almost invisibility. "Come in, dear," she said to her daughter.

"Disagreeing with the majority, Ma?" Kuarta said, smiling nervously. She could not yet bring herself to introduce the subject she had come to discuss. She needed a few moments with her mother. She entered the room and shut the door behind her. Relief flooded into her when she was finally alone with her mother, away from the argie eyes.

"My life's work, dear," was Jene's immediate rejoinder. She opened her mouth to speak again, but Kuarta stopped her.

"What is it this time?"

Jene sighed. "Oh, some of the Commissars want to relax legislation on industrial waste recycling. They say that the laws are antiquated and we are more than ready to move into a new era of industrial expansion. I say we're still on an alien planet that can kill us with a single lungful of its atmosphere." She looked shrewdly at her daughter. "But you know all about that, don't you?"

Kuarta did not answer.

"Come on, dear, did you really think I wouldn't find out? I've got my friends, you know." She snorted, then softened her tone. "Everything all right?"

Her mother had obviously heard about Yallia's experience at the school. Not through any official channels, of course, but just from the shippie grapevine. Kuarta should have guessed that would have happened and told her herself. Dolen could be excused—he was ignorant of the true nature of shippie solidarity among argies. But Kuarta should not have tried to keep the news from her mother.

Kuarta answered her mother's question. "Medically, I think so. She's been fine since coming back from the hospital. Did you get a report?"

"I saw what I needed to. It doesn't make sense. I know Wajanowitz; he's a good man and doesn't make mistakes. So if you came to me for my medical know-how to try to explain this, I'm afraid you've come to the wrong sawbones."

"No, Ma. That's not it." Kuarta looked at the closed door behind her. Jene raised an eyebrow but said nothing.

"Dr. Onizaka pulled the records for Yallia from New Chicago's Central Genebank," Kuarta said quietly.

"What?" Jene's eyes widened and she leaned forward. Until that moment, she had shown routine maternal interest in her daughter's story—Kuarta suspected that Jene had assumed her daughter was coming to her just for the comfort of being with Ma. "Onizaka doesn't have that kind of authority."

Kuarta nodded. "I didn't think so. I wasn't sure, but I knew you would know. Who can authorize that kind of investigation?"

Jene did not answer, but stared at a corner of her office, her mind obviously racing ahead of the question. Kuarta watched her for a moment, then said, "Ma?"

"What? Oh, sorry, dear. Ordinarily, no one has the authority. Technically, the Commissar-General can declare a genefile open to select members of his staff, but only to contain a quarantine or other epidemic."

The two women stared at each other for a beat, then Jene added, "It has to be related to what happened to Yallia at school."

"I imagine so."

"And it was definitely native biomatter she ate?

"No question. She was exhaling chlorine gas. From the smell, it had to be had to be as high as five p.p.m. or more."

"But her blood gasses were normal. So were all her respiratory functions, mucous membranes, and so on. Did she have any eye problems?"

Kuarta shook her head. "No. Some of the onlookers started to blink and rub their eyes, now that I think of it, but Kuarta is fine."

"She should be dead. Or very, very sick."

"I know."

The two women, both trained in the field of medicine and both quite aware of the only answer that fit all the facts, fought with their intellects to keep the conclusion from themselves.

"She metabolized the chlorine," Kuarta said softly.

CHAPTER
8

Yallia looked with envy at the other children in the Crèche. They were mostly argie boys and girls, though there were a handful of shippies there too. Ordinarily, she would not have made special note of the difference, but the incident at school yesterday had sharpened her awareness of the invisible caste to which she belonged. She was by no means sophisticated enough to understand much of the social fabric of her world, but she had turned an important corner in her education: she knew she was different.

"Yallia, dear, how are you feeling today?" Mr. Rice asked, bending down to her level. Mr. Rice was one of her favorite grown-ups, and despite the obvious evidence of his dark complexion and impressive stature, she did not notice he was an argie. Yallia had left the Crèche last year to attend school and had missed Mr. Rice as a result—she was glad to be back here, even if she suspected it was only for a little while.

"I'm kinda thirsty, Mr. Rice," she said boldly. "Can I have a drink of water?"

"Sure you can, my dear," he said. He drew the water for Yallia, saying as he did so, "I'm glad your mom and dad brought you here to see me today." He handed Yallia the water.

"Thank you," Yallia said, and gulped it down. When she was finished, she handed him the tumbler again. "Could I have some more, please?"

Rice refilled the glass. He handed it to Yalli and said, "That's a lot of water you are drinking today, hon. Do you have to go to the bathroom?"

Yallia accepted the water gratefully. "Nah," she said breathlessly. "But, Mr. Rice? The water tastes funny."

Rice took the glass from her and sniffed it. "Really?" He drank down what was left. "Tastes okay to me. Do you feel sick? Your mom told me you were sick yesterday." He looked suspiciously at the cup brim. "Are you sure you are feeling well, Yallia?"

"Yeah. It's just the water." She thought for a moment, then added brightly, "I know!" She hopped down from the step on which she had been sitting, grabbed the cup from his hands, and raced to the kitchenette.

"Don't make a mess in there," he called after her. Yallia rooted around in the cupboards for a few moments before emerging with a cylindrical container.

"What do you have there, dear?"

She had to hurry—he had stood up and was coming towards the kitchenette.

"You'll see," she said puckishly, drawing some more water from the tap and adding the contents of the cylinder.

"Oh. Sugar, huh?" Rice said.

Yallia added more and more to the cup of water until Rice finally arrived and took the container. "I think that's enough, dear," he said kindly. Yallia took the cup and drank most of the water in a sustained gulp.

Yallia smiled brightly at him when she had finished. She laughed at the grimace on his face.

"*That's* better," Yallia said, wiping her mouth with her sleeve. "Here, Mr. Rice, you take some."

"That's okay, Yallia." He pushed the tumbler away.

"No, go ahead. It's really good."

Rice looked uncertainly at the cup.

"Go ahead, Mr. Rice."

Rice downed the remainder of the drink, then coughed and spluttered, spraying the water out amid gales of laughter from Yallia.

"Salt!" he managed to croak. He recovered enough to laugh. "That's disgusting! Why did you drink that, Yallia?"

"I told you. Because the water tasted funny before." She eyed the salt container on the kitchenette counter. "But this made it better." She stared at the salt container for a few more seconds, feeling a strange hunger. When she looked back at Rice, she was a little surprised to see what looked like fear in his eyes.

* * *

Dr. Onizaka had only spent four hours analyzing the genedata from Central, but she knew Tann would be pleased with what she had already found. She had not looked gene by gene but instead concentrated her search in the sectors of the DNA that would reveal if the project had produced a success. And it had.

She leaned back in her chair and savored the discovery for a moment before reaching for her intercom and calling Tann.

"Carll Tann," his flat voice answered.

"We got it," she said triumphantly.

"I'll be right there."

Twenty minutes later, Carll Tann entered her office and pointedly shut and locked the door behind him. He gave the holo a brief glance before rounding on her. "Well?"

"Yallia Verdafner's DNA shows many of the same changes as the gengineered mammals I've made in the lab." Onizaka said it simply, but the effect on Carll Tann was quite remarkable.

He balled his fist and pounded it into his hand, once, twice. If she didn't know better, she would have thought the gesture was one of revenge finally realized.

"She's a chlorine-breather?"

"That's what the DNA says. I haven't done a full analysis, of course—that'll be a project for several years yet. But—"

"Will she breed true?"

The question surprised Onizaka. "Uh, I'm not sure. I guess so. This isn't a radiation-induced mutation, so there shouldn't be any side effects like sterility." She stopped at the strange glare he shot at her. "What?"

Tann's face swiftly regained its composure. "Nothing. Congratulations, Doctor. And will we be seeing more and more of this from other children?"

"From the hybrids, you mean. Yes, we will. Though I'm not sure the mutation doesn't need a trigger of some kind."

Tann thought for a moment. "Yes, but that would be easy to arrange, yes?" He swatted the potential problem away with a wave of his hand. "Have there been any reports of true shippie children showing signs of the mutation?"

Onizaka smiled. "I knew you'd ask me that. No, Carll. You and I agreed that we wanted to limit the exposure to hybrids only. Even though I didn't agree at first, you convinced me. And now, I'm glad I agreed."

"Why?"

"We couldn't do anything to the argies—that was obvious. There would have been no way to force them all to submit to any kind of new immunization program. We had to use the shippies."

Tann listened without comment, his face unreadable.

Onizaka went on. "But I had my doubts about a self-canceling virus, at first. I wanted to use the entire shippie population. More test data to work with."

"Doctor, we've been through this. The then Commissar-General would never have approved such a project without some safeguards."

"Oh, I know. I understand, I suppose. Still—" Onizaka trailed off, thinking of what might have been. How many more subjects could she have had?

Tann let the silence grow for a while, then asked, "So will this mutation breed true?"

Onizaka returned to the here and now. "It's not a mutation like you are thinking, but...yes," she hazarded. She had not even begun to analyze the relevant data on Yallia, but her instinct told her that there was no reason why the mutation would not breed true.

"How soon before the mutation is noticeable?"

Onizaka shrugged. "I don't know that. It all depends on how efficient her body is."

"When can she go outside?"

Onizaka's eyes grew wide. "Outside? You mean, outside the Dome?"

"Yes."

Onizaka could not answer immediately—not because she did not know the answer but because the very idea of sending her only test subject outside the controlled environment of the Dome unsettled her.

Tann added, "For testing, I mean."

Onizaka paused before answering. "We wouldn't need to do that. We would just do it in the lab." She watched him intently, her unease fading.

Tann nodded. "Of course. What was I thinking? Is the little girl all right at this moment? Do you think she is experiencing any discomfort?"

"I doubt it. The incident at the school was almost certainly the trigger that activated the gene, sort of like puberty activates certain functions in the body. She might have odd cravings or tastes, but she ought to be fine." Onizaka shrugged off the last remnants of unease when she heard Tann's sincerity. "Part of the mutation involves adaptations—improvements, really—to the organism's electrochemical system. Once the chlorine is liberated from the salts in which it exists as a solid, it would ordinarily place a high demand on the body for electrons. That would do serious damage to an unaltered metabolism, but the mutation allows the organism to form complex compounds using the H+ atom, which it then either metabolizes or expels. If she survived the exposure to such a high concentration of chlorine, that means the mutation is working perfectly."

"Good. I'm already ashamed enough that we had to do it this way— I'd hate to think some sweet child is suffering as well." Tann smiled and said, "You did it, Doctor. Your name will be remembered forever now. You've created the first new humans who will one day live and work on this planet outside the protection of the Domes."

Elated at the thought, Onizaka looked away from Tann to indulge in fantasy. When she looked back some moments later, he had gone.

* * *

Jene was able, with surprisingly little difficulty, to clear her schedule for the next few days and return with her daughter to New Chicago. She had wanted to contact Commissar-General Newfield from her office, but Kuarta had seemed...reluctant.

Jene looked at her daughter as they rode the wirebus back home. The fire that had burned in Jene when she had been younger wasn't as bright in her daughter. Perhaps that was not the right analogy—Kuarta was dedicated to her job as fiercely as Jene had been to hers, and by all accounts, loved Yallia as much as Jene had loved Kuarta as a child. But there was more of Renold in Kuarta than Jene cared to admit. It was easy to forget him. Looking at Kuarta sitting stoically in her seat on the wirebus, Jene realized that he was very much a part of her.

"I should tell Dolen as soon as we get back," Kuarta said, her eyes still turned toward the scenery outside the tunnel.

"Kuarta, I know you sealed the medical data, but you don't really think this will stay quiet, do you?"

"What do you mean?"

"I found out about it rather easily."

"But you're her grandmother and a Commissar."

Jene snorted. "So? You don't think the girl who did this to her will keep quiet, do you? Or the school personnel? If it hasn't already, news will leak out."

Kuarta appeared to think before answering. "I—I haven't thought about that yet. I've been thinking about Yallia."

"People in New Chicago will talk."

"You're right," Kuarta sighed. "But you don't think people will suspect what we suspect, do you? Most people who hear the story will think Yallia was very lucky to be alive and unhurt, but that's all."

"Yes, but we can do our part to encourage that view. Tell people that she didn't really eat that much and that what she did eat she threw up. That'll help keep things calm." Jene was already thinking about the public fallout. In a sectioned-off corner of her mind, she worried about Yallia's health, but her training as, first, a doctor, and now a political leader, had given her the ability to compartmentalize such thoughts, to be dealt with as appropriate. Kuarta did not have Jene's experience nor her ability.

"But, Ma, we're not going to keep this a secret forever," Kuarta said suddenly. Jene looked at her daughter quizzically.

"What?"

"This business of the genedata investigation. How did Newfield know about the incident so quickly? And why would he want the genedata if there were no reports of colony-wide problems? No, Ma. Someone was watching all this, and someone has done something to our family. Someone has to answer for it."

"Now, Kuarta, don't jump to conclusions. I'm sure that—"

Kuarta cut her off. "I can't believe you are going to step in to defend the government! You, of all people!"

"Government is not always a bad thing, dear," Jene said softly. "If you think I'm some kind of anarchist, you must have me confused with someone else."

"Why did you start the war on Ship then?" Kuarta said bitterly.

Jene felt herself rock backwards mentally. Kuarta had never asked that question before. When she had finished asking it, Jene knew that there was an unasked question behind it that Kuarta did not trust herself to pose. But it screamed loudly in her mind: *"Why did you kill my father?"*

Jene didn't answer for a long moment. She had been asked that question, in many different forms, throughout the twelve years. It had been the only armed conflict her society had known in over one hundred years. The question had been the central one at her largely ceremonial "trial" held just before planet-fall while Ship was still a sovereign body.

Perrault had been the adjudicator and had been overtly friendly to Jene. No one seemed to mind, though—there were few friends of the old Council regime left, and those quickly renounced and reversed their views when Jene told them all what Eduard Costellan had told her. She told them of the already-established colony on Epsilon Eridani III and of Arnson's knowledge of it. She told them that Arnson's plan to slowly cut away at the weaker, more dependent members of the colony had been put forward while he himself knew how unnecessary it was—the colony on EE3 was a well-established one and had been in place for sixty Ship years and would be more than able to care for the Class D children.

She had been officially absolved for any possible wrongdoing in the affair, but nothing the newly elected and very temporary provisional government on board Ship could do would bring back her husband.

And now Kuarta asked her the same question she had asked herself, unconsciously, every day of her life since. She had not needed to start the war—Arnson's plan could not possibly have succeeded with the colony in place. The dozens of deaths she had caused weighed heavily on her in ways Kuarta would never understand.

"I thought I had to," she whispered to her daughter.

"You knew he and I were hostages. You knew what could happen," Kuarta said. "I've been told the story many times and read about it extensively in the colony library. It was filed under 'Ship History.'"

"Yes. Kuarta, you have to understand—I was fighting a larger fight. I had more to think about than just myself. Ship had been my entire world—I couldn't just watch while innocent children were left to die."

"So you sacrificed my father for them?" Kuarta fairly shouted this, half rising from her seat.

Jene glanced at the other passengers only to find them watching the exchange carefully. Dozens of argie eyes were on her and her daughter, and their expressions indicated they had been watching and listening for quite some time.

Jene kept her voice low as she said, "Yes." The word shocked both of them. Jene knew it was the truth—she had known what she was doing when she made that terrible speech over the comweb. She knew what she was setting in motion for her world and family. "I don't expect you to understand because I don't fully understand. Maybe I felt guilty for you—for your having escaped genetic damage while scores of children of your generation were born horribly deformed. I don't know. I miss your father, even though I never speak of him. He was a good man."

Kuarta could not hold on to her bitterness. "I...can't remember him."

"I can."

The argie eyes turned away as the two women talked in soft tones about Renold Halfner.

* * *

Mr. Rice raised his ordinarily calm voice when he saw Yallia sneaking into the kitchenette again. "Yallia! Come back here!" She disappeared behind a cupboard, and Mr. Rice excused himself from the play of the suddenly giggling argie children to pursue her. He entered the kitchenette, wondering what had possessed Yallia to try to eat salt straight out of the container so many times. She was doing it again when he entered—she had upended the salt canister and was frantically pouring the granules into her mouth.

"Stop that!" Mr. Rice said, making a grab for the salt canister. Yallia dodged him, spilling some of the salt on the floor but quickly adjusting her position to continue eating. Mr. Rice made another grab for the canister and got it this time.

For a moment, he forgot himself. "What the hell is the matter with you?" he said, noting how little salt was left in the two-kilo container.

Yallia did not answer. She darted to the floor and started to lick up the small amount of salt that had spilled from Rice's first attempt on the container.

Rice watched, feeling sick. Yallia's behavior had become bizarre to the point of serious concern. He bent down to pick her up and heard laughing coming from the entry to the kitchenette. Six or seven argie children were watching, pointing and laughing at Yallia as she lapped at the salt like an animal.

"Come on, dear. Get up now." Rice said, recovering his calm. He wanted to protect Yallia's dignity as well as her body. "You kids go back to the playroom. I'll be there soon," he said over his shoulder. He managed to pick Yallia up and took her into the staff room beyond the kitchenette.

"Yallia, why don't you lie down here on the sofa. I don't want you to move from here. I'm going to call your daddy," he said. Yallia nodded mutely, her eyes glazed.

It took Rice an agonizingly long time to reach Dolen, who was in class, lecturing. Presently, Dolen answered the call on his headphone.

"Yes?"

"Professor, this is Langis Rice at Emerald City Crèche. Uh, Yallia has eaten an awful lot of salt just now and I'm worried about her. I was going to call medical services but I thought I'd call you first."

"Salt?" was Dolen's only question.

"Yes. She had the container upside down and was literally pouring it into her mouth. Earlier, she drank salt water and even though I tried to keep her out of it. I've got more children to—"

"No, no, I understand. I'll be right there."

"Should I call medical services?"

"No," Dolen said with enough conviction as to cause Rice to frown in surprise. "I'll handle it. Thank you so much." Rice heard the connection break and blinked. He looked at Yallia—despite Dolen's wishes, if she looked to be in distress, he would call medserv on his own. But the girl seemed all right, if a bit listless. She had risen from the couch and was standing calmly next to him.

"Yallia, honey, how are you feeling?"

Yallia was a moment before answering. "I feel okay. My stomach is rumbling a little."

"I guess so." Rice had no idea what that much salt would do to a child, aside from making him or her ill. But Yallia was not complaining of anything serious.

"Can I go back and play?" she asked brightly.

"Well, why don't you stay here until your daddy gets here. He's coming now to pick you up."

"Why?"

"Honey, you ate so much salt I'm afraid you'll get sick."

"No I won't. I'm fine," she said, with enough girlish enthusiasm as to make Rice doubt his own common sense. She couldn't be covering any kind of distress—she wasn't guarding her stomach, wincing, or acting in any way like a child in pain. Still, he suspected that the salt would affect her suddenly and that he would have to clean it up. He wanted to localize the problem.

"I need you to stay back here, dear. I'll go get you something to play with while you wait."

Yallia looked dejected, but Rice assured her it would not be for long and she seemed to accept the situation. He went back into the main playroom where the other children were playing. One of them, a pudgy argie boy named Pem, looked up at Rice.

"Where's Yallia?" Pem asked. Rice frowned inwardly. Pem was an aggressive boy who was really too old for the Crèche—his parents coddled him too much. While Rice treated all his charges fairly and with love, he did not *like* Pem.

"She's in the back. I'm going to take her a puzzle,"

"I'll take it to her," Pem offered. Rice's inward frown intensified. Pem was uncomfortable with Yallia in the Crèche—attention he might have had from Rice was diverted to her and Pem resented it. Pem was also a troublemaker—Rice's instincts were to tell him 'thank you, no.' As he opened his mouth to say just that, he heard a child's shout of anger in another corner of the Crèche. Two youngsters had begun a rough-and-tumble over a toy, a commonplace event but one that demanded his instant attention. He dropped the puzzle and headed off to end the skirmish and adjudicate.

Pem quietly sneaked out of the main room to deliver the puzzle to the weird shippie girl.

Yallia was waiting in the room, sitting on the couch and kicking her feet against the cushions. She got up when Pem entered with the holopuzzle.

"*You* brought it," she said in a half statement, half question.

"Yeah. Are you coming back tomorrow?" Pem asked as pointedly as only a child could.

"I don't know," Yallia said, reaching for the puzzle.

Pem held it out of her reach. "You can only have this if you promise not to come back. You smell funny," he added, wrinkling his nose in disgust.

"That's not nice," Yallia said quietly. She stopped reaching for the puzzle and a curious expression came over her face. She felt a slight swelling in her stomach.

Pem pressed the attack. "So? You're *weird*. You have funny hair. I hope you get lost outside and never come back to the Dome."

Yallia felt the strangeness inside her growing. It was as if a bubble of fire were rapidly erupting in volume inside her lungs. She spoke to Pem in a whisper. "You should stop talking," she said, looking at him with barely concealed hate.

"*You* stop. I hate you. I hate all you stupid shippies. I hope you *die!*" He punctuated his wishes with a violent shove that almost knocked Yallia down.

It was, of course, a child's threat, but in that moment, Pem Wenakasaki meant what he said, even if he did not fully understand the nature of death. It was enough to know that he wished her out of his life entirely, and if that meant death, so be it. In that, his desires were not too incompatible with those of the adult argies around him, even if his expression of them was more direct.

The shove shattered the delicate equilibrium Yallia had been trying to maintain in her midsection. The fire inside her grew quickly, and she instinctively opened her mouth as it rose through her throat. She had no choice in the matter—she could no longer contain the pressure.

She expelled a green-yellow jet of gas at the older boy, heaving her body grotesquely to do so. The jet of gas ignited brilliantly a few inches away from her mouth and covered Pem in a wash of lime-colored flame. He dropped to the floor and screamed in agony as Yallia turned the fire on his writhing body. Pem rolled helplessly on the carpet, which was also aflame by now, and abruptly stopped screaming as the superheated gas choked off his breath.

Yallia ran out of breath, and the flame stopped. As if waiting for her wrath to end, the building's heat-sensitive sprinkler system began dousing the room with water. An urgent computer voice spoke loudly in the Crèche: "Fire! Evacuate the building! Fire! Evacuate the building! Fire! Evac—"

Another computer voice added to the first one. "Atmosphere warning! Chlorine detected in toxic amounts. Evacuate the area!" The low hum of blowers added to the noise.

Rice burst into the staff room and hesitated a fraction of a second, trying to put together what he saw through the rain. His eyes stung when the chlorine and smoke assaulted them. Pem was still ablaze on the ground, silently rolling on the carpet. Yallia seemed all right, so Rice jumped on top of

Pem and tried to smother the flames with his body. It was all he could do to stay in contact with the boy and fight off the agonizing pain of the fire as it burned his own flesh. It seemed to take hours to put the fire out, but Rice, coughing and choking in the stinging air, extinguished most of the flames and patted away the pockets that still smoldered. Pem lay motionless in his arms, and Rice started CPR, knowing emergency services had been alerted by the Crèche computer. He was only able to complete three cycles when his own breath gave out, and he collapsed on the floor, coughing and holding his tearing eyes.

Yallia watched him as if in a dream—her child mind was putting the events of the past few seconds together. She was not aware of the chlorine in the room, nor was she affected by the smoke that obscured the upper half of the office. She saw Pem's body, curled in the mantis-like fighting stance all burn victims assumed, and felt...nothing. She knew, intellectually, that she had burned him, but at that moment, her sympathy was reserved for Mr. Rice. She bent down and shook him.

"Mr. Rice! Get up, Mr. Rice!" she shouted above the din of the computer warnings and sprinklers. Rice coughed and screamed at the same time, pressing his palms into his eye sockets. "I'm burning!" he managed to shout between coughs.

"You have to get out of the room! There's bad air in here," Yallia said, trying to lift him from the floor. Rice fought her off, insane with the pain of his melting eyeballs. Yallia continued to tug at his arm but she could not budge him. Rice buried his head in the now-soaking carpet and tried to hide his eyes from the air.

Yallia could think of nothing to do but try to lift his body, to carry him out of the room. She tried for several minutes but could not move him. Part of her failure was due to her youth and Rice's weight, but she was also hampered by a growing realization of horror at what she had done.

"Watch out, there!" Voices behind her startled Yallia. Two firefighters in environment suits had entered the room, their faces ugly, insect-like behind their scrubber masks. One of them snatched up Yallia in a gauntleted hand and removed her from the scene. As she left, Yallia caught a glimpse of the other firefighter bending over Pem's body. She could see, for a fraction of an instant, the firefighter's expression through his faceplate as he lifted the boy from the carpet. Yallia saw the hope in the man's eyes vanish.

And then she was outside, cradled gently in the other firefighter's arms. He set her down outside the Crèche where the other children wailed in mindless terror. The firefighter removed her mask and looked intently at Yallia. "My name's Ioli. What's yours?"

"Yallia."

"Hello, Yallia. Are you having trouble breathing?"

"No. Is Mr. Rice—?"

"He'll be fine. I need to put this on you, okay?" the firefighter said, withdrawing a plastic mask from her belt. A thin loop of plastic stretched to a small tank. She unclipped the tank and dropped it on the ground next to Yallia.

"Oxygen?" Yallia asked.

"Yes. It'll make you feel better."

"But I feel fine."

The woman nodded dismissively. "Well, just put it on and keep it on." She slipped the mask over Yallia's face and looked to someone outside Yallia's field of vision. "Make sure she keeps this on. She seems okay, but I want her on the oxygen until she gets to the hospital." The firefighter got up and dashed back into the Crèche

An adult whom Yallia did not recognize came around to face her. "Hi," he said uneasily. He was an older argie man with wrinkles. "My name is Suth. Are you okay?"

"I'm fine," Yallia said, through the mask.

"Good. We'll just wait here until the doctors come, all right?"

Yallia just nodded.

Inside the Crèche, Ioli's partner had run an intubation tube into Pem and was securing the area for field treatment. Ioli checked the atmosphere reading displayed on the inside of her faceplate. "Chlorine's down to three p.p.m. in here," she said through the radio to her partner. She took off her mask and blinked. The air was still acrid from the smoke, but whatever chlorine smell might have been present earlier was almost undetectable now. The computer warnings had ceased, and the sprinkler system shut down even as Ioli took her mask off. She bent to Rice and shook him. "Can you speak?"

"Yeah," he croaked, and coughed.

Ioli fastened her facemask on Rice's head and opened the valve. Rice immediately started coughing again.

"It's going to hurt, but you'll need to take deep breaths if you can," Ioli said. She waited for him to stop coughing, then added, "I'm going to help carry you out. Just relax and let me do the work." She slipped one arm under him and lifted him off the ground. "Karem, stabilize the kid as soon as you—" A look from her partner stopped her in mid-sentence.

"Stay with CPR, then," she said in a low voice and left the room, carrying Rice over her shoulder.

"How is he?" Rice asked when Ioli placed him gently on the ground outside. His eyes were still closed.

"He's in trouble," Ioli said simply. "We can't tell anything yet."

"Is he dead?" Yallia asked through her mask.

Ioli stared at her. The girl was perhaps three, maybe a young four, she estimated. Time enough to know the truth. "He is now," she said, "but the doctors at the hospital might be able to bring him back."

"Ms. Ioli?" Yallia said timidly.

"Yes?"

"I have to tell you something."

"What?"

"I killed him."

Ioli felt something melt inside her stoic heart. Unlike her partner, she had seen death by fire before. Three years ago, when the Dome had been victim to an unprecedented storm which had opened a three-foot split in both inner and outer shells near Botanical Preserve Two, five people had died instantly when chlorine poured into the sector before the dome could be brought to overpressure. But thirteen people had been blinded. They had since been fitted with artificial eyes, but the initial pain of burning membranes had expressed itself in ghastly screams. Ioli thought she had hardened herself to anything after that, but now this child's expression of guilt melted her again.

"Oh, no, sweetie, you didn't—"

"Yes, I did. I threw up fire on him," Yallia said, tears forming in her eyes as she finally admitted to herself what she had done.

"No, no," Ioli said, not really listening.

"Yes, I did! I got mad at him and I felt it inside me and I ate all that salt today and I just—just—spit it at him and he was on fire and screaming—" Yallia broke down. The old man named Suth wrapped his arms around her and made soothing sounds.

Ioli watched Suth comfort the girl, then forced herself to turn to Rice. "You need to do something for me," she said carefully. "You need to open your eyes."

Rice shook his head in terror.

"Yes. I need to see them." She removed the faceplate and grabbed his cheeks.

Rice opened his eyes slightly, mere slits.

"Farther," she said.

Rice opened his eyes and Ioli placed her fingers above and below one eyelid, jamming it open and holding his face in her hands.

Rice yelped but otherwise kept his composure.

"Can you see anything?" Ioli asked.

"I—No, not really. I see light, but nothing distinct."

"Good," Ioli lied. "You can close them again."

"Will it come back?" Rice asked.

"The doctors will work on you," Ioli said. She looked up at the commotion behind the standing spectators. A crew of second-aid rescuers had arrived with a portable operating room. Ioli stood up and gave her report to the physician.

"Three victims, one female approximately three years old, no symptoms, on oh-two right now. One male, approximately—" she glanced at Rice, "twenty-two years old, mild chlorine and smoke inhalation, severe optical damage. Also on oh-two."

"Where's the third one?" The doctor looked about him.

Ioli's voice became even crisper as she covered the severity of the situation with formality. "Third victim is still inside with Mfuse," she said, leading the doctor and a team of three assistants, who wheeled the equipment inside the Crèche. "Male, approximately four years old, third degree chlorine burns over sixty percent torso and limbs, ninety percent head."

The doctor swore softly. He entered the room and saw Mfuse still performing CPR.

"Vitals flat-line," Ioli added unnecessarily. "Mfuse intubated him immediately. He's been on pulmonary bypass for about three minutes."

"EKG?"

"Flat."

The doctor bent down and worked around Mfuse. He pried open Pem's eyelids.

One of the assistants asked, "Pupils fixed and dilated?"

"Can't tell. They've been...melted," the doctor said, a note of shock in his voice. "I'll have to go in with the remote, see if there's anything left inside." Another assistant withdrew a tiny sphere on a flexible tube. The doctor maneuvered around Mfsue again and inserted the sphere into the intubation tube from the supply side, using an aperture on the pulmonary machine for just that purpose. The assistant hooked the probe's telemetry into a monitor and all save Mfuse watched as the probe explored Pem's blasted trachea and lung tissue.

"Damn. It's all burned," the doctor mumbled. The probe flashed data in the monitor as it took samples of tissue and transmitted the findings to the computer. "Nothing left in there. The chlorine stripped away everything."

The monitor flickered once and then died.

"What's that?" Ioli asked, startled.

The doctor pulled the probe out of Pem's lungs and shut off the pulmonary machine. "Probe got burned up in the chlorine," he said softly. He placed a hand on Mfuse's shoulder. "That's enough. He's gone."

The six people paused for a fraction of a second and considered what had happened. The doctor consulted his wristwatch and said quietly, "Time of death: fourteen-fourteen." He looked up at Ioli. "You say the other two are on oxygen?"

"Yes. The adult male is complaining of impaired vision."

"What about the girl?" The doctor gestured for his crew to begin removing the intubation tube from Pem's body.

"Physically, she's all right. No symptoms. She's shaken up, of course."

"Sure." The doctor looked around the room, seeing it for the first time. "What the hell happened in here?"

Ioli had not examined the room yet. She turned to look, really look, at the blast pattern of the fire. "I don't know. Looks like it started here," she pointed at the carpet where Pem lay, "but how it started, I don't...."

"What?"

"Look at the wall here," she said, pointing to a vaguely humanoid shape on the wall nearest Pem's body. "The boy's body shielded this part of the wall. Was he hit from the side?" Yallia's words came back to her: "*I spit it at him.*" But what? How? Had she been holding some flammable liquid? The image of a circus fire-eater came unbidden to her mind, and she dismissed the thought as ludicrous. Besides, she thought, it didn't explain the chlorine.

"Let's get back to the other two," the doctor said suddenly. He directed two of his assistants to bag Pem's body while Ioli continued to stare at the burn pattern. Mfuse stood up, still panting. He looked at Ioli for direction.

"We'd better go with them," she said absently, and left the two technicians to put the little boy's body in a bag.

Dolen arrived on one of the intra-dome wire-buses and leapt off before it had a chance to come to a stop. There was a crowd of perhaps eighty people being kept away from the Crèche by New Chicago police. Dolen fought his way to the inner ring of onlookers, hearing snatches of conversation as he went:

"...Fire in the Crèche...."

"Little girl sitting outside...."

"...Shippie girl started it all..."

"...Hope it doesn't spread...."

He pushed to the front and encountered the cream uniform of the police sergeant blocking his path.

"Sorry, sir, you'll have to...Professor?" the officer squinted at him.

Dolen turned his gaze from the scene outside the Crèche to the face of the young officer. He was surprised to find one of his former students, an uninspired young man named Rober, looking back at him.

"Let me through, Rober."

"Can't, sir. There's—"

"My daughter is in there."

Rober glanced behind him, as if to check the resemblance. Yallia sat on the ground perhaps twenty meters away, a doctor and a female firefighter squatting next to her, talking to her. As Dolen and the officer watched, the doctor took what had to be an oxygen mask off her face.

"Oh. Uh..." Rober managed. Dolen cursed him under his breath and forced his way past.

The doctor and firefighter exchanged glances.

"Look, sir, why don't you..." the firefighter began.

"Thank you for everything," Dolen snapped and carried his daughter away. Rober hurried to him before he reached the crowd's perimeter.

"Uh, professor? You'll have to stay here so we can, uh, ask her some questions. Go on back to the Crèche so we can—"

"She's going home," Dolen said, not checking his stride.

Rober hesitated, then said, "I'm sorry, Professor, but—"

Now Dolen stopped and glared at Rober. "Look. You know where we live. We're certainly not going anywhere. You want answers, you come to us. But I'm taking her home. Now." Before Rober could answer, Dolen pushed his way through the crowd. This time through, he heard a different set of fragments of conversations:

"...Hope she's all right...."

"...Where's he going with...?"

"...The same girl from...."

"...Shippie girl from the school...."

And when he had broken free of the crowd, he heard behind him: "That girl's the center of the trouble."

As he left the scene and started the walk home, Dolen knew his daughter was different. He did not have a degree in biochemistry, but recent events could no longer hide the inescapable conclusion: he was cradling in his arms something that was not the daughter he had known.

CHAPTER 9

Kuarta stared at her mother and at her husband that night after Yallia had gone to bed. The small family room in their cramped but cozy apartment had never been so solemn. Dolen listened as Jene and Kuarta had explained for an hour, in language as free from technical jargon as was possible, what Yallia had become. Now all three stared blankly at each other.

"There's going to be hell to pay," Kuarta said.

Dolen stared back. "I still don't believe it. She's a chlorine-breather? How could such a thing have happened?"

Kuarta and Jene traded glances. "It's not a natural mutation," Kuarta said quietly.

"Not a chance," Jene said.

"Wait a minute. Why couldn't it be...uh...." Dolen stammered.

Jene scowled at him. "Radiation? You mean effects of the trip?"

"Yes," Dolen said, not meeting her gaze. He knew the word carried strong connotations of inferiority and weakness when applied to any of the immigrants or Ship-descended, but the question had to be raised.

Jene waited for him to look at her before answering. "The chances that random genetic mutation would result in such a complex and useful trait are so astronomical as to be impossible. Radiation almost invariably produces harmful or, at best, useless mutations."

"So it has to be something that has been done to her," Kuarta added.

Dolen looked at the two women with increasing horror. "Done to her? You can't mean that. Who would do such a thing? Who could?"

Jene laughed bitterly. "Dolen, I like you. You've been a good husband to my daughter. But, for Ship's sake, man, haven't you learned anything from your damn history books?" She leaned in close to his wide-eyed stare. "Governments obey their own laws when it is advantageous to do so—and only then. If there is something to be gained by a little illicit genetic modification here or there, don't think your precious Commissar-General would hesitate. And it's even easier to hack away at a few shippie chromosomes since we're not quite as human as you."

"You don't mean that, Jene," Dolen said softly. "The part about being less human than me, I mean."

Jene didn't answer.

Dolen said finally, "Still—you think the government did this? Why?"

"They're the only ones with the means to do so."

Kuarta interrupted. "Look, this had to be a retrovirus, right?"

Jene paused before answering. "That's all it could be. I can't see how else it could have been done."

"What's a retrovirus?" Dolen asked.

Kuarta said, "A virus that is tailored to alter the subject's DNA. The virus sort of hijacks the cell and deposits the new gene inside."

Dolen still looked befuddled. Kuarta waggled her fingers, trying to prompt her memory. "In one of your history lessons, you asked me once about the AIDS epidemics of the late twentieth and early twenty-first centuries, remember?"

"Yes. I think I asked you why the epidemic happened at all. The medical technology of the age should have been sufficient to wipe it out or at least contain the—"

"Yeah, yeah," Kuarta flapped away his digression with her hand. "The AIDS condition was brought about through the human immunodeficiency virus, or HIV. That's a retrovirus."

"But...AIDS killed millions of people!"

"No, no! HIV was a different kind of retrovirus. It didn't simply deposit a gene in the cell—it forced the cell to make more viruses. But the idea is the same."

"So...Yallia is going to die?"

"We don't know anything right now," Jene said gruffly, shooting a warning glance at her daughter. "If she gets sick, we'll be able to handle it through gene therapy."

"Look, we're missing the point," Kuarta said, standing up suddenly and turning away from the table. "The traits Yallia possesses are far too complex and useful to be random. That means she has been the subject of some kind of genetic experiment. How was it done?"

Dolen asked, "You mean, they gave her an injection or something?"

Kuarta looked at Jene, who shrugged. Kuarta said, "Not necessarily an injection—it could have been in capsule or liquid form, I suppose. Or possibly airborne."

"Airborne delivery would be very risky," Jene said. "Unless she were in some kind of hermetically sealed room, there'd be risk of contamination of the surroundings. And if this was slipped in a drink or given to her in some other form, like in food, there'd be a danger again of contamination. In her urine and feces, for instance, assuming there wasn't some other mishap. Like dropping the food or spilling the drink. I say it was an injection. That's how I would have done it."

"You think someone injected Yallia with some kind of retrovirus to turn her into a chlorine-breather?" Dolen's tone was incredulous.

"No," Kuarta said at the same time her mother said, "Yes." Kuarta rounded on her mother, but Jene spoke first.

"Come on, Kuarta. You said yourself that this cannot be a natural mutation, and the delivery of the retrovirus would most logically be an injection. How else could it have been done?"

"Ma, you've been out of medicine for ten years or more. You're forgetting your basic genetics. There is no way any retrovirus could possibly have affected Yallia so completely after her birth. There are simply too many cells for the virus to infect. A human baby is a complex organism that has undergone nine months of painstaking development. No retrovirus could have altered her basic pulmonary system like that."

The living room clock chimed fourteen. All three adults turned to look at it. They were in time-slip now for the next eight minutes. New Earth's day was twenty-eight hours and eight minutes long—the extra eight minutes were wedged between days, starting at midnight. For eight minutes, human time stood still.

"She wasn't altered," Kuarta said softly.

"You mean now you think it's just a fluke or something?"

"No, Dolen. She wasn't altered. I was."

"What?"

Kuarta sighed. "The retrovirus couldn't have been tailored to affect the recipient—just the offspring. The gene was deposited in my DNA so that when I passed it on to my child, she would have the trait."

Jene nodded. "Yes. That makes sense."

Dolen looked from his wife to his mother-in-law. "Makes sense? Do you realize you are saying that the government purposefully did this so that Yallia would be a mutant? Why?"

The women were not listening to him. "The only injection I can remember getting at the hands of the government was my initial battery of vaccines and booster shots when we first arrived."

"Yes. But we all got those," Jene said. Her eyes widened. "Do you think...?"

Dolen's voice lowered in utter disbelief. "You can't be saying what I think you're saying. Now you think the government did this to every immigrant some twelve years ago?"

"Twenty years ago," Jene said. "Ship years, I mean. And yes, Dolen, I find it not only possible, but plausible."

Kuarta nodded and rose. "I agree with Ma—the government did this to us and therefore to Yallia."

Now Dolen raised his voice. "This is madness. I have sat here listening to the two of you concoct your theories without a shred of empirical evidence. You call yourselves scientists? Everything you have said is conjecture, speculation, and unsupported by facts. Why would the government infect its own citizens? You say 'the government did this' as if the government is some kind of living, breathing entity instead of a body of separate individuals. You of all people ought to know how government works, Jene."

"I know very well how it works. I've been on both sides of it. Yes, government is made up of individuals. But I've seen the act of governing turn moral, ethical people into unprincipled monsters more times than I care to count. Government has the potential to do great good—or great evil." She paused and looked at Dolen, then softened her tone. "You said something in that little speech of yours that betrays your thinking. You asked why the government would infect its own citizens. Dolen, haven't you realized by now that there are many of you people who do not think of us as citizens?"

"It sounds more like you are doing the dividing, Jene. *You* people?"

They looked at each other for a while across the table before Dolen said, "You disapprove of my union with your daughter, don't you, Jene?"

"That's enough!' Kuarta slammed her fist down on the table. "Dolen, this isn't the time for that. And Ma," she turned to face her mother, "shut up. I'm sick to death of all your anarchist's talk. You can't let go of what Arnson did to Dad twenty years ago, and now you're putting all your hate towards the argies. I say this with all love, Mother, but *get over it!*"

Jene stared at her daughter for a long moment. Jene had unpacked the memory of Renold Halfner during the wirebus ride earlier, but that had been different somehow. She had wallowed selfishly in memory and nostalgia while talking to Kuarta about him, and now her daughter was asking her to do something quite different. She was not asking her to forget Renold, but to release the anger and bitterness that had welled in her for twenty years and now manifested in a hatred of government.

Then why have I become a part of it? Jene wondered.

Kuarta spoke again, dissolving Jene's unasked question. "Yallia is in there, mutated, different, and someone did this to her. Let's try to remember that."

The silence that followed was broken by the soft chiming of the living room clock. Time-slip was over.

"I say we were all injected during our initial quarantine," Kuarta said.

"Maybe," Jene said.

"I wish to point out," Dolen said with noticeable formality, "that there were approximately eight thousand immigrants twelve years ago. You are suggesting that the government had eight thousand samples of this mystery retrovirus prepared, tested, and ready to deliver, and all of this was done in secret. The conspiracy involved is so massive as to be impossible."

Jene and Kuarta were silent. Dolen continued. "There is another factor to consider. I am not a medical expert"—this with considerable disdain—"but if all immigrants were infected with the virus, why is Yallia the only child to exhibit tendencies? There have been thousands of children born in the past twelve years. And why are the changes not reflected in her face or body?"

Kuarta answered with eyes glazed in thought. "I see no reason for an outward physiological change. Her ability to metabolize chlorine is a biochemical one. I'm sure her insides look quite different, if one knows what to look for—probably she has some kind of protective coating in her mouth, trachea, bronchial passages, and so on."

"That still doesn't answer my other question. Why weren't other children affected?"

"She's one of the few children so far born of an argie father and a shippie mother," Jene said.

Dolen rose slowly, trying to keep his rage in check. "I've already been accused of racism twice tonight. Are you now implicating me in this bizarre plot to turn my daughter into some kind of freak?"

"Mommy?"

The three adults whirled to see Yallia, her eyes half opened and face half-turned from the light of the living room lamp, standing in the hallway.

"Oh, Yallia," Kuarta said, advancing on her daughter, "what are you doing up?"

"I heard you and Daddy and Gram talking. Did Daddy call me a freak?"

"He—" Kuarta stopped, trying to control herself lest she burst into sobbing in front of her daughter.

"Because that's what the other kids at school and in the Crèche called me."

"Oh, honey child," Jene said, getting up from her chair in turn and coming to comfort her granddaughter, "we talked about that. Those people at school and in the Crèche are just...well, they're just dummies. That's all."

Yallia shook her head. "No. They're right. I am a freak. And I killed that boy. Pem." Yallia's eyes, still red and swollen form a night's crying, started to tear up again.

Kuarta held her daughter close, blinking back tears herself as the pungent smell of chlorine from Yallia's tears filled the apartment.

* * *

"You're sure they went home?" Tann asked the lantern-jawed face that floated in front of him in holographic representation.

"That's what the officer at the scene said he was told. But, Mr. Tann, even if they didn't, we can find them. They can't hide." Police Captain Dunbarston was not happy at the prospect of talking with him, Tann knew. His ugliness was particularly effective against the burly, handsome police captain.

"I realize that, Captain. But I don't want every dome turned upside-down in a search. I want to contain this. Your officers are ready?"

"We can go to the house at any time."

Tann looked at his desk clock. It was only a few minutes past time-slip.

"All right. I'll be at your constabulary in one hour. We'll go from there. And Captain," he added before Dunbarston could disconnect, "your orders come directly from the Commissar-General. Should you meet Commissar Halfner there, you are to politely but firmly refer her to my office. Understood?"

"Yes," Dunbarston said, and switched off.

Tann stared at the air where the policeman's face had been for a moment, then called Onizaka on a secure line.

Onizaka appeared haggard when she turned from her work to answer the call. "Oh, Carll. I'm really busy right now. Can you call back?"

"This will only take a moment," he said, settling back in his chair in contradiction. "You didn't tell me about the more...incendiary aspects of the mutation, doctor."

"Carll, look, I have no idea what happened. I'm still looking into it now. And I'm doing it alone, of course, so I'm—"

"Rather an important trait, wouldn't you say?" He did not need to manufacture anger.

"It's something to do with the way she can manipulate sodium, hydrogen, and chlorine. Chlorine gas is very reactive to light. I've looked at the data, but...."

"A little argie boy died, Doctor. And from what I've been told, died rather painfully."

Onizaka lowered her head. "I know. I'm sorry, Carll. I just had no idea—"

Tann stared at her head, waiting for her to look up. When she did, he met her frightened gaze with his furious one, then slowly allowed it to soften. "Well. I know you meant well. You should know that the mutant is, for the moment, at her residence. Dome police have been dispatched to collect her."

"Did you send them in with environment suits? She could burn them, too."

"No. I think she will refrain. Besides, I cannot tell the police to take extra precautions without revealing too much of what we have done. Afterwards, when she is in our care, we can release some data on her mutation."

Tann considered the dead boy. His death was a tragedy, to be sure, but one which Tann could use to his advantage. Tann sympathized with the parents and felt for them, but at the same time he knew he would be a fool not to exploit the situation. He was an able and experienced politician. capable of divorcing his personal feelings from his work.

"I have one more question: why haven't the six or seven other hybrid children shown signs?"

"I'm not sure. We have sketchy, anecdotal data only. The one difference I can find is that the Verdafner child was exposed to high concentrations of chlorine. That might have acted as a catalyst for the mutation."

"So the others may never manifest themselves?"

"Carll," Onizaka said in an exasperated tone, "what I've told you is pure speculation. I don't really know what happened, or if it will happen again. But I promise I'll get back to you as soon as I have more. Okay?"

"Very well. Go back to work, Doctor," Tann said, and switched off. He got up from his desk and headed for the door. Before he reached it, he stopped, turned, and went back to his desk. He withdrew a small, slim weapon from his desk drawer and pocketed it before leaving the office.

He arrived in New Chicago with plenty of time to spare. He was the only passenger on the wirebus at this late hour; there were, of course, vital colonial functions and services that had to be maintained twenty-eight hours a day, but by and large, the colony slept at night and was active in the day.

Captain Dunbarston was waiting for him in the nearly-deserted lobby of the constabulary wing, which made up one part of the administrative and medical center of the Dome. Tann nodded curtly at the blocky peace officer, noting his nervousness. "Are your men ready, Captain?"

"Yes. I've got myself and four others." Dunbarston indicated the young officers, two men and two women, who stood nearby. The only other officer in sight was the desk clerk, who watched the affair with interest.

"Then let's go." Tann commanded.

Dunbarston cleared his throat and headed towards the motor pool area, his officers and Tann in tow. The six piled into a police transport, used primarily to shuttle large numbers of officers to disturbances, and headed toward the Verdafner's building.

Dunbarston spoke to his men. "All right, let's go over this again. We are to secure a young shippie girl named Yallia Verdafner and take her to Valhalla Dome where she will be turned over to Valhalla constables. There may be one or more adults present—her mother, Kuarta Verdafner; her father, Dolen Verdafner; and possibly Jene Halfner, the Commissar from New Chicago."

The four young officers could not help but glance at each other briefly. Dunbarston licked his lips before continuing. "We are under the direct orders of the Commissar-General, as represented by Mr. Carll Tann." Dunbarston motioned towards Tann, hesitated, and looked at Tann. "Perhaps you would like to add something here, Mr. Tann,' he said. The pleading in his voice was almost pathetic.

Tann spoke quietly but firmly. "You are charged with apprehending the girl. Do not harm her, of course, and do not harm any of the persons you may find in the apartment, but take her to Valhalla. If this means she needs to be separated from her family momentarily, so be it."

"Isn't this girl the same one involved in that fire in the Crèche?" the light-haired female officer asked.

"Yes." Tann said it with such an air of finality that the woman sank back into her seat. "Any other questions?" Again, his voice denied any further queries even as his words asked for them. The officers shifted in their seats and looked everywhere but at the short, balding man with such fire in his eyes.

Surprisingly, one of them spoke. As if he was trying to imagine himself alone in the car, his question directed at no one in particular. "Has this kid done anything wrong?"

Tann stared at the officer. "Hasn't your Captain briefed you on the circumstances?" He glared at Dunbarston, who, like the other officers, was looking the other way.

"I see," Tann said. The question had been rhetorical, but Tann decided he would answer it anyway. "You are uncomfortable with this assignment, aren't you?"

The three officers in the passenger section nodded, and Tann was sure, even without turning his head to look, that the driver had as well.

"You wanted to be constables in order to serve the public trust, yes?"

Nodding.

"And you think kidnapping little girls in the middle of the night isn't nice."

This time, the officers looked at him for a moment. Tann could see their thoughts. This, too, would require his oratorical skills.

"All right, then. I had hoped to avoid this, because I thought it might cloud your judgment and efficiency, but I can see you are not just men and women who will blindly follow orders. This little girl is a shippie, as the vernacular goes, who has for some reason been targeted by the local argie population. We in the Commissar-General's office have been watching the developments in New Chicago and have become concerned with the level of antagonism directed towards her. We are therefore taking steps to ensure her safety while at the same time keeping the public calm. We felt taking her quietly, in the night, would be best."

Dunbarston leaned forward. "You didn't tell me that, Mr. Tann." His voice had a definite edge to it.

"No, I didn't. I was hoping we could take her, secure her in a secret location, and then try to defuse the situation here in New Chicago."

"But why didn't the Commissar-General just address the—"

Tann smiled. "Captain, you don't understand. There is a point when the general public ceases to be a thinking body and turns to a mob. There is no reasoning with a mob; no series of syllogisms or arguments will quell a mob's fanaticism. The Commissar-General feels that the undercurrent of hatred towards shippies in general, and toward this girl in particular, is so great that any overt action on the part of the administration would result in violence."

"Do you think the fire at the Crèche was an example of that?" a young male officer asked.

Tann blinked. He had never thought to try that angle. He had prepared the cover story of taking the girl away for her own safety some time ago, but this was a new wrinkle he could use. He had to be careful, though.

"I leave that to local authorities to discover," he said disingenuously. He glanced significantly at Dunbarston and knew the Captain would immediately launch an investigation—one dedicated to finding out that the fire was arson.

"So now you know," Tann said to all of them. "Does that make you feel better?" He said the last with such expectation that all nodded and seemed to relax a bit. Tann did as well. These officers would talk, of course, and the rumors would start to circulate. People would begin to think there was a vast argie underground of activists—there might even be one now, for all Tann knew—who were dedicated to shippie destruction. Better yet, if he played the next few days properly, he could either expose a real underground or claim to have done so.

"Here we are," the driver said unnecessarily as he slowed the transport. The officers filed out of the truck, Tann behind them, content to let the local authorities lead the way. He was under no illusions as to his role here. He did not need to be in the front to be in control—as had been demonstrated by the last twelve years on New Earth.

The officers and Tann made their way to the ninth floor using the stairways. Tann was the only one a bit winded when the group reached their destination. Dunbarston pressed the doorbell and presented himself to the door eye.

Dolen opened the door. "Yes, officers?" He took in the sight before him and narrowed his brow. "What is this?"

"Sorry, Professor. We've come for your daughter," Dunbarston said.

"You've what?" Behind him, Jene rose from the living room chair where she had been stroking the crying body of her granddaughter. Kuarta was holding Yallia and tightened her grip when she heard Dunbarston's answer.

"Officer, I presume you know who I am," Jene said, approaching the police with clear distaste.

From behind the officers, Carll Tann pushed his way forward. "And I presume you know who I am, Commissar Halfner."

"Mr. Tann?" Jene was taken aback. "What are—?"

"I'm here as a representative of the Commissar-General. He has ordered the immediate arrest of Yallia Verdafner for her own safety."

"Her own safety?"

"He has reason to believe that she is in danger from a growing anti-shippie movement. The girl will be taken to Valhalla Dome where she will be placed in protective custody."

Jene's face grew beet-red in apoplexy. "He can't just order a little girl taken away from her family! He's—"

Tann matched her fury with coolness. "The Commissar-General's emergency powers are quite broad, as you know. Captain?" Tann directed the last remark to Dunbarston, who seemed to be in a trance.

"Commissar Halfner, please. We don't want any trouble," Dunbarston said.

"Then you shouldn't have come here." Jene tried to slam the door on them, but Dunbarston blocked it with his gauntleted hand. Jene hurried back past the still-stunned Dolen to the living room where she hugged her daughter and granddaughter with ferocity.

Dunbarston sighed and motioned to his officers to enter the house. They pushed past Dolen and surrounded the three females in the living room. For a moment, the officers simply stared at the sight—three generations of women huddled together against the authority they represented.

"Mommy, Gramma, you guys are squishing me!" Yallia's muffled voice said from within their arms.

"Sorry, honey," Kuarta said, and relaxed her grip slightly. She glared at the officers with almost feral hate.

The tableau was broken by Tann's imperious voice. "Captain! Order your officers to—" He stopped when Dunbarston flashed him a look of loathing that far transcended simple aesthetic disgust. For an uncertain moment, Tann wondered if Dunbarston would falter, order his officers away.

"This is madness!" Dolen's shrill voice said from the hallway. He strode to the living room and squatted down next to his wife, child, and mother-in-law. "You can't win. We can go with her, I assume," Dolen said, glancing at Dunbarston, who in turn looked at Tann.

"If you wish. But we must go now."

Dolen spoke softly. "Come on, Kuarta, Jene. Let go. What are you trying to prove by resisting?"

"If they want my granddaughter, they'll have to break my arms to get her," Jene said through clenched teeth.

"What good will that do? You'll have two broken arms and Yallia will still be in custody."

"What's custody, Daddy?" Yallia asked from the huddle. "Why are the police here?"

"I'll know I did everything I could to save her," Jene said.

"Let her go. We'll be with her," Dolen said again.

"Ma, he's right. We can't win here, now. Let's save our resistance for a time when it can do some good."

Jene looked at both her daughter and son-in-law. "Resistance to authority always does good, children." But her grip loosened on Yallia.

Freed from the embrace of her family, Yallia looked with wide-eyed fear at the officers ranged around her. "Mommy, what is it?" she said, trying to burrow back into the cocoon.

The officers advanced and helped Kuarta and Yallia rise from the floor. "Let's go, Doctor," Tann said.

"Where are we going, Mommy?"

"For a ride, honey. Listen," Kuarta said, taking Yallia by both shoulders and simultaneously shrugging off the guiding hand of one of the officers, "it's very important that you try to stay calm. If you feel anything...happening inside you, you just tell me, okay?"

Yallia nodded, comprehension coming slowly. "You mean like at the Crèche?"

Kuarta quickly placed her finger over Yallia's mouth. "Shhh. Yes, like at the Crèche. Hush, now."

The officers escorted their charges down to their transport, while Carll Tann fingered the slim weapon in his pocket, watching Yallia carefully.

CHAPTER 10

"Release her immediately!" Newfield thundered at Tann as the latter spread his hands in front of him as if to deflect the force of his superior's wrath. "You had no authority to order the New Chicago constabulary to take her from her house!"

Tann had come to Newfield's office immediately after arriving in Valhalla with the Verdafners. They were under detention in the Valhalla constabulary now, and Tann did not want to think what the Valhalla police captain was going through trying to keep Commissar Halfner under control. First things first, though—he had to calm Newfield down. Tann had acted before speaking to him, using the formula that had worked so well for him during his career as advisor to the office of the Commissar-General: better to beg forgiveness than ask for permission.

"Sir, please listen to me. I know what I did was technically illegal—"

"Technically? It was wrong, Tann."

"—but let me explain to you why I did it. If, after I'm through, you still don't agree with my reasoning, I shall of course release the girl and furthermore submit to disciplinary action."

Newfield held his fury visibly in check and folded his arms. "Go ahead."

"Thank you. We had already agreed that there was a potential epidemic to deal with, and it appeared that this girl, Yallia Verdafner, was the key. After Dr. Onizaka studied the data you released to her, she found that the child was not just a genetic anomaly as I had feared, but was a functional mutant." Tann paused to let the word sink in. Newfield blinked and his arms fell to his sides.

Tann pressed his advantage. "Somehow, this child has the ability to metabolize chlorine."

Newfield shook his head slightly, as if to deny the data. "She can...." He wasn't able to continue. "How did this happen?"

Tann scowled. "Dr. Onizaka is still working on that, sir. Her data is sketchy and very preliminary, but she is convinced that the girl is a danger to herself and others."

"Danger? How so?"

"Dr. Onizaka feels that the girl can use the chlorine, along with other elements in her body, as a sort of catalyst for exothermic reactions."

"Exothermic…heat producing?"

"Yes. It's my belief that she caused the fire in the Crèche using her mutation. Onizaka concurs. I thought I'd best get her in custody quickly— what Onizaka could discover, so could others. Can you imagine what people would do to her if they suspected she was a dangerous mutant? I thought it best to act quickly, instead of wasting time taking the data to you and the whole government. I thought you would arrive at the same conclusion I did, sir, but I also believed that we had little time to waste."

Newfield hesitated before answering. Tann could see the confusion in the man's face—he was caught between fury at having been ignored and shock at the news of the mutation. When he spoke, his voice carried evidence of his ambivalence.

"Onizaka's studying her now, I suppose?"

"No, sir. I did not want to proceed further without your authorization. Now that the situation is more secure, I mean. In addition, I've broken enough laws already."

The joke had its intended effect. Newfield grinned slightly, and Tann knew once again he had won.

"All right. I see your point. I suppose I'll have to convene the Assembly now to decide what is to be done."

Tann said nothing, but scowled enough to prompt Newfield to ask, "What's wrong now?"

"The girl's grandmother. Commissar Halfner. She'll make trouble, sir. If you convene the whole Assembly, Halfner will derail the government with wild accusations and charges—charges that, while false, will be uncomfortable for you to refute entirely."

Newfield blew air out through his cheeks. Tann waited a calculated few seconds and asked, "What do you want me to do, sir?" He was confident he knew what his instructions would be.

"I want the girl examined by Dr. Onizaka. And I want you to send Commissar Halfner to me. I'll straighten her out on this. No need for you to try to do it."

"Thank you, sir." Tann summoned up false relief. "Truthfully, I was hoping you'd say that. She respects you and will follow your lead. To her, I'm just a flunky. It's a wonder I've been able to keep her in line as far as this."

"Well. You'll keep this quiet for now, Tann. I want no one but Onizaka in on this. Report back to me personally, later when you know more. At some point, I'll have to convene the Assembly, but before then I want the situation secure. Understood?" Newfield spoke with a confident tone of command.

Tann listened with all the respect he could muster and nodded when his superior was finished. "Yes, sir. I'll get back to you." He bowed out of the office and headed to the constabulary.

"Yallia, I'm going to go ahead and increase the chlorine to three hundred p.p.m.," Onizaka said without turning from the double-paned glass behind which Yallia Verdafner sat. The girl had been in the isolation room for the better part of the day, undergoing increasing levels of chlorine saturation. She had been breathing two hundred and seventy-five parts per million for a few hours now and had reported no discomfort, other than boredom. The faint green tinge of the air about her gave testimony to the lethal nature of the gas inside the cell.

"Doctor, when can I get out?" Yallia's voice echoed in the chamber, even through the intercom.

Onizaka had stopped counting the number of times the girl had asked that question hours ago. Without turning from the atmosphere display, she answered, "Soon. Now take deep breaths, just like before."

"Okay," came the morose reply. "But I'm still hungry."

Onizaka ignored this last comment and studied the various readouts on the display panel. So absorbed was she in her work that she did not hear the lab door open.

"Damn it, Karin, I told you to lock your door!" Tann growled.

Onizaka started when she heard him and turned her head to the door. "Oh, yes...sorry about that. I must have gone out and—"

"Keep it locked. I don't want anyone in here. I also don't want to post guards." Tann looked at Yallia without waiting for a response to his order. He strode to the glass and switched off the intercom. "What have you learned?" The question was directed at Onizaka, although the advisor's eyes were on the girl. She started back at him uncertainly.

"She's breathing the chlorine," Onizaka said simply.

"How much?"

"I just upped it to three hundred."

Tann looked at Onizaka. "Three hundred?"

"Enough to kill both of us in about two breaths."

Tann looked back at Yallia. "What about the fire?"

Onizaka sighed. "Her body is using the chlorine like we use oxygen, only more efficiently. Her respiratory and digestive systems have some kind of protective lining, like glass but more flexible, to protect them against the action of the chlorine. If she breathes chlorine, I think she is somehow able to keep it separate from the hydrogen she's also breathing, and can kick them back out together, forming a sort of hydrochloric acid vapor. I'm not sure how she ignites it. Maybe she follows the stream with a sodium vapor somehow which reacts to the water vapor in the air."

"What happens when she eats chlorine?"

Onizaka hesitated. "I haven't done that to her. I wasn't sure what it would do."

Tann continued to stare at Yallia. "That's rather the point of experimentation, isn't it, Doctor?"

Yallia was mouthing something. Onizaka started hesitantly toward the intercom, looking at Tann. He watched the girl for a moment more, then nodded slightly. Onizaka turned on the intercom.

"Yes, Yallia?"

"Doctor Onizaka? I'm feeling hungry still."

Tann looked at Onizaka. "You had best feed her, Doctor." He stared at her to be certain she would understand. Onizaka wet her lips nervously, glanced at Tann, then back at Yallia, then back to Tann. She nodded.

"I'll get you some food, dear," she said.

Tann smiled and turned off the intercom again. "I'm going to see the family. I'm sure they've been causing trouble in the constabulary. Call me immediately if anything happens." He glared one more time at the girl in the isolation booth and left.

Kuarta watched her mother and her husband pacing in the conference room and resisted the impulse to scream at them. Jene was still murmuring obscenities at the government, her rage sharpened by impotence. Dolen wandered aimlessly about the room, his hands busy with chair backs, the doorjamb, an irregularity on the wall, anything to keep them occupied.

A soft knock on the door startled all three of them. The door guard, a young woman with a girlish charm that even her severe Valhalla Constabulary uniform could not diminish, opened the door and entered. Carll Tann entered with her.

Jene went into action instantly. "Where is she?" She said it as she took three quick strides towards Tann, who did not shrink from her. The door guard put one of her arms up to keep Jene away from Tann, but Jene brushed it aside. "Get your hands off me!"

Dolen pulled Jene back from behind, grabbing her shoulders and using a considerable amount of strength. Jene shrugged off his hands but stepped back.

"Ma." Kuarta said softly. She looked at Tann. "Are you taking us to see her?" She asked the question softly but with audible iron behind her words.

"I am. You should be made aware of some developments, first. She—"

He got no further. Jene snarled and lunged forward. The constable, caught by surprise, hesitated for an instant, thus allowing Jene to strike Tann once across the face with a half-closed fist. His head snapped sideways with the force of the blow, and he took a step to steady himself. The door guard tackled Jene and rolled on top of her, pinning her head to the ground and lifting her arms back. "Calm down, Commissar. I don't want to hurt you."

"You goddam bastard! What have you done to her?" Jene managed to choke out.

Tann felt his jaw for blood and, finding none, turned to the guard. "Take her to a cell for now. I want her to cool off."

The guard hesitated. Tann raised his voice. "Now!"

"Sir, with all respect, you do not have authority here. Please stay out of this." The guard spoke to Jene. "I'm going to let you up, Commissar. But I will still be here. If you try anything like that again, I'll have to put you in a tank. Do you understand?" The guard spoke precisely, with respect due a Commissar, but also with firmness.

Jene mumbled something that passed for assent. The guard rose from astride her and took up position next to Tann again. Dolen helped Jene up while Kuarta watched impassively.

"I'll ignore that," Tann said calmly. "Let me finish. Yallia is under Dr. Onizaka's care right now. She is being examined."

"We know that," Kuarta said, almost inaudibly. "You gave us your personal assurance that she would not be harmed. You asked us if we would stay here and wait for your return. We have done as you asked. Now it's your turn. Take me to my daughter."

"Very well. I have no intention of keeping you from her, Doctor. I just wanted to—"

"I'm sure you mean well, Mr. Tann," Dolen said quickly, before Jene could respond. "We want to cooperate with you."

Jene murmured something. Tann turned to her. "What was that?"

"I said I don't believe you."

"What don't you believe?"

"The Commissar-General would not order all of this. I demand to see him."

"As it happens, he wishes to see you, too, Commissar. Or would you prefer to see your granddaughter first?"

Jene hesitated. Kuarta spoke in the vacuum. "Ma, go to Newfield. Dolen and I will be fine."

Jene nodded.

Tann spoke to the guard. "Presumably I am not overstepping my authority to request that additional guards accompany Commissar Halfner in light of her assault on me?"

The guard stared at him with not-quite-concealed loathing, then called for back-up on her radio. Tann nodded in satisfaction, then gestured to the door. The party left the conference room, three of them for Dr. Onizaka's lab, Jene to the administrative center of the planet.

* * *

Yallia scrambled to her feet and dashed towards the glass wall that kept her from her mother and father, who had just entered the room with Tann. She stirred up faint green eddies of gas in her wake. Dolen, too, ran to his side of the glass enclosure and pressed his hands up to hers. There was a thin section of vacuum between the panes as an extra layer of security in the unthinkable event of a breakdown in barrier integrity. Yallia was clearly shouting "Mommy! Daddy!" even though no sound came through the glass.

"What are you doing to her?" Kuarta said, turning to Onizaka.

Onizaka had begun to approach the parents, a half-smile on her lips that vanished immediately under Kuarta's withering stare.

"She's not in any pain or danger, Doctor."

"What are you doing to her?" The question was repeated in the same frigid tone.

Onizaka looked at Tann, who nodded indifferently and studied the panel readout. Onizaka said, "She's in Dome-normal atmosphere with an admixture of chlorine gas."

"How much?"

"Right now, she's at four hundred parts per million."

Kuarta gasped. "Four hundred?"

"What? What does that mean?" Dolen said, his hands still pressed against the glass opposite Yallia's.

"She's breathing chlorine at almost three times lethal amounts," Kuarta said over her shoulder.

"But she is showing absolutely no adverse effects. See for yourself," Onizaka said, gesturing to the wall readout that Tann was idly examining. He moved off, hands behind his back, as Kuarta and Onizaka spoke in low tones about the data.

"She's been in here for three hours?" Kuarta said, scrolling back through the experiment history.

"Yes, but she's only been in this level of exposure for about twenty minutes."

"And she's given no signs of distress?"

"None at all. Oh, she said she's hungry, but that's almost certainly not test-related."

"Have you fed her?" Dolen said from his position at the glass.

Onizaka looked at him. "We have. We gave her four hundred calories, give or take a few, and—"

Kuarta blurted out, "Ninety thousand milligrams of salt?" She turned from the readout on which the meal specifics were displayed.

"She wanted more, but I wanted to limit it at first."

"Let me speak to her," Kuarta said, glancing about her for the intercom switch.

Tann himself flicked the toggle from his place near the corner of the room. "Go ahead, Doctor. Professor. She can hear you."

"Mommy?"

"Sweetie, are you all right?"

"I want to get out of here. I want to go home."

"Soon, dear. Mommy will take you home soon." Kuarta rose from where she was squatting and turned to Tann. "I want her out of there."

"We're not done with the testing," Onizaka said.

"Yes, you are."

Tann's hands unclasped from behind him as he approached Kuarta. "Doctor, you don't seem to understand. The girl behind the glass is more than just your daughter."

"What?" This, suddenly, from Dolen.

"She's a member of this colony, and a potentially dangerous one at that." Tann's eyes did not blink.

Kuarta matched his stare. "You know what happened to her."

"Yes. And we know what happened in the Crèche."

Kuarta's eyes widened. "You'd use that to keep my daughter here?"

"I'd use anything in my power to keep a dangerous mutant out of the general population. I would invent facts if it suited me. Fortunately, I do not need to. The girl has provided me with reason enough." He did not smile, exactly, but his expression changed subtly. He was satisfied.

There was silence for a moment, then Kuarta spoke again. Her voice was almost tender, even as a deep hatred for this misshapen man swelled in her. "I know what you did to her. I know what you did to me, to all the other Ship women twenty years ago when we arrived. And now it is affecting my daughter."

Onizaka gasped. Kuarta ignored her. "You tell me she is a dangerous mutant. But you are responsible."

Tann snorted. "You are irrational, Doctor. I am responsible? And to what do you refer when you say you know what I did to all shippie women twelve years ago?" Tann placed slight emphasis on the number, as if to reinforce the distinction between argie and shippie. "You are inventing conspiracies out of worry for your daughter." He turned to Dolen. "Professor, can't you speak to your wife? Assure her we have only the best interests of your daughter and the colony at heart."

"My wife is her own person, Mr. Tann."

Kuarta started at Dolen at this unexpected show of resistance.

Tann, too, was taken slightly aback. "Surely, you don't believe her wild—"

"Why not? Because I'm argie, like you?"

Tann cocked his head slightly in affected surprise. "No, because I thought you more rational than your wife. Perhaps I misjudged you." He loaded his voice with contempt, but Dolen did not rise to the bait. Kuarta stepped forward and addressed Tann.

"The evidence is clear. Yallia's mutation cannot be a natural one."

"Why not?" Tann looked at Onizaka. "Doctor? Can you rule out natural causes for the child's mutation?"

Onizaka's unease was clear. She started to speak, stopped, then finally mumbled, "Carll, maybe we should call Newfield."

Tann scowled at her. "Why?"

Onizaka fumbled for a response. "Well, I...."

"You want to consult with the Commissar-General? I can tell you what he will decide. Do you really suppose that the colony can take any course of action other than expulsion of all hybrid children?"

"Expulsion? To where?" Kuarta said.

"Outside, of course." Into the stunned silence of the laboratory Tann continued, "The child is dangerous—the incident at the Crèche shows that clearly. You've told me that other children will soon manifest their mutations, posing an even greater threat to the colony. Furthermore, we cannot know if the mutation will not eventually make the oxygen atmosphere of the domes toxic to these children. With all these facts in mind, I see no alternative to expulsion from the colony."

As Kuarta listened, she watched Dolen's face change. In a sudden flash of insight in the deep recesses of her mind, she realized that her husband was receiving a far greater shock than she. Kuarta had lived her entire life suspicious of government—her mother's involvement in politics served to strengthen her wariness, not diminish it—but Dolen had always believed implicitly in the goodness of all who served in administration. He was the perfect citizen—conscientious, loyal, blind to fault or malice in his government. Kuarta saw his almost childlike trust in appointed authority shattered by Tann's words. She saw something twist and break inside of him as the lines on his once-soft face hardened almost imperceptibly, and Kuarta knew he would never be the same man again.

"You...why did you do this?" Dolen said, rising unsteadily from the glass barrier, using it to support his weight.

"You keep saying that," Tann answered, turning to look at him. "I will put it down to grief and shock, but I assure you, I had nothing to do with this. It must have been something in your shippie genes."

Kuarta reacted without thinking. She leapt at him. The attack was not precise; as she lashed out at him, she had no plan, no goal. She merely wanted to end the words and somehow smash this nightmare she knew Tann had created.

Tann easily sidestepped Kuarta's charging body, producing a weapon from his pocket. He smoothly brought it to bear on Kuarta as she slammed against the glass a meter away from him.

"Get back, Doctor. You too, Professor," he said, keeping his eyes on Kuarta. "I'd rather not use this on you. As you can see, it is not a paralyzer. Your deaths would be inconvenient to explain, though not impossible."

Kuarta's shoulders slumped. She and Dolen moved slowly away from Tann and his weapon.

Tann kept his gaze on Kuarta and Dolen and said to Onizaka over his shoulder, "Karin, call the constables. I think it's time for the parents to go so you can finish your work." He waited for a few seconds, and suddenly saw Kuarta's eyes grow large as they spied movement to his left. Tann turned in alarm, only to receive a vicious blow to the face as Onizaka brought a heavy lab chair down on him. Tann crumpled to the ground with dull thud, the weapon flying from his hand to land a few feet from Dolen.

Dolen and Kuarta watched, frozen for a moment, as Onizaka raised the chair again and brought it crashing down on Tann's supine body. Tann partially deflected the force of the blow with his arms, but one of the chair supports struck his face. Tann's head cracked onto the floor of the lab and he lay still.

Onizaka raised the chair yet again, but Kuarta recovered her presence of mind fast enough to intervene. "Stop! Karin, leave him! You've done enough."

Onizaka stared at Kuarta for a moment, her eyes wild, unseeing. Then she seemed to recover her wits and slowly lowered the chair. She stared down at Tann's unmoving body. "You'd better get out of here," she said quietly and pressed the cycle button on the chamber airlock. Blowers whirred to life, pumping the airlock to overpressure.

Dolen had scooped up the weapon and now turned on the intercom to Yallia's chamber. Immediately, the sound of hysterical crying filled the air. Yallia was pressed up against the glass, red-faced and terrified.

"Dear, you need to come out now. Go to the door and go inside. There will be a little wind, but that's okay. Just go into the little room over here," Kuarta tapped the glass of the airlock outer door. Yallia hurried to the airlock and entered. Onizaka closed the door remotely when she was inside and checked the airlock gauge. "Only trace chlorine in the lock. About 20 ppm," she said and opened the outer door.

A strong chlorine smell from Yallia's clothes made the three adults blink as the girl rushed to her mother's and father's arms.

"I want to go home," Yallia kept repeating.

Onizaka smiled faintly and moved to Dolen. She held her hand out for the weapon. Dolen placed it in her hand, and it disappeared into one of the lab coat's pockets. "I'm sorry, Yallia," she said.

Yallia blubbered for a few more seconds and turned a tear-streaked face to her. "For what?"

"Everything." Onizaka looked at Tann. "I don't know why I did it."

Kuarta started at her, then looked stupidly at the overturned chair. "What?"

"You were right, of course. About the mutation. I was just trying...I thought I could make the colony better."

Kuarta did not try to console her. "We've got to get out of here."

"And go where?" Dolen answered. "We can't hide. Tann will regroup and organize a search. While I appreciate what you did for us, Doctor, it may prove futile." All three adults stared at Tann's body. It took a full twenty seconds before Dolen added quietly, "Maybe one of you should check to see if he's alive."

It was Onizaka who knelt down and pressed a hand to his neck. "Pulse steady. He probably has a concussion, maybe a fractured skull."

"What about internal bleeding?" Kuarta asked, still clasping her daughter tightly.

"Can't tell. I'll have to get him to Valhalla Hospital."

"Couldn't you just treat him here?" Dolen asked.

"I wouldn't chance it. This isn't an operating room, Professor. He'll need to go to the hospital."

"Then what happens?" Dolen asked. No one answered.

"I want to go home," Yallia said again and started crying anew. Kuarta and Dolen looked at each other, helplessly.

"Why not?" Kuarta said. "We can't run, and it's better than staying here. Maybe Ma will have some luck with Newfield," she said, not believing her own words. Dolen hesitated a moment, then nodded.

So Kuarta and Dolen, because they could not think of anywhere else to go, took their daughter home, perhaps for the last time.

The trip home was uneventful: Tann's swift action and secrecy in apprehending Yallia now worked to the Verdafners' advantage. No constable stopped them as they took the wirebus back to New Chicago in the early morning. Yallia slept fitfully in her mother's lap as the wirebus glided smoothly through the outskirts of Valhalla and into the transfer tube joining one Dome complex to another.

"Should we call Jene?" Dolen whispered when the wirebus left Valhalla Dome. The two had been almost completely silent while in Valhalla, as if speech itself would somehow call attention to them and result in their recapture.

"I don't know. I suppose so," Kuarta said. She carefully dug out her phone from her belt sheath and handed it to Dolen. He hid the phone behind his hand and spoke quietly into it, careful not to wake his daughter.

"Jene Halfner," he said, and the phone automatically connected him. He heard Jene's recorded voice tell him she was unavailable right now. Dolen said, "Urgent," and the phone connected again. Presently, Jene's voice came through the receiver.

"Dolen?"

"Jene, we've had an...event. We're headed back to New Chicago. With Yallia."

"What? How?"

Dolen chose his words with care. In his newfound attitude towards his government, he suspected everything. Someone might be listening in. "That's all I can tell you now."

There was a short silence before Jene said slowly, "All right. I'm still with the Commissar-General. I'll be in touch when I'm done."

Dolen could not resist one question. "Any progress?"

"Some. I'll finish here soon." She clicked off and Dolen put the phone in his own pouch, thoughtfully gazing off towards the green-tinged landscape.

"Anything?" Kuarta whispered.

"Not really. She'll come home soon." Dolen looked back out on the landscape. Would his daughter live out there, in the swirling green gas? Would she be the only one?

Kuarta stroked Yallia's hair and noted it had a definite copper tinge that it had not had mere weeks ago.

* * *

"Before I leave you, sir, I wish to make it clear one more time that I intend to bring this matter before the general Assembly in special session. I fully expect you to call the Assembly soon. If you do not, I will contact Commissars personally to bring the matter into the open." Jene found Newfield surprisingly haggard even though he was younger than Jene herself. It struck Jene suddenly that Newfield was not a natural leader. He had been placed into this position on recommendation from the last Commissar-General, a man whom Jene had never served under but who had a reputation for listening overmuch to his advisors instead of his own conscience. Already, murmurings of a similar nature had begun to surface about Newfield.

"I understand. Commissar Halfner, you seem to think that I enjoyed presiding over this mess. Nothing could be further from the truth. I expect this crisis to ruin me politically. I don't know what I could have done differently, but I know that any solution I applied would have resulted in my ruin. But better, I think, for that to happen than the colony itself to be jeopardized."

Jene had come into the meeting full of fire, blazing away at her superior without hindrance. And he had listened to her. He had made no statement defending his actions other than to say, repeatedly, "I had to make a choice." Even under the circumstances, Jene could not but feel pity for the man before her. His had not been the hand behind this, Jene knew. Newfield was simply weak. Tann controlled him.

Jene's voice lost some of its hardness. "I would like to return to my home now, sir. Is there anything else?"

"No. We'll keep good care of your granddaughter, Jene," Newfield said with sincerity. Jene kept her face impassive.

As if on cue, a muted buzzing sounded on Newfield's desk. He said to the air, "Go ahead," and the Valhalla Police Captain's head and shoulders materialized in mid-air before his desk.

"Sir, Captain Sheihr speaking."

Newfield narrowed his eyes. Jene did not move. The Commissar-General either did not mind that she was still here or had already mentally dismissed her. In any case, she would listen in unless ordered to leave. "Yes?"

"Sir, I'm at Valhalla Hospital. Staff called us to respond to...an unusual case. Doctor Karin Onizaka has asked to be placed under arrest for assault on Carll Tann."

Newfield leaned in to the hologram. "Explain that."

"Sir, Tann is under doctor's care now. I am told he suffered blunt trauma to the skull and received a mild concussion as a result. I think they're checking his brain function now. Doctor Onizaka says she hit him with a chair."

"Why?"

"She won't say, sir."

Newfield considered for a moment, then said, "I want to speak with her." Sheihr's head and shoulders moved out of pickup to be replaced by Onizaka.

"Yes, sir?" she said. Jene thought she could hear satisfaction in her voice.

"What the hell is going on? Why did you attack Tann?"

"He was going to put the Verdafner child outside."

"What?" Jene exploded.

Newfield snapped his head up and looked at Jene. "We're done here. I'll call you if I need you." Jene nodded and left the office. As she backed out the doorway, she saw Newfield bury his head in his hands for a moment before turning to face Onizaka's image again.

* * *

"So there was no fracture?" Tann asked the doctor.

"No, but you had a fairly serious concussion. You might want to stay here for a few days." The doctor knew there were special circumstances in this case—the Valhalla police had been all over the ward, and their arrest of Doctor Onizaka was the talk of the entire hospital. Still, he did not let that cloud his treatment recommendations.

"That does not suit my needs, Doctor, though I thank you for your care. Now, is there further therapy you wish me to participate in? If so," Tann continued before the doctor could respond, "please contact my office at your earliest convenience." Tann slid off the exam table and suppressed a wince. His head still throbbed even through the pain-blocking medication he had been supplied with. He smiled as best he could at the doctor and strode from the exam room. Four burly Valhalla constables were waiting in the hallway, their captain among them.

"Where are they?" Tann snapped, turning sharply as he left the exam room and heading towards the hospital exit. The constables fell into step behind him even as the captain shuffled to Tann's side.

"We don't know, sir. No one saw them leave."

Tann's lip twitched in irritation. "All right. I want all of Valhalla dome searched. Discreetly, Captain. Begin by contacting any constables who might be on patrol near the transfer tube. Perhaps one of them saw something." Tann knew how unlikely that was, but it was worth trying.

"Sir, what if they're not in Valhalla?"

"Oh, I rather think they are not, Captain. But you do your job here, just in case. While you're checking on the transfer tube, I want you to place Commissar Halfner under arrest if she is still in Valhalla. Look in her office first."

"Yes, sir."

"Remember, Captain—discretion is paramount here. We don't want to alarm the public."

"I understand." The captain added, "What about Doctor Onizaka?"

"She's already in custody. Leave her for now, but I want her isolated from all visitors."

"All visitors? She has the right to visitors as she pleases, sir."

"I'm rescinding that right as of now."

The captain's stride faltered a moment. "I—I don't think you have the authority to do that, sir. I'll have to contact the Commissar-General."

Tann shrugged casually. "Go ahead. I'm sure he will be happy to hear from you. He's got a dangerous mutant loose in the colony somewhere. I'm sure he'll want to discuss jurisprudence with you. Oh, perhaps it would be wise to select a successor before you call him, just in case."

The captain cleared his throat nervously. "I'll see to Onizaka, sir."

"Good." Tann dismissed the officers with a wave of his hand and continued out of the hospital. His memory was fragmentary—he remembered having the accursed shippie women right where he had wanted them for twelve years when all went black. He had awakened in the hospital and had to be filled in by that imbecile police captain.

He had enough of his faculties to remember where Kuarta Verdafner lived, however.

CHAPTER
11

Dunbarston had gathered his entire twelve-person force and had equipped them with full riot ordinance. Tann could not help but nod in satisfaction when he met the New Chicago police captain at the transfer tube precisely at noon. It had been a scant twelve hours since the raid on the Halfner apartment and only five since Onizaka's treachery.

"Sir. We're all ready. We've got both our transports prepared," Dunbarston explained, his eyes darting to the few wirebus passengers who looked at the assemblage with curiosity. The wirebus had stopped to pick up and drop off passengers and light freight at the New Chicago/Valhalla transfer tube. At least a dozen people were seated in the bus with their windows open, all looking intently at Dunbarston and his riot force. He shifted in his armor, adjusting his screamer carbine slung over his shoulder. The man's discomfort was obvious—he was anxious to get Tann and his force inside the transports.

"You have verified the mutant is in the Verdafner's apartment?" Tann said casually, making no attempt to keep his comment from the civilian passengers. He had deliberately designated the transfer tube as the staging area for Dunbarston's officers, aware of the civilian traffic they would encounter.

Dunbarston stammered, "Yes, sir. Two of our constables confirm that the two parents and the child entered the apartment building about four hours ago. We're ready to get into the transports," he repeated lamely. Again, he glanced at the wirebus and saw that at least some of the passengers had heard the comment. There was a general commotion inside the bus. Dunbarston swore silently, then added, "Sir, we should get going. If you are worried about a riot, the more time we delay, the more—"

"Oh, I'm not particularly worried about a riot. If one was going to happen, it would have happened by now, right, Captain?"

"I'm not sure, sir. If—"

"No matter. Let's go," he said, and, almost cheerfully, entered the nearest of the two transports. Dunbarston directed his force to their trucks and the fourteen men and women headed to New Chicago's residential sector.

This time, the officers did not cast their eyes downwards in shame for what they were about to do. This time, they looked at each other with bold camaraderie. They checked each other's gear and made minor adjustments to armor straps and helmet fittings. They checked and rechecked communications gear with a businesslike air. Tann watched with detached interest. An officer sitting opposite him on one of the seats caught his eye.

"Didn't think we'd be back here so soon, Mr. Tann," she said, grinning behind her faceplate.

"Nor did I."

She grunted and cast her eyes over Tann's bruised forehead. She gestured with her chin and said, "How'd you pick that up?"

"A disagreement with a colleague."

She stuck out her lower lip and nodded crookedly. "Must have been some disagreement. Have anything to do with this mutant?"

Tann was spared the necessity of fabricating another lie by Dunbarston's angry voice. "Kolski! Quiet down and stay focused."

Kolski glanced at Dunbarston. "Yes, sir," she said, but Tann's practiced ears heard the disrespect behind her words. He watched her as she settled back into her seat. She had said the word "mutant." Obviously, Dunbarston would not have briefed his police using loaded language such as that—this Kolski must have picked up the term elsewhere. Tann smiled. He had made a few calculatedly injudicious remarks to prominent people in New Chicago before leaving Valhalla, and the rumors were already flying. The rest of his plan could not be far from fruition.

Only a few minutes later, Tann heard the driver grunt something in the forward compartment.

"What?" Dunbarston said.

"A disturbance ahead, sir. Looks like rioters." The driver slowed the vehicle as the five officers in the back of the truck tensed.

Dunbarston twisted in his seat and studied the vehicle's tactical display. "Dammit! All right, let us out. I don't want to take the truck into them." Dunbarston grabbed the radio and ordered the second police vehicle to stop as well. Tann grabbed hold of a strap above him to steady himself as the truck braked to a stop.

The rear door opened and the five officers scrambled out and formed a double-file line with their counterparts from the other van. By the time Tann had climbed out of the truck, all twelve of them were assembled and awaited

Dunbarston's orders. Tann could hear the distant din of angry humanity from ahead. The two drivers had placed their vehicles behind one of the other apartment towers in the residential sector, out of sight.

Dunbarston shouted his instructions to the force. "Squad A will disperse the riot using screamers when possible, paralyzers when they must. Squad B will break into three pairs and detain or arrest anyone who openly defy police or deface public property. Any threats to Dome integrity take precedence—if you see anyone with a weapon that could conceivably damage the Dome, you are to take action immediately to prevent such destruction. That goes for squad A, too. If we get into a fight with the rioters, form up into a phalanx and assume full defensive posture. We'll use numbjel if it gets too wild." He looked the group over. "Any questions?"

There were none, or if there were, no officer voiced them. Dunbarston nodded to the two women (one of whom was Kolski, Tann noted) at the head of the lines. They started off towards the rioters, the group designated as squad A forming a horizontal line and advancing behind their clear plastic shields. The second group paired up and followed them.

Dunbarston motioned to Tann. "Come inside with me. We can monitor from there," he said, climbing back inside the truck. He switched on a bank of monitors positioned in the upper corners of the truck and adjusted some other controls. The view on the monitors was evidently from the helmets of the police officers. The shots were clear and steady, and as Tann watched, he could see the lead officer of squad A round a corner and come face to face with the riot.

Dunbarston switched a toggle and the truck was filled with angry shouts.

"Kolski, go ahead and break it up," Dunbarston said. Tann looked at the screen, leaning forward in his seat to do so. Something was wrong here— almost all the rioters he could see were facing the building but had not gone inside. Kolski's viewpoint was blocked past one or two layers of people; Tann could not see closer.

Dunbarston said, "Kolski, float your camera. I need a top-down." As he spoke, he grabbed a joystick controller on the panel before him. The picture shook a bit, then everything in the shot descended, as the camera flew upwards. The ground tilted crazily, and then the remote camera was floating above the riot, under Dunbarston's control. Now Tann could see why the rioters had not entered the building. There were perhaps fifty people outside trying to get in, but Tann could see a line of people, argies and shippies, blocking entrance to the apartment building, their arms linked together at the elbows.

Kolski and her officers started to shove their way past the outermost layer of the crowd to the building itself. Tann followed their progress on the bird's-eye view he was afforded by the floatercam.

"Kolski, get up to the door and disperse this mob. Everyone—including those people guarding the door—is to vacate the area."

"Yes, sir." Kolski grunted, working her way through the crowd. No one jostled her—in fact, most of the rioters, once they realized who was pushing them from behind, moved aside with minimal resistance. Kolski and a brace of officers made it to the front and shouted for the crowd to go home.

"There's a mutant in there!" several people shouted back.

"She's already killed a child!"

"What are you going to do about her?"

The other officers had by now arrived with Kolski at the front and were slowly but steadily pushing everyone back, using their shields and occasionally jabbing at particularly recalcitrant rioters with their stun rods. Kolski muttered into her mike as she pushed, "Captain, I think we need some help here. They're not violent, but we can only push them back so far before our wedge breaks down." She moved her mike away from her face and shouted at her officers to stop where they were. Tann saw the distance between them was already dangerously great—as the officers pushed the rioters back in a semicircle, the bubble of safety between the police and the building grew, but so did the perimeter. There were perhaps ten meters of space where nobody stood, only the twenty defenders, arms still linked. Now that the riot had moved off a bit, Tann could hear the defenders singing quietly.

A young voice came over the radio. "Captain, this is Galmeade. There's a wirebus on its way here, packed full. About forty more people on it."

Dunbarston worked his controls and pivoted the floating camera towards the wirebus track. He zoomed in on a moving speck in the distance and saw two of his officers accessing a small box mounted on a pole near the wirebus stop.

"What are they doing?" Tann asked.

"They're stopping the bus." As Dunbarston spoke, the wirebus slowed gradually to a stop. It was perhaps two hundred meters away from the apartment building and one hundred away from the stop.

The two officers moved towards the bus. Galmeade's voice came through again. "They're getting out. Captain, I don't think we'll be able to stop them. You've got a few minutes before they arrive."

"Opechui here, Captain. Rioters coming in on foot from the rest of the residential sector. I make it about two hundred."

"Captain? Baghdassarian reporting in. I think there are more people coming, sir. Looks like from the University complex. Students, mainly, I'd guess. About fifty of them. Me and Franco can't hold them back."

As Dunbarston listened to the reports, his head sank lower and lower. Tann watched him—there could be no doubt: the man was simply not suited for this work. He could police a quiet community very well, Tann supposed, but as soon as he was called upon to act decisively and perhaps violently, he became paralyzed. All the better.

Tann leaned towards him and said, "Perhaps I had better speak to the crowd. Can you get me in there?"

Dunbarston's head snapped up and there was a moment of relief in his eyes that faded almost as quickly as it came. "No, no. Too dangerous. I can't risk getting you hurt."

"I take the risk, Captain. Besides, as a member of the government, I might be able to quiet them down. After all, we are here to deal with the mutant, as they are asking. They will welcome the news."

Dunbarston did not move for perhaps ten seconds. Then he nodded and lowered his head again. Tann waited. Dunbarston snapped his head back up, as if that would give him the courage he needed to face the mob and his force, and escorted Tann out of the truck.

It was perhaps a minute's walk to the edge of the mob, which could now be seen from around the residential building behind which the transport trucks were parked. Tann spent that minute in fierce thought.

The mob had indeed gathered as he had planned, but who were these people staked out in front of the building, preventing entrance? Could Halfner have mobilized a counterforce so quickly? Tann dismissed the thought. She had been busy with the Commissar-General, and besides, how could she know Tann had planted information to encourage a riot?

"All right, make way there. Move aside," Dunbarston started pushing the outermost levels of the crowd out of his way. Tann followed in his wake.

When they reached the perimeter and were permitted to pass, Tann headed for the line of people in front of the building. One of the officers stood nearby, watching the group but taking no action. Dunbarston stepped over to her and conferred quietly. Tann approached one of the argie defenders.

"What are you people doing here?"

The person to whom Tann spoke was a young argie adult, perhaps thirteen years old. She answered, "We're exercising our right to assembly." That brought a murmur of support from her twenty or so comrades nearby.

Tann glanced up and down the line. For the first time, he noticed that the members in the line alternated shippie and argie almost to the very end, where three shippie defenders clung to one another to complete the chain.

The mob on the other side of the police barricade had been all argie, of course. Tann looked back at the argie woman in front of him.

"You must disperse. The police need to enter this building."

"To take the child away? No. You'll have to go through us."

"Don't make this harder than it has to be. We're taking the child for her own safety. You can see—"

The woman snorted. "Don't lie to us, Tann. We know perfectly well why you're here. Yallia has done nothing wrong. You can't have her."

"Nothing wrong?" Tann shouted, quite aware that his words would be heard by the crowd. He needed this stalemate broken, and quickly, before more supporters to the mutant's cause arrived. If that meant utilizing the raw power of the mob, he would do so. He half-turned so the crowd could better hear his words. "The mutant inside this building killed a little boy! How many more children must die before you allow your government to act for the safety of its citizens?"

Dunbarston strode quickly to Tan and hissed, "What're you doing? You want to start a riot?"

"Yes, Captain, he does," the argie woman said. "I'd call for medical services while it's still quiet. You might not get the chance if Tann has his way."

Tann shook off Dunbarston's hand on his shoulder. "Go back to your officers, Captain. I'll handle this."

"Not like this, you won't. I'm getting reports that more and more people are on their way here. I've got to stop this now before it's more than we can handle."

Tann could feel his control of the situation slipping away. He turned back to the argie woman. "What do you think you're accomplishing here? Do you think you can stay here forever? The child will have to be examined and quarantined. We don't know what we're dealing with yet."

The woman did not answer, but just looked at Tann with maddening satisfaction.

Tann growled and turned away to look back at the mob. There was only one thing left he could do.

"I can see more people coming from the University," Dolen said, his face pressed up against the glass of the living room window. The University complex was perhaps three hundred meters away from their building, near the outskirts of the populated section of the Dome. Beyond the University were the botanical sections. As Dolen watched, another floater cam zoomed up to his level, joining the two that already hovered outside the window. Dolen had long since adjusted the glass to one-way transparency, and although the technology existed to penetrate the opacity of the window, extreme reluctance to violate personal privacy kept the newscams outside. The newsweb would wait for its story.

"Come over here, dear. The newsweb has shots from all around the Dome," Kuarta said. She and her mother were watching the newsweb screen as it displayed pictures of people giving their reactions to the disturbance. Most were unfavorable and seemed to blame the Verdafners themselves for the civil unrest.

"Mommy, are all those people mad at me?" Yallia said, snuggling up to Kuarta on the sofa.

"No, dear. No one's mad at you."

"I heard them say my name and they looked mad."

Kuarta looked at her daughter with what she hoped was a reassuring smile. "No one's mad at you."

"Then what are they mad at?"

"Nothing, dear," Kuarta hugged her daughter closer.

"Mommy?"

"Yes?"

"I'm sorry I killed that boy." Yallia said it with a sincerity few adults ever reached. Kuarta looked at her daughter again, wondering why she had to grow up so fast.

"Kuarta," Dolen said softly. He was gesturing at the screen. Kuarta turned her head to see the outside of their own building on the newsweb. As the shot returned to the front of the building, Kuarta saw Tann talking animatedly with an argie woman she vaguely recognized. She was one of the chain of defenders at the building's entrance.

"Tann's here." Dolen said.

Kuarta was not looking at him—she was trying to place the woman. She knew her from somewhere.

"Shhh," Jene said, and Dolen fell silent. The three adults listened to Tann's exchange with the young woman and saw Tann try to incite the crowd with his rhetoric.

"My God," Dolen said, "he's actually trying to start something. He's going to kill someone if he keeps this up."

Kuarta turned to her mother to ask her if Newfield knew about this, but the expression on Jene's face took her words away. Her mother was sitting transfixed—her face was looking at the screen, but her eyes were elsewhere. Kuarta could see that her mother was lost in memory.

"Ma?"

Jene did not answer immediately. Kuarta said, more loudly, "Ma?"

Jene shook her head a bit and turned to Kuarta. "What? Oh, sorry. What was it?"

"You were thinking about Ship, weren't you, Ma?" Kuarta asked quietly.

Jene was silent for a moment. When she did speak, her voice was husky. "It's happening again. I can't let it happen again."

"It's not your fight this time, Ma."

"It wasn't mine then, either. I had no right—"

"You had every right to do what you did."

Jene shook her head slowly. "No, no. It wasn't necessary. All we had to do was land and it would have been fine. No one needed to die. Not Rik. Not Bobby. Not your father."

"You didn't know that. You couldn't have known that." Kuarta spoke soothingly, even as the throng outside threatened to rip their family and their world apart. The two women were together in the past, trying to heal a wound that had festered for twenty years.

"My God!" Dolen shouted suddenly, leaping from the sofa. He was pointing at the screen. Kuarta and Jene watched as Tann pulled a small flechette gun from his pocket and shot the argie woman squarely in the chest. She slumped to the ground, taking the defenders on either side of her down with her. The weapon had made little sound and had not caused any visible signs of trauma to the woman save for her collapse.

It was at that moment that Kuarta recognized the woman—she had been at the museum a few days ago when Yallia had been pushed to the ground. Hers had been the face of compassion for Yallia and hatred for what the others were doing to her. She had not had the strength to act then. Now she was dead.

As Kuarta and her family watched, Tann grabbed the police captain and whispered something to him the floating recorders could not quite pick up. The captain looked at Tann with uncertainty for a moment, then called to the one officer standing nearby to remove the limp body of the woman from the building.

"If you do not disperse immediately," Tann said calmly to the remaining wide-eyed defenders, "the police will take similar action against all of you. You will be detained and brought to trial for incitement. If you leave now, no such charges will be brought."

The defenders started at each other and at the spot where the woman had stood. Before any of them could answer, however, a disturbance in the crowd erupted. The shot changed abruptly to a vantage point above the crowd, where perhaps five hundred people milled about. Within the mob, a fight had broken out, and as the hovercam zoomed in for a closer look, Dolen mumbled, "Oh, no."

"What is it?" Kuarta asked, her eyes fixed to the screen.

"Those are students," Dolen said, pointing. Dozens of young argie men and women were hand fighting with many more argie adults in the crowd. The hovercam picked up occasional snatches of shouted invective. It seemed the fighting students were themselves defending the Verdafners while a significant majority of colonists were demanding Yallia's incarceration.

The fight could not find release, having started in the middle of a huge crowd. In a matter of seconds, the melee grew as onlookers chose sides and started throwing punches and elbows.

A moan of despair was wrenched out of Jene as she stood watching the image. She buried her face in her hands.

Another camera shift—quickly back to the front of the building, not lingering long—he or she only allowed a brief shot to establish what was happening at the scene before cutting back to the action, but in those few seconds, Kuarta saw Tann looking not towards the fight, but up towards the Verdafner's apartment. For a split second, the hovercam lens caught his eyes and he was suddenly staring through the screen right into the Verdafner living room. Kuarta imagined she could hear him taunting her, asking, *how much longer are you going to let this continue?*

"No longer," Kuarta mumbled.

Jene looked at her. "What?"

"We've got to stop this."

"How?" Jene said, and her eyes went immediately to Yallia. "No."

"Look, Ma. Look at what is happening. Tann will keep this riot going for as long as it takes. He'll kill dozens, hundreds of people if he has to."

"Newfield will stop it. The government will stop it." Jene said.

"When? After how many deaths and what kind of irreparable damage to our world?"

"The world will recover."

"So would have Ship."

Jene looked at Yallia again. The little girl looked back, her eyes large. "What is it, Gramma?" Jene looked away before she started to cry. She looked at Dolen, who was still watching the screen. If he had heard the exchange, he gave no sign. "Dolen, you talk to her."

Dolen did not move his eyes from the violent images as he said, "What should I say? That I love my daughter more than I love my world?"

"The public will not allow a little girl to be—" Jene stopped with a glance at Yallia. Even now, she thought of protecting her granddaughter.

"To be what, Gramma?" Yallia said.

"There's the public, Jene," Dolen said, pointing to the screen where many of the students had been knocked to the ground, protected from kicks and blows by the remaining upright students. All were bleeding. "If we don't give up now, the government might not be able to protect us. Then we'll lose her forever. If we give her up, she might...have a chance." Dolen's voice was steady until the end.

"I can't do it," Jene said.

"You don't have to." Kuarta stroked Yallia's hair a few times. "I'll go outside. Don't worry," she added to Jene while still looking at Yallia, "It'll be different this time." She started to get up, trying to deflect and hush Yallia's anxious cries. Dolen and Jene comforted her as best they could, but Yallia would not be pacified. She wailed piteously as her mother walked out the door to the waiting mob below.

Kuarta stepped down the last stair to see Tann facing the glass entrance. One of the panes was cracked in a spider-web pattern where a demonstrator had no doubt thrown something against it. Tann stood patiently, hands behind his back, while behind him the crowd surged against the police barricade. A roar of unidentifiable emotion came from the crowd as Kuarta stepped out of the building.

"Doctor Verdafner," Tann said simply. His words were all but soundless in the din.

Kuarta surveyed the crowd. She could not see the fights breaking out in the thick of the mob—all she could see in the front were apoplectic argie faces screaming with rage, argie arms and hands clawing past the police in a vain effort to reach the object of their loathing.

Tann spoke again. Kuarta had to look at his face when he spoke in order to read his lips. "You know why I am here," he said.

Kuarta nodded.

"Are you prepared to surrender the girl?"

Kuarta looked at the crowd. She could not make out any individual words, but the overall tenor of the mob was quite clear. Had the police not been there, she would surely have been attacked, her daughter taken forcibly from her, her family beaten.

"You did this," Kuarta said to Tann, her eyes still on the mob.

"Does that matter?" Tann said louder. "They are here, and I cannot control them."

"The police could disperse them."

"Perhaps. But the police are under my orders not to interfere. They have no experience with riots, you know. They are only too happy to oblige me in this." He laughed. "One of the unexpected weaknesses of a peaceful, egalitarian society is a fairly ineffective police force."

"Egalitarian?" Kuarta turned to him, her resignation giving way to anger. "How can you call our society egalitarian? You have experimented on me, on thousands of human beings to produce a mutant. And now that you have done so, you want to exile her. And you call your society egalitarian?"

"You still persist in that ridiculous fantasy. Let us not argue politics, Doctor. The crowd behind me grows more restless by the minute."

"How would you stop me from broadcasting what you have done all over the newsweb?"

"I would not stop you."

Kuarta blinked. She had expected Tann to have blocked her transmission privileges (illegal, but a trifle compared to the egregious illegalities he had already perpetrated) or arranged some other technological barrier.

Tann continued. "Who would believe you, Doctor? Oh, I'm certain a small percentage of the population would," he said, preempting her answer, "but the vast majority would see your words as a desperate attempt to smear the government and save your child." Tann stepped closer and unclasped his hands from behind his back. "In any case, would it matter? Even if you convinced the world that what you say is the truth, the facts would remain the same: your daughter is a dangerous mutant, responsible for the brutal murder of an innocent argie child. How long do you think it would take me, even if your rhetoric had its intended effect, to get my way? And how many deaths out there," he waved a hand behind him to the roiling crowd, "would result?"

He was right, Kuarta thought, even as she damned her analytical mind for concluding so. Yallia was a mutant, and the colony would not tolerate her. If she stayed in the Dome, even under constant supervision and detention, public sentiment would be so against her that she would live in constant fear of attack.

Kuarta felt her shoulders droop a little. She saw Tann's at the gesture. Both knew that she would surrender, and Tann would have his victory.

"How did this happen?" Kuarta said, looking again at the mob.

Tann seemed to understand. "It was always there, Doctor. Behind the façade of civility and tolerance, there has always been hatred and fear of those who are different." His eyes darkened. "I know about that." He regained his composure and said, "All I needed to do was mobilize it, spur it on."

"Why?"

Tann glowered. "You will not ask me that. My motives are not for you to question. You will turn over the girl immediately, or I shall release the crowd."

Kuarta took a deep breath and nodded. Tann nodded in return and turned to face the mob. As he did so, Kuarta had a vision of herself leaping upon him and pummeling him mercilessly. She saw his head slam against the hard pavement over and over as the vision of herself relentlessly attacked him. She saw his head open up, black bile ooze out, and somehow everything was all right. The crowd smiled and cheered and hugged one another and there was the sun, inside the Dome? No, there was no Dome—she was outside. And Yallia was with her, and they were smiling and laughing.

The vision abruptly ended as a missile, a rock of substantial weight, whistled past her to crash into the already-cracked glass of the lobby. Kuarta felt heavy as she turned to reenter the building and give her daughter away.

CHAPTER
12

"You'll be a hero, Doctor Verdafner," Tann said hours later back in his office in Valhalla Dome. Yallia had been safely transported to Onizaka's labs again, which were now under the temporary supervision of a promising young geneticist named Parvin from Nirvana Dome. The young argie scientist was bright, to be sure, but more importantly had been thoroughly checked for any anti-government sentiment in his writings or personal relationships and found extremely patriotic. He would begin where Onizaka left off.

Kuarta, Dolen, and Jene sat opposite Tann in various stages of numb defeat. "The populace will be told of your sacrifice for the good of the colony."

"Mr. Tann," Dolen said, "you are either wholly ignorant of the social dynamics of this colony or you are purposefully trying to mislead us. Since I cannot believe a man could rise to your level of power in the government without at least a basic understanding of sociopolitical science, I must conclude the latter. You know the population will not see my wife in that light."

"I thought you were a historian, not a sociologist, Professor Verdafner."

"A good historian must be both. We learn about social structures by studying history."

"Oh?" Tann leaned back and steepled his fingers. "And what does history teach us in this case, Professor?"

"My wife and her mother are members of a lower caste. Don't deny it, Mr. Tann," Dolen said as Tann opened his mouth to object. "You've already had your security team search us for weapons and recording devices. There is no need to continue the façade."

Tann smiled. "Well spoken. Very well, I agree. Shippies are a hated underclass."

"No, sir. Not an underclass. Class implies fluidity. Shippies will remain hated and despised no matter what they do. They are a caste—a social group from which there is no escape."

Tann bristled at the correction but said nothing. Dolen continued. "In such a situation, no single action by any member of the lower caste can result in respect from the upper caste. Our family's surrender will only confirm what the argie caste already whispers among itself—that the shippies are not fundamentally human. They are monsters who give up their babies in a vain attempt to placate the masses."

"You're saying that if we had kept Yallia, we might have avoided all this?" Kuarta said.

Dolen looked at her with kindness. "No, Kuarta. Anything we did would have been twisted to put us in the worst light possible."

"You mean shippies, don't you, Dolen?" Jene said with unconcealed bitterness. "You're argie. You won't be tarred with the same brush."

"Jene, you know as well as I do how the argies will treat me. I'm the worst of all possible cases—someone who was once human who chose to become subhuman by marrying a shippie. You can be pitied. I will only be hated."

There was silence for a moment before Tann broke it. "I won't lie to you anymore. I think Professor Verdafner is right. The best you two can hope for is pity," he said, indicating Jene and Kuarta.

"We'd rather be hated," Kuarta said.

"You won't get the choice, I'm afraid."

Again, Kuarta knew Tann was right. She looked at him and spoke in a steady monotone. "You said you will not lie to us. Will you then tell us the truth about what you did to us? To the shippie women twelve years ago?"

"I see no reason to do that. We are not living in the past."

"You know we will continue to fight you. We'll spread news of what was done to us twelve years ago. We will tell everyone of your actions during the crisis, and we will never stop. The rest of your political career will be an ongoing battle to keep the truth hidden. If you try to silence us, we will shout louder."

"Silence you?" Tann chuckled. "My dear Doctor, of course I would not try to silence you. I'm sure your husband can find dozens of examples of regimes that tried that foolhardy strategy of silencing dissenters. No, Doctor, I shall do much worse. I will let you speak. Oh, yes, your movement will grow in power and stature for a few years, but eventually it will die of its own familiarity. You will be in a public relations war that I will not fight. And I will win as a result."

Tann stood up and walked around his desk to stand directly in front of Kuarta. "Your husband is quite correct, shippie. You are subhuman. Every time you look out of the Dome, remember your daughter and the others of her ilk to follow." Tann glanced at Dolen, then looked back at Kuarta, his calculatedly urbane manner dissolving in venomous rage. "You came here thinking you could take for free what we and our descendants built over the course of thirty-six years. I want you to remember what happened when you tried to make your daughter one of us."

Tann and Kuarta stared at each other for a long moment. Dolen broke the stalemate.

"I want to live with her."

Tann smiled slightly, his composure regained. "I'm afraid, Professor, the Dome cannot afford to support you, your wife, and whoever else decides they wish to live at public expense while producing nothing in return. The price of socialism, sir, is participation in the whole."

"We will be allowed to visit her at will?"

Tann continued to look at Kuarta for a moment before walking back to his desk. "Yes, Professor. Subject to environmental conditions, of course. You'll have full access. Plus we'll arrange for electronic conferencing at your request."

"And how far away will she be?"

"Dolen," Jene said, "we've been through this before."

"I know. But I want to hear it again. I may have forgotten to ask something."

Tann answered Dolen's question. "The atmospheric testing station in the Green Valley is even now being expanded to house a permanent staff for the child. It's about sixty kilometers to the east and one kilometer lower in elevation."

"What about the other children?" Kuarta asked.

"Other children?"

"There will be others, Tann. There are others right now, but their mutations haven't manifested themselves yet. Will you send them to the same facility?"

"We shall make that decision when the time comes. I expect we will, but I cannot confirm that at this time." He looked at all three adults. "If there is nothing more, I imagine you will want to say goodbye to her. She is scheduled to be transported in a few hours." Tann spoke dismissively, and the family members understood the message. All rose wearily from their chairs.

Dolen and Kuarta supported each other as they exited the office, hands on one another's shoulders. Tann called to Jene as the Commissar was about to step over the threshold.

"Commissar Halfner?"

Jene turned.

"You may be interested to know that the Assembly is contemplating a vote regarding your future as a member of this government. I have it on good authority that you will no longer be a Commissar in fifty-two hours. Perhaps you had better begin preparations for career reassignment. Gengineering specialists will be in demand, no doubt."

Jene stared at the floor as she spoke. "I underestimated you, Mr. Tann. Even in my utter distrust of government, I never believed any government could be so driven by hate to plan the forced genocide of a group of people it hadn't even met. You had this planned since before our arrival."

"Certainly, but you give this administration, and the one of twelve years ago, far too much credit, Commissar. The government did not plan this—well, I hate to call it genocide; perhaps we should say, reorganization of caste—in any way. I did. I used the talents of Doctor Karin Onizaka, then a promising young gengineer, and set my plan in motion without the government's knowledge." He smiled at her. "We both distrust government, Commissar. You think it perpetrates evil at every step through draconian action against its citizens. I distrust government because it seldom acts with decision in critical moments. Our society has been building to a crisis over the shippie immigrant issue since before your arrival. I merely found a way to end the crisis before it could do any real damage to the colony."

Jene considered this. "No. That's too easy. You're making yourself too altruistic, too concerned with the public good. If you were truly concerned with the welfare of the colony, you would have donated your gametes for reproduction."

Tann's eyes widened momentarily, and a look of fury passed across his face for an instant.

Jene spoke in almost a whisper. "I've checked the records. I had to pull some strings here and there, but if you can do it, so can I. You've never fathered a child."

Tann had regained his composure again with admirable alacrity. "That has nothing to do with the case." His face was a mask of stolid inscrutability, and his voice was unnaturally even.

Jene studied the man for a moment, and with a flash of insight, she knew what he was hiding. His homosexuality was merely a cover for a secret so shameful that he would do anything to hide it.

"You're sterile."

Tann's mask almost held. "And if I am, Doctor? Does this make you feel superior to me?" A flush slowly grew on his face and the veins on his bald head began to stand out. "The meanest shippie immigrant, with no skills save those which we have taught her, can produce dozens of children to populate the planet while argie laborers work a few hours more each day to support the increase. And the mother is applauded for her efforts! 'Children are our future' says the slogan. Perhaps they are, but one thing is certain, Doctor Jene Halfner," he took three quick steps until he was almost nose to nose with the taller woman, "there will always be a difference between argie children and shippie ones."

"Why not just sterilize all of the shippies?" Jene asked quietly.

Tann laughed, almost crazed. "Do you think something like that would have gone unnoticed? Besides, we need shippie children. Professor Dolen's underclass needs workers. There is a phrase from Old Earth—"the world needs ditch-diggers too.'"

To her surprise, Jene found herself growing calmer and calmer as Tann lost control. She stared at the man, watching him breathe deeply in his underdeveloped chest. "You realize that by creating a new breed of human who can survive outside, you are giving the hybrids an advantage."

Tann sneered. "What advantage? The terraforming process will be complete in a few generations. In one hundred years, all of us will be able to live outside. What use is their mutation then? And they will always have the social stigma of the outcast—I have found that sociology always outlasts biology, Doctor."

"I won't argue," Jene said quietly. "There is no point in arguing with you; our fundamental beliefs are too different." She turned again to go but threw a final barb over her shoulder. "But you will regret what you have done. You have not ended a crisis—you have set events in motion that will precipitate a far worse one." And she left. Kuarta and Dolen were waiting some distance down the corridor from Tann's office.

"What was that about?" Kuarta asked.

"Nothing important," Jene sighed. Kuarta opened her mouth to say something, but thought better of it. The three continued towards the lab where Yallia was being readied for transport.

She was sitting morosely in the outer lab, wearing a shapeless grey jumpsuit that had all manner of biomed sensor patches on it. Three technicians were also present, looking at a holo display of Yallia's vital signs as broadcast by her suit sensors. Yallia looked up when the door opened to admit her family and broke into a faint smile. For an instant, Kuarta saw an eerie wisdom in the child's eyes, as if Yallia understood why her mother had consigned her to exile. Then the illusion was gone, and Yallia was just her frightened child.

Kuarta and Dolen hugged her. One of the technicians started to move forward to admonish them to back off—their embrace was distorting the sensor images—but Jene waved her off. The technician hesitated, then returned to her compatriots.

"Mommy? Daddy?" Yallia said, her voice muffled by their arms.

"Yes, dear?" Kuarta said.

"Are you mad at me?"

Kuarta felt the tears trickling down her face. She and Dolen had already talked to her at length about what was to happen and why. But Yallia, as all children, needed assurance of certain facts.

"No, of course not, darling. We love you very, very much."

"Then why are you sending me away?"

Dolen handled this question. "We are not sending you away, sweetie. You are going to live outside and we will come see you all the time."

"Promise?"

"Promise."

Yallia hugged her parents and cried again. The hysteria, the fighting, had all ended hours ago. Yallia accepted what was to happen now, since she had no choice. She even understood a tiny fraction.

"Is this because of Pem?" she said between sniffles.

Kuarta said, "No. You are a very good girl. Sometimes...people have to go away for a while. It just happens. One day, you'll understand." And Kuarta could not help but to glance at her mother. "Like I do," she added, her eyes locked on Jene's.

There were more questions concerning the nature and frequency of their visits, and there was more pleading, but in the end, Kuarta, Dolen, and Jene left the child to the hands of the transport technicians.

Jene was the last to speak with her. Even as the techs closed in to take her away, she held her granddaughter and whispered, "Don't forget any of this, child. Come back one day. No matter whom you have to hurt. Come back."

And Yallia was taken away.

It was a long time before Jene and Kuarta spoke privately again. The next few hours were spent in silent lamentation as the three grieved for Yallia. But the time came when the two women were alone, late at night, after Dolen had crawled into bed.

"You're coming with us tomorrow morning to see where they're putting her?" Kuarta asked her mother over coffee at the kitchen table. When Jene did not answer immediately, Kuarta asked, "Aren't you?"

"I...I have to see someone."

"Ma, you've seen everyone. There's no way to reverse this now."

"No, not to reverse this. There's one person I need to see. I need to ask him some questions."

"Who?"

"Eduard Costellan."

"Who?"

"You probably don't think of him much. He was the leader of the Flight Crew on Ship."

Kuarta snapped her head back in surprise. "Ship's just an observation satellite now. Is it still staffed?"

"Yes. The Flight Crew could never leave their null-g environment. We left the central core in orbit after we stripped away most of the rest of Ship. They're self-sufficient up there."

"But Costellan must be...how old?"

"I don't know. One hundred and fifty. Old Earth years, of course."

"He can't still be alive."

Jene shrugged. "Maybe not. But I would have thought his death would have been reported to us. Shippies, I mean—not Commissars."

"Why do you need to see him?"

"There are some loose ends that need tying up."

Kuarta did not pry further. Jene's relationship with the Crossing was wholly different from Kuarta's, of course. Kuarta had enough respect for her mother to leave the issue alone. "I have some loose ends of my own to tie up, Ma."

Jene looked at her expectantly. Kuarta dropped her gaze to the brown liquid swirling in her cup. "I...I never really understood why you sacrificed Renold and me all those years ago. Until now." She looked up at her mother. "I know the circumstances where different, but...I just want you to know...I forgive you."

Jene took a deep breath. "Thank you, dear."

"I hope Yallia will do the same for me in her time."

Jene started to say, "I'm sure she will," but something held her back. She simply took her daughter's hand. The two women gazed at each other for a long time as their coffee cooled slowly in the time-slip.

* * *

"You are expected," the tall, reed like woman said to Jene as the latter exited the airlock. Jene had been able to secure a trip to the orbiting relic with little difficulty—Tann evidently was willing to let her have her way in matters unimportant to him.

The woman before Jene was wraithlike in her gauntness. Jene tried not to stare. The woman was at least two and a half meters tall but so thin she could not have weighed more than fifty kilos planet-side. She wore no clothes and only the absence of a penis marked her as female. "My name is Heaven-watcher Eee. Welcome."

"Thank you," Jene murmured. As she strove to keep her glances at the woman within the bounds of decency, Jene noticed her scrutiny, an expression of barely concealed disgust on her elongated features.

"Something wrong?" Jene said pointedly.

The woman made no show of embarrassment. "I was examining you. I have never seen a ground-crawler before."

"Ground-crawler, eh? Well, that's a new one." After the stresses of events planet-side, Jene found this whole situation mildly humorous. "Take a good look, sweetheart. But while you gawk at me, perhaps we could head over to Mr. Costellan. I think he's waiting for me."

"Of course." The escort turned gracefully and floated down the access tunnel that Jene vaguely recognized as the same tunnel she had navigated many years before.

"Since you were so bold in your exam, may I ask you how old you are?" Jene said at the woman's back. As she spoke, she watched the interplay of bones in the woman's arms. There was a thin but noticeable flap of skin connecting the woman's tricep to her latissimus dorsi, forming a small triangular sail on either side. As Heaven-watcher floated, she flapped her arms slightly, and Jene immediately saw the purpose of the flaps—they were for movement in microgravity.

"I am only a child. Merely forty-three years old."

"Old Earth years or New Earth?"

Heaven-watcher pivoted in air and looked at Jene angrily. "Year: the amount of time it takes the planet Earth to make one complete revolution around its star." She spun back around again.

"Right." Jene shut up.

The two entered a vast chamber that should have been the control room. Instead, it had been converted to a three-dimensional plaza. A dozen men and women, all unclothed, flew gracefully to and fro, and Jene even saw a child swooping down from above to some destination on the other side of the sphere. The chamber was perhaps one hundred meters in diameter, dotted with innumerable outcroppings on all sides whose functions Jene could only guess at. Jene grabbed at a stanchion and gawked at the spectacle.

"Our Father is waiting on the other side. Do you think you can fly over?" Heaven-watcher asked.

"I think I can make it," Jene answered and pushed off awkwardly. The two slowly floated towards an opening in the opposite wall, and when it became apparent that Jene had misjudged her aim and was going to collide with the far wall some distance from the opening, she appealed to her guide.

"Uh, I think I might have missed. Can you shove me over?"

Heaven-watcher stared at her in shock. "Use the wall and pull yourself over. I will wait." Jene thought she saw the woman shudder in disgust.

Jene slowly and painfully made her way to the opening, aware that the inhabitants of the plaza were watching her with wide-eyed stares. Despite the beauty of the sphere, she was glad to escape into the tunnel.

"Continue straight ahead. He is waiting for you. Tell the sentinels who you are," Heaven-watcher said.

"Thank you. I—" Jene started to add a comment that she had known Costellan before, in an attempt to explain her presence here, but Heaven-watcher launched herself into the plaza and did not look back.

Jene grunted and propelled herself towards the end of the tunnel. It was well-lit, and before long she could make out two humanoid forms (men, a brief glance downward told her) at the other end. Both held weapons that resembled ancient blunderbusses.

"I am Jene Halfner. I am expected," she said nervously.

One of the two men nodded and pressed a contact. An iris valve, the panels of which had not been visible a moment before, opened and revealed a darkened room.

"Enter," the other sentinel said.

Jene nodded and floated inside, careful not to bounce off either of the two guards. As she entered the room, the iris valve closed behind her, plunging the room into near-darkness.

Her eyes took a moment to adjust to the dimness of the room. She thought she could hear...wheezing? She began to make out a dim outline of a figure floating horizontally before her.

"Costellan?" she said softly.

"Doctor Halfner," breathed a man's voice. The voice carried with it the unmistakable impression of extreme age. "I am glad you came. I would not have summoned you for my death, but the fates conspired, eh?"

Slowly, Costellan's face came into view as Jene floated closer. It was his face—Jene could recognize it even through twenty years and despite the dimness. The room was slowly revealing itself as her eyes adjusted—an elaborately furnished bedroom in a style that once would have been called Victorian. Jene was surprised to discover that Costellan was floating a few feet above a four-poster bed.

"Impractical, isn't it?" Costellan laughed, catching her gaze. "In my old age, I found myself growing increasingly...homesick. A word I'm afraid you won't understand, my dear."

"Why not? Ship was my home, Mr. Costellan."

"Eduard, please. I get enough honorifics here as it is. Yes, Ship was your home, but not the same way Earth was mine. You knew Ship was artificial and temporary. You never had a home like I did."

Jene resisted the impulse to argue. "Maybe not. But we are trying to build one now."

"So I see."

"You see?"

"Yes. You know we watch you, don't you, Doctor? Surely, you don't think we just serve as a survey satellite, weather satellite, communications hub, and all that without keeping you under surveillance?"

"I never really thought about it."

"Which is as we wish. We do not want to meddle in your affairs."

Jene wanted to move closer but was afraid to do so lest she bump into Costellan. She lowered her voice instead. "Nothing has changed, then, from twenty years ago."

Costellan didn't answer, but Jene could see him close his eyes.

"I have a question for you, Eduard. I need to know the answer before you die."

"You had best ask it now."

"There were more communications between EE3 and Ship than you told me about twenty years ago," Jene said simply.

"That's not a question," Costellan said.

"Don't bandy words, Eduard. It's not like you."

"True. Forgive me, Jene. I have been keeping the secret for a long time. The wheels of revelation need lubricating. Yes. There were more communications between Arnson and an official planet-side."

"What was the official's name?" Jene asked. She had come all this way to ask, even as the answer burned in her brain. But she had to *know*.

"Carll Tann."

She thought she had steeled herself against the truth she had come to suspect these past few days. But when Costellan spoke the name in his husky, dying voice, Jene reeled nonetheless. Even a confirmed believer in conspiracy has, in the dark recesses of the mind, a glimmer of doubt—a tiny spark of optimism that defies the evil all around it. To have that spark finally arrested and killed is a powerful blow, one that Jene Halfner could not have prepared herself for.

"He knew all along," Jene said. "Arnson. He knew."

"Yes," Costellan confirmed, but his voice was hesitant, as if there was still much more unsaid.

Jene focused her eyes again on the present, to the man floating before her above his deathbed. "And so did you, Eduard."

"Yes. We all knew."

"Why didn't you tell us?"

Costellan's voice rose in pitch. "Tell whom? The public? We told the leader of the Ship government. What he did with the knowledge cannot be laid at our feet."

"But you knew he was keeping the secret. You could have broadcast to all of Ship and stopped the war!"

"It is not for us to meddle. We turn our eyes outward."

"You...." Jene stopped, unable to find words to express her frustration. Here the truth had been known: had she known what Arnson had known then, she would have—

Jene frowned. "You say Arnson knew of Tann's intentions?"

"Yes."

"Then why didn't he stop the fighting? Why did he continue to plead his case for prioritizing medical services and materials?"

Costellan did not answer immediately. Jene grabbed one of the bedposts and maneuvered herself closer to him. "Why?"

"Arnson tried to strike a deal with Tann," Costellan said slowly. "Tann agreed to abandon his plan for infection if Arnson agreed to wipe out all...undesirables from Ship before it started sending colonists down."

Jene whispered, "Genocide?"

"That was the final solution."

"And what for Arnson in return?"

Costellan sighed. "Power, of course. A seat in the Assembly, prestige among the argies."

"Tann wouldn't have kept his side of the bargain," Jene mused. "He just wanted Arnson's cooperation in ridding Ship of the Class D's. But how could he have expected to accomplish that in just a few months?"

"Arnson asked Flight Crew to help."

"Help?"

"He asked us—ordered us—to engage the light-pressure sails earlier than necessary for added braking as we approached Epsilon Eridani. He wanted us to also alter course through the Oort cloud in the system."

"The Oort cloud?"

"A ring of cometary debris and assorted particles some distance away from a star."

"Why through the cloud?"

"He never told us. However, such a course correction would have drastically increased the chance of striking debris. We would have experienced a hull breach similar to the one we had back in S.Y. 55."

"He wanted to cause a hull breach?"

"In our opinion, yes."

"To try to increase the crisis, I suppose." Jene looked away. "To place a demand on the medical staff that they could not possibly meet and thus abandon then and there the Class D's. He wanted to force the decision. He was ready to kill hundreds." Jene's head snapped back to Costellan. "But you didn't do it."

"No. We refused. Our charge was to take Ship safely to the third planet of the Epsilon Eridani system, and we would not obey any order that placed the mission in jeopardy."

"So he tried to take it public before he was ready."

"And you were there to meet him. So you see, we did not need to interfere."

Jene shuddered. "But the conflict! The war—all those deaths. They didn't need to happen."

"Yes, they did, Jene. You saved more people than you could possibly have known. Arnson would have cooperated with Tann to exterminate hundreds, even thousands of *Odyssey* colonists in orbit or even on the planet. Under his leadership, the colonists would have willingly, but unknowingly, walked into death. Arnson would have been the shepherd leading his flock to the slaughterhouse. Tann's slaughterhouse. But for you."

Redemption did not come easily to Jene. She fought it off as desperately as she had sought it for twenty years lest it prove false. "If we had known, no one would have died."

"Those who died had to. They were all willing combatants."

"You could have told us. Told me."

Costellan's voice showed signs of life. "What would have happened if we had told you all that was planned? How long do you suppose the Flight Crew could have remained inviolate? The colony would have stormed the Control Deck at precisely the time we needed to be left alone. The delicate calculations and procedures involved in braking Ship and approaching our destination were almost more than we could handle as it was. And assuming somehow that shipmates did not molest us, do you suppose that Arnson would have left us alone if we betrayed him? Any disturbance to our operations during the last six months could have been disastrous. The civil unrest alone was quite distracting. I am proud of my Flight Crew for focusing on their tasks and guiding Ship to its destination."

Bitterness came easily to Jene. After years of self-hatred, she was used to the taste. "I'm glad you're proud of them. But you and your Flight Crew were worse than Arnson and his council."

To Jene's mild surprise, Costellan did not object to this characterization. He merely sank into himself and seemed to withdraw. Jene felt a tiny twinge of regret for her words, but pressed on nonetheless. "Arnson, at least, was doing what he believed in. In his mind, he was doing nothing wrong or evil. But you believed he was wrong and did nothing to stop him. Nothing! You let innocent people die." Jene fought off tears at the sudden thought of Renold.

"I did not call you here, Jene. I thought you might feel this way. I am still human enough to want...to need...your forgiveness. But I can't ask you to forgive. All that I have told you is rationalization. Looking back, now, I wish I had spoken."

Costellan drew in a deep shuddering breath, and Jene knew he was close to death. The tiny pang of regret she had experienced earlier returned and started to gnaw at her.

"There was a writer on old Earth named Dante. He wrote something called *The Inferno*. In it, he claimed that the hottest places in Hell were reserved for those who, in time of crisis, did nothing. I will die soon, perhaps even today. I hope he was wrong."

Costellan sighed again. Jene could not look at him, ashamed at her own feelings. She could not forgive him, and she did not like herself for that.

Costellan spoke again. "You should leave me soon. But before you do, you must take one thing from our meeting. The revolution you sparked was necessary—you must believe that. I know what it cost you: your husband and now your granddaughter. But think of the magnitude of evil you thwarted. Arnson and Tann were planning mass murder. You stopped that. You must release yourself from guilt."

Jene stared at him but did not see him. She was looking through her memory. There was no sharp twist in her point of view on the past, but she felt within her the beginning of a change. She felt the pain of twenty years fading. She knew it would never vanish: Renold would still be dead, and Yallia would still be in exile. But Jene knew that eventually she would be able to live with her past.

Jene reached for Costellan's hand, but the old man moved away slightly and accessed a control panel on the wall behind him. He depressed a button and without warning, a section of wall slid away and the room was flooded with light. Jene squinted into the glare and recognized, after a moment, New Earth hanging in space above them.

"One of the perks of being the patriarch of my little kingdom. A view like no other, Doctor."

Jene and Costellan looked out at New Earth for a long moment before Jene murmured, "What's going to happen to us?" When Costellan didn't answer, Jene turned to him. He was floating as he had been, but his eyes were closed and his arms were hanging awkwardly away from his body.

Weeks later, a package from Ship would arrive for her on New Earth. It would be an old-style journal that was beginning to yellow slightly despite its nearly acid-free paper containing hundreds of short poems written by Costellan. The poems in the leather-bound journal would be written in an ancient form from Old Earth called haiku. Jene would spend days reading them and would soon understand Costellan: he was an observer. Like a haiku poet, he strove to remove himself entirely from what he was observing. To meddle, to inject oneself into a process or a setting was anathema to haiku poetry and to Costellan's life. Jene would come to understand the man from his poems.

But that was all still to come. Now, as she saw him floating there, eyes closed and unresponsive, she found it within herself to forgive him for his inaction. It was as if she was borrowing knowledge from the future.

"I forgive you, Eduard." She said to the floating body.

Sometimes, the universe conspires to smile upon the humble creatures crawling within it. Costellan smiled and nodded. His lips moved, but no sound came out; still, she knew he thanked her.

He died, taking Jene's pain with him.

BOOK THREE
PLANET

CHAPTER
13

Yallia looked up to the sound of children calling her name. She brushed a wisp of still-brown hair that had escaped from beneath her wide-brimmed straw hat and squinted through the green haze. She was almost in the center of the acre-wide potato field but could still see the cart near her farmhouse. Ten or twelve adults stood in and around the cart, lifting children out of the hay-lined bed and placing them on the ground. Almost like wind-up toys, the children scampered off towards Yallia as soon as the adults let go of them, and soon there were dozens of little bodies moving awkwardly in her direction.

Yallia could not help but smile at the welcome intrusion. She had not seen this part of her family for many weeks. No doubt they had heard the news and were coming to cheer her.

The little boys and girls stumbled over roots and fell into the soft dirt, laughed, brushed themselves off, caromed off each other on the uneven ground, and bit by bit made their unsteady way to their grandonlymother. The children were all almost the same age; three years old.

Twenty-six children in all, Yallia knew. She could recite each of their names and relationships to her, despite the similarity of appearance and manner. Sirra was the first to reach her, truedaughter of Emme, who was Yallia's truedaughter. Sirra was almost always first in whatever she did.

"Grandonly!" Sirra said, launching herself bodily at Yallia and knocking the older woman to the ground. Yallia fell, laughing, her arms around the little girl to protect her from the impact.

"Ooof!" Yallia grunted. "My, you are getting big! Hey!" she said as the other children closed in. Yallia was soon buried under a loving pile of arms and legs.

"Children! Get off your Grandonly!" Yallia faintly heard Emme shouting. Slowly, the pressure on her chest lifted and daylight returned. Yallia got up from the ground with a momentary headache that quickly subsided. She smiled at the gaggle of children. "Well, there are a lot of children here!" She put her hands on her hips in an affected manner. "I wonder if any of them would like to have some salgar cookies?

There was an immediate and predictable response. They raced back towards the adults, who were picking their way through the potato field with dignity befitting their fifteen years, and shouted at their respective parents, "Grandonly said we can have salgar cookies!"

Sirra did not leave her grandonly, however. She was the same age as her siblings, but Emme and Yallia had both noticed the girl possessed an unusual empathy. It was why Emme had petitioned the Genetic Council for a full genome exam a few days ago.

Sirra looked at Yallia and said, "I'm sorry that your grandonly is dead."

Yallia smiled back and kissed her. "Thank you, Sirra. But she wasn't my grandonly—she was my grandmother."

"Oh. I'm still sad for you."

"That's okay, dear."

"How old was she?"

"She was very old. She was fifty-seven."

Sirra considered this. "Is that old?"

"Sort of."

"How old are you?"

"I'm twenty-seven."

"Oh." Sirra thought for a moment, and Yallia knew what must be going through the young girl's mind.

Yallia leaned in close to her. "Don't worry, Sirra. I'm not going to die."

"Ever?"

Yallia laughed. "Not for a very, very long time. Long enough to see your children and their children and their children!"

Sirra brightened. "And you'll make cookies for them, too?"

"Of course. Speaking of cookies," Yallia rose and patted Sirra on the rump, "you had better get moving, kiddo. There might not be any left!"

Sirra smiled knowingly and started off at a moderate pace towards the farmhouse. Yallia watched her go, and as her eyes followed the girl's progress, they met those of Sirra's onlymother.

Emma did not look like her onlymother. Of course, if a holo of a fifteen-year old Yallia were to be superimposed on a similar one of Emme, the two would appear identical, but in the moment-to-moment fluidity of expression all faces undergo, Yallia and Emme were quite different. Emme did not have the same hardness, the same outward-looking, searching expression on her face that Yallia did. Emme could only partially explain her onlymother's demeanor by her status as an Original. Not all Originals had the same questing look about them, but it was a common enough trait.

Yallia watched Emme's approach and knew exactly what her truedaughter was thinking. Emme did not know what effect the news of Jene Halfner's death would have on her onlymother. No one except an Original could understand the death of an ancestor due to old age.

"How are you, onlymother?" Emme said when Sirra was out of earshot.

Yallia looked at her truedaughter and smiled crookedly. "'How are you, onlymother?'" she repeated with sarcasm. "You think I'm so fragile as to burst into hysterical tears at the thought that my fifty-seven year old grandmother, one of my family who sent me here twenty-three years ago, has finally died?"

Emme said soothingly, "Now, Yallia, no need to get mean about it. I just thought we'd bring some of your grandkids along to see you. They haven't visited you in a few weeks."

Yallia softened. "Thank you, Truedaughter," she said, this time using the honorific as a gentle barb. "Whom else did you bring?" She squinted into the distance where the other adults were rounding up the children preparatory to entering the farmhouse.

"All your trues."

Yallia nodded. She could see the tall, spare figures of her three truesons organizing the children while her other two truedaughters talked and laughed with one another. Yallia snorted. Poene and Voer had always been talkers instead of doers.

"Just them, eh?" Yallia knew she was being difficult. It must have taken considerable effort to organize the twenty-six grandchildren and six truechildren as it was. There was no need to expect Emme to bring the rest of her family as well. Still, the whole thing smacked of favoritism—

Yallia loved all her children, whether they had come from her alone or from a union with another.

"I should probably see the rest soon too. I don't want them to feel neglected."

"Sure, Only." Emme said it with just enough condescension to irritate Yallia.

"Look, Emme," Yallia said, rounding on her truedaughter, "I know you think you are somehow better than my other children because you're a clone," Yallia used the taboo word on purpose to see her truedaughter's gasping reaction, "but everyone on the Outside is equally important. As soon as we start deciding who is better or more worthy of respect and love, we might as well move back into the Domes."

Emme did not answer immediately. Yallia could see her truedaughter's eyes searching her, looking for herself in her onlymother's face. When she did speak, she matched Yallia's anger with softness. "As you wish, Onlymother."

"And that's another thing. I'm tired of everyone treating me like I'm some kind of goddomed prophet. Argue with me, tell me I'm a crazy old woman, but don't just bow your head and say 'as you wish, Onlymother' like I'm a saint."

Emme sighed. "I know you're upset about your grandmother. If you want us to leave, we can come back later."

"Domeit, I'm not upset!" Yallia shouted, the lie almost refusing to come out.

Emme looked at her, waiting.

Yallia felt a smile creep onto her face. "All right. But I tell you one thing. I'm not going to let those children eat all the cookies. Come on," she said and headed towards the farmhouse.

The farmhouse, like all structures the Family built, seemed to rise naturally out of the ground. There was a certain amount of inefficiency in the sloping curves of the house, but the aesthetic effect was well worth it. The house looked as if it had been produced by the planet itself, and indeed the house had been constructed largely with materials already nearby—stone, saltclay bricks, pieces of dead wood cured naturally—so as to minimize the impact on the environment. The farmhouse, like the Family themselves, sought to make only the lightest stamp upon the world on which they lived.

"Lawson!" Yallia called and waved. A burly man filled the farmhouse doorway, holding a bucket in one hand and a cloth in the other. He waved back. Yallia and Emme approached him.

"Your brood just went inside," Markh Lawson said, jerking a thumb over his shoulder. "I think I heard them talking about salgar cookies?" He looked at Yallia with bushy, grey, raised eyebrows. He glanced at Emme. "Hello, Emme."

Emme nodded at him, lowering her eyes for a full second before looking up again, paying him the respect due an Original.

"Thanks, Law," Yallia said. She moved towards the doorway and patted his brawny arm as he moved aside.

"Yallia," he said hesitantly.

"I'm okay, Law," Yallia said, not meeting his gaze.

"The household wants to call a Session."

"About Jene?" Yallia said, this time turning to look at him.

"Well, sort of. I think Kahlman wants to bring up some policy issues."

Yallia grunted. "All right. Go ahead and call the Session. I'll be there in a few minutes, ok?"

"Sure." Lawson glanced at Emme with an unreadable expression and disappeared through an interior doorway to Emme's right.

Emme and Yallia proceeded to their left to the dining area. The farmhouse was home to eighteen Originals, but as one or more generally had lines visiting them, much space had been dedicated to common gathering areas. Emme heard the sounds of children playing in the next room. Yallia and Emme entered the dining hall to see a bedlam of children running, playing, chasing one another, knocking down chairs, and otherwise keeping their five adult supervisors very busy.

"All right! Who is making a big noise in my house?" Yallia shouted with mock-seriousness. The nearest children flocked to her and hugged her about the legs. Others laughed and shouted back, "We are!"

"Everyone who is staying for the night raise your hand," Yallia said. A forest of arms waved frantically in front of her. Her eyes widened in pretend horror. "All of you? Where will you sleep? I know—you can sleep with the piggies!"

Laughter and a chorus of "no's" greeted that suggestion.

"No? Well, then, you'd better find rooms and put away your things. Your mommies and daddies and onlies and birthers will help you. Off you go, now."

The children scattered every which way to the nearest parent. It did not matter if the person they latched onto was a genetic donor in their makeup—all were equal partners in their upbringing.

Sirra stayed near Yallia. "Where are you going, Gramma?" Yallia smiled behind a straight face. She alone saw through Yallia's ruse.

"I have a meeting to go to. But it won't take long, so you just wait for me, okay?"

"Okay," Sirra said, but Yallia saw the uncertainty in her face. "Why are you angry at your own Gramma?"

The question caught Yallia off-guard. She recovered quickly, though, and managed to smile reassuringly at the child.

"I'm not, Sirra. Now you go find a bed to put your things on." She swatted her playfully on the rump and Sirra giggled, then moved away.

Yallia watched her go with interest. Sirra's question had been a most penetrating one—it had cut deep into Yallia, through the insulating years and experiences, almost to the knot of bitter resentment that still gnawed at her.

Perceptive as Sirra was, however, she was still a child. She could not know that she had overshot the mark by one generation.

Session was of course not underway when Yallia entered the bare room. The other seventeen Originals sat at their places, talking quietly to one another. The Presiding chair had been pulled back for Yallia, and she slid smoothly into it, glancing at the others ranged around her.

"All right. What's so domed important that it has to pull me away from my children?"

The other Originals shifted in their seats. Without turning more than a few degrees, sixteen individuals managed to give the floor to a handsome man three seats to Yallia's left.

"I apologize, Yallia. I'd have spoken to you about it personally, but I thought a Session would be more...official." Franc Kahlman had a resonant voice and a youthful appearance although he was in fact a year older than Yallia. Like all the other Originals, he had joined Yallia already in exile, but he had been expelled from the Dome at an older age.

"Official?" Yallia snapped.

"Yes. We've received word that your mother wishes to see you."

Yallia gripped the table edge to keep the room from spinning. She had not expected that, although as soon as she heard the news, she realized such was inevitable.

"I haven't seen her in six years," Yallia said quietly, half to herself. She ruminated for a moment, then jerked her head up to meet Kahlman's level gaze. "Why is this a matter for Session? Are you planning to call a Grand Session too? Why not? Let's make this open to all. Ask the Family—should Yallia meet with her mother?" Yallia saw the effect her sarcasm had on the rest of the Originals. None of them looked at her— they simply stared at the table and fidgeted with their fingers. Kahlman was the only one to respond, his eyes never leaving Yallia's.

"Yallia, this is a Family issue. Your mother is the only direct source of intelligence left to us for Domer activity."

Yallia stood up slowly. "Is there anything else? Am I excused to see my grandchildren, or do I need Session permission for that, too?"

"Oh, sit down and stop acting like a fool," came Lawson's voice from the far end of the table. There was not quite a gasp from the other members of the table at this outburst of disrespect from their most junior member. Lawson had only joined the Outside four years ago, having manifested his mutation at the remarkably old age of twelve, and was still not quite ensconced into Original favor. Yallia herself, however, had taken a liking to the outspoken man and had extended him every kindness.

"I'm not the fool here, Lawson," Yallia said, but there was a glint in her eye as she sat back down.

"You know very well that a visit from your mother was coming, and you knew a Session would be called to convince you to see her."

"I have nothing to say to her," Yallia said, her voice maintaining a warning tone.

Kahlman said, "But she brings with her information about the Domers. We need that information."

"Why?" Yallia asked, turning to him. "All we do is collect data. I've wanted to strike at the Research Enclave for over a year now, and Grand Session just keeps voting to delay, to collect more information. And you usually lead that faction, Lawson." Yallia swiveled her head and pointed an accusing finger at him. "What's the current census report?" She asked the table in general.

A woman named Marbe spoke up. "There are ten thousand, nine hundred and eighty-four Family members as of this morning," she said in precise tones.

"How many have reached Age?" Yallia asked.

Marbe did not hesitate. "One thousand, one hundred and two."

Yallia surveyed the table, silently allowing the numbers to sink in. The number of battle-ready Family had remained almost constant for several years, but rarely was the exact number mentioned. "We are ready to attack the Enclave. We've been ready. We don't need any more information, and we don't need to wait seven years for our grandchildren to come of Age."

"We can always use more information. There's no such thing as too much intelligence," Lawson rumbled.

"By that so-called logic, we'll never attack," Yallia shot back.

"I submit that this argument can wait," Kahlman interjected. "Right now, I put the question to you directly, Madame Prime"—Kuhlman used her official title without rancor or irony—"will you speak to your mother?"

Yallia had not moved her eyes from Lawson's even as Kalhman spoke.

"Yes. But I'm going alone. No braintap this time."

Kuhlman seemed satisfied at this and sank back deeper into his chair. Yallia saw Lawson shift his weight.

"You don't like that, Lawson?"

"No, but I suppose I'll have to live with it."

"Dome right you will. When does she want to come?" Yallia asked the table itself, looking around at the Originals around it.

"Tomorrow, just after daybreak," Kuhlman answered. "Standard procedure—she'll meet you in the Enclave. She made the usual request to see her grandchildren—"

"She doesn't have any grandchildren," Yallia mumbled.

Kulhman swept on as if she hadn't spoken. "—but did not indicate she would venture Outside. The Enclave is ready for the visit."

Yallia got up, suddenly tired. The rest of the Originals got to their feet.

"All right," Yallia said. "If there's nothing else, I'm adjourning this Session." She gave a cursory look around the table, then waved the other Originals away. They left hurriedly.

"Law," Yallia said to the muscled young man as he passed her to leave the chamber. She reached out and seized his arm.

He looked at her expectantly.

Yallia hesitated the barest second before speaking. He was a good man, despite his youth and inexperience—no, because of it. He was what the Family needed, a reminder that they were pioneers in every sense of the word. These Sessions were becoming staid. They were robbing the Family of the initiative to act. Lawson, and people like him, were their best hope. She had to convince him, above all the others, to abandon passivity and act.

"I've been thinking about having another child. A boy, this time. I'd like you to be the father." She looked at him without irony, without any of the hardness she displayed in Session. Lawson had fathered one of her children already—a girl named Renne who had gone into the arts and was a moderately successful poet. Yallia knew he knew that she had had six children and had been cloned six times.

"Me, again?" Lawson was taken by surprise.

"I know. It's unusual, but I like what we made in Renne. I'd like to see what comes of a boy between us." Yallia knew what Lawson must be thinking. It was indeed highly unusual, and somewhat indecent, to have multiple children with the same partner, but Yallia was the Prime Original. She did not only follow fashion, she helped shape it. Besides, there was something fascinating in Lawson that drew her to him. He himself had only had four children so far—two by female Originals, one by a native Family woman, and one by an Original man from a different farmhouse. The latter had had minor difficulties during its gengineering process, but Yallia had managed to pull it through without too much trouble. All four children were shaping up to be excellent Family citizens of superior stock. But Yallia knew that was not all that drove her to seek another union with Lawson. He was different. He did not bow unquestioningly to her whims but stood in disagreement with her on many points. Yallia found herself inexplicably drawn to that facet of his personality.

"I see no reason to refuse, Yallia. Let me know when you are—"

"I'm ovulating in six days. We should try for the next few. If we don't catch this cycle, we'll keep trying."

"Sexually?" Lawson asked, with no hint of expectation or lechery in his voice. The question was purely an information-seeking one.

"For a few cycles, at least. If that doesn't work, then we'll give science a chance." Yallia looked at him and smiled. This time, her smile was not sarcastic or bittersweet. "I'll see you tonight," she said, and started back to the common area where her children and grandchildren waited.

* * *

"You're looking very well, Yali," Kuarta said when she saw her daughter. She tried not to notice the hatred riding high in her offspring's eyes or feel the almost palpable resentment that seemed to come off Yallia's very skin. Kuarta had seen her daughter hundreds of times since her exile more than twenty-four years before, but the visits had been increasingly hostile and therefore less frequent as Yallia grew older. It had been almost a quarteryear since her last visit.

"I've asked you not to call me that," Yallia said venomously. The two stood facing one another in the small Dome that was the Research Enclave. The research staff was sympathetic to Kuarta's wishes and had provided her a small room, an unused lab, to meet with her daughter. They were alone.

"Sorry," Kuarta said and sank heavily onto a chair.

"I suppose you're here to find out how I'm doing. I heard about your mother's death, of course."

"Of course. But something tells me you don't want me to ask, do you?"

Yallia was not biting. "No, I do not. I do not understand why such news should affect me. I barely knew her, and what little I do know of her makes me think I should be jubilant at her passing."

"Like you would be at my own?" Kuarta sank the barb deep.

Yallia shrugged. "You bore me, you raised me for a short time, then you abandoned me here. Your death would mean nothing more than a loss of another Domer. Something we *Outsiders* do not mourn." Yallia placed a bit of extra emphasis on the Domer term for the Family.

Kuarta did not let the hurt show. The last several visits had been almost as bad. But she did not wonder why her daughter saw her regardless of her feelings. She had hoped, years and years ago, it was out of some vague sense of family or even love, but her pragmatic mind had dismissed those thoughts. Yallia needed her mother for information about Dome society.

"Speaking of the Domes, what shall I tell you this time?" Kuarta said, a hint of sarcasm entering her voice.

"What are your numbers like?" Yallia asked without hesitation.

"I think there are about a quarter million or so."

"Any more you are planning to exile?"

Kuarta winced at the accusation, but answered. "There are no new hybrids that I know of. Oh, you might be interested in this. Dr. Onizaka was honored at the seventy-fifth anniversary ball about ten days ago."

Yallia nodded with mock enthusiasm. "Oh, fabulous. Nice to see the Domers appreciate good work. What's she working on now—goats?"

Kuarta understood the reference. It was an Old Earth legend about transferring sins onto an animal. Dolen would probably be able to track down the exact story. "I'm not sure," she answered.

"Wonderful. How wonderful for her. Why should a single instance of attempted genocide spoil an otherwise brilliant career raping an entire planet?"

Kuarta sighed and said, "Look, dear, if you want me to go, I'll go. I can bring a detailed report on Dome activity for you the next time I come, all right?"

"But, Mother," Yallia said with sickly sweet acidity, "how will you assuage your feelings of guilt and remorse if you don't see me periodically?"

"You think this does that for me? You think I'm here so I can receive your abuse and feel like I have somehow atoned for what I did?" Kuarta was breathing heavily, trying to fight back tears. "I've spent almost twenty-five years in agony thinking about what I've done, thinking what I could have done differently. I see you not to atone, but because I love you."

"You Domers must have a different definition for that term," Yallia said dryly. "I don't want to hear about your feelings, Kuarta. I need to collect data for my Family. This Research Enclave—how important is it to your Domes?

Kuarta searched her daughter's face for a long time—looking for something she herself didn't even understand. Perhaps she was looking for the remains of a young girl of three who had once been happy.

The question and its implications slowly sank into Kuarta's mind. "What do you mean, how important is the Enclave?"

"If something were to happen to it, I mean. How would your Domes look upon the loss?"

Kuarta mulled the question over, then said, "You're going to destroy it."

"We're tired of being studied."

"When are you going to attack?"

"That hasn't been decided yet."

Kuarta leaned back in her chair. "It'll be soon. Before I return to the Dome to warn them."

Yallia smiled wolfishly. "Very good. When I go back to my own government, I will tell them you are warning the Dome of our actions. There will be no other choice but to attack immediately."

"You're using me to leverage your own government."

"A small repayment for your actions years ago."

The sudden return to personal attack caught Kuarta unprepared. She stood violently, the chair behind her crashing to the ground. "That's why you're going to kill a dozen people in the Enclave? To get back at me?"

"Don't be melodramatic, Mother. It's a military maneuver, nothing more."

"Let me arrange for the Enclave personnel to leave with me, at least."

"Why? What's a few dead Domers?"

"I don't believe you. You can't be this cavalier about human life."

Yallia snorted. "Domer life, you mean."

"*Human* life." Kuarta said, angrily. She was suddenly reminded of Jene and Dolen arguing a similar point twenty-four years ago.

"Domers would see a distinction."

Kuarta did not dispute that: Yallia was right. But there were still twelve lives at stake. She took another tack. "If you kill the scientists inside the Enclave, the Domes will respond with force. Do you want that?"

Yallia looked uncertain for a half second, then her face returned to stoic resolve. She rose and said, "All right. Your Domers won't be killed. I'd tell them to leave now, because we won't wait. Unless they want to see our...mutations in action." Kuarta was momentarily frozen in terror. What had her little girl become?

"I—I'll start the evacuation," Kuarta said, and found her arms preparing themselves for a hug. She put them back down awkwardly. Yallia watched her with scorn, then left the room swiftly, not looking back.

CHAPTER 14

"You've got a predator eyeing us," Khadre said to her companion, looking over his shoulder at the instrument panel.

"I know. I'm secreting countermeasures right now," Viktur said, manipulating the controls of the biomech submersible.

Khadre watched the monitors intently, keeping close watch on the sleek, shark-like animal that had been gliding towards the sub. As she watched, the predator slowed, then veered off sharply, disappearing into the darkness.

"It worked. He's gone," she reported.

Viktur grunted. "How much have we got left?"

"Enough. In a few hours, we'll be full again." Khadre watched the display for a few seconds, noting the slow increase in countermeasure fluid as the biomech sub's glandular system churned out more of the foul milky substance. The sub was capable of staying under for quite a long time, although many of the more mechanical systems would have to shut down and recharge periodically.

"You need to eat soon," Khadre noted, pointing at a sector on the holographic readout.

"I know. But I've got a good hour left before power-down. I just want to clear this ridge first," Viktur said, eyes locked on the drone's forward sensor image. The visual sensor was almost useless at this depth of four kilometers—the drone's bioluminescence provided light for only a few meters, even with the supersensitive photoelectric sensors the drone was equipped with. High frequency sonar was far more effective at this depth, but Viktur hesitated to use it. Khadre's working theory that at least some of the marine life must use sonar to communicate kept him skittish about broadcasting inadvertent messages to the underwater population.

"Still nothing?" Khadre asked softly. Viktur didn't answer, though from his body language she could guess the answer was "no."

Khadre looked down at the pressure-glass bottom of the tiny research skiff. Somewhere down there was the biomech drone the two had nicknamed "Nimmo," after a character in a book Viktur had claimed to have read. She had designed the drone with her dother Rann, an Original who had raised her as a dother despite having no genetic connection to her. Rann had been skilled in biomechanology and had trained Khadre well. "The Domers don't go in for deep marine studies," Rann had told her during one of their many late-night sessions in the lab. "They have only scratched the edge of the ocean so far."

"Why not?" Khadre had asked her.

"I don't know. Not enough people, too much cost, I suppose. Keeping those Domes functional is their main concern. That and terraforming the planet. Doesn't leave a lot of energy or interest for the sea."

Rann knew what she was talking about. No one was really studying the sea, at least not the deep ocean, the way Khadre and Viktur were. That was what had pushed Khadre to the water. She could be a pioneer here. Although, she had to admit, there were many days on which she wondered if the Domers weren't right to ignore the sea. She had spent the last nine months studying various marine flora and fauna, categorizing, labeling (the novelty of naming the creatures herself had long since worn off, although her companion still delighted in the game) and otherwise classifying organism after organism, without anything truly revolutionary happening. She knew from countless discussions with the older scientists that discovery often came after years of study, not months; still, she was beginning to wonder if the sea would reveal anything of interest to those outside her field. She longed for the day when what she discovered would truly be her own.

Except, of course, for Viktur. She looked up at him and smiled. He was a good man, he just never saw further ahead than a few hours. He could solve almost any task that was set him because of his single-mindedness, but a visionary he was not. That was what had drawn Khadre to him. She planned on asking him soon for a child, hoping his practicality would balance her idealism and result in a perfect blend of genes. She was not in love with him—Viktur did not rouse passion or lust. Khadre was under no illusions as to why she was attracted to him; he would make a good father. That was more than enough for her.

The two had been working on the skiff for nine months, but had known each other for many years, having gone through upper school together. He had been impressed by her "calm fire," as he had put it. "You always seem ready to jump for joy at some discovery," he had said on the night he had proposed the working partnership. "I want to be there when it happens." Khadre had kissed him then—not emotionlessly, but affectionately.

"Uh, Khad?" Viktur said suddenly in a tone of voice that brought the young scientist back to the present with jarring abruptness. "Something's up. Take a look at that," he said, keeping his hands steady within their direction gloves and indicating the holo in front of him with a nod of his head. Khadre looked at the holographic representation of Nimmo's sensor image. She raised her eyebrows when she saw that Viktur had engaged the high frequency sonar for better image resolution.

"Looks like a kelp bed. So?"

"It's a big one."

Khadre shrugged. "We've seen big beds before. What's...." She stopped and leaned in closer. "Back up. Gimme a full field view."

Viktur adjusted a control, and the image slowly pulled back as Nimmo reversed.

The two stared at the image for a full ten seconds before Khadre said in a hushed whisper, "Could that be a natural formation?"

"You're asking me? I'm the sub jock. You're supposed to be the scientist."

Khadre did not answer. What she was seeing was not possible— every instinct in her said that. But it was there. No malfunction in Nimmo's sensors could account for what she was seeing.

Pale green strands of kelp waved gently in the current of the water, rising perhaps ten meters above the surface of the ocean floor. This, by itself, was unremarkable. The sea plants had been studied by scientists before Khadre and rapidly dismissed as simple vegetation of the deep, unworthy of serious study.

What was impossible was the neat arrangement of the kelp bed— rows upon rows of kelp in straight lines formed an almost perfect square about two hundred meters on a side, if Nimmo's high-frequency sonar could be trusted.

"Recorders on?" Khadre asked urgently.

"Never been shut off. We're getting all of this."

"Swing us around. Try and get the whole bed."

Viktur manipulated the controls, and Nimmo's scullers propelled the drone forward. Viktur backed away from the bed formation until the whole square was visible on sonar.

"What's that?" Khadre said, pointing to a collection of sliver-thin objects at the extreme northern edge of Nimmo's view-field. Viktur swung Nimmo about and closed slowly on the objects.

"Looks like a school of sea cows," Viktur said, using the informal nomenclature he had devised for the fat, dirigible-like creatures he and Khadre saw occasionally. There were about twenty of them.

"This deep? We've never seen them past three hundred meters before." Khadre stared at the slowly growing images. "Why aren't they moving?"

As the images on Nimmo's sensors grew larger and sharper, one of the creatures stood out as different. Khadre pointed anxiously. "There! Another predator?"

"I don't think so," Viktur said after a hesitation. "It's too small. And it has…tentacles, I think. Let me get a little closer." A few seconds later, Khadre nodded. "Yeah, those look like tentacles. I don't believe we've ever seen this one before, Viktur," she said proudly. "Another new species." Khadre was still giddy with the anticipation of discovery. First, the strange vision of the square kelp bed, now this new species.

"I get to name it, since I found it," Viktur said. Khadre could hear his smile.

"Why don't you stick to nicknames instead. I'll catalog it officially."

"Then no one will ever use that name again. All right, I hereby dub thee…." Viktur took a good look at the creature. Khadre did as well. The first impression she had was of an Earth dolphin (she had seen holos in the library texts) but there were many differences. The creature's head was disproportionally bulbous and shaped like a slightly flattened sphere. Six tentacles drooped downward from its underside, but when the animal moved, they became flush with its body. The animal used a sculler for propulsion. As they watched, fascinated, the animal moved towards the sea cows. The bloated sea cows started moving, as a body, away from the dolphin-creature, which began darting here and there, retarding their progress in some directions and only allowing the cows to move as a unit.

"Khad, I think he's herding them," Viktur said.

"You're right," she answered. "Terrestrial fish and mammals do that too, but…."

"What?"

"It is a sign of sophistication. Intelligence." Khadre said quietly. "How close are you?"

"Two hundred meters, give or take."

"Bring us closer."

Viktur adjusted the controls and Nimmo surged ahead, towards the retreating herd and its shepherd.

The animals were headed for a cliff face that resembled nothing more than a blank wall to Nimmo's sensors. A momentary flicker on the screen caused Khadre to jump.

"What was that?

"I don't know. Sudden power loss or surge, I guess. We're okay," Viktur said, eyes intent on the shepherd.

"What do you—my God!" Khadre said. A swarm of dolphin-creatures came out of the cliff wall, all emerging from the same spot. Nimmo's sensors still reported the wall as solid, but dolphin-creatures were coming out of it as if it were not there. As the two human onlookers watched, the still-unnamed dolphin-creatures swam around the sea cows, encircling them. There were perhaps fifty dolphin-creatures surrounding the sea cows, which appeared quite docile.

"We're within one hundred meters." Viktur said. "Nimmo's picking up interference from somewhere. On the VHF sonar band."

"Lots of it?"

"Yeah."

Khadre thought for a moment, trying to exhaust all other possibilities before arriving at the one she was hoping for. She was a determined scientist, but even so, she was also a human being and could not help prejudicing her views even slightly. "Could be the animals' speech."

"On VHF sonar?"

"Why not? How else are they going to talk? They can't—" she broke off as she saw one of the dolphin-creatures separate itself from the pack. "Something's up."

"What's wrong with that one?" Viktur said. "He's got a growth or something on his head."

Khadre looked closely. "A horn, maybe?" The projection was a thin rod that extended about a meter in front of the animal's eyes. Nimmo's sonar could not make out details at this range. "Closer."

"If I get much closer, we'll be visible," Viktur said, but complied. Khadre did not answer immediately but let Nimmo close the distance a bit.

"Not at this depth, it's too dark," she finally said. "The only way they could spot us is with...." Before she finished, her eyes widened as a thought struck her. "Turn off the sonar! Now!"

"What?"

Khadre reached over him and slapped the kill switch on the drone's sonar projector. The sensor image died.

"Khad, what're you—"

"Go to infrared."

"Why?"

"Just do it."

Viktur sighed and activated another set of controls. The screen lit up in a completely different configuration. It took Khadre a few seconds to recognize what she was seeing.

"This is next to useless at this depth. Too much cold, and the infrared gets confused by eddies and currents, anyway," Viktur said.

"But if those animals use sonar to talk, they might have heard Nimmo's."

Viktur thought about it. "So now what?"

"Now we bring Nimmo back and head to shore."

"What for?"

"We have to study the data. But if what I think happened happened, we won't have any trouble getting the Family to fund more research." Khadre could not contain her enthusiasm, but a small part of her felt fear. She had set out to discover and explore, but she had not been prepared for what she might find.

"Why, what do you think we saw? I saw a bunch of dolphin-things herding other fish around. So? You said yourself Terrestrial fish do that too."

"But I also said it was a sign of intelligence."

Viktur shrugged. "Rudimentary, maybe. Or maybe it's just instinct."

Khadre shook her head.

"Why not?"

"The kelp bed. And the dolphin's horn."

"What about them?"

"The kelp bed was not a natural phenomenon. It was crafted that way."

"By whom?"

Khadre smiled, ignoring his question. "And that was not a horn. It was a weapon—a spear."

Viktur looked at her quizzically.

"We just saw a farmer and his farm."

CHAPTER
15

When Yallia came down the next morning to the common area, she saw her truedaughter eyeing her with clear distaste over the phalanx of children who sat at the long breakfast table.

Yallia was in too good a mood to let Emme's discomfort bother her. Yallia knew the reason for Emme's anger: she was upset that her truemother had had intercourse with a man that had already fathered one of her children. Yallia knew the news would spread; almost everything a Family member did was public knowledge. Yallia herself had helped build such openness into the society as a direct reaction to the Dome's privacy laws. Openness led to scrutiny, which led to honesty. Yallia did not believe in the inherent goodness of the human race or of individual humans. Only through constant vigilance could people be expected to act moral. Even she, herself.

"Good morning, Gramma," Sirra said to her. The girl had stopped eating and was looking at her intently. The other children looked up from their plates, mouths sticky with food, and mumbled greetings.

"Hello, Sirra. Hello, everyone," Yallia said.

"Did you and Lawson have another baby?"

Yallia knew the glances Emme and the other adults were shooting her way. "I don't know yet."

"Can you make it another girl?"

"I suppose I could. But this time, I thought I might have a boy. Remember, though, I might not be pregnant. It doesn't happen every time, you know."

"Like with Opima?"

Emme almost dropped the serving platter. Yallia heard a faint gasp.

"You're not supposed to talk about her, dear."

"Why?"

"Because it's not nice."

"She doesn't have any children," Sirra announced. "Just truesons and truedaughters."

"That's right." Yallia gestured to Sirra's breakfast plate. "Finish your breakfast, dear."

Sirra hopped back onto her chair and dug into the half-eaten meal. Yallia sighed, thankful that Sirra had not pressed the matter. Opima was one of very few Family members who did not wish to breed. Such was their legal right: Yallia refused to compel anyone on such a serious issue, but the community itself had demanded she procreate, and when Opima had refused, Yallia found the solution in cloning. It was not a perfect solution—Opima was not adding to the genetic diversity needed to keep Family viable—but it calmed the masses. That had been six years ago, and it had set the precedent that although an individual Family member had control of their own reproductive organs, their basic genetic structure belonged to the Family. It was a decision necessary to ensure the future of the community, but one which had privately troubled Yallia.

"Gramma?" Sirra said politely.

Yallia moved closer to her to hear over the clamor of the common room. "Yes?"

"Is Mister Lawson still here?"

"No, he left before you got up. Why?"

"No reason." Sirra turned back to her plate.

Yallia started to inquire further, but stopped herself. If the matter became important, Sirra would bring it up again.

Yallia sat in the common area for a while longer, conversing halfheartedly with her grandchildren and truechildren. Emme stayed aloof, however. Whenever Yallia caught her eye, the young clone looked away in disgust.

"Madam Prime?" Franc Kahlman's voice startled her. She turned to see him looking at her with a pinched expression that in the past had meant trouble. "We've had an...unusual development with a research skiff in the Bitter Sea."

"What?" Yallia blinked. "What research skiff?"

Kahlman looked around the common area. "I think you should call a Session, Madam Prime."

His formality did not worry her—Kahlman was always formal. But his unerring sense of protocol would have told him not to bother her at breakfast unless there was an emergency. She nodded and got up. "Alert the Originals. We'll meet in fifteen minutes."

Kahlman did not speak, but his expression indicated he was still not satisfied.

"What's the matter?"

"Madame Prime, I think a Grand Session is called for."

Yallia's eyes widened. "Why, for Ship's sake?"

"The research skiff has made a discovery that changes...everything." Kahlman spoke softly, looking around the common area as he did so.

Yallia weighed her options. A Grand Session was reserved for important, Family-wide decisions or issues. The last time all the Originals had met was fifty days ago to discuss once again attacking the Enclave, and that had been a rather perfunctory, let's-wait-and-see meeting. Yallia preferred action to the slow, pondering deliberation of the Grand Session.

But Kahlman was as level-headed as they came. On the few occasions she had gone against his advice, she had regretted her decisions. He was a good man.

"All right, Franc. Call an emergency Grand Session. We'll meet in one hour."

She stood to leave and caught Sirra's eye as she did so. The little girl had a look of fear on her face that struck Yallia like a blow.

"It's all right, dear," Yallia said. "I'll be back soon. There's nothing to be afraid of."

Even as she spoke, she realized that Sirra was not looking at her, but over her shoulder at Franc Kahlman. And she realized that the look on Sirra's face was not one of fear, but of hatred.

Yallia hesitated, torn between trying to understand Sirra's expression of loathing and the pressing matter Kahlman had brought to her. She stood at the breakfast table, the knuckles of her left hand resting gently on the table top, her body trembling with indecision.

Emme spoke suddenly. "Sirra, are you finished with breakfast?"

The comment seemed to break Sirra's concentration, and she snapped her head towards her truemother. "Yes."

"Then clean your plate, please."

The girl obeyed, and as Yallia watched her at the sink, Kahlman mumbled, "Madame Prime?"

Yallia tore her eyes off of Sirra and left with Kahlman.

* * *

Khadre took a deep breath and glanced at Viktur. She had never addressed the Grand Session before—all one hundred and eight Originals assembled together for only the most important of issues. The thought that they were meeting to discuss the discovery she and Viktur had made was not one she could grasp fully. "I wonder what she'll be like," Khadre said.

"Who?"

"The Prime Original." Khadre stared into space. She herself was not related to Yallia in any genetic fashion, though Viktur, she knew, had a paternal fratern who could trace his lineage to Yallia. This in itself was by no means unusual, and Viktur had not met the woman with whom his father had had a son.

"We're not here to bask in the glory of the sun that is the Prime Original, Khad," Viktur chided. "We need—"

He was interrupted by the opening of the massive doors that led to the Originals' Chamber. A grey-clad intern looked around and saw the two scientists. "You can come in now. The Session is ready."

Khadre breathed deeply and started toward the door, Viktur content to fall in behind her. She passed through the archway to the chamber and was profoundly disappointed. The room was brightly lit, not dim and smoky as she had imagined it. The Originals did not wear robes of scarlet or gold, but wore the same common clothes all Family members did. Khadre's dother had told her often enough that the Sessions were very informal, but until now, Khadre had always held out hope that her nonbirth mother had been hiding the truth. The conference area was a circular pit holding the hundred-plus Originals who were seated in subgroups at round tables. The whole room had the air of a cocktail party rather than a governing council.

Just as Khadre's disenchantment had reached a point of near-disgust, she saw a new figure enter the room from a distant door. Instantly, the babble in the room ceased and Khadre knew without doubt who the new person was. Even if she had not recognized her from various holos and news reports, the air with which she commanded the room was unmistakable.

"It's her," she whispered to Viktur.

Yallia's mouth was set in a grim line as she approached a small raised dais near the entrance. She surveyed the group quickly and commanded silence with her eyes.

"Are we all present?" she asked.

"Yes, Madame Prime," responded a man Khadre recognized as Franc Kahlman, the Original to whom she had first brought her findings.

"Good. Let's hear from the two scientists first. Khadre Seelith, daughter to Ciol Seeloki and Loni Jaysmith," Yallia said, nodding at two of the female Originals in the room, who were seated at different tables, "and Viktur Ljarbazz, son to Ennex Ljarsen and Abdelle Shabazz." Yallia found the two parents and smiled slightly when she spotted the father, Ennex. Yallia fixed her stare at Khadre and said, "What have you found?"

Khadre swallowed nervously. She had known that Ciol and Loni would be here, naturally, but had attached no special significance to that. They were her genetic parents, but they had not raised her as her dother had. It was not her geneparents' attendance that had thrown her, but the directness of Yallia's question.

"Well," Khadre croaked, then cleared her throat noisily and began again. "Well, Madame Prime, we, that is, my research partner and myself"—Khadre motioned to Viktur, who smiled and waved dumbly—"have been researching some of the native marine life in the Bitter Sea. And what we've found out there...." She shook her head and could not stop herself from laughing in a combination of nervousness and the sheer joy of discovery. "Well, I think it would be best if we showed you. I've arranged with Original Kahlman for a holo." she and looked vaguely at Kahlman, who nodded and rose from his seat. He gestured to the chamber attendant, and the room lighting dimmed.

The VHF sonar image filled the air above the pit, and Khadre cleared her throat again. "Uh, this image is just before the encounter. You can see...there," she said when the kelp bed hove into view. "The kelp bed is almost a perfect square, about one hundred and eighty-eight meters by one hundred and ninety-six. We do not think this is a natural phenomenon."

"Why not?" a voice Khadre did not recognize called out from the pit.

"Well, as you will soon see, there are a number of sea cows tethered nearby which—"

"Sea cows?"

"What do you mean, 'tethered?'"

The two questions came almost simultaneously, and Khadre heard a slight rustling of bodies and the sounds of brief comments from the Originals. She could not make out all of the speech, but the undercurrent was clearly unfriendly. She licked her lips, fearful that she was losing credibility.

"If you'll be a little patient, all your questions will be—"

"There!" Viktur said. He was pointing to the holo where the distant images of the "livestock" could be seen.

Khadre did not speak for a few seconds, letting the holo image speak for itself. She still heard mumbling from the pit, but it sounded more expectant now, less skeptical. The originals watched as the "farmer" herded his sea-cows towards the cliff face.

"Keep your eyes on the right-hand side of the image," Khadre said. No sooner had she spoken than the swarm of dolphin-like creatures appeared and surrounded the herd. The holo froze on the image of the farmer armed with its spear-like horn poised to attack one of the herd animals.

Khadre approached the holo and spoke from inside it. "Viktur and I have spent considerable time analyzing the holo, especially this image. From what we have been able to determine, the horn is part of some kind of yoke the farmer slipped on outside sonar pickup. The horn is quite obviously artificial," Khadre said, indicating key points on the holo, computer-enhanced discolorations she and Viktur had decided were crude straps attaching the implement to the creature's head, "and is a tool, most likely for slaughtering the herd animals."

The implications of her remarks were not lost on the Originals.

"You're saying that there's intelligent life in the sea," Yallia said, her voice soft. She was not asking a question.

"I am," Khadre said, straightening a little and looking at the assembled Originals. Few returned her glance—they were busily whispering to each other at their various tables.

"Originals, please. We have a lot to discuss here," Yallia said and the whispering stopped. Yallia turned to Khadre. "I will want you and your partner to submit a full report as soon as you're able. Send a copy to all of us in the room. Better yet, send a copy to the whole Family."

"Madame Prime, is that wise?" Kahlman said. "We don't really know anything about these animals. Should we be broadcasting our meager data to the Family at this time? Perhaps we should review the report first, and then decide what—"

Yallia cut him off angrily. "Decide what the Family can be trusted with? Why don't we just erect a Dome while we're at it, Franc? I will not have the Family denied information that could affect them."

Khadre watched Kahlman hesitate, then say gently, "Madame Prime, I—"

"It's not just the Family we have to worry about, Madame Prime," A new voice from the back of the gallery said. Khadre recognized Lawson, the newest Original, as he rose from his seat. "I assume that the Domers have no idea these animals exist?"

He looked at Khadre, who, surprised at having been thus appealed to, spluttered, "Uh, not that I can see. They have never sent surface vessels that we know of, and certainly no submersibles. Robot probes and shallow-water drones only, mainly for commercial fishing near the desalinization plants. I doubt they know."

"And we should keep it that way for as long as possible."

"Why?" Khadre said, then tried to shrink back into herself. She hadn't meant to challenge the Originals, but the question had been shocked out of her. She could feel Yallia's eyes on her before the Prime Original spoke.

"Young woman, you are thinking that such knowledge is beyond petty national politics. You are thinking that the knowledge that we are not alone on this planet should be enough to unite the Domers and the Family. You think we should tell them, don't you?"

Khadre nodded slowly, her eyes wide with awe.

Yallia sighed. "You youngsters are all alike. We are on the brink of war with the Domers—a war they started twenty-five years ago and which only now is turning in our favor. The Domers will never accept us, never consider us fully human. Nothing will ever change that. We must take this planet from them before they are able to fully adapt it to their alien bodies. We must destroy the terraforming stations."

Silence echoed in the hall as the assembled Originals allowed Yallia to regain her composure. Khadre had heard the naked emotion in her voice—her hatred of the Dome and all inside, particularly of her mother. This was no secret, even outside the Original caste.

Khadre swallowed her fear and spoke in a shaky voice. "If we share the information, the Domers might stop their terraforming process on their own. To spare the native life."

"On the contrary—they will redouble their efforts. The discovery will only scare the Domers into action."

"Madame Prime? I agree with Khadre," Lawson said. Yallia blinked at him. Lawson continued. "But not for the same reasons. We should delay our attacks on the terraforming stations until we can fully study this new phenomenon. In light of this, I further suggest that the information be held temporarily secret," he placed considerable emphasis on the word 'temporarily,' "until we can study it."

"I agree, Madame Prime," Kahlman said. There were general nods of agreement from the Originals, and Yallia looked at them in obvious anger.

"We must strike now! The discovery of the native life is all the more reason for us to stop the terraforming process as quickly as possible!"

"Another few days will make no difference, Yallia," Lawson said, his voice soft.

Khadre watched Yallia's expression melt from rage to resignation. Khadre could see the pain of defeat in her face, and from it knew this was not the first time she had lost against the other Originals.

"Very well. I ask for consensus: shall we postpone action, again, against the terraforming stations until such time as the Grand Session can study the report from Khadre Seelith and Viktur Ljarbazz?"

No one objected, and Yallia said softly, "so ordered." She looked down at her shoes for a moment, appearing to gather herself.

It was in Khadre at that moment to shout out, "No! Attack now! Do what this woman says, though it defies sense!" Such was her admiration for this Original who wanted so much to fight. She instead translated her impulse to anger at the other Originals, and for herself, for doing what was sensible and right, because it conflicted with what Yallia wanted.

* * *

The Commissar-General's office was dim. Two figures, one seated, one standing, looked out at the dusky landscape beyond Valhalla Dome.

"You have seen much more than I, of course, but I can't help feeling life inside the Domes was somehow...more orderly before," Commissar-General Ludith Nessel said to the old man who sat near her.

The man harrumphed. "And will be again. If you follow through. Do you have the intelligence report?" His voice was a harsh, throaty growl. It demanded instead of requested.

"I do. Our operative sent it a few hours ago." Nessel retrieved a thin folder from her desk and offered it to the man. He ignored the folder.

"What does it say? In brief."

"The Family has discovered some kind of quasi-intelligent life in the oceans. They are planning to investigate and, in fact, are probably doing so now."

"Hmph. So they are suspending any further attack plans on other Dome installations?"

"Yes."

The old man nodded. "Good. Reinforce those stations, Nessel. Send troops, no matter how green, to defend them."

"You think I should send untrained troops?" Nessel's voice was uncertain.

"What other kind do you have? A few dozen internal security officers? You'll need those for the Domes in the days to come. Besides, the outcasts will not press the attack when they see you have prepared to meet them. Guerrilla tactics," he snorted derisively.

"What about the discovery?"

The man waved away the comment with a single motion of his gnarled hand. "It is of no consequence."

"I think it might become so. I don't want the Family to discover something they can use against us."

"It won't matter. Once the terraforming process is complete, native life will have been replaced by our own flora and fauna. Whatever the outcasts have discovered will remain as a curiosity only."

"Still, I want to send a flyer over there to disable or destroy any research vessel they send."

At this, the man's eyes flashed with interest. "Do that, and you reveal our weapon. The outcasts do not realize a traitor lives among them. Any action taken against their research operations will cause suspicion. For what you hope to gain, it is not worth the risk. When the terraforming operation is complete, we will be able to eradicate the exiles easily."

Nessel did not look convinced. She was a woman who did not like questions. She did not know what would become of the discovery, but she did know nothing would change if she prevented further research.

"I'm going to send a flyer anyway. I think you're wrong about this one," she said, trying to make her voice playful. She was frankly scared of this man who had become both a legend and a curse. Would he grow angry at the comment?

The man simply shrugged. "Others have said so in the past. But they have ignored my advice at their peril. Send your flyer, then. I shall arrange to minimize the damage to our intelligence-gathering operation." He stood up, slowly, and shuffled toward the Commissar-General's door without asking for permission to depart.

Nessel watched him make his slow, painful way to her door. He did not use a cane. When he had opened the door and started through the jamb, Nessel said softly, "Thank you for your advice."

Without turning, he growled, "I will not live to see the project completed. But I do not wish to die until I see all threats to its fruition eliminated. I have shepherded this colony to this crucial point for almost forty years. Do not ignore my advice lightly."

Nessel swallowed and said, "I won't, Mr. Tann."

Carll Tann grunted and left the room.

CHAPTER 16

Sirra knew that if one of the adults looked in her direction for long enough, she would be in serious trouble. Grandonly Yallia would be very angry with her, and the thought was nearly enough to make Sirra abort her mission. But something was afoot, and Sirra wanted to know what it was. She could see the dim figures of the Originals through the sliver-thin crack in the door she had opened with extraordinary care. She stood with the absolute silence only an eavesdropping child can achieve and listened to the adults argue in the "grown-ups' room," as her onlymother called it.

"There's nothing you can do on the ship, but there's more than enough for you to do here," Lawson was saying.

"That's nonsense," Sirra heard Yallia reply. "I'm a geneticist, one of the best in the Family. I say that without boasting." Sirra was proud of her Grandonly's matter-of-fact manner, even if she was not sure what a geneticist was. "Besides, one of us should be out there to make any kind of instant decision those two young eggheads will need. I might as well go."

"I concur, Madam Prime." This from Kahlman. Sirra had never liked him. He was always cordial to her, as he was to everyone, but there seemed to be no warmth to the man. Sirra felt a shiver run down her spine, which she attributed to the clandestine nature of her mission. "While I might dispute the claim that your scientific knowledge is quite the incentive you are suggesting—" A ripple of laughter sounded in the room and Sirra frowned. She hadn't heard a joke—why were they laughing? Maybe Grandonly made a funny face or something, she concluded.

Kahlman was saying, "...and I would submit that any of the Originals would serve as on-the-spot authority, I do think you are strong in both the prerequisites."

"Jill of all trades, mistress of none, Franc?" Yallia said.

"I wouldn't say that, Madam Prime." Sirra could imagine Mr. Kahlman smiling that little smile of his.

"This is madness," Lawson broke in again. "Holo representation could easily—"

"We've been through that, Law. Holos can break up, especially from such a distance in a rickety research skiff. And the Domers may intercept the transmission. We want to keep this a secret for as long as we can."

Sirra squirmed in delight. She had understood that, at least—a secret! And she was listening!

She heard someone get up and momentarily froze. She listened intently to hear if the footsteps were approaching the door. After a breathless interval, she decided that someone was pacing around in the room.

"Why are you so worried, Law?" Yallia asked softly.

"Something could happen."

"Like what? A tsunami?"

Sirra didn't know what a tsunami was, but it must have been something funny because again there was the ripple of laughter in the room.

Yallia continued. "There's nothing out there that's dangerous. As for what you said earlier about there being plenty for me to do here—" Sirra heard bitterness enter her Grandonly's voice. Bitterness and that same anger that she heard from time to time. Sirra felt that she was on the edge of understanding why her Grandonly hated the Domes so much, if only she could talk to her Grandonly about it.

"—the Assembly made it very clear they are only too happy to postpone action again until this matter of the sea creatures is settled. So I want to go out there to figure it out so we can get back to the business at hand."

Sirra blinked. Sea creatures? What was Grandonly talking about?

Lawson again. "You still don't agree that we can learn something from these things?"

"Oh, sure, Law, but they're not going anywhere. The Domers, on the other hand, might be doing any number of things. They are not static like this problem before us. The only reason I submitted to the will of the Assembly is that it is possible, however domed unlikely, that something about these creatures will help us in our inevitable military campaign. And if there is a chance of a military advantage coming of this, however slight, I'll agree to wait. For a short time. We should be able to figure out if these creatures can offer us anything immediate rather quickly. If not, I will return to the Assembly, and I *will* have my way."

Sirra had not heard this part of her Grandonly before—she was very serious. Sirra knew that if her Grandonly ever spoke to her that way, she would jump at her voice so fast she might leave her skin behind. But what was all this talk about sea creatures and attacking the Domes? There was—

"Madame Prime? We have a small, and very young, security breach," Mr. Kahlman said, and something in his voice told Sirra that he was looking right at her. She slowly turned her head, eyes wide, and met Kahlman's unreadable gaze not three meters from her.

"What's the matter, Sirra?" Yallia asked, coming around the table and kneeling in front of her. "Can't you sleep?"

The temptation to use sleeplessness as an excuse, especially when it was being provided by her Grandonly, was almost too much for Sirra. She nodded slightly, then shook her head.

"I wanted to hear what you were talking about," Sirra said quietly.

Yallia sighed. "How long have you been there?"

"I heard that you are going to see some fish. And maybe use them to fight the people in the Domes."

"Long enough," Lawson's voice floated through the dimness.

Yallia threw a disapproving look over her shoulder, then looked back at her grandclone. "Listen, Sirra. You heard us talking about a secret. You can't tell anyone else, okay?"

"Can I come with you?"

Yallia's shoulders slumped. "What? No, dear. I have to go by myself."

"Please?"

Franc Kahlman got up from his seat and approached Sirra. "Young lady, your Grandonly asked you a question. Do you understand that what you heard in here is confidential? Secret, I mean?" he added quickly at Sirra's look of confusion.

"Can I tell my onlymother?"

"You mustn't tell anyone, dear. It's very important." Yallia grabbed both her hands to emphasize the point.

"Okay, Grandonly. I'll try."

Kahlman sighed softly. "Madam Prime, I submit we have a new problem. I am not sanguine about her sudden new status as an illuminate," he said, his inflated vocabulary leaving Sirra far behind.

Sirra could not understand the words, but her intuitive sense served her well. "I'll try, Mr. Kahlman. I really will. Buy why is it such a secret? Are you in trouble, Grandonly?"

Yallia shook her head and looked up at Kahlman. "I agree, Franc. But what can we do? Keep her under house arrest until I get back?" Yallia's disgust at the idea was clear even to Sirra.

Kahlman did not answer but looked thoughtfully at Sirra.

"Arrest?" Sirra squeaked.

Yallia patted her hands. "No, not like that," she said vaguely. She looked at Kahlman for a moment, then muttered, "I suppose she could just come with me. There's no danger, really."

Lawson exploded, "What? You can't take her with you! Yallia, for Ship's sake, think about it! What if—"

Yallia stood up and let go of Sirra's hands simultaneously. She whirled to face Lawson, her expression alone silencing him. "What if what? We'll be out on a boat. We're not going to do any diving or blockade running, Law."

"But...." Lawson stammered his objection, his arms waving in the air before him, trying to indicate danger where his words could not.

Yallia smiled at him in a way that made Sirra uneasy—she felt jealousy well up in her as her grandonly paid that kind of attention to him. Yallia stepped closer to him. She spoke softly so only he and Sirra could hear, and Sirra got the impression that she herself was not meant to listen. "Law, I understand what you're trying to say. But I haven't been tested yet—we don't know whether I'm pregnant. But even if I am, you don't think two days' growth will hinder me? If there's a baby in there, he or she is about as big as the head of a pin. Your gallantry is noted, Law, but it is also about a thousand years out of date." Still, she smiled and resisted the urge to touch him on the cheek. She backed away and said in her normal voice to the rest of the Originals, "Sirra and I will go on the research vessel."

"A good decision, if I may say so, Madam Prime. We hardly need a cover story now—you and your grandclone are going to the Bitter Sea for a day of, shall we say, 'girl talk.'" Kahlman said, a small smile on his face. He looked at Sirra and winked so quickly the girl was not even sure it had happened.

The meeting broke up. Yallia turned to Sirra and said, "Now go to sleep, little one. I'll wake you early in the morning before everyone else is up and we'll go sailing. All right?"

"Thank you, Grandonly. I'm sorry if I messed everything up."

"No. It'll be fun," Yallia said. "Now, off with you," she turned Sirra around and swatted her playfully on the backside.

Sirra giggled and made as if to leave, but she could feel eyes on her back. She turned her head to see Lawson staring at her, an unreadable expression on his face. For a moment, Sirra got the impression the man was fighting inside himself, as if he wanted to say something but at the same time did not want to say it.

Then the moment passed and she started to go. On her way out, she bumped into Kahlman.

"Excuse me, Mr. Kahlman."

"Excuse me, little one," he said, patting her on the head, and he left. Sirra still did not know what to make of him. He seemed sometimes to be nice, but other times he seemed...like a computer. Like he was always working problems in his head.

She shrugged and headed upstairs to her room. She did not know how she was going to sleep.

* * *

Khadre gave the tiny cabin on the skiff another worried look. Was that a bit of grime in the corner? She moved towards the suspicious smudge, her lower lip firmly caught between her front teeth. No, it was a shadow.

"Khad, please," Viktur said, his tone far past exasperation now. He was working topside, watching Khadre through the opening to the cabin below.

"Just giving the room a once-over," she said, her eyes darting from corner to corner.

"Tenth-over, you mean."

"It's not every day we have the Prime Original here, you know. I just want to make sure everything's in order for her."

"You gonna sweep the ocean, too?"

Khadre stuck her tongue at him. Despite appearances, she was thrilled at the prospect of taking Yallia aboard and showing her their discovery firsthand. If all went well, she and Viktur would finally get the recognition necessary to continue their studies. The Family had made little secret of their priorities—marine research ranked near the bottom of a very long list. If she thought about the matter hard enough, she knew she would discover that warfare was increasingly becoming the main focus of the Originals. But Khadre preferred not to think that hard. Instead, she concentrated on the mission ahead. Perhaps, somehow, their discovery could avert a war. She did not know how, but as a scientist, a *pure* scientist, she believed that knowledge ultimately led to peace.

"There they are," Viktur said, pointing from his vantage point topside.

Khadre scrambled out of the cabin and nearly tripped on the top stair.

"Easy, killer," Viktur said, laughing.

"What do you mean, there 'they' are? Who's with her?" Khadre squinted into the predawn gloom and made out two figures—an adult and a child. She gave Viktur a worried look and leaped lightly off the skiff onto the pier.

"Madam Prime?"

Yallia emerged from the fog, her right hand grasping the strap of a knapsack slung over her shoulder, her left holding the hand of the little girl at her side. She nodded gravely to Khadre and said, "Hello, Khadre Seelith. This is my granddaughter Sirra. I would like her to come along."

There was little doubt that Yallia did not expect a refusal, and Khadre immediately responded with more enthusiasm than was sincere. "Sure! Hello, Sirra. I'm glad you could come. Would you like to see the fishies?" She bent down to the girl and thrust their faces close, as if the girl was hard of hearing or mentally deficient or both.

Sirra blinked at her. Khadre knew how foolish she looked, but she could not start over and reintroduce herself to the girl. To her relief, however, Sirra smiled brightly, and Khadre felt the little girl take an instant liking to her.

"Fish," Sirra said. "There's no such word as 'fishies.' Or 'fishes,' either," she added.

"Actually, there is such a word, Sirra. 'Fish' can mean one fish or many fish of the same kind. 'Fishes' means many fish of different kinds." Khadre said, smiling. She, too, liked the little girl, even if she could not say why.

Sirra said, "Oh!" and looked up at her grandonly with glee.

Khadre caught the glance and took a chance. "You already knew that, didn't you?"

Sirra laughed openly. "Yes, I did. Can we go on the boat now?"

Khadre looked at Yallia. "Are there any more preparations to make?"

"Not from me. I am ready to leave as soon as you are," she said, her tone indicating that she expected the moment of departure to be right away.

"Then take my hand, Sirra, and we'll go aboard," Khadre said, holding her hand out to the girl. Khadre straddled the skiff and the pier and helped Sirra step aboard, then looked uncertainly at Yallia. "Do you need— should I—" Khadre said, her hand neither at her side nor extended far enough out for Yallia to hold.

"I think I can manage," Yallia grumbled, then boarded without holding Khadre's hand. She looked around the skiff with an air of disdain. Sirra had introduced herself to Viktur, who had started giving her a tour of the vessel. "Tell me about your safety precautions," Yallia barked.

Khadre coughed. "We have a signal beacon that broadcasts our position to a monitoring station on land, and we have some emergency rafts, rations, emergency medical supplies—"

"No life jackets?"

"Life jackets?" Khadre blinked. "Well, no, ma'am."

"Why not?"

"You can't really drown in this water, ma'am. The salt content is so high that a person floats quite comfortably without effort. The real danger comes from cold, not drowning. And we have chemical warmers for that."

"Hmm." Yallia did not seem satisfied.

Khadre looked at her in exasperation. "I can probably fashion some life jackets if you want, ma'am."

"Eh? No, I was thinking about something else. Your beacon. What would happen if you turned it off?"

"Well, the station would not know where we were. Unless we radioed in."

"Surely they would have some idea. You know where you are going to find the creatures, yes? And the station knows it, too, right?"

"I believe so. There is pretty tight security, but I think Del, our station monitor, knows."

"Then we will turn off the beacon. If you need to inform your partner at the monitoring station, do so."

Khadre swallowed. "Yes, ma'am." She squeezed past Yallia, who seemed disinclined to move, and climbed up to the conning platform. She activated the skiff's radio and told Del of the change in plans. He accepted the new data without comment, wished her luck, and switched off.

"Grandonly!" Sirra called from the bow, "Look! I think the sun's coming up!" The morning had grown gradually brighter, and the green-grey fog had diffused the light of Epsilon Eridani to an emerald glow.

Viktur bent down and whispered something to Sirra, who giggled and shouted again, "Cast off mooring lines, you swabbie!" She looked at Viktur who, laughing, gave her a thumbs-up. "You want to drive the boat?" he asked her. Sirra's eyes grew into saucers and she nodded vigorously. Viktur and Sirra started towards the conning platform.

Khadre happened to be looking at Yallia after Viktur's exchange with Sirra, and saw the Original attempt, unsuccessfully, to suppress a smile. Khadre felt warmth course through her, and it was only then that she realized how tense she had been with Sirra on board. The old woman was powerful and knew it well. Until the moment she smiled at her grandonly's antics with Viktur, Khadre had wondered if the formidable woman had a softer side. Now she knew, and the knowledge simply added another level of awe to Khadre's attitude.

Khadre climbed down from the conning platform and untied the ropes from the starboard cleats, throwing the rope onto the pier. Khadre saw out of the corner of her eye Yallia watching her and thought she saw grudging admiration in her expression. When Khadre finished untying the ropes, she pushed off from the pier with her foot and called out to Viktur, "We're clear!"

Viktur engaged the screws and the boat started forward. Sirra held on to the helm, eyes fixed ahead, while Viktur stood behind her, judiciously holding onto the wheel under Sirra's right hand.

"Look, Grandonly! I'm driving!" Sirra shouted.

"You sure are," Yallia shouted back. She turned to Khadre. "How long until we reach your creatures?"

"About two hours."

Yallia nodded and continued to watch Sirra at the helm. Khadre followed her gaze. The girl seemed oddly comfortable there, even though she had probably never been on a boat in her short life. As the women watched, Viktur said something to Sirra, and she released the wheel. Viktur threw a few switches and took Sirra's hand to lead her down from the conning platform.

"We're on auto now," he explained. "I thought Captain Sirra would like to see the drone."

"Can I, Grandonly?"

"Of course, dear. But don't touch."

"I won't." Viktur led Sirra aft to look at the cyborg submersible.

Khadre and Yallia stood perhaps two meters apart and watched. Khadre had dozens of questions to ask the Prime Original but could not begin to frame them properly. Mostly, she wanted to know why the Originals had taken such an interest in the creatures. She was not naïve—pure science for its own sake was rarely held in high esteem by politicians, even ones as enlightened as the Originals. Why, then, the sudden interest, to the point of sending the highest-ranking member of the Family to personally oversee the study?

Khadre could not ask the questions. It was not for her to receive explanations from her elders. She simply did as she was told and hoped for encouragement and praise.

The next two hours were uneventful. To Viktur's obvious surprise, Sirra did not tire of the novelty of being on board the skiff—she still thrilled at the buck and spray of the sea. She spent most of time near the bowsprit, bracing her teeth into the wind and laughing as the ship heaved gently, its internal gyros absorbing much, but not all, of the roll of the sea.

"Coming up on target area," Khadre called out form the conning platform. "I'm going to slow us down to one-third." The hum of the motor changed pitch and the craft gradually decelerated.

"Khad, put her back on auto and come down to help me with Nimmo."

"I want to get closer manually. Less work for Nimmo."

"I'll help you, Viktur," Sirra said, advancing toward the cyborg.

"No, skipper, this is for me and Khadre to do. You have to watch out for monsters, remember?"

Sirra smiled at Yallia and turned back to the bowsprit and looked out at the sky. Yallia looked fondly at her back. The girl was too old to believe in monsters, but she was willing to humor the young man.

Khadre eventually came down from the conning platform and helped secure Nimmo to the hoist. She activated the winch and lowered the drone into the water.

"Now we go into the control cabin to monitor and guide the drone," Khadre said to Yallia, who nodded gravely and turned to Sirra.

"We're going to go into the cabin now, Sirra. Come on."

"Okay," she said, but something in the sky caught her attention. "Hey, Vik, a bird!"

Yallia began, "Sirra, come on. We've no—"

"Wait a moment, Madame Prime," Viktur interrupted. "What do you see, Sirra?" He scrambled past a startled Yallia and came up next to Sirra. She pointed to the sky where a black speck hovered near the horizon.

"What is it? Why such excitement over a bird?" Yallia said, annoyed, despite her own protestations against her pseudo-noble status, that Viktur would so causally interrupt her.

"We're over one hundred and fifty kilometers from land. Much too far away for solo birds. We've never encountered any this far out," Khadre said.

Yallia wondered at the worry in her voice, but before she could comment on it Viktur shouted from the bow, "Khad! Can you get the binocs and take a look at this?"

Khadre bounded to the conning platform and opened a compartment, withdrew a pair of binoculars, and focused them on the speck.

"It's not a bird," Khadre said, unable to convey any emotion save surprise. "It's a flyer. Coming at us."

"A flyer?" Yallia said, shocked. She came to the bottom step of the conning platform and reached for the binoculars. Khadre handed them over without a word.

Viktur said to Sirra, "Okay, I'm going to show you something fun now. It's down in the cabin, though. Come with me?" He said, trying to keep his voice calm but firm.

His very playfulness and rapport with the girl now worked against him as Sirra reacted to the almost undetectable hint of anxiety in his voice. She broke from him and ran to Yallia.

"Grandonly, what is it?"

Yallia lowered the binocs and held Sirra with her free hand.

Viktur took the binoculars from her and watched the flyer. "If it keeps coming at this speed, it'll be over us in about a minute." He lowered the binoculars and added, "We'd better hail them, see what they want."

"Mister Ljarbazz," Yallia said softly but with iron in her voice, "that is a Dome flyer."

Viktur started at her. "Of course, Madame Prime."

"It is almost certainly a drone, like your submersible. There's no one on board."

"But surely if we hail them, whoever is controlling it will hear."

"Hear us? Certainly. But that won't stop them. You don't have anything we can use on them, do you?" she asked calmly.

It took Viktur a moment to understand what she meant—she had refrained from speaking directly because of Sirra. But as realization dawned on him he shook his head.

"Do you want me to hail them or not?" Khadre said from the conning platform, her eyes glued to the approaching flyer. There was no need of binoculars now—the outline of the machine was clearly visible to the naked eye.

Yallia hesitated. She was loath to give away their position, but the flyer was obviously approaching them. Whatever secrecy the mission had started under had been lost. She looked up at Khadre and said, "Go ahead."

Khadre immediately switched on the communicator and spoke into it. "To unidentified flyer: this is the research vessel *Beagle*. What can we do for you?" The flyer had slowed, its twin engines changing configuration to turn it into a sort of helicopter. When it was completely transformed, it hovered perhaps one hundred meters above the skiff.

Yallia let go of Sirra suddenly and strode up to the conning tower while Khadre still waited for a response. Viktur held Sirra, who let out a fearful whimper.

Yallia snatched the transmitter out of Khadre's hands and snapped, "Dome flyer! You are interfering with peaceful Family scientific research! You will withdraw immediately!" Khadre could barely hear her, despite her shouting, above the roar of the flyer's engines.

Khadre looked at Yallia, startled. What was she doing? She sounded as if she wanted a confrontation with this thing.

There was still no answer from the flyer. Khadre shouted to Yallia, "What do they want? Do you think they'll try to board us?"

"There's no one in it," Yallia shouted back. "It's a drone."

"But what—" Khadre's eyes widened suddenly. "Get down!" she screamed, pushing Yallia off the conning platform as the two slug-thrower emplacements on the flyer shed their camouflage and spat projectiles at the *Beagle*.

Viktur and Sirra crumpled to the ground as soon as the shooting started. Yallia and Khadre crawled down the steps of the conning platform, scraping skin off their elbows and forearms as they went, making their way to Viktur and Sirra.

The flyer rotated to cover them and continued to pump high-velocity bullets into the skiff. Most of the slugs tore through the flimsy materials of which the skiff was constructed—only a few bounced off the tougher metallic elements of the craft.

"Over the side!" Khadre said. She started to push Yallia over the railing, but could not accomplish this without getting to her knees and lifting the older woman. She knew that by getting up, she would lose whatever soft cover she had behind the conning platform, but she needed to save the Prime Original. Yallia entered the water gracelessly but at least now had the bulk of the skiff between her and the flyer.

The deafening roar of the autocannons ceased, and Khadre wasted a split second in looking at the flyer in renewed horror. A new weapon sloughed off its camouflage and began to track the skiff. Khadre did not know weaponry, but this belly-mounted cylinder looked distinctly more powerful than the slug-throwers. With a sudden flash of understanding she knew the flyer's cybernetic brain (or human pilot back in the Dome) had decided the time for antipersonnel weapons was over. Khadre saw the flame shoot out of the flyer's belly turret and strike the skiff mid-ship. The heat of the blast almost knocked her out and the air displacement sent her skidding against the portside railing. The skiff was ablaze and would soon founder. She crawled towards where Viktur had sheltered Sirra with his body and grabbed her partner by the shoulder. He fell away from Sirra, his face reduced to a pinkish mass of bone pulp. He must have been hit by one of the first bursts from the flyer's autocannons as he had dived to save Sirra. Khadre forced herself to look away from Viktur and saw Sirra huddled under the lower stair of the conning platform. She was still alive—her eyes met Khadre's in terror.

Khadre reached out and grabbed Sirra. The heat from the burning skiff was intense enough to cause Khadre to lose consciousness for a split second. When she came to, she was back at the portside railing somehow, still holding Sirra. She rolled over the side and entered the blessedly cold waters of the Bitter Sea. Instantly, Yallia's arms were around her granddaughter.

Khadre looked back up at the flyer and saw it slowly lose altitude, as if searching the wreckage. Khadre realized that its infrared sensors were no use in the heat—the craft was forced to use visible spectra to search for survivors.

The fire must have reached some of the diving pressure tanks just then, for a titanic explosion shattered the skiff from inside. Khadre, Yallia, and Sirra were only a few meters away from the port side of the boat when the vessel exploded—much of the debris slammed into them and sent them rushing away from the skiff. Khadre was stunned momentarily when a chunk of the skiff smashed into her head, but she had the presence of mind to hang on and ride the wave. When her head was clear, she searched frantically for Yallia and Sirra and saw them several meters away, amid more wreckage. They were both unconscious but floating in the saltwater. Khadre was about to move towards them when the whine of the flyer's engines changed pitch. As she watched, the flyer hovered shakily, then began to change configuration. The flyer seemed to be having trouble morphing back into its high-velocity shape, though Khadre could not see any external damage. If the flyer had been alive, Khadre would have called the erratic behavior indecisive. The machine turned unsteadily, then moved back away, more slowly now but still quick.

Khadre did not watch it for long. She made her way painfully through the debris to where Yallia and Sirra floated and checked their vitals. They were both alive and seemed strong, just unconscious. Khadre looked around her at the shattered remains of the skiff and cried, since there was no one to stop her.

CHAPTER
17

Tann scowled at Nessel when she entered her office. She gasped to find him there, then hardened her features to cover her surprise.

"What is the result?" Tann snapped.

Nessel didn't answer until she had placed herself behind her desk. Tann was far too seasoned a politician to be deceived at her action—she wanted him to think she was taking her time and establishing herself as the dominant one in the conversation by moving to her official seat, but her stiff posture betrayed her fear. She wanted a desk between herself and this old, gnarled adviser. So be it.

"The flyer destroyed the research ship. There were four people on board."

"Dead?"

"Presumably."

Tann's eyes flashed. "What do you mean? Are they dead or aren't they?"

"The flyer was damaged in the attack. An explosion on the research craft. The flyer was forced to withdraw back to base for repairs. We'll send another one out as soon as possible."

"Why?"

Nessel looked at him quizzically. "To confirm they are dead, of course. Or to pick up survivors."

"Why would we do that? Leave them be. Dead or not, it doesn't matter. Our attack on the scientists is enough."

"They weren't all scientists, Mr. Tann."

"Whatever they were," he said in annoyance.

"One was a child." She said this with unnatural distinctness, and again Tann saw through her. She had waited to reveal this fact out of some perverse sense of revenge. Hers had been the command to attack, it was true—she saw herself as the final authority in the Domes, no matter what this Carll Tann thought. He met her iron with steel.

"Whatever they were," Tann said again, clearly and forcefully, "the exiles will seek revenge." He smiled a crooked half-smile. "And we will be ready for them."

"But to leave them out there...."

"So? Were you not aware that this is a military action, Nessel? People die in wars, or hadn't you been told?"

"Not children and civilians."

Tann shook his head. "Especially children and civilians. That's what makes war ugly. That's why we must do this—to stop a greater ugliness. The death of a few innocents now will prevent mass slaughter later." Tann started to add that only mutant outcasts were dying now, but he refrained. Nessel was not of a mind to hear that line of reasoning.

Tann sighed inwardly as he watched Nessel grapple with what she had set in motion. Again, he thought, I am forced to do my work from underneath a weak, vacillating fool. Left to the likes of her, this colony would be destroyed by internal warfare in a generation. Left to the old, departed Commissar-General Jalen Newfield, the colony would have been torn to pieces by genetic class struggles. And had Tann not acted all those years ago when he first put this plan in motion, the colony would surely be in ruins now. He had to stay alive and keep working until this crisis was past.

He had heard the talk in the Domes from the various left-wing movements preaching 'integration' of the outcasts and a reintroduction into Dome society. He had even heard vague talk of 'reparations' to them. His spy network had the various leaders and orators of the "People's Party," as they liked to call themselves, under surveillance. Aside from the outcast group itself, this proletarian movement represented the greatest threat to society he could imagine. Eliminate the outcasts, and the movement would have to dissolve—there would be nothing to champion except a memory.

He cursed inwardly. Daydreaming like a child! His fifty-seven-year-old brain was still sharp, but it required an exercise of will sometimes to keep it focused. He closed the door on his ruminations about politics and social upheaval, but not before he made a mental note to increase the level of surveillance on the People's Party leadership.

* * *

Yallia woke slowly. She opened her eyes to slits and winced at the bright midday sun through green clouds. Her eyes became accustomed to the light after a few seconds, and she could make out Khadre and Sirra looking at her intently.

"Grandonly!" Sirra said, her voice a combination of relief and fear. The girl started to move toward Yallia, but the swaying of the makeshift raft the three were on stopped her.

"Easy, sweetie," Khadre said. She turned to Yallia. "Glad to see you're back with us, Madame Prime." Her voice was flat, emotionless.

"Where—" Yallia croaked, then caught herself. She swallowed and began again in a more forceful tone. "Report, please."

Khadre sighed. "There's not much to report. The skiff is destroyed. Sirra and I are not seriously hurt. You might have a concussion, you might not. I don't really know."

"How long have I been unconscious?"

"Not long. Maybe twenty minutes."

Yallia absorbed those few facts, her still-foggy brain slow. "What about Viktur?"

Khadre glanced at Sirra, who had begun to cry again. "He's dead," Khadre said in the same monotone as before.

"Grandonly," Sirra said through sobs, "he saved me! When that flying thing shot at us he...he...protected me. He put himself on top of me...and...and...." Sirra's next few words were indecipherable.

Yallia forced herself to attend to urgent matters first. "Is the skiff completely destroyed? Nothing left?"

Khadre swept her eyes across the horizon where the scattered remains of the skiff still floated. "I haven't really been able to find much, just some of the larger bits for us to rest on. I had Sirra to look after, and you, too. But now that you're awake, I'd like to suggest something."

"Go ahead."

"The only device that is likely to still be intact is Nimmo. The drone submersible. We might be able to use that."

"How?"

"If I can find it, I'll be able to use it to get us motive power back towards the mainland. It'll be slow—extremely slow—but perhaps we can paddle, too."

"How far out do you think we are?"

"We found the creatures about one hundred and fifty kilometers out. We haven't drifted far, if at all."

"And we can get back using the sub?" Yallia did not try to hide her doubts.

"I agree, it isn't much. But it'll help. It's all we've got."

Yallia paused before answering. "You're thinking we should have kept our beacon on."

Khadre shook her head. "No, Madame Prime, I never—"

"You should be. I was wrong about that."

"As you say, Madame Prime. I'm going to go look for the sub now." Khadre rolled carefully off the debris that served as their raft and started swimming in increasingly wide circles around Sirra and Yallia. Yallia watched her go, thankful that the young scientist had proven tough despite her initial impression at the Grand Session. She could have easily fallen into uselessness from the attack and Viktur's death, but she seemed to understand without explanation why the three of them must return to the mainland. Another flyer was certain to return to the site of the attack.

It was not long before Khadre returned with the submersible. Yallia could tell, however, that it had been a fruitless search when she saw the drone's sculler—it had been almost completely sheared away from the main body. The sub would never move under its own power.

Khadre gave the sub's other systems a halfhearted examination and found them in working order. Sonar was on, and had presumably been on since Viktur had lowered it into the water. The drone's chemical camouflage was on as well. But the drone was useless to them now.

Sirra asked, "Nimmo is broken?"

Khadre said, "That's right. We'll just have to paddle our way back, Sirra." She looked in the debris. "I'll go find some boards we can use."

"Khadre," Yallia said. Khadre turned and waited. Yallia said softly, "We'll need some way to attach Viktur's body to our raft."

Khadre glanced quickly at Sirra, who was listening with wide eyes. "Why?"

"He can still contribute to the Family." Yallia said it quietly but with determination.

Khadre nodded slowly, and Yallia understood what she was thinking. Viktur's genes belonged to everyone, and the Family had the right to clone him. Yallia was not being ghoulish, but practical. In her way, she was honoring the fallen scientist. Khadre was thinking that she could still have a child by him after all. Yallia slid into the water and swam to Viktur's body.

Khadre's search for paddles and rope turned up three more-or-less straight, lightweight boards and a bit of rigging. When she returned to the raft, Sirra was staring disconsolately into the water while Yallia appeared deep in thought.

"Here we go," Khadre said. She put the boards on the raft and helped Yallia lash Viktur's body to the side using the rigging. Yallia tried not to think about what she was doing. She had not known the man for long, but he had obviously been close to Khadre. She was surprised to find the young scientist had managed to attach Viktur's body without crying.

"Which way do we go?" Yallia asked.

Khadre looked up, Yallia following her gaze. It was midmorning—the sun was moderately high in the sky. Khadre angled the raft slightly, checking the sky as she did so. The expression on her face did not give Yallia a great deal of confidence.

"Grandonly?" Sirra's voice called out. She was still looking at the water, but her face had a curious expression on it.

"What?"

"Look," she said, pointing down.

Both women looked into the water and saw figures below them—three torpedo shapes swimming about perhaps five meters under the surface. All three wore the spear-helmets they had seen the farmer use on one of his livestock. The creatures circled below the humans in tight, interweaving patterns.

"What does this mean, Khadre?" Yallia asked, her eyes never leaving the creatures.

Khadre stared for a few moments before answering. "They're armed but not attacking. Why, then, have they come up to the surface at all? And how?"

"Are they air-breathers, like Terrestrial dolphins or whales?"

Khadre shook her head slowly. "We discovered them about four kilometers below the surface with what appeared to be a farm. If they were air-breathers, they wouldn't establish a settlement so far down. Or would they?" She looked away from the creatures and stared into the sky, obviously deep in thought.

"Let's solve that later," Yallia said, and when there was no answer from Khadre, she barked, "Khadre! Get your paddle and let's go!"

Sirra spoke up then, in an odd little voice. "No, Grandonly. I want to watch the fish."

Yallia ignored her and started paddling, inexpertly churning the water but making little progress.

Khadre dipped her paddle in the water and began rowing, then shouted, "Madame Prime! I need to retrieve Nimmo!"

"No. Remain in the raft. We're going back."

"I don't think these creatures will hurt us. And Nimmo...Viktur and I spent a lot of time working with it." She looked uncertainly at Yallia.

"All right. Get it. But hurry."

Khadre slid off the raft and started towards the drone. Yallia continued to watch the creatures below. They had been swimming in their complex pattern immediately below the sub, and as Khadre closed in on it she called back to Yallia, "I think they're attracted to the active sonar."

"Khadre, get the sub and get back in the raft. You don't know what those things will do to you."

Khadre did not need prompting. She started back, towing Nimmo behind her.

"Can you shut off the sonar?" Yallia called.

"I want to see how far they'll follow me."

Despite the situation, Yallia accepted Khadre's position. She had spoken without reverence for the first time in their brief relationship—she was curious and heedless of danger. Yallia could respect that, though she would prefer the scientist showed her courage some other time.

Khadre splashed back aboard the raft and seized her paddle. She and Yallia made slow progress through the debris field, while Sirra hung her head over the back and watched the pursuing animals.

"Sirra! Get back!" Yallia snapped.

"But, Grandonly, they're curious."

"They are dangerous," Yallia corrected.

"No, they're not," Sirra said with uncanny confidence.

Khadre glanced at her. "How do you know, Sirra?"

"Just look at them!" Sirra pointed. "The way they swim around and the way they talk to each other."

Yallia almost dropped her paddle. "Talk to each other? Can you hear them?"

Sirra's face pinched in puzzlement. "No, but they're talking. You can tell." She spread her hands slightly, as if unable to comprehend Khadre's lack of understanding.

Yallia did not answer but continued to watch Sirra observe the sea creatures. The raft was moving at no better than a meter per second in the debris field, and the sea creatures had no trouble keeping pace. Sirra hung her head over the back of the raft and watched.

Yallia gasped suddenly as one of the creatures changed course and shot upwards, rising at an alarming rate.

"Sirra! Get back!" Khadre shouted as the creature's lance emerged from the water. It missed Sirra by perhaps a meter and a half. The girl did not draw back but reached her hand into the water.

"Sirra!" Yallia had stopped rowing and reached behind her to grab the girl but lost her balance on the unsteady raft and fell into the sea. Khadre scrambled to the side of the raft to help Yallia back on while Sirra reached down and touched one of the creatures on its smooth back.

When the two touched, Sirra felt a piercing pain in her head, as if someone had stabbed her with micro-thin needles through the inner ear. She slapped her hands over her ears, trying to block the pain, but even as she did so the needles withdrew, and she was left with only the memory. It lasted perhaps a half second. When it was over, she looked at Khadre and knew instantly that she, too, had felt the sensation.

Yallia made her way back onto the raft, then lunged forward and grabbed Sirra by the shoulders, almost knocking both of them into the water as the raft tipped crazily. Khadre lifted Sirra's arm out of the water, watching the creature just below the surface. Its lance was almost perpendicular to the raft now, bobbing gently with the creature's motion. As they watched, other sea creatures swam to the one Sirra had touched and nudged it back down deeper. The intent was unmistakable—they wanted their fellow sea-creature to have no further contact with the strange organisms floating on the surface.

Khadre looked at Sirra. "Is she all right?"

"Seems so. Sirra? Are you okay?"

Sirra did not answer immediately. She looked at Yallia with a strange expression, as if she were trying to hear something just beyond audible range. "What? Oh, I'm fine."

Yallia said, "We have to get out of here. If we can't outdistance them, maybe we can discourage them from following. Perhaps if we beat at the surface of the water with the paddles, we—"

Khadre shook her head. "No. They're following us because of Nimmo's sonar, I think." Khadre leaned towards the drone, her eyes darting back and forth between the drone's manual switches and the depths to which the creatures had retreated, and turned off the submersible's sonar.

The effect was not immediate, but after a few seconds, the creatures' swim pattern changed.

"Ohhh," Sirra said, her voice conveying pity. "They're sad now."

Yallia paid no attention to her but watched the creatures gradually sink lower and lower until they were no longer visible. "Let's go," she said, and grabbed her paddle.

She and Khadre rowed for what must have been well over three hours, until Khadre could no more. Viktur's body was on the raft with them—Khadre had said she was afraid of predators and also that his body would produce drag. She had nothing to cover him with and so simply turned him over, face down on the deck.

Yallia was a machine. Every stroke was identical; every stroke brought her closer to shore. She and Khadre did not speak but saved their energy for their makeshift paddles. Khadre kept the raft pointed in the rough direction of land, as determined by the sun that had crawled to a position almost directly overhead. When Khadre felt she could no longer navigate by the sun, she called out to Yallia.

"All right, Madame Prime, I think we can take a rest."

"I'm not tired," Yallia shot back over her shoulder.

"I can't navigate now. I have to wait a few hours."

"Why can't we just keep going the direction we are going in now?"

"Well, I...." was Khadre's only answer.

"All right," Yallia agreed, placing her paddle on the raft and arching her back. "We'll rest here. But we get going again in an hour." She dipped her hand into the seawater and took a few gulps. They had been drinking regularly, as the salt posed no special problem for them— indeed, it gave them a slight boost in energy as their bodies naturally metabolized the chlorine. They would not want for water, at least. Yallia turned back to Khadre when she had finished drinking. "How far do you estimate we are from shore?"

Khadre looked into the distance. "Tough to say. If we were making about three meters per second, we can cover a kilometer in about five minutes. We were out about two hundred kilometers."

"So we are about thirteen more hours away from shore." Yallia said calmly.

"Give or take. Of course, that's not accounting for drift and fatigue."

"Fatigue is not a factor," Yallia said dismissively. "And I trust you will correct for drift." Yallia looked into the distance, towards where the shore was, assuming Khadre's navigation was right. "We need to get back as soon as possible. The Family must learn of this."

"Of what? The sea cr—?" Khadre began, stopping at Yallia's icy stare.

Yallia started to open her mouth to snap at the scientist but held her tongue. She reminded herself that Khadre was just that—a scientist. It meant nothing that the woman's first thought was of the marine life.

Yallia saw that Khadre had correctly interpreted her expression. There was no need to speak. Khadre looked away, towards Sirra. Yallia followed her gaze thoughtfully. The girl had not helped paddle but had instead lain down on the raft and dragged her fingers in the wake. Neither Khadre nor Yallia had disturbed her.

Sirra caught Khadre looking at her and offered the scientist a faint smile. She looked past her at Yallia. She screwed her face up in a question and asked, "Grandonly? Is there a God?"

The question begat stunned silence. The Family had a few members who adhered to a sort of Unitarian religion, but by and large the Family was truly agnostic. The overriding belief was that the question of the existence or nonexistence of God was an inherently unanswerable one. Yallia had encouraged this "belief," thinking that escapism and abdication of responsibility to a god (or a God) were unacceptable by-products of religion.

Yallia cocked her head slightly and said, "Why do you ask that?"

"Because the fish think there is." She looked down at the water and said, sadly, "They think it's me."

Khadre and Yalli were spared the necessity of a response by the faint but unmistakable sound of an air horn in the distance. They whirled around towards the direction of the sound. Khadre saw it first.

"There. One of the fishing fleet," she said, pointing at the ship's mast.

"Good." Yallia said and reached for her paddle.

Khadre did not object, although the speed of the fishing boat was at least twenty times the speed they could make with their pathetic makeshift oars.

The two paddled for a few minutes, then Yallia spoke suddenly. "Khadre, why is that boat coming towards us?"

"What do you mean?"

"How did it know to investigate us? Did you turn the beacon off as I ordered?"

"Yes, Madame Prime. I don't know why it's here."

"Could it simply be fishing?"

Khadre shook her head between strokes. "Not out this far. I'll ask Del, the dock-master, what's going on when we get in. But I'm more interested in the sea creatures' behavior."

"Why?"

Khadre took a breath and spoke rapidly. "Why did they investigate Nimmo's sonar, and is there a way to use sonar to establish communication? Why did the lone animal surface, or nearly surface, towards us?"

"Towards Sirra," Yallia corrected her. And her correction sent a chill through her. Why had the animals been so fascinated with Sirra, and what had the little girl meant about God? What was different about her?

"Could the animals have sent scouts to warn the fishing boat to pick us up?"

Khadre hesitated only a moment. "I don't see how, or why. Even if they could understand what had happened, and for some reason sent one of their own to help, there is no way the fishing crew could understand any message."

Yallia sighed and cast her gaze downward. She caught sight of Viktur on the raft and her thoughts immediately grew darker. The death would hit Khadre sooner or later, even as it now hit Yallia, though on a different level.

Yallia paddled mechanically, with one thought growing stronger and stronger in her mind, crowding out all others. The Domers had pinpointed their location and sent one of their few assault flyers to kill all aboard. There could be only one explanation: there was a traitor in the Family, and with a shock that almost caused her to cry out in alarm and rage, Yallia knew who it was.

The trip back on board the fishing vessel *Lady Gwenevere* was uneventful and blessedly short. Khadre had learned surprisingly little from the captain and her three-person crew. They had received word about two hours ago that the *Beagle* had "come to distress" and needed assistance. The *Lady Gwen* had been dispatched at full speed to investigate. Khadre called Del at the harbormaster's office, and the mystery had deepened.

"You called us," Del said indignantly. "You sent a general distress message."

Khadre assured Del she had done no such thing. She could almost hear Del shrugging on the other side.

"Whatever you say. You want us to throw you overboard and leave you to paddle back?" Del was nothing if not a thoroughly practical man.

Khadre switched off. Had Viktur managed to send a distress message before he died? She shook her head. No, he had not even been up on the conning platform. But it was the only solution that made sense.

The mystery nagged at her nevertheless. The pieces didn't fit.

Khadre watched Sirra as the girl continued to stare out to sea. Land was in sight off the bow, but Sirra was still at the stern, looking almost wistful.

"How are you, Sirra?" Khadre asked, putting her arms around the girl's shoulders.

"I'm sad."

"Me, too. It's all right to be sad, Sirra. It's even all right to cry. Viktur was a nice man," she said and choked up. Despite her words to Sirra about grief, she found herself trying to deny her own emotions.

"I'm sad about the fish, too," Sirra said.

Khadre suddenly remembered Sirra's enigmatic comment before the *Lady Gwen* had picked them up. "Sirra? What did you mean that the fish think you are God?"

"When I petted the one fish, I could sort of hear what he said. It wasn't like hearing people talk. But I could still understand what the fish said."

"What did he say?"

"*She.*" Sirra said with quiet emphasis. "She said...I don't know the words. But she was...." Sirra stopped and looked at Khadre slyly. "She was like you are with my Grandonly, sort of. But more."

"Like I am with your Grandonly?" Khadre considered that. "You mean, like how I am nice to her? Respectful?"

"What's 'respectful?'"

"Respectful is when you think someone else is very important and smart," Khadre answered, thinking that the definition would suffice for the young girl.

"That's what the fish were doing. Respectful. But...."

"What?"

"It was more. They wanted to do things for me, I think. Like they wanted to make me happy."

"Why?"

"I don't know. They thought I could make things happen to them, and they wanted to make me happy so I would make only good things happen to them."

Khadre felt a chill as she realized that Sirra was right when she said the 'fish' thought she was God. The chill passed when rationality took hold—there was no way Sirra could have learned all this from the sea creatures. Her overly fertile imagination, distorted by the violence that preceded it, must be creating all this. She decided to test her theory.

"Sirra? Did the fish say anything about Viktur?"

"Viktur?" Sirra thought. "No."

"Did they say that he would be all right?" Khadre knew she was leading Sirra, but she had to dispel the effects of the girl's experience.

"No." Sirra said plainly.

"You know the fish can't make him alive again."

"I know." Sirra spoke so clearly, so plainly, that Khadre began again to doubt her carefully constructed analysis of the girl's psyche. This problem was beyond her—Sirra would have to see Doctor Jakielies when they returned.

"Did you hear the one fish sing to me?" Sirra said suddenly.

"No, dear, I didn't," Khadre said, then added, mostly to herself, "unless that was the one who broadcast the high-frequency whine."

"She wasn't whining. She was singing. It kinda hurt my head, but it was still nice."

"How did you know she was singing?"

Sirra spread her hands. "I just know."

Khadre stared at her for a moment, then shook her head slightly. The girl was in need of help. And yet....

Khadre did not complete the thought.

Yallia stepped off the boat when it docked and saw Kahlman and Lawson waiting for her on the pier. She waved once to them and helped

Sirra off, then waited as Khadre disembarked. The three watched reverently as Viktur's body, covered with one of the spare sails from the *Lady Gwen*, was removed by two of the crewmembers. Yallia strode purposefully to Kahlman and said quietly, "I want this man's body taken care of, Franc. Harvest what can be saved, especially sperm. We'll have a burial after that."

"A burial?" Kahlman said, his eyebrows rising.

"Yes." Yallia knew what she had requested. Family corpses were not buried—they were harvested for cell types and gametes, which were stored in the vast central genebank for later use. The corpses themselves were ground into a fine loam and spread in fields as fertilizer. Ritual played no part in the disposal of corpses—Yallia had frequently spoken against "death-worship," as she called the Dome practice of funeral rites. She looked significantly at Kahlman. "He was killed by the Domers. We need to use his murder to galvanize the Family."

Kahlman did not answer, but his expression indicated his extreme displeasure at Yallia's disposition. He understood what she was trying to do, and although he saw the wisdom in her approach, it nevertheless unsettled him.

Yallia did not wait for Kahlman to respond but instead turned to Lawson. A tiny smile crept onto her face as she saw the control Lawson was enforcing on himself to keep from wrapping her in a loving, relieved embrace.

"Madame Prime. I am glad to see you," he said with excessive formality.

"And I you, Mr. Lawson."

The two stared at each other for a while before Yallia said to Kahlman, her eyes still on Lawson, "Arrange a Grand Session, Mr. Kahlman. I intend to hold a vote. You had also better prepare our forces for an immediate attack."

She continued to stare at Lawson, while out of the corner of her eye she saw Kalhman move off with the two crewmembers carrying Viktur's body. Khadre touched Yallia lightly on the shoulder.

"Madame Prime," she said softly, "I am sorry to interrupt, but I have...things to attend to. May I—"

"Of course." Yallia turned and knelt down to Sirra. "Sirra, you're going back home for a little. I'll see you there soon, all right?"

Sirra nodded, but her eyes were elsewhere. Yallia looked at Khadre.

Khadre said, "I think she should see Jakielies."

Yallia rose and nodded slightly, then thought better of it and shook her head. "No. She has to come to grips with this. This is the world she lives in. The sooner she understands that, the better off she will be."

"But, Madame Prime! No one should have to—"

"—face the harshness of the world at such a young age? See what cruelty adults are capable of? I consider Sirra lucky to have seen all this at her age. She will be better able to form a true picture of humanity."

"She will lose her childhood. She will die a worse death than Viktur did."

Yallia stared at Khadre, whose face betrayed her considerable surprised at speaking out so forcefully against the Prime Original. Yallia wondered if Khadre realized, as she now did, that she had been speaking not about Sirra, but herself.

"Childhood." Yallia said with disgust. "A period of time in which an organism is dependent, socially and to some extent physically, upon the charity of the community in which he or she lives. The sooner that period can be ended, the better for the organism and the community at large."

Yallia had never spoken like this before, and she was sure Khadre had never heard such heresy from a Family member, least of all the Prime Original. Yallia had spent her life building up the belief that children represented all that was best in humanity and were the central focus of any civilization. As a result, Yallia knew, because she had founded a nation almost singlehandedly, she was in danger of being elevated to near-goddesshood herself. She was her own iconoclast.

"Come on, Yallia. We have an Assembly to run," Lawson said, drawing his arm around Yallia and leading her away.

Sirra watched them go and reached her hand out to Khadre, who took it and led the girl slowly back to the Family.

CHAPTER 18

"This Assembly has waited long enough. It is clear that the Domers have no compunctions about escalating a war—and make no mistake, this is a war we are in. Shall we wait for the Domes' flyers to descend upon our city and surrounding farmland? We have no defense against the Domers should they decide to attack; our only weapon is aggression itself. We must destroy the atmosphere stations now!" Yallia fairly shouted the last word.

The Assembly had spent the previous few hours listening to and discussing the reports from Khadre and Yallia about the attack on the *Beagle*. The general consensus was that the Dome had tapped into the skiff's locator beacon on its first trip and was waiting for the research vessel to return before destroying it. Yallia encouraged that view and took careful note of who had first advanced it—Franc Kahlman.

She stared out at them in the discussion pit below her. Presently, Kahlman stood up and waited to be recognized.

"Mr. Kahlman," Yallia said, yielding the floor.

Kahlman nodded to her. "Thank you. I, too, am shocked at the behavior of the Domers. But I am also astounded by the discovery Doctor Seelith has made. Under ordinary circumstances, I would suggest suspending all other projects and devoting all our resources to investigating this potentially life-changing discovery."

He paused gravely. "But these are not ordinary circumstances. I agree with Madame Prime. Attack." He said it with such suddenness and force that, although quiet, his words had perhaps more effect than Yallia's near-scream.

Yallia listened impassively, her face blank. Kahlman returned her level gaze with one of his own. "Any other discussion?" she asked the multitude. In the crowd, she could see Lawson fidgeting in his chair, but he did not stand.

"Then I shall call the vote. All in favor of—"

"Madame Prime!" Lawson called out. Yallia could hear the anguish in his voice. She turned and looked at him expectantly. He said, in a strangled voice, "I request a short recess before the vote is taken."

Yallia lowered her eyes to find Kahlman shaking his head slightly. "Irregular procedure, Madame Prime," he muttered.

Yallia was aware that Lawson's suggestion was out of order, but she was inclined to follow it. She needed to speak with him. "So ordered. Fifteen minutes." She stepped down from the speaker's rostrum and intercepted Lawson, who was moving hastily in her direction.

He approached her, his face uncomfortably close to hers, and whispered, "I've got to talk to you. Now."

"Yes. Outside," she added. The two left the Session chamber. Yallia thought she saw Kahlman eyeing them suspiciously as they left, but she did not dare turn around to confirm her fears.

Once outside the chamber in the entrance hall, Lawson looked around and dismissed the page at the door. When the page had left, Lawson seized Yallia roughly by the shoulders and said, "Yallia, don't attack now."

She had expected this from him. She had made no secret of her intention to personally lead the charge on the terraforming stations—none of the Originals, including Kahlman, had voiced any objection. They knew her history with the Domes and dared not interfere.

"Law," she began softly, "you might think you have some special prerogative with me, since you are the only father to two of my children...."

His eyes widened and she nodded in confirmation, then continued. "...And, truthfully, you probably do. But not in this."

"Yallia, you don't understand. I...I know something. I've kept it secret for too long as it is because...." he didn't finish.

Yallia filled the silence. "There's a spy among us," she said, and grinned as Lawson's eyes widened. "And I know who it is."

"How long have you known?"

"Not long. Since the attack on the *Beagle*."

Lawson didn't answer immediately. He studied her face for a long moment before muttering, "What are you going to do?"

"Nothing, now. Franc is in the Assembly room—he's not going anywhere."

"Kahlman?" Lawson spluttered.

"Of course. Who did you think it was?"

"I...." Again, Lawson didn't answer but instead lowered his eyes. He was wrestling with something—that much was obvious. Yallia decided to soothe his inner turmoil.

"It's all right, Law. I know you feel responsible for Viktur's death. You're thinking if you had told me of your suspicions before the trip, he would be alive now. But don't you see, we needed this to happen."

He looked up suddenly and began to speak, but Yallia stopped him. "I am sorry Viktur is dead, but his death will mean action. It will not have been in vain. We'll smash the terraforming stations inside of thirteen hours, before the Domers know what's hitting them."

Lawson continued looking at her. When he spoke, it was a husky whisper. "You are an amazing woman, Yallia. I wish...." He fumbled for words. "I wish I could be like you."

"Don't," she said. "You are like me." And she leaned in and kissed him.

When they parted some seconds later, she spoke fondly. "We need to go back in now. The vote will be unanimous. Afterward, I'll put Kahlman in isolation where he won't be able to report back on our decision. When the attack is over, the Assembly will decide what to do with the traitor." She started back in, but Lawson remained in the hall. "Coming?"

"I just—in a minute. There's a lot I have to adjust to."

"All right," she said, then entered the Assembly room.

The vote was, indeed, unanimous. Yallia put herself in the attack group, which included a high number of Originals. Evidently hers was not the only score to settle with the Domers, she thought. Volunteer soldiers from the ranks of the Family had been drawn up some time ago, and the armed forces organization table had been prepared. Yallia resisted the urge to displace one of the tactical group leaders—her strength was strategy, not tactics. During the Session, Yallia saw Lawson's expression remain pained, especially when she placed herself on the assault team, but he did not speak out against her. Other Originals seemed to be content to let Lawson's silence speak for them, and the Session continued smoothly. When all had been prepared, Yallia adjourned the meeting and called Kahlman over.

"Franc, I need to see you. We'll talk at our house," she said. Together, they walked back to the farm. At some point along the way, two young members of the Family police force fell in behind them. Yallia noticed them but made no comment. Lawson walked behind them. Yallia shrugged mentally. Lawson must have alerted the police during his time in the hallway. No matter.

When they entered the farm, Yallia took Kahlman to the meeting room. Lawson and the two police officers started to follow, but Yallia waved them off. "I'll meet with Franc for a moment in private, first," she said. Lawson started to object, but Yallia cut him off. "I'll be fine, Law. Just a few minutes." She closed the door and turned to Kahlman. He had seated himself in one of the conference chairs and looked at her with an expression of mild surprise.

"How may I serve you, Madame Prime?"

Yallia took a deep breath. She was not sure how he would react and found herself glad the police officers were outside.

Yallia came out of the meeting room a few minutes later and closed the door behind her. She turned to the burly officers and said, "I need Mr. Kahlman to stay inside until I return. If I do not return, Mr. Lawson has authority."

The police officers looked at each other nervously. These were obviously Family members who had only recently been appointed—Lawson must have deputized them only a few hours ago. Yallia continued. "He won't give you any trouble, but he must not be allowed to leave this room. No one is to enter until I come back."

One of the officers said stiffly, "Yes, ma'am." Then he added, "Good luck, ma'am."

"Thank you." Yallia turned to Lawson. "You are not going with us on the mission." She ignored his raised eyebrows. "I need you to stay here and lead the Family if I am killed. You must hold elections for a new Prime. One thing I ask—do not take any action against Kahlman until I come back. Leave him to me."

Lawson nodded but did not look at her. Yallia started to reach out to touch him again, but drew back. "I'll be back, Law. Go and help assemble the troops, please. I want to attack tonight."

"What are you going to do?" Lawson asked.

"I need to talk to Sirra before I go."

Lawson started back towards the city, where even now the first volunteers were reporting in for the raid.

Yallia watched him go, then brushed past the two sentries at the door of the meeting room on her way upstairs to Sirra's room.

Sirra and Emme were inside. "Grandonly!" Sirra said and rushed her. Sirra hugged her tight around the legs while Yallia patted her back.

Yallia looked at Emme. "Where is everyone?"

"Some are still here, but most are back at their own farms. We all heard the announcement from the Originals' Council. Lots of your children and onlies are volunteering."

"But not you," Yallia said, her voice neutral.

"No." She stared at Yallia for a moment, then added, "Someone needs to stay behind to help raise the children."

"The raid will not take longer than a few hours, Emme."

"Many of you will be killed," Emme said. Yallia felt Sirra let go of her legs.

She looked down at Sirra and said, "No, we won't, Sirra. That's what I came to tell you."

"You're going to die?" Sirra asked, her eyes moist.

"No. I can't tell you why, but Grandonly has fixed things. None of us will die."

"Don't tell her that," Emme said angrily. "You've already shown her death by violence—why hide it from her now?"

Yallia felt the sting of her words but did not dispute them. She did not feel like arguing the point that she was not responsible for the Dome's attack on the skiff. "Emme, listen. This isn't just an onlymother's soothing words. I have fixed things."

"How?"

Yallia sighed. "I can't tell you. But we will all be back. I promise."

Emme looked at her onlymother and thought, not for the first time, how different they were. Genetically identical, of course, but with different experiences. "Yallia, you don't have to do this."

"Don't start that. The Family is under attack. We—"

"I mean *you*. You personally."

Yallia did not answer.

"You're not a soldier."

"None of us are."

"But you are the leader of the Family."

"All the more reason I should be in the attacking force."

Sirra spoke up suddenly. "Grandonly, don't go."

Yallia stroked her hair. "I have to."

Emme exploded. "You won't prove anything! You can destroy all the Dome installations you want, and it won't change what happened to you!"

Yallia was spared an answer by Sirra's gentle question. "What happened to you, Grandonly?"

At that moment, despite the fresh memory of Viktur's death, despite the fear that her Grandonly would die in some unknown fashion, Sirra sought to relieve whatever pain her Grandonly felt, even if she could not understand it.

"Something happened a long time ago. When I was a girl, like you."

"You are a girl like me."

Yallia smiled. "A little girl."

"What was it?"

Yallia paused to think away some of her emotion. "My mother sent me away."

"Why?"

"I don't really know. She thought she was doing something important."

"I love you, Grandonly. I don't want you to go away." Sirra hugged her again, then added, "Did your mommy send you out of the Domes?"

"Yes."

"Do you want to go back there?"

"No, of course not," Yallia said, thinking that Sirra had asked a question far more complex than she realized.

To her shock, Sirra said, "I think we should live with the Dome people."

"What?" Yallia said, taking the girl's arms from her legs and squatting down next to her.

"We should live together. They should come out or we should go in. I don't know why we live apart."

"We can't, dear."

"Why not?"

Yallia hesitated and looked at Emme. Emme stared back at her, faintly challenging.

Sirra continued. "We could live with the fishes, too."

"The fishes?"

"Yes. I think...I think that would be a good idea." Sirra said. As she spoke, her eyes unfocused slightly and she trailed off.

Yallia looked at her for a moment, then stood up. "I have to go. But I will be back soon. Take care." She hesitated, then approached her onlydaughter. The two embraced for a long moment.

"Come back," Emme whispered. "For her."

Yallia left the farm to join the raiding party.

Hours later, Lawson, Yallia, and some of the other Originals had marshaled the troops into their three sections of sixty each. None wore uniforms, although Yallia saw occasional colorful armbands signifying rank on some of the soldiers. Each section was in ragged ranks, casually policed by a blue-arm-banded soldier. Six flatbed halftracks sat nearby, their solar collectors folded against their sides. It was already dusk—the yellow-green sunset cast a mustard-emerald pallor over the scene.

"Everything is ready, Madame Prime," Lawson said. "Section commanders have all reported in. The transports are in operational order, and all weapons are prepared. Uh...." He searched the assembled force for more to report on, but Yallia stopped him.

"Good. I'm sure the section commanders have everything under control. Which section am I in?"

Lawson pointed, and Yallia squeezed his arm before trotting off to join her group. As she settled in the ranks, she felt a wave of relief settle over her. Here, she was just another soldier—she had, for the moment, no responsibilities. She looked forward to the next few hours as the section made its way towards its target under someone else's command. There would be much for her to do soon, but just now, she relaxed.

"Section Two!" she heard her section commander bawl, "Board your transports!" The men and woman scrambled onto the halftracks designated Section Two. In a few minutes, all the troops had boarded their transports, most of them sitting in the open bed in the backs. The electric engines started up with an almost inaudible hum, and they were off.

Yallia did not look at Lawson as her transport rumbled by. She could not continue her façade any longer.

The transports covered distance steadily, losing little speed over rough terrain. Yallia did not speak to the other soldiers. There was an invisible sphere around her into which they would not enter, and none of them initiated conversation with her. Their own conversations were mostly speculations about the attack on the skiff and what the Domers would do as a reaction to the current raid.

"They'll have to surrender," one of the soldiers was saying in response to his companion's opinion. "With the atmosphere project disrupted, they'll realize that they haven't a chance to live here."

"You're wrong," his fellow soldier said, her voice a rich contralto. "They'll try and attack our city with their flyers. Anyway, there are plenty of Dome installations around the globe—destroying one won't disrupt the atmosphere project enough to—"

"Sure it will!"

"Look, you domed moron, do know how many years this project is gonna take if we were to let it happen? About sixty more years," she said, smugly answering her own question. "We have to get them all before the Domers will even think about negotiating terms."

"You're full of it. You think to Domers have the stomach for a fight? They can't even breathe out here."

"That's why they'll send their flyers. And who knows what else they've got."

The male soldier grunted. "They haven't got nothing. They barely have an army, I'll bet. This will be as easy as salt," he said, and settled back in his seat, putting his hands behind his head with an air of finality.

His female debate partner looked at him for a moment, then shook her head. Her eye caught Yallia's and she seemed about to ask something but did not.

Yallia prompted her. "You have a comment, soldier?"

The woman's tongue darted out for a second and touched her upper lip, then withdrew. She said, "Well, yeah. But I don't mean anything by it, ma'am."

"Go ahead."

"Well," she paused, then blurted, "don't you think we should have left some troops behind? In case the Domers attack?"

"They won't."

The woman chafed. "Uh, no offense, ma'am, but how do you know that? I mean, we'll be way out at one of the terraforming installations. If they've got their flyers and whatever else at the Domes, we won't be able to get back in time to defend the city."

"True, but we won't be at the terraforming installation."

Yallia saw those nearby soldiers who heard the comment turn to look at her in surprise. Yallia did not give them time to ask what she meant, but instead excused herself and made her way towards the control cab of her transport. She stopped outside the window and knocked.

The relief driver looked behind him in annoyance. When he recognized the face behind the glass, he fumbled to open the window. "Yes, Madame Prime?"

"I need to speak to the section commander."

The relief driver blinked, then reached for the transmitter on the control panel. "Section Two lead transport, this is Transport Two-Two."

"Two-One here."

The relief driver glanced nervously at Yallia, and said, "Uh, I need Commander Didosken. Now."

There was a pause and Didosken's voice came over the speaker. "Didosken here."

The relief driver handed the transmitter to Yallia through the cab window. Yallia had to shout to make herself heard over the wind. "This is Prime Original Yallia. Commander, we have a change in battle plans. All transports will redirect towards Valhalla Dome."

"Madame Prime? Did I hear you correctly? You are changing targets?" Didosken asked.

"You heard correctly, Commander. Issue what orders you need to, but we are attacking the Dome itself. But, Commander?" She paused for emphasis. "You are not, under any circumstances, to contact the Family to inform them of the change. I repeat: do *not* tell the Family of the change."

There was a considerable pause from the other end. Yallia sighed. She did not want to have to get nasty with this man, but it might be necessary if he balked at the change in order. Yallia knew she was trying to use the very idolatry she claimed to reject as leverage, but at the moment, she felt it necessary.

Didosken came back on. His voice sounded distant. "Orders understood, Madame Prime. I'll devise a new battle plan and get back to you. Didosken out."

"No need to get back to me. When you devise your battle plan, factor in minimal resistance from the Dome."

"Minimal resistance, Madame Prime? With all due respect, I think—"

"Dome troops are in the installations, Commander. The Domes themselves will be lightly defended, if at all."

"As you say, Madame Prime." He paused, then said, "New estimated travel time is two hours."

"Very good. Good-bye." Yallia handed the relief driver the transmitter. "Thanks," she said, and made her way back to her place in the bed of the halftrack. All around her she heard the news spreading, first as unbelieving questions, then as confirmed data.

She sat back down in her seat and let the conversations flow.

The female soldier that had spoken to her earlier finally addressed her directly. "Madame Prime?"

"Yes?"

"Are we...uh, did you...?"

"Don't worry, soldier. You didn't talk me into anything. This was always the plan."

"It was?"

"Yes. I just...kept it secret for a while." She sat back, mimicking the gesture the male soldier had made to end the conversation, and thought of Kahlman and Lawson back in the city.

The revised battle plan had been told to the troops only half an hour before the transports arrived at the Domes. Yallia listened with half an ear as the lieutenant on the transport detailed directions to the assembled troops. It wouldn't matter if the plan was well-conceived or not—the Domes would be caught completely unprepared. Almost two hundred Family soldiers massed outside with explosives would be enough to make the Domers listen. And if necessary, a demonstration of Family resolve would force the Domers to their knees.

Valhalla Dome was smaller than Yallia thought it would be. She knew its dimensions from careful study, but those numbers had not translated into the awesome presence she had expected. In fact, the Dome looked shabby and bleached, no doubt a by-product of years of exposure to the withering chlorine atmosphere.

Yallia heard the force commanders shouting instructions to their troops. She stared at the Dome for a moment longer, then strode towards one of the transports that had been unpacked and now served as a communications base for the attack.

Three young Family soldiers bent over communications gear, listening intently and cross-routing information to officers. Yallia waited a moment, then caught the eye of one of the operators. "Pardon me, young man, but I wonder if I might have one of your transmitters for a while."

The operator hesitated only a fraction of a second, then cleared his board and shoved the transmitter into Yallia's hands. "Yes, ma'am!"

"Thank you. Can you please connect me to the Dome frequency? I think some of them inside might be wondering what we want." She spoke sweetly, and the operator grinned.

"Yes, ma'am," he said and adjusted some controls, then nodded to her.

Yallia's tone hardened perceptibly. "This is Yallia, leader of the outcast group that is now outside your Valhalla Dome. I stand ready to dictate terms for your surrender."

The other two operators gasped while Yallia's technician made an incoherent but identifiable sound of exultation.

There was a considerable pause before the receiver crackled to life. "This is Commissar-General Nessel. You will disperse the mob outside our Dome immediately or we shall consider it an act of war and retaliate appropriately."

"I'm sorry, Nessel, have we not made ourselves clear? This is already an act of war. The last act. If you do not agree to an immediate and unconditional surrender, my soldiers will blow a hole in your Valhalla Dome and kill everyone inside. If you try to send soldiers or police out of the Dome in environment suits, rest assured that they will be taken care of by sharpshooters who are even now at every Dome exit. If you send one of your flying drones after us, I shall set off the explosives."

Yallia loved the irony. The explosives had not yet been set, and the "sharpshooters" were just Family men and woman armed with rifles. But the bluff was a good one precisely because it was so near the truth. Yallia knew that all available Dome personnel were at the nearest terraforming station waiting for an attack that would never come. She was taking a slight risk that the Dome did not have automatic defenses, but she was comforted by the presence of the spy amongst the Family. For the Domers to think they needed up-to-date intelligence meant they were not wholly certain of their own military superiority. Yallia was taking a chance, but it was a good one.

Again, a long pause preceded Nessel's reply. "Nothing will be gained, for either of us, through violence. We agree to negotiations on whatever point you wish, but we will not submit to—"

Yallia interrupted angrily, "No negotiations. We demand your surrender. Open the Dome to us peacefully and we shall take over your administration without bloodshed. Refuse us and we will blast our way in and take over in any case. You have three minutes to decide." She switched off the transmitter and tossed it back to the operator. "You might want to dial up the commanders, or do whatever it is you do to get in touch with them. Tell them what I've done."

She listened indifferently to the three operators relay the story quickly and efficiently to the various commanders of the ragtag army. Presently, one of the technicians turned to her and said, "Ma'am, incoming message from Valhalla."

Yallia nodded and Nessel's voice once again filled the cabin. "We agree to your demands. You may enter through the southwest lock. We will offer no resistance unless you violate your part of the bargain, in which case we will have to defend ourselves."

Despite herself, Yallia felt a grudging sense of admiration for her counterpart in the Dome. This Nessel knew she had been outmaneuvered but refused to give up completely. Yallia felt she was a woman with whom she could work.

"You have my word, Commissar-General: we will not initiate violence." Yallia looked at the radio operator. "Get the force commanders on this. I want to talk to all of them at the same time." When the technician indicated she was patched in, she issued instructions to the commanders. There was little debate—the commanders under her were in awe of her sudden, swift victory.

Scarcely an hour later, Yallia, accompanied by six of the Family's most able soldiers, stepped into the offices of Commissar-General Liduth Nessel.

Nessel had chosen to meet Yallia with four of her own guards, taken from Valhalla's police force, flanking her. Her office had not been designed for large meetings: the dozen people crowded the room and were forced to stand uncomfortably close to one another.

Yallia grinned as she saw Nessel and her men try not to grimace at the smell of chlorine. She knew that she and her entourage reeked of the stuff—it would give her even more of an edge in the conference. She decided to take the initiative and speak first.

"Commissar-General, I thank you for meeting with me in such a peaceful setting," she said, eyeing the Domer's guards pointedly. Yallia ignored Nessel's returning stare at the Family guards stationed around her and continued. "Our demands are simple. You will turn over control of the Domes to the Family."

"As exercised by you, no doubt?" said a scratchy voice that momentarily made Yallia's spine shiver. She knew that voice...as she turned to face the speaker, her eyes confirmed the knowledge of her ears.

Carll Tann emerged from a side room and made his way to the center of Nessel's office to stand face-to-face with Yallia. He gave no sign that he noticed her powerful odor. "I take it you speak for the entire Family, Yallia Verdafner?"

"I do not use that name," Yallia said, her voice shaky.

"As you wish," he said dismissively. He did not speak for a few moments, but he managed to convey disgust and contempt for Yallia, her guards, and the entire Family with a few facial gestures. He stopped his harrowing review and turned back to Yallia. "You want to control the Domes, do you?"

Yallia swallowed. She did not understand her own reactions. Why was this man affecting her so much? Could she still be frightened of him, after almost twenty-five years? He was a desiccated old man, on the brink of death—why was she so afraid of him? "You have perpetrated war on us, and we—"

"Ah. The classic rationalization of the barbarian: 'you started it!'" he said in a faint imitation of a child's indignant squeal. "And now, you come to take your vengeance on us, eh? You, Yallia Verdafner, will settle an old score even if it means you have to sacrifice your followers to do so."

"That's not it," she said, and cursed herself for her defensive attitude. She did not have to explain herself to this man! She said, stridently, "We are taking control of this planet. You have nothing to say about it."

"You would take control? You? You threatened to kill thousands of innocent people, children even, if we did not let you in. You come to us armed with explosives and demand to govern?"

Yallia was uncomfortably aware that her guards had shifted their positions somewhat—a bit of shuffling here, and nervous cough there—it all added up to uncertainty. She needed to recapture this conversation.

"You sent a robot flyer to kill four people. One of them was a child."

Tann did not flinch from the accusation. "True," he said softly, "and for that, we are truly sorry. We were investigating the scientific anomaly as you were. Our flyer reacted inappropriately. We understand that one of your Family members was killed as a result. You have the Dome's complete apology." He paused to let the words sink in. "Now," he said, his voice firm once more, "will you agree to negotiations? You must have grievances to come her so forcefully. We will hear them."

Yallia ground her teeth. Here, now, at the very moment of her triumph, this man threatened to take it all away with sugared words. "We will not be deflected. You are willing to listen now, because you have no choice. As soon as we withdraw our forces, you will not listen. You will send troops to crush us. I have had a taste of your diplomacy before, Carll Tann. You will not fool me as you did my parents."

"Your parents were quite wise, Yallia. They made a sacrifice to preserve the entire colony. Here, in the Domes at least, they are revered as heroes. Will you make even the smallest gesture of goodwill towards your fellow humans in the Domes? Or will you kill as many as you have to in order to be heard? I am listening now—Commissar-General Nessel is listening now. What more do you want?"

Yallia stopped herself from answering. What did she want? Why had she come here? She realized that she had wanted, like all children, to come home again. She had done so—was she not back inside the Domes?—but she could never turn the clock back. There was no going backwards. Only forwards.

At that instant of realization, she suddenly understood to whom this planet truly belonged. An image of Sirra, sitting quietly in the makeshift raft, looking down at the sea-creatures below, floated in her mind.

"I want the terraforming project abandoned." Yallia said.

Tann smiled. He had obviously been expecting that answer. "Madam Verdafner, surely you see the benefits of the project. You and your kind can survive quite comfortably in an atmosphere devoid of chlorine. We cannot. Would you refuse your fellow humans, who, I might add, outnumber you ten to one, access to this world on a footing equal to your own? The future of the colony depends on the terraforming project."

"No, Tann. You've got it wrong. You've been thinking of the colony as the 'pure' humans in the Domes. Can't you see that the Family is the colony? You Domers can create chlorine-adapted people at will instead of changing the planet to suit your needs."

"And what of those hundred thousand people who will never be chlorine-breathers?"

"The Domes will support them for the rest of their lives. But the future belongs to us."

Tann shook his head sadly. "Yallia, the tragedy here is that I think you truly believe what you are saying." He sighed and suddenly seemed very old. "I had not wanted to reveal this next datum, for fear of being accused of bribery, but I can see I must." He looked at the entire Family assemblage and said, "Our scientists have developed a way to reverse your mutation. We stand ready to accept you all back into the Domes. All will be forgiven."

CHAPTER 19

Yallia stared at Tann for a long moment. True or not, the statement was a master stroke. She felt something within her leap in anticipation of a grand welcome back to a mystical "home" even as the rational part of her fought for control. Images of a joyous home life, her parents, magically young again, and friends laughing with her at a party crowded out her inner protests. Tann had managed to tap into a deep desire she had not even realized she possessed.

She suspected the six guards, none of whom were Originals, did not share her feelings—having been born outside, they would not see Tann's offer as a homecoming. Tann had managed to offer a bribe that would be tantalizing to Family leadership, but not the majority of the outsiders. If even a fraction of the Originals accepted the offer, the Family would never be the same. Those who stayed would forever question their decision and would spend their remaining days looking up at the Dome, wondering if they could go back. Yallia knew in that moment that this was precisely what she had been doing for her twenty-four year exile. Her emotions boiled away at the realization and what remained was the hard residue of hatred for Carll Tann—but not for the man of twenty-four years ago; for the man before her now who threatened to take away what he had inadvertently given her.

She found her voice. "All will be forgiven, you say. You will forgive us, the outcasts, the exiles, their crimes?" Yallia's eyes bored into Tann's. "What crimes are we guilty of? *You* cast us out, *you* drove us from our homes, and *you* attacked and killed Viktur Ljarbazz." As she said the name, the thought of the sea-creatures and Sirra's affection for them reentered her mind. She tried to maintain her focus, but the image of the little girl talking to the sea-creatures persisted.

"Come back to us," Tann was saying. His voice was almost hypnotic.

Yallia saw herself suddenly on a precipice. She imagined that before her was the sea, crashing violently against rocks below her. Behind her, she knew, was safety and comfort. She could step away from the edge and rejoin her fellows on the solid ground at any time. But to go backwards, she knew, meant the future would be forever closed to humanity. Safety and order was stultifying.

In her mind's eye, she leapt off the precipice into the sea.

Carll Tann's eyes widened almost imperceptibly as he saw Yallia's face grow hard again. In that moment, both Yallia and Tann knew that he had lost her. And the war.

"I will grant permission for anyone who wishes to return to the Domes for your...treatment," Yallia said. "Don't expect many customers, Tann." She smiled wolfishly. "Furthermore, Family policy is unchanged— we will accept any of your children you care to send us. We will integrate them into our culture—"

"You will integrate them? Why should Domers have to integrate into anything?"

"Integration is a mutual process, Tann. Both sides adapt," Yallia said, then added. "But the terraforming project is finished."

Tann was beaten, but he stubbornly refused to admit defeat. "And how will you stop the project?" His voice was no longer silky. "You discovered our agent among you, obviously, and used him against us. But because of that agent, we took precautions to protect our terraforming installations. They are well defended. Your motley band of so-called soldiers would suffer very heavy casualties should you attempt an attack."

"All of them?" Yallia sneered. There were thousands of the installations churning out gengineered microorganisms every day. Tann could not possibly defend all of them, or even most of them. That wasn't the point, however. "I have no intention of attacking the installations. Commissar-General Nessel will simply order them dismantled."

Before Nessel could answer, Tann said, "She will do nothing of the kind."

"Then I will detonate the explosives and kill all inside this Dome. All the Domers, that is."

There was a moment of shocked silence before Tann said, "You will not do that. Kill thousands of innocent people? Such an act of barbarism is beyond even you."

Yallia took a step closer to Tann and said quietly, dangerously, "Do not make the mistake of underestimating me, Tann. I am not my mother." She snorted. "You certainly remember my grandmother? Perhaps resolve skips a generation. I am prepared to kill thousands, hundreds of thousands, in order to safeguard the future of the Family."

"Do you hear this woman?" Tann almost shouted at the others in Nessel's office. "She is openly advocating terrorism and mass murder in the name of genealogy!"

"No less than what you have done, Tann," Yallia said, matching his shouts with near-whispers.

Tann swiveled his head to look at her with newfound awareness. "What I did I did for the future of humanity here."

"Segregation is never the answer. I offer you two choices: destruction at the hands of the Family, or unification."

Tann started at her. Yallia had never seen such hatred in another human being. She wondered which he hated more—the fact that he had lost, finally, after all these years, or that it was an outcast that had defeated him.

Or a Verdafner?

"I choose destruction," Tann growled.

Nessel interjected with such force as to make the rest of those present jump in surprise. "You do not speak for the Domes, Carll. We will agree to Yallia's demands, subject to negotiation of certain points."

Yallia ignored the last. Nessel could have her way in many things—Yallia could afford to be generous now. She kept her eyes on Tann.

"I understand, Commissar-General," Tann said. "I was speaking for myself only. I choose destruction. For myself."

Yallia felt no sense of loss as the old, old man hobbled out of the room, far more ancient a man now than when he had entered.

Nessel was droning something about sending an emissary to the Family for negotiations, but Yallia cut her off. "We will send someone here. In the meantime, I suggest you arrange for the surrender of your armed forces and make whatever administrative maneuvers you have to in order to turn the government over to the Family temporarily. I will send one of my best men here to take over."

Nessel looked at her inquiringly, and Yallia added, "I have...matters to attend to."

Yallia made quick arrangements with the most capable of the three force commanders to act as interim military governor until she sent the permanent man in his place. She left as many details to the force commander as possible and commandeered one of the transports for a trip back to the Family.

"I know why you did it," Yallia said to him before he could speak. They were alone in the Assembly room adjoining her farm. "And you still have the option to return. I made sure of that. The Domers will still...change you back, if you wish." She spoke calmly, not trusting herself to admit to emotion. She did not even know what emotion would win out—anger? Love? Disappointment?

He did not answer. Yallia felt anger winning out in her.

"In retrospect, I was a fool not to see it earlier. I had enough signs. All your suggestions and ideas, in Session and in private, pointed to it. I suppose I didn't want to believe. But the flyer attack was proof. That was Tann's mistake."

"It should have killed you."

"Yes, I suppose so. Still, it didn't." Yallia had ceased to wonder about that. The flyer had malfunctioned, and she knew why. She knew how the fishing boat had found them, as well. But none of that mattered now. She was alive; that was all that mattered.

"I'm glad it didn't."

Yallia looked at him. "Are you?" The comment did not really surprise her. She shrugged. "You cannot remain here. If you want to go back to the Domes, I will not stop you. If you want to just wander off into the hills, I won't stop you. I'll even give you some supplies."

"I want to...."

"What?"

"I want to see your child grow." He said it in a small voice, not looking at her.

"No." It was a flat denial from which there could be no appeal. "I must warn you—I will not allow you any contact with her."

"Her? I thought we...you were having a boy?"

"I changed my mind." Yallia paused to let the implications sink in, then continued on her original subject. "You will not be allowed back here for any reason. Kahlman will have full control of the Domes in every other way, but I will not allow him to release you back to us." She paused. "And I will never tell the child of her father." She sighed and stepped closer to him. Her voice became soft, almost kind. "Despite appearances, I am not angry at you, Lawson. You are just…weak."

"I told you I wanted to be more like you."

"And I said you were like me. You still are, Lawson. We are all alike, Domers and Family, shippie and argie. I am not going to deny you existence, but I will deny you association with us."

Lawson looked at her with longing. He made abortive movements with his hand, as if wanting to touch her but afraid of doing so. "I love you, Yallia."

"I know."

Lawson stared at her for a moment longer, but she did not speak. He started to stand up and head for the door where Kahlman's guards were waiting. "I am curious, Yallia, about one thing. Why are you keeping the baby?"

"The baby has done nothing, Lawson. As I said, I am not denying you existence. You will live on through your child. Perhaps, one day, she will help to erase your sin. She will be your salvation." She paused, then looked up at the ceiling, looking through it to another time, another place. "My mother told me once, years ago, about an encounter my grandmother had with a man who told her something that you need to hear. The man said that 'hell is a place where those who do nothing go.' You had an opportunity to redeem yourself, Lawson, but you chose to do nothing."

Lawson swallowed his answer and left the room.

Khadre knocked on the frame of Sirra's dormitory room and entered when the girl looked up. "Khadre!" Sirra shouted and rushed at the young scientist, hugging her tightly around the legs.

"Hello, little one." Khadre returned the hug, bending over somewhat awkwardly, then knelt down and grasped Sirra's arms. "How are you?" she said, looking into the girl's eyes.

"I'm all right, Khadre. How are you?" The girl returned the soul-searching gaze.

Khadre sighed. "I think I'll be all right, too. I just wanted to tell you something."

"What?"

"Viktur and I are going to have a baby."

Sirra's eyes widened. "Really? A girl or a boy?" She did not ask how.

"I thought I'd have a boy. For him."

Sirra nodded. "Yes. A boy will be good."

The two did not speak for a few seconds, then Sirra said, "I was thinking about the boat. And the fish. I want to go back there."

"We will, Sirra. We still have a lot to learn from the sea-creatures."

"Khadre?"

"Yes?"

"Shouldn't they have a name?"

"I guess so. Do you want to name them?"

"Uh, well, I thought that Viktur should get to name them. He found them, didn't he?"

Khadre nodded. She felt emotion welling inside her and did not want to speak.

"So I think we should call them 'Vikturs' or something. Or maybe 'Vicks.'"

Khadre smiled. "How about V-i-x?"

Sirra nodded slowly. "Yes. Vix. I think he would have liked that."

Khadre got up from the ground and rubbed her knees. "Well, I have to go. But I promise I will come back."

"Will you take me with you when you go back to see the vix?"

"I promise."

Sirra hugged her again for a long time.

"She wants to go with me on the next expedition," Khadre said to Yallia as they sat over strong tea in the Assembly room.

Yallia nodded. "I see no harm in that."

Khadre sipped her drink and added more salgar. "Madame Prime," she began carefully, "I have been thinking about what happened out there."

"Yes?"

"The rescue. The flyer malfunction."

"Don't you believe in luck, Khadre?" Yallia said with a smile.

Khadre smiled back. "No, ma'am. Not when I can explain it away in other ways. I have been thinking that both events are connected."

"How so? And stop calling me 'ma'am.'"

Khadre blushed. "Sorry. Well, first I thought the vix were doing something with their sonar, but—"

"Vix?"

Khadre looked up from her cup sheepishly. "Oh, uh, that's a name Sirra thought up for the sea-creatures. Their official name in the taxonomy is "Neocetacean-octopii Ljarbazzii."

"Vix is better," Yallia said.

"I agree. I was thinking they had something to do with it, but...."

"What?"

"Well, there's no way I can imagine their sonar reaching far enough to be heard by the harbormaster's station. And even if somehow they could focus their sonar to reach such distances, how could Del have interpreted the message? So I don't see how it could have been the vix."

"No. It wasn't."

Khadre looked up sharply. "You have an idea?"

Yallia sighed quickly. "Khadre, I hesitate to tell you this, because I am frankly not sure what you youngsters will do with the knowledge."

Khadre looked at her in astonishment but did not interrupt.

"You have heard the stories, I'm sure, but how many of you believe them?"

"Stories?"

Yallia looked up briefly, then focused her eyes back on Khadre. "You know, of course, that the first voyage launched to this planet was the second to get here. The *Odyssey* arrived here about thirty-five, thirty-six years ago, long after the *Argo* had already colonized. The *Argo* had been dismantled to provide raw materials for the colony. When the *Odyssey* arrived, it was not needed any longer. It was stripped, but a section of it was left in orbit."

Khadre nodded. "Of course I've heard that. So? It's just an empty hulk up there, right?"

Yallia cursed under her breath. She herself had long ago emphasized to the other Originals that the history of the Family began with their exile from the Domes, and therefore all other history need not be taught or studied. There had been no formal ban on study, but most of the Family chose not to examine the past too closely. History had turned to legend and was already on its way toward myth. Yallia had often felt pangs of regret at the loss, but she saw too much danger in a connection to a recent past. When the crisis was past, she had often told herself, historians could once again study what they wished.

Yallia answered Khadre's question with a sigh. "No. It's still staffed. My grandmother visited it about twenty-four years ago. I think they are still watching us."

Khadre said slowly, "They sent the message to Del?"

"And they disrupted the flyer."

"Why?"

Yallia looked up again. "I think they are trying to...atone for something they did, or didn't do, in the far past."

Khadre didn't answer, but looked upwards.

* * *

Kuarta and Dolen received their daughter in strikingly different ways. Yallia smiled indulgently at her father and hugged him warmly. The two looked at each other for a while, saying nothing, before Yallia whispered something to him. He nodded, looked at his wife, and left the two women alone.

"I told him I'd see him later," Yallia said, preempting Kuarta's question.

"But you have to unload some of your venom on me first," Kuarta said.

Yallia didn't rise to the bait.

"I heard about your...takeover," Kuarta said carefully. She had thought to use the word 'rebellion' but instead chose a word that did not have familial implications.

"Of course. Life won't really change much for a while in the Domes," Yallia said. "Franc Kahlman will make a fine administrator."

"But life will change."

Yallia shrugged. "Eventually. There will be many more children of shippies and argies. We'll take any of them you want to send."

"I'm surprised."

"Why?"

Kuarta said icily, "You've had such anger at me for doing the same thing. Why would you endorse it now?"

"Kuarta, do you really think it's the same? You abandoned me twenty-four years ago. Now, we're a thriving community. Children sent to us will be cared for, nurtured. Loved." This last word she said with bitter emphasis.

"You think I didn't love you?"

Yallia looked away, but said, "Your actions answered that."

"You think because I sent you away I didn't love you." Kuarta waited for a response, but when none came, she continued. "If I had tried to hold you with me, Tann would have killed hundreds. Thousands. And he still would have taken you."

"I would have appreciated the fight."

Kuarta stared at her. "Even though the result would have been the same? You still would have been exiled, you still would—"

"But you would have fought!" Yallia shouted. "Don't you see, Mother? I don't want logic; I didn't want it then. I know, rationally, that you did the only thing you could have done. But since when is love rational?"

Kuarta listened and answered, quietly, "You never met Renold Halfner."

It took Yallia a moment to place the name. "My grandfather? Of course not."

"He could have answered that question."

"That's convenient."

Kuarta shot an angry glare at her daughter. "He was my father, Yallia. I hardly knew him, but Jene did. She told me about him. He was the most rational person she knew, and yet he loved me and loved Jene. To him, love was the most rational emotion, if there is such a thing, the human mind was capable of."

"You're hiding behind a dead man," Yallia said, but there was uncertainty in her voice.

"I'm answering your question. You asked 'since when is love rational?' I'm telling you that it always is. Dolen, your kind, loving father, never saw that, either. He would have kept you and fought off Tann's men on his own if I hadn't been there. And when I acted, he knew I was right."

Yallia's voice was considerably shakier as she said, "It doesn't matter. You still did it. You can't argue me out of my...."

"Your what? Hate?" Kuarta searched her daughter's face—a face she did not know well enough to read. "Why are you still holding on to it?"

"You did not fight for me."

"Would you have fought for your Family? The explosives you planted, would you have detonated them if Nessel hadn't surrendered?"

Yallia looked at her with narrowed eyes. "How do you know—"

"Most of the Domers know. Things leak out, Yallia." She returned to the question. "Would you have killed to save your Family?"

Yallia looked away again. She had thought about that as much as her tortured mind would allow in the past few hours. She always kept coming back to the same answer. "No." She looked up at her mother. "But I tried. I was willing to bluff him."

"You had an army. I had only your father, your grandmother, and a few unorganized supporters outside. I had nothing to bluff with."

Yallia felt her emotions weakening. She wanted, desperately wanted, to hate her mother. It would solve so many problems. Her feeling of injustice would have more than one target. Hating Carll Tann was easy and therefore offered no solace. She had more hate than she could comfortably place on one man. If she released her mother, her hate would have nowhere to go. She did not wish to believe the universe was inherently unjust.

Realization crept slowly upon Yallia. Rationality was taking over—the natural enemy of hatred.

"Mother, I—"

"You don't have to say it, Yallia," Kuarta started to gather her up in her arms, but Yallia pushed her away.

"I still hate you. But...." She looked into her mother's eyes. "I know it will not always be that way. You'll have to give me some time."

Kuarta put her arms back in her lap. "I think I can do that."

The two looked at each other for a long time as the green mist rolled past the Dome.

BOOK FOUR
HOME

CHAPTER
20

She was glad no one could read her mind.

It would not do to have anyone else, human or otherwise, know that at times, she thought of the vix as her children.

Sirra reluctantly answered the summons that had been buzzing in her headphone for nearly a minute. She knew what the message would be.

"Yes?" she said, disingenuously.

"Sirra, we read your life support has redlined. You need to return to base immediately." Fozzoli's voice was balanced on the razor edge between respect and demand.

"Oh, really? Are you sure you're not reading a malfunction, Foz?"

"Domeit, Sirra, you've been out for almost six hours!"

"I am fully aware of my suit's capabilities, Foz. There's a forty-minute grace period built into these things."

"It'll take you forty minutes to get back, plus another ninety seconds to flush the lock, plus—"

"All *right*, Foz. I'll come back. Sirra out." She switched off, not really angry at Fozzoli; he was a capable man. She looked at the vix nearest her and reached out to touch him. He was a young male whom Sirra had privately dubbed Vogel, after an ancient Ship philosopher who had proved empirically that his "world" was on a journey. Sirra could feel the vix even through her armored sense-glove: he was warm and smooth. She found she could always communicate more clearly if she was touching them.

"*I have to go now. I will return,*" she said. She tapped the appropriate keys on her vixvox to amplify her message, though she suspected that Vogel could understand her thoughts almost as well as he understood the high-frequency squeals coming out of the transmitter on her shoulder.

"*Thank you for your presence.*" She felt the answer come back. The vix' speech was just outside normal human hearing range, but Sirra could feel the waves deep inside her head. She had "listened" to their speech for the past thirty-five years, ever since her first encounter with them after that awful flyer attack—she knew what the native creatures were saying. Others used her translation device exclusively. Sirra used it in tandem with her mind and its sense of understanding for the sea creatures.

"I will think about what you said, Speaker-From-Above." Sirra recognized the name Vogel had given her recently. She approved; it was at least secular, or rather less overtly religious, than some of the other names she had heard.

Vogel swam away, back to his settlement. Sirra knew he had taken a considerable risk in coming this far, but he was an adventuresome type and seemed to be able to tolerate separation from the oxygen vent for longer periods than his tribal partners.

Sirra watched him go, then set her buoyancy control to maximum and swam upwards to the lab with a certain degree of alacrity. Foz was right—she had redlined some time ago and would now have to hustle into the lock. Thirty-eight and one-half-minutes later, she entered it and started the cycle. During the ninety-second cycle, her helmet computer warned her, "Life support has run out. Return to surface immediately." The warning continued—there was no way to shut it off. Sirra cursed softly to herself. The grace period had just begun; she could have stayed out with Vogel for at least thirty more minutes. The lock completed its cycle and Sirra started to climb out, only slightly encumbered by her deep-suit.

The laboratory was essentially a floating platform, maintaining its position over the vix settlement some four thousand meters below. It was constructed like a daisy, with a large central lab and several pods (power, machine shop, two subsidiary labs, and three habitation pods) surrounding it. The lab was home to seventeen researchers who rotated in and out on a three-month schedule. Only five were present at any given time, not counting Sirra, who had the right to come and go as she pleased. It was her project, after all.

Sirra finished her ascent into the spacious main lab to find Abromo Fozzoli staring disapprovingly at her.

"You can't keep cutting it that close, Sirra. We've—"

"Here are your recordings, Foz," Sirra said, withdrawing a small data disk from her belt computer pouch and tossing it to him as he spoke. Fozzoli stopped midsentence to catch the disk.

"Anything good?" he asked, his expression changing instantly from angry concern to hopeful curiosity. Fozzoli was the only member of the research crew who was more committed to deciphering the vix' language than Sirra herself.

"I think so. Some stuff on philosophy this time. I managed to get Vogel to live up to his name."

Fozzoli had slipped the disk into its proper slot on the lab's main computer console and was downloading the information into the mainframe. "Oh? How so?"

"He started thinking—in the vaguest terms, of course—about proving his own existence."

Fozzoli looked at Sirra, his eyes widening. He whistled softly. "That's pretty deep stuff."

"Well, it wasn't all that deep. But at least he's starting to develop his rational mind."

"Anything more on their religion?"

Sirra sighed. "Not much. Oh, but he did use the name 'Speaker-From-Above' for me this time."

Fozzoli grunted. "Better than 'Divine Avatar.'"

Sirra grimaced. She had always hated that translation, but she knew it was correct. She had been called any number of permutations of that name: 'Voice-of-God,' 'Celestial Messenger,' even 'Most Holy Fish from the Silence,' although this last name had never been translated to her complete satisfaction.

Sirra watched as Fozzoli tapped the holographic keys and integrated her recorder's data into his already considerable database. He frowned vaguely while she watched.

"What's wrong?" Sirra asked.

Fozzoli jumped in his chair, and Sirra laughed. "Sorry, Foz, I didn't mean to scare you."

"No, that's okay." His voice was distracted, distant.

"But what is it?"

Fozzoli turned in his seat and looked off into a corner of the lab. "These discussions you have with the vix...." Fozzoli stopped. Sirra let him finish at his own pace. For a linguist, she noted with irony, he was having difficulty expressing himself. Fozzoli took a deep breath and blurted, "I think I'm sometimes on entirely the wrong tack."

Sirra's gentle smile faded. "What do you mean?"

"Well...." Fozzoli punched up a display that hung before them in mid-air. "Look here. This is a listing of all the names given to you or any other researcher by the vix. I've indexed them by frequency. Not Hertz, but how often they are used."

Sirra studied the list. She saw no surprises on it—all the names were variations of some kind of God-representative, ranging from the mildly religious to the profoundly sacred. There were even examples of names that carried tabu within themselves: "(S)he-who-must-not-be-named," "(S)he-of-the-Unspeakable," and so on.

"We've been analyzing these names as if they contain semantic elements that relate to awe. Sort of a combination fear and respect," Fozzoli continued. He must have been aware that Sirra understood all of this without explanation—she waited patiently for him to get to his point. Fozzoli continued, "But when I have correlated the phonemes used to name the swimmers with phonemes in more secular constructions, they didn't match."

"Why not?"

"Here," Fozzoli said, and tapped in on his keyboard. Presently, a different screen hung in space before them. Fozzoli pointed to it. "This is a listing of the phonemes in religious and in secular constructions."

Sirra examined the table and frowned as well. "You've assigned most of them a fairly high negative index," she noted. "Are the other settlements the same?"

Fozzoli sighed mightily. "We've only really begun to get substantial readings on one other vent-settlement. Khadre's there now. The vix there have a different language."

"They do? I suppose that's to be expected. They have had no contact with one another. Could they have?" She asked the question half to herself, but Fozzoli answered.

"Not a chance. The nearest vent to this one is about eight hundred kilometers away. A vix would have to make a journey on low oxygen for at least five hundred of those klicks. And even then, he or she would still have to find the vent by chance. No. I'm certain—each vix settlement is isolated at its particular vent."

Sirra nodded. She had reached the same conclusion years ago herself, but Vogel's intrepid travels to the edges of the vix settlement had caused her to wonder. The volcanic fissures deep down in the ocean floor were easy enough to spot from the surface—the higher water temperature gave away a vent's presence on infrared scans. Somewhere deep in the trench that bisected the vix settlement like a river was the volcano, Sirra knew. And in its violent, superheated state, it was spewing forth high concentrations of elements from the rock it melted. One of those elements was oxygen. The concentration of oxygen was fifty to sixty times higher near the vent than it was in the open sea, and although the oxygen diffused quickly into the water as it ascended, vix settlements were still very oxygen-rich. The vix were only able to survive near vents where their gills could take in the oxygen they needed to fuel their highly demanding brains.

"So you only have this one settlement to draw language from?" Sirra said.

"Sort of. What little I'm getting from Khadre's settlement just confirms my findings here."

"Wait—you said the languages are completely different."

"That's another thing. Different, I said. Not completely different."

"Like dialects?"

"More than that. Rather like different languages with similar roots."

Sirra nodded slowly, then frowned. "But if these vix have no contact with each other, how can—?"

"That's a good question. What I suspect is happening is that I simply don't have enough data from Khadre's team. She doesn't publish much."

Sirra looked back at the display. "You said you think we're on a wrong tack."

Fozzoli turned back to the hologram. "That's right. You said the words are negative? Well, one of two things is going on. Either they are able through grammatical placement to alter the meanings of a huge number of their words for what they consider "holy," or we have grossly misanalysed their language."

Sirra scowled at him. "You mean to tell me that you think they are not in awe of us?"

"No, not at all."

"Then what?"

"I assigned a negative index to the terms I did despite your feelings. Could it be that…domeit, Sirra, couldn't you be wrong?"

Sirra stared at him for a full second, then threw her head back and laughed. "Foz, come on. I've been swimming with the vix for almost thirty years. I know them. I can understand their language almost better than our computers can. I'm the best expert on their language we have, and I've never felt or sensed anything but…well, love."

"What about fear?"

Sirra shrugged. "Sure. But that's understandable, right? I mean, we are coming from On High, literally, in a different form, and speaking to them. We appear from the void in which they cannot travel, visit them briefly, and are gone to our heavens. We've made miracles by curing their sick, increasing their crop production, and bringing peace to their world."

"I sometimes wonder if we should have left well enough alone," Fozzoli grumbled.

"Let's not get into that debate again," Sirra said. "We have improved their standard of living by a hundredfold in a single generation. How else could they see us but as angels?"

Fozzoli shook his head slowly. "I know all of that. But when they use the sounds for us in other contexts, there is a definite trend towards negativity. I can't explain it. Unless…."

"What?"

"Well, the terraforming project did quite a bit of damage to their environment. Not as much as it did to the land, but we are still seeing evidence of mass extinctions in just the past sixty years."

"How is it now?"

"Slowly returning to normal. We might be able to repopulate some of the extinctions if we can find organic material to clone from. But I wonder if the vix don't know what we did, or almost did, to them."

"Come *on*, Foz." Sirra laughed, but it sounded strangely hollow to her. "How could they conceive of such a thing? They don't even have an awareness of other vix, let alone the land, let alone the terraforming process. "

"But the language—"

"Foz, we're still learning the language. Unfortunately, there's no Rosetta Stone of the deep to help us. We'll just have to keep muddling through, making mistakes along the way, and gradually understanding the vix better. Meanwhile, I'm not worried. Besides, if they really did think we were hurting them and their planet, wouldn't they have attacked us by now?"

"That's what I'm afraid of," Fozzoli said, looking thoughtfully through the window into the unfathomable water beyond.

* * *

Kiv surveyed the latest reports from his representatives among the Tannites. How could such a small group—there couldn't have been more than five thousand of them, about one percent of the total population of Newerth—cause so much trouble? Their demands had not changed: a voice in the government, to be secured with formal appointment of one of their number to the Assembly. Kiv noted that his agent, a capable young man named Wollam Jaymoskim, did not foresee any great danger.

Jaymoskim operated in the open, his status as investigator fully known to the Tannites. The Kalhman Doctrine explicitly prohibited espionage. Kiv knew the reasons behind the twenty-year old edict, but it did make his job considerably more difficult. However capable Jaymoskin was, he could not possibly be privy to all the Tannite movements as long as his identity was fully known. Not for the first time, Kiv toyed with the notion of breaking the Kahlman Doctrine. After all, he reasoned, if his agents were successful, no one would know of the transgression. With a slight shake of his head a moment later he dislodged the thought.

Kiv put the report aside and watched a bright green finger of crepe paper flutter in the slight breeze from the ventilator. The paper was all that remained, physically, of the surprise birthday party his office staff had thrown him. He was thirty-six, and the "three dozen mark" still carried considerable cultural weight. He was an "elder statesman," as his coworkers had called him several times today.

The thoughts of his birthday led him to thoughts of his birth, and of his birthmother, and of his father. Khadre had told him of Viktur often enough, but she always seemed annoyed or disappointed at his anger at the Domers, as they had been called in her time, who had killed his father.

"Mother, why aren't you angry at them?" he had said the last time they had had this argument.

Because they don't exist anymore. There are no Domers."

"You know what I mean. And they do exist. Tannites still live in the Domes."

Khadre shrugged. "Not many of them anymore. And they only live in one Dome. The rest of them live among us."

"With implants. Or biogenetics." Kiv said it with considerable disgust.

Khadre shrugged again. "So? Are they less human because they were not born able to breathe the air?"

"Less human," Kiv repeated the phrase with derision. "That's what we were to them."

"You were never persecuted by them, Kiv. Don't assume the mantle of hatred like it's an inheritance." She reached out to touch his arm, but he withdrew it. Khadre's voice grew stern. "So you're saying we should return the favor, eh? The shoe is on the other foot? Should we do to them what they did to us? Treat them like animals, exiles?"

Kiv turned on her and fixed her with a steely glare. "They killed my father. Shot him down in cold blood because they wanted to provoke us."

"He wasn't your father then."

Kiv bristled. "Yes, he was. You just hadn't conceived me, that's all." The seeming paradox did not bother either of them. Kiv went on, "You could show respect for him."

"How? By hating Carll Tann? He's been dead for thirty-five years. He and I were only alive at the same time for a short while."

Kiv stared at his mother for a long moment. "Are you going to hide behind the conveniences of time?"

Khadre's patience had evidently run out. She almost shouted, "I'm not hiding, Kiv. You want me to hate a man who doesn't exist for killing a man who died before you were conceived!"

"I want you to respect my father. Carll Tann killed him. You knew Viktur was dead when you harvested his sperm and conceived me," Kiv had said, and mother and son had stared at each other over the sudden revelation of Kiv's true feelings.

Khadre and Kiv hadn't spoken to each other about anything even remotely related for the better part of a year. Her congratulatory birthday message (delivered by holo, as Khadre was still conducting her research two thousand kilometers away) had been loving, sweet, and superficial. Kiv had received it and had recorded a brief response in which he had mentioned coming out to see her if he could get away. He hadn't meant to try very hard. But the constant repetition of "elder statesman," however facetious, had made him feel just a bit more powerful.

Kiv stared at the crepe paper for a moment, then activated his adjutant. "Display schedule for next two days," he said. In the air before him hung a dizzying array of conferences, briefings, and reports in multicolored hues. None of them were urgent pink. Kiv smiled devilishly and said, "Reschedule all entries for today and tomorrow. Add new event: 'Visit mother.'"

The schedule changed appropriately, lines of text disappearing one by one as the computer placed them automatically in vacant slots in upcoming days. The men and women whom his choice affected would be informed of the changes and would have to adjust their schedules.

Kiv leaned back in his chair and sang softly, "Philosophers may sing of the troubles of a king, but the duties are delightful and the privileges great...."

* * *

Iede finished the Ritual of Contact and opened her eyes. The communications equipment lay in front of her, and, as always, she felt a slight distaste at the necessity of its existence. She should be able to make contact without such...devices, she thought. Her annoyance was almost immediately suppressed by doctrine: if Those Above wanted to make contact through the communications gear, then who was she to question Their motives?

She rose smoothly despite her thirty-five years and glided toward the machinery. Iede had not built the machine—such was far beyond her capabilities. It was enough that she knew how to use it. She was alone in the small chamber, of course—while it was not yet forbidden for others to enter, her parishioners had taken it upon themselves to restrict entry to herself alone. Those Above would not speak to any but Iede, and she felt pride, then shame at feeling pride, at the fact. She was their servant—she was not a God.

Iede touched the gleaming controls on the communications gear and drew a breath before speaking. "Those Above, Who watch over us with benign grace, I humbly beg audience with You."

An answer came through the speaker almost immediately. "Iede. Speak."

"Lords of the Above, I ask humbly for Your guidance. As You have guided me in the past and protected me from the beginning of my existence, I beg Your wisdom now." Iede paused, collected herself, and made her request. "I ask for an audience in Your august presence."

This time, there was hesitation. Iede was fully aware that the pantheon to which she prayed was not made up of a single God but a collection of personalities. She heard only one voice whenever she spoke to Those Above, but she had nevertheless deduced long ago that They were not a single mind.

"Why do you ask this?"

"I...My Lords, I do not feel...adequate to the tasks You have set me. I beg an audience so that I might learn Your will more directly."

"We have not set you any tasks, Iede."

Iede did not dare argue. Instead, she fought with herself to interpret this comment. Her understanding was, of course, imperfect compared with her gods': Those Above could not possibly be wrong, so it must have been her flawed understanding that caused the miscommunication.

"I beg forgiveness, Lords of the Above. I am but a planet-bound creature. I do not always understand Your words. Did You not command me to spread Your word among my people?"

Again, hesitation from the communications gear. Iede watched nervously—had she angered Them?

"We have been watching you and your people, Iede. For a long time. Longer than you realize. Sometimes, it is a frustrating existence."

Iede did not comment, but amazement flashed through her brain. Those Above could feel frustration? Why?

The voice continued. "Perhaps you should come see us. It will require some...adaptations, both for you and for us. But we can arrange it."

Iede fought to control her elation. "Lords Above, I thank You for Your grace. I do not deserve the honor You bestow upon me, Your most vile servant."

"That is something we must discuss. In order to minimize the...disruption to your people your visit would inevitably cause, we caution you to tell no one in advance of your departure."

Iede felt a fleeting pang of regret that she could not tell her parish of her assumption to the Above Place, but it was overridden instantly by joy and awe. She would stand in the presence of the Lords!

"We will send a...vehicle to bring you to us. Here is the location and time," the voice said, and Iede saw the specifics in an image on the communications gear.

"I thank you, Lords."

"Prepare yourself, Iede. You have only the faintest glimmer of an idea what you will experience here."

"I shall, My Lords."

"Ship out," the voice said, and the communications gear went dead.

And Iede, daughter of the Prime Original and he whom the Family had called Desdichado—the disinherited one—turned her eyes reverentially ceilingward.

CHAPTER
21

Sirra crept through the dark corridor between her quarters and the dive pool, feeling like a little girl again. For a moment, she was in the past, eavesdropping on her mother and the Session of Originals those thirty-five years ago. She could see Franc Kahlman's startled look as he had turned to face her. She smiled at the memory. Then she thought of Yallia.

That thought was enough to sober her. Time had dulled the severity of the pain she felt recalling her mother's death three years ago, but the pain was there nevertheless. The whole Family had mourned for her, but Sirra felt the loss especially.

She shrugged it off and continued her mission. The dive pool was just beyond the observation bubble in the main lab. Sirra entered the lab and looked around. Faint, blue-green light from the few active control panels shed enough of a glow for her to make out the dim outlines of dive equipment. She half-felt her way towards the suit rack and stopped when her hand touched the sleeve of her still-damp gear.

Sirra frowned. Familiar as she was with diving, she was not completely confident in her ability to dress for the water in darkness. After only a moment's hesitation, she decided to risk turning on the lights. The lab complex was understaffed right now with only six scientists, not including Sirra herself, in it.

Sirra whispered, "Lights on." Nothing happened. She tried again in a stage whisper, but the room computer was either asleep or could not hear her. She rolled her eyes and took a breath preparatory to speaking normally.

"Lights on." The voice was not hers. Sirra jumped, then squinted as the dive room lit up to reveal Fozzoli, clad in only a one-piece sleeper, standing near the dive room entrance.

"Hi, Foz," Sirra said.

"Yeah."

"I was going for a quick swim."

"Uh-huh."

"Since you're here, you can help me with the check." This, with as much cheer as she could muster. Sirra looked at him expectantly.

Fozzoli wiped his face with one hand, starting at his forehead and scraping downward, and punctuated the action with a drawn-out wheeze. "You were going out alone."

"I'm not now. You can keep watch from here."

"But you were going to go alone."

Sirra shrugged. "Yeah, but that was, what, ten seconds ago, Foz. What's past is past. Are you going to help me, or not?" She unhooked the first layer of her deep-suit from the rack and began opening it.

Fozzoli looked at her with an expression that betrayed his understanding of the situation. His face seemed to reflect the fact that he was going to lose this argument, as he had lost so many others with this determined woman. His sleep-sluggish brain was only a few seconds behind his face in its realization.

He shuffled towards Sirra and stared at her for a moment while she struggled to put her suit on. Presently, he reached out and helped her with the shoulders.

"What is this dive for? A late night tryst?"

Sirra snorted once. "Yes, as a matter of fact. I'm going to try to find Vogel. I promised him I'd be back."

"Get some good tape on him. And be back before you redline, please."

"Sure, sure."

"I'll monitor you from the lab. Might as well get some language work done while I'm up."

"Thanks, Foz."

"Yeah, yeah."

Sirra wished, not for the first time, that she could swim amongst the vix without the suit between them. The suit was as thin as was possible, while still keeping pressure out and air and heat in (to a depth of almost five kilometers, according to specifications) but it encumbered her attempts at true communication.

The vix were still active—they had their own sleep cycle that did not, of course, correspond to any surface night or day. As far as research had been able to determine, individual vix slept when it suited them. The changelessness of their environment allowed for such individuality.

It was not long before Sirra "saw" the faint outlines of a vix as she descended from the dive pool. High-frequency sonar (carefully tuned to not interfere with vix' speech tones) relayed images to her faceplate. She could have used visible light from the suit's powerful flood, but she always chose to swim among the vix using only those senses they themselves possessed.

"*Greetings and praise, Hallowed-Fish-From-Above.*" A vix the suit computer could not identify swam near her. Despite Fozzoli's theory, the vix' greeting sounded reverential and awestruck to Sirra's suit translator.

Sirra tapped back, "*Greetings to you. I am looking for one of your kin. He-Who-Searches.*" Sirra used one of the many names Vogel had used for himself.

"*Most Holy One, I was sent here to wait for You. I will take You to him.*"

Sirra followed the vix as it dove swiftly towards the settlement below. She had to strain to keep up with the native. It wouldn't do to let this supplicant believe a god was out of shape, she thought wryly.

The vix town was bustling with activity at her arrival. Several vix were "farming" in the kelp beds, cutting down stalk after stalk with scythes attached to their heads. As the kelp was cut, the vix used their low-hanging tentacles to gather the stalks together. Sirra knew the routine from years of study. The vix would then tie the stalks and attach a weight, usually a rock, and drop the bundle to baskets on the ledge floor.

Although she had watched the vix at their farms for years, Sirra was still amazed at the skill the vix showed in accurately dropping the kelp twenty or thirty meters to the waiting receptacles. They appeared to have an instinctual awareness of the currents in the water, despite the passage of other vix. As Sirra watched, she saw that one of the gently falling bundles was off-target and would miss its intended basket.

She thought to say something but did not know to whom she should speak. There was so much activity that she simply watched. Sirra's sonar told her that several vix were abandoning their tasks as they detected her presence and were gathering a respectful distance from her. She continued to watch the farmers, most of whom had not spotted her yet.

A small, presumably very young, vix, its last pair of arms not fully developed yet, darted from behind her and swam towards the wayward kelp. The young vix passed nearby and thrashed its tailfin twice. The kelp bobbed in the vix' wake and settled gently down, squarely into the receiving basket.

"*Most Holy One, is all as it should be?*"

Sirra turned toward her guide. "How should I know?" she said to herself, then tapped into her vixvox, "*Yes. Your city is good.*" She was hampered by the limited vocabulary in the translator.

The vix emitted a squeal that apparently overtaxed the translator, for Sirra heard her computer's voice after a slight hesitation say, "Untranslatable utterance."

"*Here is he whom You requested, Your Sublime Reverence,*" her guide vix said, then swam away to a respectful distance to join the growing number of vix who were assembled perhaps twenty meters away.

Vogel swam towards her, showing little of the reverence the other vix did. Sirra recognized the vix's sonar signature through long association. She tapped, "*I have returned, as I promised*"

"*I thank You.*"

Sirra blinked. Vogel had not added an honorific.

The vix spoke again. "*I am glad you are here. Much has been happening. The—*" Sirra's computer voice cut in with "untranslatable utterance" as Vogel continued, "*—are becoming angry.*"

Sirra swam closer to Vogel and pressed her hands against his head. The vix did not shrink from her touch. She felt the other vix squeal in supersonic frequencies. Her computer voice said, "Untranslatable utterance due to low resolution and multiple sources." Sirra translated in her mind—the many vix who were still gathered in the distance had reacted to her contact with Vogel. Her computer could not make out their excited squeals, but it did not matter. She wanted to know what Vogel had said.

"*Tell me again what you just told me.*"

This time, Vogel's answer came to her mind directly.

"*Your presence here is welcome and necessary. The plot has reached a critical stage. The Crusaders are restless.*" Her computer voice continued to translate as before, still unable to find a match in its lexicon for "crusader." Sirra made a mental note to tell Fozzoli—he would be pleased at the new word.

Then Sirra frowned as the implications of Vogel's remark sank in. Crusaders? She felt the word fit, but how could Vogel have meant that? Sirra activated her link to the lab above her.

"Foz, have you been listening?"

"Yes. What did Vogel say? I got some very odd guesses by the computer."

"I think he said 'the Crusaders are restless.'"

Fozzoli did not answer immediately. "Hm. That matches some of what I'm reading here. Religious overtones, violence, a pilgrimage. Crusader sounds about right."

"I'm going with him."

"What? Sirra, don't. I said that there was violence in what he was talking about."

"How else are we going to find out what he means?"

"By sending a fully equipped team."

Sirra hesitated. Fozzoli was speaking sensibly. She should withdraw and return with the other scientists, and she should be armed. Whatever Vogel wanted to show her would wait.

She had felt nothing but benign eagerness from the vix when she had touched him, however. He did not want to hurt her, and she felt he would not knowingly lead her into danger. She was his God, after all.

But was he hoping she would solve whatever problem was developing with the crusaders?

"No. I'm going. Keep an eye on me." She clicked off before Fozzoli could argue her out of her decision.

Vogel was still waiting patiently when Sirra turned back to him. She tapped, *"Take me to them."*

Vogel spun around and down, spiraling towards the crevasse that bisected the vix settlement. Sirra adjusted her buoyancy and followed him. The two descended towards the ocean floor where the vix town lay sprawled in a pair of half-circles, split by the trench to which Vogel led her. Sirra suppressed her nervousness as she descended below the floor on which the vix town was built and entered the trench. A glance at her depth indicator told her that she was reaching the suit's nominal limit of forty-eight hundred meters. In all her exploring, she had never gone below forty-six hundred, even though she knew the suits could handle deeper. Vogel continued to dive, seemingly unaffected by the increasing depth.

Sirra's sonar, which had been quiet since she had descended past the floor, sounded faintly. On her faceplate she saw the dim outlines of another ledge below. Vogel was clearly heading for it. She checked her rangefinder—the ledge was 4,882 meters below the surface.

Sirra continued down. At eighteen hundred meters, her suit warned her to resurface, but she turned off the warning. She also noted that Fozzoli was trying to contact her, but she ignored that, too.

The ledge was small—perhaps fifty meters long and only ten or twelve meters wide. Sirra's sonar picked up multiple vix swimming around the ledge, all of whom were wearing helmet-spears.

Vogel stopped and hovered in front of a pair of vix who had risen to meet him, their spears bobbing a few meters before him. Sirra caught some of the exchange—the two armed vix were questioning Vogel about his purpose here. Vogel's answers had something to do with Sirra, for she heard him utter one of his more religious labels for her. She suppressed a chill. She had not been down this far, and the limited drone reconnaissance the scientists had conducted in the trench had revealed little.

The argument between the armed vix and Vogel halted abruptly, and a moment later, Sirra saw another vix approaching. He was moving slowly, and Sirra's sonar picked up a deep irregularity on his otherwise smooth surface—a scar? The two guardian vix separated slightly to allow the new vix access to Vogel. Sirra moved carefully closer to catch what he was saying.

"You brought the Divine Heathen."

Sirra puzzled at the oxymoron. She checked her computer for other translations, but all were similar.

Vogel answered. *"Yes. You may ask her your questions now."*

Sirra felt a thrill of anticipation. In her previous dealings with the vix, she had assumed Vogel was the tribe's shaman and spiritual spokesman. The other vix seemed content to let him speak with her, and she had taken to escorting him to the outskirts of the settlement to discuss all manner of vix culture. No doubt that had increased his status in his tribe, but now Sirra suspected the real seat of religious power lay not on the ocean floor, but here in the trench.

This new vix, whom Sirra felt it appropriate to dub "Bishop," turned to face her.

"Why do you return now?"

Sirra mentally ran through other interpretations of the utterance, but a quick glance at her helmet display insisted that it was accurate. She tapped back, *"I have never been here before."*

"The [untranslatable utterance] *told me you would come back."*

Sirra hesitated. She had to know what Bishop had said, but she would have to touch him. She tapped, *"I do not understand you. May I touch you?"*

A flurry of activity followed her request. Bishop squealed untranslatable sounds at her while Vogel swam forward and made his own sounds. Even the two armed vix got into the argument. Her computer was hopelessly overmatched for several seconds, before the noise settled down and she heard Vogel saying, *"I have been touched, and I am not* [untranslatable utterance]."

Bishop said, *"That will be decided later."* He turned again to Sirra. *"If you think that by touching me, you can* [untranslatable utterance], *then you are wrong."*

Sirra wasn't sure if Bishop had given her permission or not. She decided to risk it. She swam forward slowly, eyeing the armed vix to either side. They seemed to be watching her closely but allowing the action, and Bishop did not lash out. She closed the distance and pressed her palm against the side of the vix' head.

Sirra tapped out, *"I am here to help you."*

"You come from Above."

"Yes."

"Then you are not here to help." Sirra felt deep confusion in Bishop when he spoke. It was as if he wanted to believe her but could not with the facts at hand. More—as if the facts he had directly contradicted his beliefs.

"I will do what I can to help." Sirra had a sudden idea. *"I will take you to the surface."*

Bishop squealed. Her translator gave the expected "untranslatable utterance" readout, but Sirra felt the meaning behind Bishop's words.

He was terrified and ecstatic at the same time. Conflicting emotion surged out of him with such strength that Sirra reeled at it. Bishop was repulsed by and attracted to Sirra's words. He both loved and hated her at that instant, and he had had his fondest hopes realized at the same time he was plunged into despair.

Sirra let go of him and he thrashed about for a moment, still squealing. Vogel moved forward but was blocked by one of the armed vix.

Presently, Bishop's speech settled down enough for Sirra's translator to catch words here and there. *"Take her to* [untranslatable]. *We will perform* [untranslatable] *there."*

The two armed vix moved towards her, slowly. Sirra activated her base link. "Foz, I'm in trouble. Foz?"

No answer.

Sirra quickly set her buoyancy to full and pumped her legs vigorously, rising quickly away from the spear-helmeted vix.

"Foz! Come in!" She could not see the upper lip of the ocean floor above her yet. Her sonar indicated that the vix were pursuing and would overtake her.

Sirra pumped even faster, but it was no use. She was outmatched here. One of the vix swam above her and prodded her menacingly with his spear. Sirra did not know if the vix could puncture the suit, but she suspected that with enough strength and speed, any vix could skewer neatly through it. And at this depth, a breach in her suit would be instantly fatal.

Sirra readjusted her buoyancy to slow sink and let the vix lead her back down to the ledge. She noted that her life support indicator had just passed the two hours remaining mark.

*   *   *

Iede had wanted to reach on foot the location given to her by Those Above, but as the rendezvous point lay some fifty kilometers away from the farthest outskirts of Arborurba, practicality dictated a vehicle of some kind. She had chosen a bicycle as a compromise between ascetic pride and pragmatic rationality.

Iede was comfortably tired as she surveyed the countryside. She could not see any sign of human habitation from where she was—even the Domes, large as they were, had faded to gentle green mist kilometers ago. The point Those Above had chosen was significantly higher than Arborurba's almost sea-level elevation, and Iede could feel the scarcity of chlorine in the air at this height. She scanned the sky for any sign of the "vehicle" Those Above had spoken of. She did not know what to expect exactly, but she knew she would recognize it when she saw it.

The fifty-kilometer journey had not dulled her sense of pride at being chosen to ascend to the gods. Iede held no delusion as to what her gods were. She had studied the history of her ancestors' journey; she knew about Ship and its mission, knew about the Flight Crew and the role they had played with her great-great-grandmother, both during the journey and after the establishment of the Family. She knew that those she called gods had started out as men and women long ago, or at least their ancestors had been so. What manner of creatures dwelt in the heavens now? What they had done for her mother thirty-seven years ago was nothing short of miraculous. And the miracle they had chosen to grant Yallia also resulted in Iede's own birth. What better way to repay the debt than to worship those who had saved her newly-conceived life?

Iede had written the Articles of Faith twenty years before, when she had been a scant fifteen years old. She had taken as her inspiration the Book of Verse that Eduard Costellan had passed on to Jene Halfner—Iede had used the thirty-nine poems as epigraphs for each separate Article. Her writings had attracted a following, and her congregation now numbered in the thousands, not including those who considered themselves "casual worshippers." Iede could not quite suppress the forlorn wish, immodest as it was, that the men and women of her congregation could see her imminent Assumption.

Iede saw the vehicle before she heard it. A speck had appeared in the air and had grown rapidly larger as she watched. She had to force herself to breathe. The vehicle was shaped like a native bird—large wings tapering from a central, ovoid shape—and was the purest white Iede had ever seen. There were no windows anywhere on the surface of the craft. Such a holy vessel could only have come from Above.

The vehicle stopped almost immediately above her, hovering perhaps twenty meters distant. It was then Iede heard the rush of the machine's engines change from a gentle hum to a deafening roar. A violent gust of hot air almost knocked her to the ground. Iede squinted into the gale to see the vehicle slide sideways a few meters and start to gently descend. The hurricane wind subsided when the craft moved from above her, though Iede still felt the hot air and could see its effects on the ground below. She refrained from shielding her eyes from the grit kicked up at the vehicle's descent—she wanted to see the landing. To her knowledge, it was the only such landing Those Above had ever made.

The craft settled to the ground and its engines quieted to an idle. Iede stared at it, wondering if she dared step towards it. She began the Lords' Prayer to calm herself.

"Iede." A flat, emotionless voice boomed out from the vehicle. Iede jumped and swallowed with a suddenly dry throat.

"Here, my Lords."

"You may enter," the voice said, and an iris valve opened in the side of the vehicle. Iede had not even seen the seams. She gathered her courage and walked towards the opening. She could not see inside—the interior of the craft was dark. She ducked her head slightly and stepped through the threshold, prepared to meet her gods.

The door closed behind her and the cabin lit up. It was empty. There was a cream-colored couch in the cabin with straps that hung limply down to the gleaming metallic floor. In front of the couch was a flat, dark panel.

"Sit down on the couch, Iede. The monitor will demonstrate how to secure your straps." The voice seemed to come from the entire cabin simultaneously. Iede was used to the ambivalent gender of the voice—all her contacts with the gods had been the same. She thought she recognized the god who spoke, but that was immaterial. She obeyed and sat down on the couch. The panel lit up, and a stylized image of a person, somewhat elongated but otherwise recognizable, appeared. As Iede watched, the image sat down on its own couch and adjusted the straps. Iede duplicated the movements carefully and found herself securely fastened in when she was done.

"Good. We will now ascend to Ship. Prepare yourself for acceleration."

Iede wasn't quite sure how she was to prepare herself, but the vehicle rose swiftly and rocketed upwards towards its destination.

Iede knew about multiple g's, even if she herself had never experienced them. The craft was not beyond mortal technology, though it did have a polish and sheen to it that was otherwise lacking in Newurth construction. Iede concentrated on breathing—she felt as if she had three people sitting on her chest. She would have to remember this sensation for her congregation, she thought. It could be seen as symbolic of the effort one must put forth in order to truly commune with the gods.

The acceleration lasted perhaps twenty minutes, then suddenly cut out entirely. Iede felt euphoria for a few seconds before she became acutely aware of a growing nausea. Her stomach, denied the gravity it had become accustomed to, threatened to rise and dislodge its contents.

Iede swallowed in a moist mouth and closed her eyes. She would not be sick. The gods would not deem her worthy. Iede repeated the thought until it was a litany. Presently, she was able to open her eyes.

The panel in front of her had lit up again and was flashing the message "DO NOT UNSTRAP" in bold letters. "Iede." Again, the flat voice. "You must remain secured to the acceleration couch. We will bring you in shortly. Remain where you are."

Iede nodded, then wondered why she'd bothered. The gods could not see her here. Or could they? She thought indignantly that surely They could, if They so wished. Iede decided to risk a question.

"My Lords?"

"Yes, Iede?" The voice did not sound angry.

"Where are You?"

"I am in Ship. So are we all, and so shall you be soon."

Iede considered this. "This vessel is but an avatar?"

"It is controlled by an onboard computer." Iede thought she heard a wry smile in the answer. She felt chagrin—she should know better than to speak to her gods in the language of a priestess.

"My Lord, may I know Your name so I might thank You in my prayers?"

"I'll tell you, but not for that reason. I am called Groundseer Aywon." The voice placed the emphasis on the last syllable in the last name.

"Thank you, my Lord." Iede smiled, pleased she had not heard the name before. This was a new God, possibly a higher order of God. Soon, she would be with Them.

She felt a slight sensation of movement and guessed that the craft was maneuvering in orbit. Her pulse quickened as she felt the vessel shudder gently. The panel still flashed the message "DO NOT UNSTRAP," but as she watched, the words disappeared to be replaced by "UNSTRAP AT WILL." The panel demonstrated how she was to remove her acceleration straps.

"You are now docked with Ship," Groundseer said. "Unstrap yourself, but be careful. You are not used to microgravity. Wait inside the craft and disrobe entirely. Then place the mask securely over your mouth and nose. I will collect you." Before Iede could ask what mask Groundseer meant, the craft's data panel slid aside to reveal a small compartment. A clear face mask lay inside.

Iede unstrapped carefully and took off her clothes, placing them neatly on the acceleration couch. She did not hesitate—she felt a vague sense of pride that her gods would choose to see her naked and alone. Iede took the mask and attached it firmly to her face. Again, she did not hesitate, though she could see no obvious breathing holes. The mask had some kind of adhesive around its edges—Iede did not need to hold it in place once attached. She found without surprise that she could breathe through the mask. The gods would not have placed her in danger. She had no choice in the matter in any case. She was sure the iris valve would not have opened for her until she had complied with Groundseer's orders. She faced where she remembered the valve to be and floated blissfully, waiting for the arrival of her gods.

The lighting in the craft changed slightly, taking on a vaguely violet hue, and Iede felt the prickly sensation of heat on her bare skin. The sensation was over before she could grow uncomfortable, and then the light changed back again. The iris valve cycled open and a tall, slender humanoid floated through. Iede could not immediately identify the humanoid's gender from facial features, and his/her body was so slight as to be almost a mockery of the human form. The humanoid was nude, but a quick, almost involuntary glance at his/her genital region did not help: Iede did not recognize the structure she saw there. She closed her eyes tightly and said with shame, "I beg forgiveness, my Lord."

"Call me Groundseer. And you'll need your eyes to get through the hatch, Iede," Groundseer said.

Iede forced her eyes open but kept them pointedly averted. She made an arbitrary decision to think of the humanoid as male until she was presented with facts to the contrary.

"Through here," Groundseer said, and launched himself back through the iris valve. Iede followed.

He led her through a short, immaculately silver-white tunnel that terminated at another iris valve. As in the shuttle, light seemed to simply *exist* in the tunnel—Iede could not determine its source. Groundseer pressed his slender fingers against a spot on the gleaming wall and the valve spiraled open. He swam effortlessly through, Iede in tow. When she cleared the valve, she gasped at what she saw.

A vast chamber, so large she could only with difficulty make out the other side, opened up in front of her. The chamber was spherical and must have been at least one hundred meters in diameter. Thin, birdlike Gods swooped through the air, using small wings that Iede had half-glimpsed on Groundseer. Iede did not know if the wings were part of the gods' bodies or mechanical contrivances of some kind. All the gods were nude, and Iede guiltily stole glances at their genitals in a sort of morbid curiosity. The nearest god was at least thirty meters distant and moving quickly, so her eyes could not quite make out what she saw. She looked away, lest the god see her and grow angry with her. She looked instead at the chamber itself.

The interior of the sphere was largely empty, save for the occasional god moving from one end of the sphere to another. As she watched, Iede saw a pair of small gods playing what appeared to be tag. She gave a short, shocked laugh when she realized these were children.

"What do you think?" Groundseer asked, his tone neutral.

"It is glorious!" The mask muffled her voice slightly.

Groundseer snorted and said, "Come on. There are some others I want you to meet." He pushed off the threshold of the iris valve and flew gracefully toward the far wall. Iede pushed off as well and saw immediately that she would miss her target.

Groundseer looked back at her and said, "When you hit the wall, crawl along it until to get to me. I don't want to have to bring you in myself."

Iede did as she was told, feeling foolish. She had wanted to show her gods that they had chosen well in preserving her life those thirty-five years ago. She was not off to a good start.

Groundseer was waiting for her at the opening. He dove down the tunnel opening before she was done maneuvering into it. She saw him disappear into a side tunnel that branched off the main one and followed him. He continued in this fashion, staying ahead of her and choosing tunnels without hesitation, until they arrived at another tunnel terminus. Groundseer paused before the blank wall and turned to look at Iede.

"We're going to the Groundseer's hub. There may be many of us in there. It is vital you do not touch any of us. When we enter, find a station near the wall immediately and stay there." He did not wait for a response but opened the valve and entered.

The room was another sphere, although one considerably less spacious than the last one she had seen. The first features that caught her eye were multicolored holograms floating in various places in the sphere. She recognized some of them as locations from around Newurth: the Assembly Building, the old Valhalla Dome, and a patch of ocean that had to be the location of the Vix Observation Lab. She also saw individuals: governmental figures, scientists, even one of her cardinals. At every holo, a god watched dispassionately.

"I said to find the wall, Iede," Groundseer's voice snapped her away from the scene. She blushed and grabbed hold of a stanchion. Groundseer moved off into the room and hovered near another god to converse. The two gods were oriented oddly to one another—Groundseer was upside down and above the god to which he spoke—but neither of them seemed to care. None of the other gods were looking at Iede or had acknowledged her presence. Iede took the opportunity to take her first good look at the bodies of her gods.

Each adult god in the chamber was at least two meters tall, and Iede could see elongated bones sheathed in brown skin. All the gods were the same shade of toast-colored tan. All were entirely bald—no hair on even their bodies. The hairless, slender bodies seemed incredibly fragile; Iede wondered if she looked hard enough, would she see their hearts beating in the thin, corrugated chests?

Iede's gaze wandered towards the genitals once again. The nearest god was situated in such a way as to afford Iede a clear look. Iede could not suppress a slight shudder as she finally understood what she had been seeing in her furtive glances: the gods were hermaphrodites. A small vagina bisected a dual scrotum in which Iede could make out tiny testicles drawn up against the god's body. As she watched, the god shifted position slightly, and Iede could see the miniature head of the god's penis peeking out from within the vagina.

"Iede." Groundseer's voice caused her to start in shame. She looked around to see him motioning her over. She let go of the stanchion and pushed off, careful that her course did not take her too close to any gods. She needn't have bothered—the gods moved blithely out of her way as she approached until she reached the other side of the chamber where Groundseer and another god waited.

"This is Groundseer Deefor. She will explain why you were brought here." He pronounced the pronoun 'shuh-he.' Iede mentally assigned the female gender to Deefor.

Deefor nodded and began in a voice that was almost identical to Groundseer Aywon's, "We in Ship, and especially those of us in the Groundseer line, believe you are embarking on a path that will lead you to ruin."

Iede blinked. "My Lord, I have been trying to bring more and more followers to Your glory. We of Newurth are but vile creatures crawling under Your grace. I thank You for Your wisdom and ask humbly how I might bring more of my fellow creatures to the truth."

Deefor and Aywon exchanged unreadable glances. Aywon said, with some gentleness, "No, Iede. We don't think Newurth is on the wrong path. You yourself are."

Iede cast her eyes downward. "Again, I thank You that You should bring me here, to your glorious Above, to correct me in—"

"Iede! Stop that!" Aywon's voice had lost what little compassion she had heard earlier and was now clearly annoyed.

Iede continued to look down. "In what way have I strayed from Your plan? How have I misinterpreted Your words and precepts?"

"Iede, you must abolish this religion. Immediately."

"As my Lord wishes. I am but a humble servant."

"Iede—" Aywon said, but Deefor interrupted.

"Ay, she will not listen. She cannot hear you." Iede heard the contempt in Deefor's voice but did not look up. The god continued, "This is what comes of interference. We should never have involved ourselves. Costellan was right."

"And I was wrong?"

Iede looked up at this. It dawned on her with incredulity that she was listening to an argument between two of her gods.

"I said so sixty years ago. I say so now again."

Iede looked at Deefor in astonishment. The god was more than sixty years old? S(he) did not look older than twenty. In the back of her mind, Iede remembered that the gods did not record the years in the same fashion as those on Newurth. She converted the figure according to the information contained in the Verses and was still astonished: Deefor was over thirty-five years old and looked much younger.

Aywon sighed in a most human fashion. "I've thought about that. I've tortured myself about it for those sixty years."

Deefor said, "You have affection for her." Iede knew that she was being referred to, although Deefor had made no motion in her direction.

"I do."

"You even feel responsible for her. You personally." Deefor said it with an air of indictment.

"Yes. How can I not?" Aywon turned to Iede and spoke directly to her. "Sixty years ago, which is thirty-six years ago to you, your mother and two other people were attacked by people you used to call Domers."

"My Lord, I have studied the histories. I know of the miracle You enacted."

"Yes. It was me."

Iede's eyes widened. "You, my Lord? You were the god who…my Lord!" She squeezed her eyes shut and clenched her fists. "I cannot…express to You—"

"Quiet, now," he said firmly. Iede calmed herself somewhat and heard Deefor mumble something under her breath. Iede could not make out the words, but Deefor's tone was unmistakably disgusted.

Aywon looked away and said, "What you don't know is that I acted without authority. I did not consult with the Arch-Captain. For that, I was assigned control of the Groundseer hub that I might correct my mistake. I have spent the last sixty years trying to do so."

"Mistake, My Lord?"

Aywon turned to Iede again. "I don't want you dead, Iede. But my superiors believe you should never have been saved. We're not supposed to meddle with your affairs."

Iede nodded and quoted from Costellan's poetry: "Verse Twelve: 'Green mist hides those below/ Only birds under the fog/ All as it should be.'"

Aywon continued as if he had not heard. "But having saved you, I set in motion a chain of events leading to this...religion. It must end."

"But My Lord, I only wish to worship You, to thank You for all You have done."

Deefor laughed—a short, derisive burst of air. "It's hopeless. You've twisted this creature so far out of shape she is no longer human. And she is twisting others."

Aywon moved closer to Iede. "Iede, I am not a god. I am a human, like you. I eat, I bleed, and one day I will die. This place you are in is just a Ship."

"My Lord, I have studied all of that. I know what You are. I still worship You—not for what You are, but for what You have done and what You will do."

"What will we do?"

"It is written in Verse Thirty-Nine, the last verse: 'The globe spins in space/ Night becomes day becomes night/ Life grows forever.'"

"What does that mean?"

Iede looked down. "My Lord, my understanding is flawed, being a lowly planetdweller, but in my limited intelligence I understand it to mean the gods will always ensure life. Whatever crisis we may face below, You will act in Your own way to keep life flourishing."

Aywon turned to Deefor. "Can you argue with that? She may have twisted Costellan's words completely out of shape, but she understands our purpose."

"Our purpose is to study. We watch, we gather data, we watch more." Deefor continued to look away from Iede.

"To what end?" Aywon asked with a sneer.

"There is no end."

Aywon stared at Deefor for a moment, then said, "You are as twisted as she is. Your blind acceptance of doctrine is no less foolish than this poor human's religion." Aywon looked at Iede, and she saw kindness in his eyes. "I have something to show you."

Deefor seized Aywon's arm. "What are you going to do?"

"She needs to see what we have discovered."

Deefor's eyes widened. In her peripheral vision, Iede could see the other Groundseers turning from their workstations to stare at Aywon. Deefor whispered, "You can't! We can't influence their growth and development in any way! Look what one small act sixty years ago has done! If you reveal any more to her than you have already...."

"She's here. We have changed her irrevocably as it is. We may as well complete the process. Unless you had in mind killing her outright rather than returning her to the surface?" Iede hoped she detected sarcasm in his voice.

Deefor murmured, "It would be the best possible solution." Then, more loudly, "Failing that, we must keep her here forever. She must not be allowed to return to the surface. Even that will not correct the problem, but it will keep our interference to a minimum."

"No. She'll learn what she needs to know, then go and tell the others below."

Deefor locked eyes with Aywon and said slowly. "I'll tell the Arch-Captain what you are doing. She will not return to the surface, and you will be rendered to the tanks."

Iede did not know the meaning of that last remark, but it chilled her nonetheless.

Aywon paused and licked his lips. "You'd do that? Yes, I see you would." He lowered his head and sighed. "All right, then. I agree. We'll keep her here." He looked at Iede. "I'm sorry, Iede, but you cannot leave. Ever."

Iede was overwhelmed with conflicting emotion. She had been assumed into Above where her gods reigned—in her own way, she was to become a god herself! She tried to dismiss the thought as unconscionable hubris, but found she could not entirely. She felt pride swelling in her even as she wept silently for all those she would leave behind and never again see or talk to. She had so much she would have taught them—but how could she question the will of the gods? She looked uneasily at Deefor. But was the will of the gods one will?

"Since she will remain here with us, there is no reason she cannot see everything we have discovered," Aywon said. Deefor blinked and looked like she was trying to formulate an objection. Eventually, she shrugged slightly and said, "I suppose not."

"Show her the city," Aywon said. Deefor swam to a nearby control panel. The holo image that had been floating beside her vanished to be replaced by a long-range view of a nondescript patch of land.

"Look carefully, Iede."

Iede stared at the holo but could not identify the landscape. She was looking at perhaps a thirty-square kilometer area, judging by the size of surface features. A river snaked through the center of the display. Most of what she saw was fairly flat and heavily wooded.

"My Lord, what—"

"Deefor, now show us the enhanced holo." He added to Iede, "We have many ways to observe, Iede. What you are seeing now is a combination of rather complex visuals, including ultraviolet, x-ray, penetration ray, and other enhancements that I'm afraid would take rather a long time to explain."

Iede stared at the holo, her mouth open. The landscape was still recognizable, although now the river shone out as a bright pink ribbon of light and the trees had faded to near transparency. The landscape revealed a ghostly image of circles and lines that Iede immediately recognized as order.

"What is it, My Lord?"

"You know what it is, Iede."

Aywon was right—she did. Her mind had simply refused to accept what was being presented to it, for the image calmly overthrew everything she had known about her home.

"It's…a city."

"Ruins of a city, yes. We estimate it is over ten thousand years old—six thousand, one hundred Newurth years."

"Who built it?"

Aywon motioned to Deefor, who pressed a key on the control panel. The image vanished. Aywon turned to Iede. "We don't know."

CHAPTER 22

Sirra examined the prison—there was no other name for the structure into which she had been placed—and thought ruefully that Fozzoli had tried to warn her. She tried her flash again in the vain hope that the vix had left an obvious weakness to their stone jail that was only visible to ordinary light. Her sonar told her that she was sealed in on all sides, and her flash confirmed this. She could see the true nature of the cell—rock walls that had been crafted with subtle angles and strange corners.

Her sonar had initially sent her contradictory messages. Depending on how she turned, the cell grew or shrank in size. Now she knew that the vix had designed this prison to torment any of their brethren placed within. Sonar bounced crazily off the walls, reflected by the oddly shaped rock, to return to the sender with false data. Only Sirra's flash had revealed the irregularities in the rock walls of the cell. It was not hermetically sealed, but the hairline cracks in the ceiling and floor allowed for "ventilation," nothing more.

She had spent the last ninety minutes alternately tapping out desperate messages to any vix who could hear her and brooding over her decision not to run when she'd had the chance. She knew the pursuing vix could have impaled her and probably would have, but that quick death would have been preferable to this slow one. She did not want to check her life-support gauge again.

When it had become clear that no messages were making it out of the cell (or if they were, they were being ignored), she had rigged her vixvox in what she hoped would prove her miracle weapon. But the weapon required the partial cooperation of the Bishop's guardian vix—she needed them to open the cell. They had stubbornly refused to do so.

Despite the impending thought of her own demise, the question of the vix' behavior still burned in her mind. Why had they done this to her? Bishop was obviously some kind of religious leader—she now suspected that

Vogel was merely a vicar at best, carrying out the orders given to him by Bishop.

Sirra's eyes widened in her helmet. Was that it? Was Bishop upset that Sirra and the rest of the scientists had usurped his authority as the shaman? Sirra almost laughed at the irony. Had a religious leader taken action against the very gods he worshipped because Their arrival had rendered him irrelevant?

Before she could further pursue the thought, her sonar image told her of a change in the environment. The great stone wall that had been rolled into place to close the cell was opening. Sirra started towards the opening, then checked herself when she saw the sonar image of a guard's spear-helm entering the cell.

"Come with me, Damned Saint."

Her right hand went immediately to her left armband controller. She knew that she should act now. Her jury-rigged vixvox was set to produce a single high-frequency howl she hoped would simultaneously blind and deafen any vix within a few meters. The cell was open, and only a lone vix floated in the opening. She would most probably not get a better chance.

Her hand did not quite activate the vixvox. She had less than fifty minutes of oxygen left and was almost certain to be herded to a place with many more vix to guard her, but her curiosity, mixed with a feeling that the sea creatures did not seriously intend to harm one of their gods, stayed her hand.

She swam towards the opening. The vix guard backed away, undulating gracefully while keeping his lance pointed directly at her chest.

"You will not touch me, Demon Angel."

Sirra tapped out, *"Where are you taking me?"*

"To your [untranslatable utterance]."

Her own instincts gave her no insight as to the vix' mysterious words. Sirra fought back frustration and asked, *"What will happen there?"* If she could get the vix to answer in pieces, her translator might be able to synthesize a meaning where her intuition failed.

"We will learn why you have come to us from Above. And we will cleanse ourselves of you."

Sirra had heard enough. She did not need her translator to feel the hatred mixed with fear in the vix' sounds. The word her computer had seemed unable to translate now burned in her mind as clearly as if the vix had spoken it in her language: she was going to her own exorcism.

The lance prodded her, none too gently, to swim forward. Sirra obeyed, keeping a worried eye on the tip of the vix' lance (or at least on the sonar image of it). The prospect of attending a religious ceremony that none of her companions in the lab had seen almost dampened the terror she felt. She kept her hand close to her vixvox controller, but did not activate it.

There were no other vix in sonar range as her guardian guided her to a destination on the extreme edge of the shelf. When they arrived, the vix maneuvered itself into position, still guarding Sirra but settling on the shelf near a low outcropping that resembled a trumpet.

"*Remain still.*" The vix said and lowered its lance. It placed its head into the outcropping and sent a loud high-frequency blast through the trumpet. Sirra found herself impressed. The device was simple but somehow amplified the vix' natural vocal ability, much like a megaphone. The guard raised his lance again and resumed his guardianship of Sirra.

Before long, other vix appeared on Sirra' sonar. She could not be certain, but she thought she recognized one of them as Bishop. Her suit sonar could not identify the vix grouped together. Seven vix swam toward her, one of whom was being guarded by three other spear-helmed warriors.

"*Wise One, I am sorry,*" the vix said. With this new data, Sirra's computer identified him as Vogel.

"*You will be silent,* [Vogel]" Bishop said.

Sirra tapped back, "*What is happening?*"

Bishop preempted Vogel's answer. "*You are to be* [untranslatable utterance]. *We will use the old ways. Spirits and demons cannot withstand the holy depths.*"

Sirra scowled inside her suit mask. If Bishop intended to try to remove her suit to test her ability to survive, she would have to try her vixvox blast. She was not sure if all seven vix were inside the blast radius or even if the contrivance would work at all.

Sirra relaxed a tiny fraction when Bishop and the three unarmed vix floated away from her, toward the edge of the shelf. At the extreme edge, all three made a curious gesture, folding their fins inward and making themselves as small as possible for an instant before uncurling slowly to their full width. The gesture reminded Sirra of vix births she had seen.

The three vix launched themselves towards the crevasse, hovering in the up-current and sending sonar messages towards Sirra that her computer was unable to make any sense out of.

Sirra looked at Vogel and decided to risk a message. "*What are they doing?*"

The guards did not answer or react in any way. Sirra concluded they were either transfixed by the macabre dance going on in the up-current by the three vix or did not care if she and Vogel spoke.

Vogel answered, "*A ritual. To ensure their communion with the Old Place.*"

"Old Place?"

"You do not know of the Old Place?"

The humans' translation equipment was not subtle enough to detect overtones such as incredulity, but Sirra was sure that Vogel had been shocked at her ignorance.

"Is the Old Place the same as the Above?"

This was evidently the wrong comment to make, for Vogel shrank away, and Sirra saw the four guards pivot towards her. One of them approached and menaced her with its lance.

"You will be silent, Celestial Demon!"

Sirra did not move. The vix kept his lance hovering centimeters from her chest for a long moment, then withdrew slightly. The tip of his spear did not move farther than a meter away from her. Sirra decided that further conversation with Vogel was out of the question.

She watched the three vix cavort in the up-current and glanced at her oxygen supply indicator. Thirty-one minutes. The trip back to the surface would take longer than forty minutes at this depth—Sirra shuddered slightly as she realized the return trip was now over nine minutes into the "grace period" of life support her suit supplied.

She returned her gaze to the three vix. What had Vogel meant, the Old Place? Evidently, the Old Place was connected with the surface in some way—the tabu Sirra had broken confirmed that. The three vix were trying to "commune" with the Old Place, Vogel had said. Perhaps it was not a place in the physical sense but a spirit world of some kind. If that was so, why had Vogel and the guards reacted with such intensity when she had suggested the Old Place was the surface?

Sirra shrugged. Even in this developing race, religion had reached a complexity that would take years for the humans to understand, if they could ever truly comprehend the spiritual lives of the natives.

One of the three vix who had been hovering in the up-current swam towards Sirra and spoke to her. Her translator caught some of the speech: "*Sacred Depths, we* [untranslatable] *ask you to* [here followed a long burst of untranslatable speech] *so that we may rid ourselves of this* [untranslatable]." Her computer identified the speaker as Bishop.

Bishop spoke again. "*You will come with me and enter the Depths.*"

Sirra glanced down into the crevasse. Her sonar did not bounce back, indicating that the bottom was too distant to be detected; she knew from probe launchings that it was several kilometers deep. At the bottom was the volcanic vent that supplied the vix settlement with its increased oxygen. Surely, the vix could not survive the conditions down there. The pressure alone would be many times greater than it was here.

"We will go together?" Sirra tapped.

"Yes. But only I will return. No Blessed Sinner from Above can survive the Depths."

Sirra pondered this. Bishop was right—her deep-suit was already below the depth for which it was rated; she could not survive more than another few dozen meters. But how could Bishop himself survive?

A quick look back at the guards made her decision for her. If she used her vixvox now, she would not get them all—many were out of range. But if she dove with Bishop, she might be able to stun him and rise to the surface faster than the guards could catch her. And she would learn more about the ritual.

"I am ready," Sirra tapped. Her air supply read twenty-seven minutes.

She launched herself off the ledge and set her buoyancy to "slow sink." Bishop circled her and dove below her. Sirra felt her competitive nature rising and resisted the impulse to show Bishop that she, too, could take the pressure.

Bishop was still visible on her sonar. "Do you feel that, Angel-Demon?"

Sirra looked at her gauges. Her pressure indicator was hard against the redline. She did not feel anything, however, nor would she unless her suit ruptured. Then she would feel instantaneous, unbearable pressure, followed by oblivion. It would not be the comparatively slow death of suffocation that awaited her should she fail to return to the surface in twenty minutes at most.

"I feel nothing," she tapped to Bishop.

Bishop made an untranslatable sound and continued down. Sirra's suit computer said, "Warning: you have descended below maximum depth. Ascend to the surface immediately." Sirra took a deep breath and continued to dive, hoping her suit's pressure indicator had the same safety margin as her oxygen gauge.

Bishop was still diving, but his rate of descent had slowed. Sirra was gaining on him, but he was still ten meters away.

"Most Holy of Places, Giver of wisdom and joy, blessed be your waters." There was an odd quality to his voice that caused Sirra's translator trouble— her computer could no longer identify Bishop from his voice. "I beg you to show me the wisdom to understand. Oh..." and Bishop lapsed into another untranslatable speech.

Sirra's depth indicator read 4,907, more than one hundred meters below maximum, but she needed to be closer to make sure Bishop got caught in the blast of her makeshift weapon. He was no longer sinking, so she lowered herself to him and moved her hand to the buttons on her armband.

She did not press them. Bishop was paying her no attention. She could easily shoot to the surface now, blasting the guards at the shelf as she went. Her oxygen supply read eleven minutes, plus her forty minutes grace period—she would just make it if she left now.

But Bishop's behavior puzzled her. He was still making incoherent sounds to no one in particular. Sirra wondered why her computer could translate none of what he was saying. Was he speaking a different language? Why would the vix be bilingual?

She moved closer, carefully, and reached out a gloved hand to touch him. She made contact and was instantly flooded with a feeling of disorienting euphoria. The pressure, her dwindling oxygen supply, all her problems dissolved into the water as she shared in Bishop's experience. Content was not enough of a word—he was *fulfilled*.

But what was he saying? Sirra shook off the feeling of euphoria and concentrated on his words. His thought processes were as confusing to her as his words were to her computer. He made no sense, and as Sirra "listened," she could feel herself growing giddy.

She let go of Bishop and shook her head. The pressure was getting to him. She did not think as she grabbed his starboard fin tightly, then reset her buoyancy to maximum. Sirra kicked away, rising swiftly back to the shelf.

Bishop seemed to shake off the effects of the deep and said, *"Release me! Sentinels! Attack this abomination!"* Three of the four guards swam quickly towards her, lances rock-steady. The remaining guard stayed with Vogel.

Sirra let go of Bishop and depressed the buttons on her armband. She could not hear the sound, but Bishop and the three guards twitched spastically for a moment, then set up a hideous caterwauling of what she hoped was pain.

Sirra did not waste time to study the effects of her blast. She kicked up and kept kicking. She cleared the crevasse and reentered the vix town. She immediately tried to activate her suit radio, only to find her weapon had overtaxed not only her vixvox but her entire communications assembly. Her sonar "eyes" still functioned, but her ears and mouth had been disabled.

She continued towards the surface and noted that three armed vix were in pursuit. Either her blast had had only a temporary effect or three new vix guards had entered the chase. Whatever the case, they were closing in. Sirra kicked as powerfully as the deep-suit allowed, aided by the suit's buoyancy. She rose through the town blindingly quick.

Her legs began to ache, then burn with effort. With several hundred meters to go she could see from her sonar that she would never reach the surface before the vix reached her. She turned to face them, preferring to meet her death than run from it.

The lead vix' lance could not have been more than ten meters away from her when all three vix suddenly broke formation and veered off, turning swiftly in the water to retreat back to the crevasse. Sirra watched, dumbfounded, as the entire vix population reacted similarly, ducking into side caves and hiding behind kelp beds. In a matter of moments, the town appeared deserted.

Sirra did not hesitate to question her good fortune but turned again towards the surface. She cried out when her sonar registered six human swimmers and the station's "waterbug," a twin-prop vehicle the station personnel used for large specimen collection.

She waved to them, then pointed to her helmet at the earpiece. She gave a thumbs-down to indicate that her communications gear was out.

The operator of the waterbug unhooked and swam to Sirra, then touched his helmet to hers. "You owe me a night's sleep, Sirra," Fozzoli's voice sounded faintly in her ears.

* * *

"I don't know how you get used to all this," Kiv said, gripping the railing and looking uneasily out to sea.

"Well, I don't know how you can stay inside your office all day," Khadre chided him. Her voice was still girlishly high, her hair still worn in a ponytail, though a touch of rasp and a lot of white had crept into them over the years. Her face was deeply wrinkled and a permanent chocolate color from years of sun exposure. Kiv could not imagine her dying.

"Someone has to push papers, Khadre."

"Hmph." Khadre tried to suppress a grimace. She was almost successful.

"You want to go below?" Kiv asked softly. Bone cancer was still painful, even through the nanoscreen, he knew.

Khadre shook her head. "Nope. Nothing down there to help me, Kiv." She smiled and looked out to sea. "I'm glad you came, son." She closed her eyes again, but this time she looked peaceful. "I'll miss this."

"What do you mean?"

Khadre opened her eyes and said, "I can't stay out here anymore. I'm just getting in the way."

Kiv did not speak but looked at her expectantly.

"Oh, everyone here has been very accommodating. They treat me well and listen respectfully. But I'm out of my league, Kiv."

"You are the one who discovered the vix. You are the founder of the whole movement."

"I'm also fifty-two years old. I'm not as sharp as I used to be." She tapped her temple.

Kiv did not answer. He knew the limitations of the antiagathic process as well as anyone else—his mother had been unusual to stave off early senescence for as long as she had. Her body might live another ten or twelve years, but her mind would slowly deteriorate despite science's best efforts.

"What do you think you might do?" Kiv asked. "You could teach marine biology at the university."

Khadre laughed. "If my mind is slowing down, the last place I should be is in front of a bunch of university students. No, Kiv, I'll find something. Maybe I'll become a spokeswoman. I'll give talks in vix language."

Kiv nodded. "Sounds good."

"I'll teach people how to speak vix."

Kiv started to laugh, but stopped when he saw she was serious. "How?"

"I'm sure some bright young engineer can rig up some kind of device so we can reach their frequency. Not through a vixvox—through ordinary speech."

Kiv thought about it. "Maybe as a curiosity. I don't see how we can ever really communicate with them. They are from a totally different world."

"So were we, once, and we got along. Look at what has happened with the Family and the Domers."

"Yes, let's look at that," Kiv said, trying to keep the annoyance out of his voice. It was all well and good for his mother to spout idealistic phraseology, but those same ideals had to be translated into action, and he was the man who had to maintain balance. "We have spent the last thirty-five years trying to integrate the Domers into society and helping them live outside. And at every step, they fight us. We strive to bring them into civilization and they thank us with demonstrations, graffiti, and near-riots."

"But look at where we have arrived. Family and Domers coexist peacefully and equally. The only way you can tell Domers apart from Family is the implant system, and that only under a scanner."

"What? Mother, you really have been out here too long. We don't coexist peacefully, we barely tolerate each other. Or rather, we reach out to them, they respond with hate. And now you speak about reaching out to the vix?" He shook his head. "We have to integrate the Domers first, if we can. We have problems already without inventing more."

Khadre did not answer. She knew better than to try to debate with her son. He was a fine politician and had a keen mind, and even if his conclusions did not match her own, he nevertheless arrived at them through careful analysis and logic.

"Kiv, you never really liked the sea, but you liked the beach. You remember?"

"I still do. I just can't get there often. Why...?"

"You remind me of one of those big rocks at the shore."

Kiv did not speak but looked at his mother, puzzled.

"Those rocks look like they are going to stand there forever. The tide washes over them, and when it's gone, the rocks are still there. But each pass of the water wears a little bit off, until...."

"I get it, Mother." Kiv was irritated now. He did not like being lectured to, even in allegory.

* * *

Iede thought she was beyond awe, but when she entered Aywon's personal quarters she found herself breathlessly excited. The wall opposite the entryway was a window, looking down on Epsilon Eridani. Iede's eyelids fluttered as she fought off a faint. Her entire world, in all its glory, as viewed from the vantage point of a god! Aywon had to gently push her forward into the room in order to fully enter himself. Iede tore her eyes away from the window to take in the rest of his quarters. The room was quite small, but Aywon had made use of all three dimensions in such a way as to maximize space. His personal taste tended towards green, and Iede was suddenly struck with a faint pang of homesickness at the familiar color.

"You'll stay here with me, Iede."

"My Lord, I am not worthy. I do not wish to intrude upon You."

Aywon waved her objection away. "Don't worry. You won't be here long."

Iede nodded and felt shame that she had even entertained the thought that the arrangements might be permanent. No doubt a meaner dwelling space was being created for her even now.

Aywon looked at her for a moment, then looked away. Iede thought she saw shame in his eyes for an instant, only to be replaced by resolve.

"I suppose you have more questions about the ruins."

"My Lord, if You wish to speak to me about them, I would be honored to listen." Iede lowered her head.

Aywon sighed. "There's not much to say. We discovered the ruins about a year ago—that's about three-fifths of a local year—but have learned little. We're in synchronous orbit," he looked at Iede and must have read the blank stare on her face, for he added, "that means we stay above the same area on the planet below. We have a satellite network around the globe, of course, and we've been using the network to search for more ruins. We've found dozens of cities."

"My Lord, I asked You in the…room with the other gods if You knew who built them. Is it possible that You know but do not wish to say?"

"No, Iede. We truly do not know." A grin spread suddenly on his face. "You know, it is indescribably invigorating talking to you."

"My Lord?"

"You're curious. You want to know…well, everything." His grin faded. "We lost that fire long ago. We're content now to observe and study, but there's no passion in us. I hope that you won't become infected with the same malaise in your stay." He looked at her for a long moment, then said brightly, "While you're here, though, you may as well soak up as much as you can. Here." He swam through the air to a wall panel and said, "Access mission log." A holo menu appeared before him. "Access Costellan speech one."

Iede noted again Aywon's implication that she would be leaving and could not help but feel a pang of regret. She was beginning to like this god—and not for His godliness, but for His…humanity.

The holo projector came to life. A young man appeared in air, standing behind a podium. He was outside, but the sky had a curiously blue tint to it. The image was frozen—the man seemed about to speak.

"This is Eduard Costellan," Aywon said.

Iede swallowed. "*The* Costellan? The same one who—"

Aywon nodded gravely.

Iede looked closely at the image. The man could not have been more than eighteen years old. "My Lord, when was this recording made?"

"This is a recording of the launch crew's speeches the day before the voyage. It was made two hundred and twenty-one years ago, Earth years. That's roughly…one hundred and thirty-five years ago the way you count years. Of course," he added reflectively, "we're a little bit out of synch with Earth time due to the slight relativistic effects of the journey."

This meant nothing to Iede. She just stared at Costellan's image hanging in space before her. Suddenly, the blue sky made sense to her. "This was recorded on Earth!"

"Of course. Not in this format, of course—but we've adapted it to our systems now."

"'Green air, wind, and sky/Not the blue of the old home/New beauty to see.'" Iede quoted. She continued to stare at Costellan. She had known, intellectually, that he was physiologically a man and as such must have had a youth as well as an old age, but her mental image of him was of an aged patriarch. She had to force herself to believe that the dashing youngster (younger than she was!) before her was the same man whom she had based a religion upon.

"Would you like to hear his speech?"

Iede turned to Aywon. "If my Lord thinks I am worthy."

Aywon opened his mouth but seemed to think better speaking. Iede saw annoyance in his jaw as he said to the wall panel, "Run."

Costellan immediately came to life and smiled at an invisible audience. He was dressed in a blue jumpsuit adorned with patches of all shapes and colors. Behind him, pennants and flags flew in a strong breeze, and Iede could even see a flock of birds in the distance.

"Thank you, Madame President. Assembled guests, my crewmates have spoken at length about what the mission ahead means to them, so I will not belabor it. What I have to say has mostly been said already. I would like to make only a few points. Of my own.

"Nineteen years ago, construction began on the vessel that hangs above us now, awaiting the order to unfurl her sails and get underway. I was eleven years old then. I did not dream that I would be standing here now, less than twenty-four hours before launch, addressing the world. Now that the moment has come, I still have trouble believing it.

"Much has been made in the news of late that the two thousand people who have chosen to make the journey are somehow abandoning Earth and the System. I know that there have been some acrimonious things said in the Systemweb about us, and about me. I was told by numerous public relations experts to ignore the comments and make today's speech idealistic, full of bright promise and hope. I could have done that, but I chose instead to answer the critics.

"The Martian Confederacy was established forty years ago this year, and the last census places its population at just over one million people, with five thousand new immigrants every Earth year. Twenty years ago, the Europan colony was founded: current population, eighteen thousand. No fewer than eight orbiting habitats provide living space for over ten thousand Earth citizens. Are these examples of traitorous cowards fleeing an overworked Earth for more fertile pastures? Or are these colonies and habitats bold pioneering strides for the greater glory of the human race? Ask a Martian or a Europan. Better still, board a System-ship and go there yourself to see what these intrepid adventurers have carved out of native rock and ice.

"Now we are prepared to make the next step. In one hundred years, humans will set foot on a planet outside their home solar system. But none of the people standing on this platform in front of you will do so."

Iede shivered slightly when Costellan said that. He had been right, but perhaps not in the way he had expected. Had he known, even then, what the future held for him? She shot a quick glance at Aywon at the wall panel. He was floating near the panel, eyes closed, his face completely at peace.

Costellan spoke again. "I know the analogy has been made before, but I think it bears repeating. We are children of Earth who have grown and who must seek our fortunes elsewhere. But, like all children, we will never forget our mother. Thank you." Costellan waved to acknowledge applause and the holo faded out.

"He was a poor public speaker," Aywon said, "and yet his words always affect me profoundly."

Iede nodded slightly. "Why, my Lord, was the journey undertaken?"

Aywon smiled indulgently. "Your question has been asked countless times by children who are beginning their true education among us. The answer is in the form of a riddle. Would you like to hear it?"

Iede nodded.

"Why did the man climb the mountain?"

Iede scowled. She felt that Aywon expected a deep, soulful answer from her, but she could not think of one. The only answers that came were somehow ugly in their pragmatism. "Because it was in his way?"

Aywon smiled again. "No. But that answer would tell your examiner much about your personality. You would have been marked for possible engineering training based on that."

"Because he wanted to see the view from the top?"

"Again, no. That answer would have possibly put you in line for the arts, or possibly the Groundseers themselves. Do you wish to hear the true answer? The answer Costellan himself gave when he was asked the same question just before his death?"

"Yes, My Lord."

"The answer is: because it was there."

Iede nodded slowly. Aywon cocked his head and stared at her for a moment.

"You don't understand, do you?"

Iede stopped nodding and licked her lips. "No, my Lord,"

"That's all right. The answer at first is disappointing, I know. In time, the answer satisfies." He paused. "But there is a corollary to the riddle that no one seems to think of."

"My Lord?"

"Why was the mountain there?"

Iede blinked and thought for a moment. An answer had presented itself immediately, but she could not imagine it was the correct one. She did not think that she could so easily solve a god's riddle.

"You are about to say something," Aywon said.

"My Lord, I do not—"

"Say it."

Iede took a breath and said, "So the man could climb it?"

Aywon smiled. "That's the answer. At least, as I see it. You've climbed a very tall mountain, Iede, as have your brothers and sisters planet-side."

Iede did not answer immediately. Aywon was hiding something—that much was obvious. No doubt there were truths that she was not yet ready to accept. She would be patient.

"My Lord?"

Again, Aywon tried to conceal a look of disgust. "Yes?"

"About the speech I heard. What kind of people set out on this journey?"

She thought she saw worry crease Aywon's features for an instant. He seemed to come to a decision, and his face cleared. "They were outcasts, Iede. Not quite criminals, for it was not yet illegal to hold such views as theirs, but pariahs, certainly."

"What views, My Lord?"

"They were what used to be called socialists. They believed that every member of society had an unbreakable obligation to every other member of society."

Iede blinked in surprise. How else could a society be run? "And they were exiled because of that belief?"

"Not quite. They were encouraged to volunteer for the mission."

Iede could not fathom a kind of civilization that would find such views as heretical. She made a feeble stab at envisioning a culture run on nonsocialist lines and could not. With a tiny shake of her head, she dismissed the almost-vision.

"The people who left, my Lord...were they...?" she did not know how to complete the question.

Aywon sighed. "We have records on every one of the original launch crew and the colonists. Would you like to see them?"

Iede's eyes went wide. "I am...allowed?"

"No, not really. But I won't tell anyone if you won't." He smiled indulgently.

"No, my Lord."

"There is one condition I must insist upon, though."

Iede thrust her face forward a bit, anxious to accept whatever Aywon said. "Yes, my Lord?"

"You must stop calling me 'my Lord.' Or anything else like it."

"My Lord, I—"

"Ah!" Aywon thrust his hand out, palm up, and waggled it about. "No more. I am Groundseer Aywon. You can call me Aywon in private, though in public I'd prefer Groundseer."

"I do not wish to show disrespect, my...." Iede caught herself.

"There's a difference between respect and reverence, Iede. Besides, what have I done to earn your respect?"

"You saved my life."

The statement did not have the effect Iede imagined it would. Aywon seemed to deflate visibly. "True. But what more could we have done? So much...so much." His eyes were far away for a moment, then he snapped them back to Iede. "Let me get the records on Ship for you. I have some things to attend to. You will remain here in my quarters until I return."

Aywon showed her how to use the holo viewer and how to advance to the next file. "I will be back before you should need to eat or drink. If you find the need to eliminate, I'm afraid I will have to ask you to hold it. We have strict recycling protocols here, and I haven't the time to show you how to use the nearest reclaimer. I'll be back soon, though."

Aywon left the small room. Iede looked at the door for a moment after he was gone, then turned her attention to the holo records. She had much to study.

CHAPTER 23

"How many times do you want me to say it, Foz? You were right." Sirra buried her face in her hands for a moment, then looked at the young linguist. "I'm sorry. I'm still a little…."

"Sure," Fozzoli said, then looked back at the holo display between them. It was a complicated mass of symbols, lines, and arcane markings intended to decipher the new data about the vix' language. Fozzoli studied the holo for a few moments, but his posture indicated he wasn't really looking at it. Sirra realized she was being childish.

"All right," she said, tearing her mind away from the near-death experience she had had six hours ago and focusing on the problem before her. "What have you got for me?"

"Here," Fozzoli said, indicating a particular line in the holo. "We used to think that this frequency was used to express awe and reverence, since it was the one we saw most often in vix utterances referring to us. But your experience, along with some other clues, makes me think it's something else."

"You're still on that, eh? What other clues?"

Fozzoli smiled sheepishly. "Well, we've seen this frequency most often when the vix refer to…uh, excrement."

"Shit?"

"Yeah. I've also seen it in references to unusual sexual practices. They seem to have a strong incest taboo."

Sirra considered this. "You say you saw the same frequency when the vix referred to me?"

Fozzoli nodded. "Or to any of us. I thought it was just a coincidence, but your recent…adventure makes me sure."

"You're saying they think we are like shit?"

Fozzoli shook his head. "No, no. I'm saying the frequency they use for excrement, deviant sexual practices, and us is the same. It doesn't mean there is a direct lexical match; it just means they think of us in the same ways. All three of those topics refer to the profane, in differing degrees."

"Which one is the worst?"

"We are."

Sirra stared at him, then slowly shook her head. "It's no good, Foz. You read the transcript—they kept referring to me as "Damned Saint" or "Demonic Angel" or something like that. They said it enough times so I'm sure there was no fault in my translator. What's that about if not religious reverence?"

"I think there is some confusion in the vix religion," Fozzoli answered wryly. He grinned. "'Course, that could be said of any religion."

Sirra ignored the comment. "I think they don't know what to do with us. It has something to do with the confusion between the Above and the Old Place."

Fozzoli shrugged. "I had assumed the Old Place was just the undersea volcano. The Above and the Old Place are opposites. That's why they took you to the Old Place—to try to reverse, or exorcise, the influence of the Above."

Fozzoli's reasoning made sense, but something did not feel right. There was something wrong with his logic, though she could not find a flaw in it. She thought back to her experience with Bishop. He had been in ecstasy as he descended—could that be purely religious?

"Foz, what's the dissolved oxygen concentration at the bottom of the fissure?"

Fozzoli blinked in surprise at the sudden change of topics. "Uh, hold on." He accessed the data and said, "We haven't gone all the way down."

"What is it where I was? Compared to the vix town depth?"

"About eight times higher. Seven-point-nine-four times."

"You think that would have an effect on one of them?"

"I imagine so. It sure would on one of us in atmosphere."

"That's why the religious leaders live below the rest of them. They have access to a higher level of oxygen than the others."

"I suppose. We know that vix settlements are found only near undersea volcanoes, and that there is a definite radius away from the volcano beyond which vix will not build."

Sirra nodded excitedly. She felt she was on to something but could not explain what it was. She would have to talk it out. "Depth means more oxygen near a volcano. Okay. That means the surface has less. Above, to them, would mean death."

"Or at least a loss of mental faculty. Kind of like lightheadedness in us. Do you think they associate the Above with death? Like heaven, or some other afterlife?"

Sirra shook her head. Again, Fozzoli made sense, but his conclusion didn't feel right. "I think it is a mistake to start ascribing human theology to the vix, though."

Fozzoli said, "But they have death rituals. We've seen them cast off vix outside their cities. Sometimes they float up, sometimes they sink down. Has anyone studied that phenomenon?"

Sirra frowned. "I'm not sure. I've never heard of a study on it. But who would study it, aside from one of us?"

"Maybe there's a reason some of them go up and down. Maybe they send the saintly, good vix up to the surface, the Above, while they make the bad vix sink below, to hell."

Sirra considered that. "It's a question I'd ask Vogel, if I didn't think my mere presence there would result in another exorcism. I'd rather not do that again. And I think we should suspend further dives until we've got this figured out."

"We could go to another settlement," Fozzoli suggested.

"Yes, but it'd take months, years to learn another language, even with the head start we've got here. Plus, there's no reason to assume a different vix settlement, completely unconnected with this one, would have similar rituals. No, we've got to stay here and figure this out ourselves." Sirra pressed the sides of her head with her knuckles. She could almost feel the answer sliding around in her brain, imprisoned by a discontinuity. There was a crucial fact she and Fozzoli were overlooking—she just didn't know what it was.

"Hang on," Sirra said finally, removing her knuckles from her temples. "Just because down signifies hell in some ancient Terrestrial religions doesn't mean the vix think the same way. Why would they take me down to exorcise me? Why not up?"

"Maybe they want to return you to where they think you came from."

"But they know we all come from the surface. The surface means something to them—something awe-inspiring but at the same time repulsive. No," she shook her head at herself, "not repulsive—profane, as you said. Like a bad memory."

"A bad memory?" Fozzoli said, puzzled.

Sirra was not listening. She could feel the answer forming in her head, but it was still cloudy. She knew what questions she had to ask. "Foz, what was that study done of vix physiology? The one that said there were no blind alleys or dead ends in the vix evolution?"

Fozzoli furrowed his brow. "You mean Doctor Seelith's piece?" At Sirra's nod, he continued. "She said something about the evolution of the vix didn't leave them with any vestigial organs. Like our appendix or our tailbone, stuff like that. The vix don't have any of that. Hang on, I'll dig it up." He turned to the computer, but Sirra waved him away.

"No, don't bother. I remember it now."

"But what does that have to do with—"

"I don't know. I don't know." Sirra squeezed her head gently, palms against her temples. "I need to talk to Khadre."

Twenty minutes later, Khadre's holo image stood before Fozzoli and Sirra. The two women exchanged a warm look. Although the two had only corresponded a dozen times in the past thirty years, the five years before that had sealed a bond between them that in some ways rivaled Sirra's relationship with Yallia.

The moment passed, and Khadre said, "My assistant told me you want to talk about 'Notes on Missing Vestigial Organs in Vix Anatomy.' This is the first time in eighteen years anyone has made comment on that paper. Not the most exciting piece of work, but I am happy to discuss it with you."

Sirra smiled back. "Thanks for taking the time to talk with me, Khadre."

"It's been too long."

Sirra was anxious to get on with her questions. The demands of nostalgia, however strong, would have to wait. "In your paper, you proposed that the vix do not have any vestigial organs or structures, like we do." Sirra had skimmed the paper while Fozzoli had been contacting Khadre's research ship. "What can you conclude about their evolutionary process as compared to ours?"

Khadre's eyebrows rose. "That's all? You get right to the point, don't you? You haven't changed." She said fondly. "Eighteen years ago, when I wrote the paper, I wasn't prepared to draw any kind of conclusions. I didn't have enough data to stick my neck and reputation out."

"But you do now?"

"No. But I find now I care less about my reputation…and my neck." She drew a breath and said, "The vix' evolutionary process was fundamentally different from ours. There had to have been outside factors involved."

"How can you be sure of that?"

Khadre shook her head. "As I said, I'm not. I have no real data to back me up, just observations and conjectures. But the vix are different from any other life on this planet. We've examined other marine life and other animals on land. All of them have vestigial structures or organs. They seem to have followed the same kind of evolutionary paths Terrestrial animals have.

Only the vix have arrived at their present state with no leftover genetic debris, so to speak."

"Couldn't the vix just be fortunate in their evolutionary path?"

"Not a chance. Organisms as complex as the vix would have vestigial structures that were once useful but are no longer. Vestigial structures aren't a sign of genetic weakness—they're more of a history, showing where the species came from and what it used to be like."

"And these vix show no signs of ever being any different than they are now?"

"Right."

"Why couldn't the vix be throwbacks from prehistory? Like the Terrestrial alligator? Unless I'm wrong, the alligator is virtually unchanged over millions of years."

Khadre sighed. "Yes. So is the shark, to some degree. That question was one of the reasons I never published what I'm telling you now. I can't disprove that with empirical evidence, but my feeling is that an organism as complex as the vix could not possibly have remained stagnant for the millions of years required to eliminate all vestigial traces of preceding forms. Also, while I'm not as expert as you on their culture, I am under the impression that their culture shows signs of rapid development over the last few thousand years."

Sirra nodded absently and looked at Fozzoli. "Yes. My colleague, Doctor Abromo Fozzoli, has studied that."

Khadre looked at him. "Oh, yes. I know Doctor Fozzoli."

Fozzoli cleared his throat and said, "We have reason to believe there was a cultural explosion on the order of eight to ten thousand years ago."

Khadre nodded. "That would tend to discredit the notion that the vix have been in their current form for millions of years."

Sirra broke in. "But if all you say is true—"

"I never claimed it was fact. Just speculation."

Sirra ignored her objection and swept on. "—the vix, as a species, are only eight to ten thousand years old."

Khadre did not answer.

Fozzoli coughed awkwardly, then said, "I'm not seriously proposing this, but have you thought of punctuated evolution, Doctor Seelith?"

"Don't be shy, Doctor Fozzoli. I've read your papers." Khadre said, and Sirra suppressed her amusement. "I have indeed thought of punctuated evolution, but no theory ever advanced with any sort of merit postulates wild evolutionary change in such a short time. When added to the changelessness of the sea, the idea is untenable."

Sirra shook her head. "But what alternative have we? Where did they come from?"

"Another good question. And that's another reason I never published. I haven't got even the beginnings of an answer to that."

"It has to have something to do with the Old Place." Sirra said absently.

Khadre's eyes narrowed. "What?"

Sirra started, then looked back at Khadre. "Oh, uh...I had a little problem a short while ago with the vix." At Khadre's curious expression, Sirra related the story of her abduction and escape.

When she had finished, Khadre blew out the air in her cheeks. "Well, I think you've got a lot of data to integrate. Do you think the Old Place, wherever that is, is where the vix come from?"

"Maybe," Sirra said, "But where is that? Bishop was descending towards the vent when Vogel told me he was trying to commune with the Old Place. But...."

Khadre completed the thought for her. "But the vix couldn't have come from the vent. If they had, you can be sure they would look quite different than they do now. The incredible heat and pressure would require quite a different type of organism."

Sirra was closer to the answer now, she knew it. But there was still a hole in her data that she needed to fill. The vix didn't come from the vent, but something about it reminded them of their original home.

Sirra and Khadre did not speak for a few moments. Khadre broke the silence. "I think, Sirra, that we had best sign off for now and think about this in isolation. Do you object to my sharing of your discovery with my colleagues on this end?"

"No, of course not."

"Good. If you need to reach me, I'll be at the same combo. Please call if you think of anything new. I'll do the same. Or, you could call just to talk."

"Thanks."

Khadre smiled. "I remember you, thirty-six years ago, reaching your hand in the water to talk to the vix after the attack." Her eyes sparkled. "I knew you would one day make something of yourself with the vix."

Sirra smiled back, but her memory was tainted with Viktur Ljarbazz, lying in a bloody heap on the heaving deck.

Khadre nodded slightly, as if in acknowledgement of the man's memory, and switched off.

Khadre was still staring the spot where Sirra's holo had stood moments before when Kiv entered the cramped comm suite. "What's up?"

Khadre did not answer immediately. She swiveled her head to face him, her mind still on the conversation. "What?"

Kiv snorted. "You been hypnotized?"

Khadre slowly focused on her son. "Hm? Oh, no. I just...." She hesitated again.

Kiv looked suspicious. His voice no longer tinged with humor, he said, "What's wrong?"

"Something's happening with the vix."

"What is?"

Khadre drew a breath and told him of Sirra's encounter, leaving out most of the speculation the two women had done minutes earlier.

"We have to stop research. Immediately," Kiv said when she had finished.

Khadre stared at him. "What?"

"The vix have attacked one of us."

"But we don't know why."

Kiv shook his head. "It doesn't matter. Any human who goes down there is subject to the same risks. I can't allow any of us to be in that kind of danger."

Khadre got up and approached her son. "Kiv, listen. We are at a crucial moment in our research. If we stop now—"

"You scientists are always at a crucial moment of research. The vix aren't going anywhere. I am ordering an immediate cessation of information-gathering. You yourself said that you have more data now than you know what to do with."

"Kiv, you can't stop us from researching." As soon as she had said it, she knew it was precisely the wrong thing to say to her son. She saw his face harden and his shoulders square at her words.

"Yes, I can. These vix have all but declared war on us."

"*What?*" Khadre's eyes widened. "Son, you don't know what you are saying."

"No?" Kiv looked away and walked to the other side of the comm suite. He stared at the ground for a moment, then looked up again. "You have told me, many times, that the vix are intelligent. You've said that they are tool-making, problem-solving animals. I think they are smarter than you give them credit for. I think they are tired of being prodded by us and are now striking back."

"Kiv—" Khadre shook her head and spread her hands wide.

"How can we be sure they don't know about the terraforming process the Domers started one hundred and ten years ago?"

"That was abandoned thirty-four years ago. The vix have roughly the same generation cycle we do—thirty-four years is between two and three generations for them. Vix lifespan is a bit shorter than ours—barring accidents, vix tend to live about forty-two to forty-five years. There'd only be a very few vix who were even alive during the terraforming process, and only a tiny number of them who were old enough at that time to think purposefully."

"Aren't we still feeling the effects of the project now? Surely, the planet hasn't returned to its original state in just thirty-four years."

Khadre chafed. "No. And it never will, not entirely. But much of the damage has been reversed. The remains of the project really aren't much of a factor in the day-to-day lives of modern native animals."

"But as I understand, during its seventy-five year duration, it had quite a profound effect on the planet's ecosystem. Isn't that right? Whole species became extinct, and others were forced to change their behaviors in rather extreme ways. Why not the vix, too?"

"I'm sure they did, but they seem to have adapted to it."

"But how do we know they don't have some deep resentment for what we've done to them?"

"How could they possibly know what we have done? The concept of terraforming is many orders of magnitude beyond their comprehension."

Kiv's eyebrows went up in scorn. "Really? You told me they are skilled in agriculture. They modify their environment to suit them. What else is terraforming but a more extreme version of basic agriculture?"

Khadre opened her mouth to answer and stopped. Kiv was right.

He smirked at her. "Just because I spend most of my time behind a desk, Mother, doesn't mean I'm not smart."

"I never said—"

Kiv waved away her objection. "It doesn't matter." But Khadre could see the hurt in his eyes. Despite the nature of the conversation, Khadre found herself replaying various encounters she had had with her son over the years. Had she shown him less love than her other children? All her other offspring were in the sciences in some way, although none of them had yet made a name for themselves. Only Kiv, her sole male child, had gone into a different field. Had she been guilty of favoritism towards her science-minded daughters? She remembered the many times she had joked with him about his job as a paper-pusher as he had risen steadily through the political ranks. On the infrequent times she had called him, she had dismissed his work as mere bureaucratic fiddling. Eventually, Khadre realized, he had stopped calling her to tell her of another political victory or legislative triumph. And she had been only too happy to distance herself from him.

"Son, I—" After all the years, she could not find the words to excise twenty-plus years of injustice.

"I'm ordering an immediate interdiction on the vix. No human is to approach them for any reason. That goes for automated machinery as well. I don't want to take the chance that they will capture some of our technology." Kiv's voice was iron. "Besides, we might need you scientists to help us against the Domers should it become necessary."

Khadre ignored the last comment. "That's a mistake, son. We won't be able to learn what they want if we don't research them more."

"Right now, we know what they want. They want to kill us. I'm not going to give them the chance."

"Kiv, listen. We'll be careful. We'll keep—"

"Domeit, Mother, you listen! I'm ordering an end to it! You'll tell the leader of this expedition to cease work immediately and return to the mainland. Or would you prefer I do that?"

"I'd prefer to keep studying them."

Kiv stared at her, and his mood changed abruptly. "Why can't you listen to me? I am the leader of this colony. I am ordering you to stop work." His words conveyed command, but his voice was almost a petulant whine.

"Are you telling me to stop because you are afraid of our safety, or are you just trying to get back at me for all the years I ignored you?"

Kiv swallowed before answering. When he did, Khadre could hear the effort he was exerting to keep his voice even. "You will cease research on the vix, effective immediately. I am declaring this an emergency, where I have broad disciplinary powers. If need be, you will be impressed into military service where you will assist in naval technologies should they become necessary to put down Dome rebellion. If you do not follow my orders, I will have you placed under arrest." His voice faltered on the final words, but he kept is eyes locked on hers.

Khadre thought to fight him—he did not have any police with him, and it would be quite a while before he could summon anyone to enforce his order. In the meantime, she and the crew of the research vessel could conduct valuable research on the vix. She might also be able to change Kiv's mind while he waited for police to arrive.

But she knew that that would hurt him more than anything else she could do. To disobey him now would ruin whatever chance she stood of correcting the damage of the past.

If, indeed, she could correct it at all.

Khadre reluctantly climbed the short ladder that led out of the comm suite and headed for the bridge.

Kiv did not speak to his mother during the trip back to shore. Had he bothered to analyze his own behavior, he might have found himself irrational, selfish, even childish. Questions hovered at the edge of his conscious mind—why had he truly suspended research on the vix? Surely the researchers could take precautions, studying the vix from remote locations or with robot submersibles. Had he simply wanted to take away something his mother found dear: more dear than she found him?

Could he truly be jealous of the vix?

He would not think that thought. He was an elder statesman, the leader of a million colonists on a world orbiting an alien star. He was more than just his mother's child.

His mind sought for a way out of the loop it threatened to lose itself in, and it turned to the Tannites. The small but troublesome faction had been unusually active lately—there had been three near-violent demonstrations (in the Dome, of course) and an unusually high number of threats. And his agents among the Tannites had been warning that there were indications that there was a much larger, more radical movement keeping itself hidden from the Family.

What did they want? At every step, it seemed, the Family offered its hand in welcome and the Tannites spat on it.

He had been approaching the problem from the wrong angle. The answer did not lie in integration, but in segregation. That was what the Tannites truly wanted. Why should he force them to live amongst people they hated? The planet was certainly large enough for multiple groups and points of view. What was wrong with the Tannites forming their own state and governing themselves? And if in future there were problems with the other factions, well, those would be solved by later administrators. Kiv would solve the problem of the Tannites now. If that meant armed conflict to ensure the safety of the Family, so be it.

* * *

Iede started when the door to Aywon's chambers raised open. It was, of course, Aywon himself. Iede tried to stand up in respect, found that she could not orient herself properly in the zero-g environment, and began a lazy cartwheel spin towards the window.

Aywon swam to her and gently righted her with a bony arm. "Steady. Small movements in zero-g."

Iede fought off shame at her behavior and mumbled, "I suppose I will have to learn how to operate in zero-g."

"No, you won't. That's what I've come back to tell you. I've found a way you can get back to the planet."

Iede stared at him. She did not fully understand her own emotions—they were a mirror image of her feelings when she had learned she would be staying on board Ship for the rest of her life: a combination of joy and regret. To her own embarrassment, she found a hard lump in her stomach had dissolved at the thought of returning to the ground.

"It won't be easy, though. You'll have to learn how to pilot one of our lifeboats and land it on the ground. I can teach you."

"My Lord...."

"I've asked you not to call me that."

"I will do as You say."

"But you want to say something, don't you? Well, go ahead. And keep the awe out of your voice."

"I do not deserve all that has happened to me. You have shown me so much already and I cannot ask for more. Yet...." Despite his encouraging face, she could not go on. What right did she have to ask the gods for anything?

"You want to stay for a bit. Well, learning how to pilot the lifeboat will take some time, and I suppose there's no harm in waiting a few days so I can better set up the caper. But when I'm ready, you'll leave. You can't stay here."

"As you will it, Lord. I have much to teach my parishioners about all of this. When I return, I hope I can impart some of your wisdom to my people." She closed her eyes for a few moments, thinking of the grand new evolution her religion would take.

When she opened her eyes, she found Aywon frowning at her.

"Have I displeased you?" Iede asked timorously.

"Maybe you're right. You're not ready to go back just yet."

Iede looked at him, wondering what she had done wrong.

Aywon sighed and said, "You've still got a lot to learn. Or unlearn." He looked out the window for a moment, then turned back to her. "Earlier, in the Groundseer hub, you were told to abandon your religion. When you return to the surface, that's what you will do."

"My Lord!" The exclamation was wrenched from her.

Aywon continued implacably. "There is no greater threat to the survival and well-being of the colony than your religion. If you have any love for your fellow colonists, or owe any obedience to me, you'll do as I say."

Iede did not answer. To put the command on that kind of footing made it impossible for her to object, but at the same time, how could she just abandon her life's work—and abandon the man who had made her life possible?

Aywon sighed and looked away, towards the window. "I realize I am using your reverence of me to order you into a course of action—don't think I'm not uncomfortable at that. But I must have your word that you will begin dismantling this religion as soon as you go back."

Iede did not answer: how could she? She was trapped in a paradox she had never dreamt of—her gods were commanding her to cease her worship of them.

Aywon continued. "You have a second job to do—almost as important as the first. You must tell the others of the ruins."

Iede blinked, nonplused. She had almost forgotten about the ruins in her awe at her surroundings. While the discovery was interesting, how could it compare with the experience of being in Ship? But her god commanded her, so the ruins must be very important.

"I will." She bit off the honorific 'my Lord' with conscious effort.

Aywon seemed to sense that she did not understand the importance of the ruins. "We in Ship have always been concerned with threats to the mission from the outside. During the voyage, that meant cosmic debris and other astronautical dangers. Now that the colony is set up, our function has largely been to observe. But the ruins represent another potential outside threat—I feel it is our duty to alert you to it and help you take action."

"But you are alone in this?" Iede ventured, remembering the argument in the Groundseer hub.

"Yes. I think we have been observing for so long we have forgotten to act. We see so much, Iede. Much of what you colonists do on the surface is laudable, but there is so much injustice, too. To float up here and simply watch...." He looked out the window again, staring down at the green-tinged planet. "Once before, our distant ancestors watched without taking action. I have studied our history. Never again."

Iede stared at him with a new reverence—one born not of religion but of genuine respect for his obvious resolve, even if she did not quite understand what he meant.

"Enough of that," he said suddenly, his voice firm again. "If you are to return to the surface, you'll need to learn how to pilot the lifeboat. I have some holos for you to watch."

Aywon swam to his wall control panel and began accessing flight simulator holograms. Iede watched him, wondering what she could possibly do to remove the threat the ruins presented that the gods themselves were powerless to thwart.

CHAPTER 24

Sirra smiled at Fozzoli and added, "For a linguist, you certainly seem at a loss for words."

The young scientist merely shook his head slowly. "There's just no way. No way am I letting you do this."

"Vogel knows what's going on. We need him."

"How many ways do you want me to demolish your line of thinking? First," Fozzoli held up a slender forefinger and violently slapped it with his opposing forefinger, "you don't know that Vogel knows anything. Second, even if he does, we don't know if he will tell us anything. Third, even if you're right and he will tell us all he knows, you don't even know where he is now. Fourth, assuming that somehow you can find him, you'll be attacked as soon as you show yourself to the vix priesthood, if not to the ordinary townsfolk."

"What's the alternative, Foz? Wait up here for something to happen?"

"Yes!" Fozzoli fairly shouted. "What's the great rush? We have a lot of data to coordinate—who knows what we'll come up with? The vix aren't going anywhere."

"I wonder."

Fozzoli's eyes narrowed, then his voice softened. "Look, Sirra, you and I have disagreed on a lot of stuff. You're always pushing the limits, trying new things, getting yourself in trouble. I know that I'm cautious. I'd rather think something through than rush in. Maybe I've lost opportunities that way—I'll never really know. But you've got to ask yourself—why do you really want to go back down there? Is it really because it will serve our research interests best?"

Sirra frowned. Fozzoli pressed his point harder.

"I'm sorry I have to say this. You're an old woman, Sirra. Your career is almost over. Are you sure you just don't want to make one last mark on the world, no matter the cost? Rather than leave the next generation to do it instead?"

"You think I'm that way, Abromo?"

"I'm not sure. But going back down to see the vix again...there's no sense to it. Other risks you've taken at least had a sort of balance between risk and benefit. This, though...what can we gain from this that is worth risking your life?"

Sirra stared at him a long time. His moist eyes stared back at her, unreadable. Fozzoli had always been a loyal assistant—no, more than an assistant. A colleague. He was poised to make some astonishing discoveries of his own and make a name for himself in the scientific community. Could it be true that he was jealous? Was he trying to gently push her aside so that he might shine more brightly?

"You think I should stay up here with all of you youngsters and try to coordinate the data? You said it yourself, Foz—I'm an old woman. I'd just be in the way. Maybe you think I should just retire altogether, is that it?" As she spoke, she watched him carefully. He squirmed at her words but held his composure.

"I never said that. Your input has always been valuable. But maybe you don't have the patience you once had, since you have so few years remaining in the field. Don't throw away a fine and distinguished career in a moment of childish weakness. Let's study the vix for a few months, and if we find we need further data, then we'll go down and get it."

"No, Foz. Something happened down there, and if we don't get back there fast, I think the vix will...." She shook her head. "I'm not sure what they'll do, but something's coming. I can feel it."

"You and your domed intuition."

Sirra thrust her hands outward, palms up, in a deprecating gesture. "It comes with age, Foz."

Fozzoli did not answer immediately. Sirra knew that he trusted her hunches almost as much as she did herself. She did not invoke her intuition often, and as a result, a statement that she was "feeling" something carried weight with the linguist.

"Then let me go instead. Or one of the other divers. The vix're hunting you now."

Sirra smiled inwardly at his change of tactics. "The vix don't make much of a distinction between us, you know that."

"A team, then. Armed. With the launch. No need to go in alone and unprotected."

"I've thought of that, too. I don't want to cause more of a disruption than necessary."

"You mean, more than rewriting their entire religious philosophy?"

"Exactly."

Fozzoli sighed. "Can I ask one thing first, since you are going to go and there's little I can do to stop you?"

"Short of pulling a gun on me."

"Oh, don't think I haven't thought of that. And I would have too, except that the weapons locker is locked and only holds tranq pistols and there's only one person with the keycode and she's a stubborn woman."

"What was your question?"

"Did I say anything that even remotely changed your mind?"

Sirra laughed suddenly. The note of pleading in Fozzoli's voice was comical.

"You got me angry with your old woman comments."

"Yes, well, I'm sorry about that. I was just trying to—"

"It's all right. But the two of us should know better than to debate one another. Two linguistics experts playing semantic and rhetorical games? What could be more pathetic?"

Fozzoli snorted. "I suppose you won't object to my monitoring you?"

"Of course not. And have a diving team ready this time. I don't want to wait around like I had to last time before you and the rest of the research team dragged their carcasses down to get my tired old body."

"Sirra, I really didn't mean what I said about your age. I just…well, I was trying to say anything to get you to reconsider."

"I know. It's all right."

"No, I want to tell you. You've done more for the study of the vix than any other living person. Including Khadre. I expect you will continue to lead the field for the next…well, for quite a while."

Sirra found herself welling up. She had dismissed Fozzoli's remarks on her age as ploys to weaken her resolve, but even though Fozzoli had just confirmed that her intuition was correct, she was nevertheless relieved that he still held her in high esteem.

"That means a lot to me, Foz." She hesitated briefly to allow her sincerity to sink in. "But before we start crying and painting each other's toenails, I've got to get ready for the dive."

Sirra checked her gauges again. The surface water temperature was as warm as it had been the last dive, but she still felt a chill as she settled down through the dive pool and swam under the lab.

"No vix in the vicinity down there, Sirra," Fozzoli's voice sounded in her ears.

"You've shut off active sonar?"

"Yes. We're listening on passive only."

Sirra nodded. She did not want any transmissions coming from the lab's remote sensors below to inflame what she knew were already high tensions among the vix. Passive sonar had a much shorter range, and was limited in resolution as well, but she would be effectively silent.

"Passing nine hundred meters," Sirra said. "I'm going to go off communications at one thousand."

"Acknowledged."

The next hundred meters passed all too swiftly. "I'm switching off, Foz. Stay sharp up there."

"Good luck, Sirra."

Sirra turned off her transmitter and her sonar beacon. Fozzoli had suggested they reconfigure her suit's communications to a higher frequency, but the modifications would have taken days, and Sirra had not been convinced that the vix could not sense the higher frequencies in the same fashion that some humans could sense dog whistles. She had opted for sonar silence instead. Fozzoli had extracted a solemn promise that if she found herself in trouble, she would reactivate her beacon. The lab would pick up her signal and come for her.

As she continued to descend, her own passive sonar began to pick up the conversations of nearby vix. Her suit lamp cast a dim glow a few meters ahead of her, which would provide her with a slight advantage in close range work, but she still was forced to rely on passive sonar for long range "seeing."

At one thousand and sixty-six meters below the lab her suit's speakers came to life.

"*Speaker-From-Above. You should not have returned.*"

Sirra did not need to glance at her HUD to know who the vix was.

"I'm glad to see you, Vogel."

The vix swam into her sonar field. "*The Crusaders remain vigilant.* "

"But I found you first. Why are you so near the Above?"

"*I do not fear it as the Crusaders do. The stories my father-by-actions told me drive me ever closer to the surface.*"

In all her discussions with Vogel, he had never once mentioned his family. Sirra knew enough of vix family custom to know that a "father-by-action" was not a child's biological father but one who raised the youngster, sometimes with the help of the mother, sometimes with the help of a mother-by-action, or even with community-parents. But children were never raised by a single parent, and rarely by only two. There were various gradations of intimacy in the words the vix had for family members—in this, the vix were not unlike the humans of the Family.

But Vogel had spoken of stories, too. "What stories do you mean?"

Vogel began swimming in slow circles around her. *"My father-by-action told me stories of his own youth. He told me that when he was a young* [untranslatable utterance] *himself, he swam towards the Above Place. Much farther than any other vix had ever done. He says he left the world for an instant.*

Sirra glanced at her translator display. The last sentence had translated directly, according to her computer. More importantly, her own intuitive sense told her Vogel was speaking literally. She could make certain of her translation, if he let her.

"Vogel, may I touch you while you tell me the story?"

The vix stopped circling, his tentacles fluttering smoothly to check his movement. He hovered there before Sirra for a moment before answering. *"You wish to touch me after what we have done to you?"*

Sirra started to tap out an answer, started to tell him that she did not hold him responsible for what he had done, started to tell him she did not even understand what had happened a few hours ago, but stopped herself. If he was right about the Crusaders, she might not have long alone with him. "Yes. I must. Please."

Vogel moved cautiously towards her. *"Will I be...Lifted?"*

It was the first time she had heard that phrase. Her translator was little help, even with Fozzoli's additions—it blinked the question symbol to indicate Vogel's utterance was an interrogative one but gave no alternate definitions for the final word. But Sirra was close enough to get an impression from him. The word had religious overtones, but she could not tell if he was fearful or eager to be "Lifted."

She answered in the safest way possible. "No," she said, and placed her gauntleted hand on his smooth surface. She closed her eyes and tapped out on her vixvox with her one free hand, "Now, tell the story." She placed her second hand on his body and felt her connection with him deepen.

"My father was, to his friends and townsmates, a simple farmer. But he was much more than that." His words came smoothly, easily, and Sirra felt the emotion behind each sonar ping. She could even hear his voice as she knew it would have sounded were he a man—a deep baritone that at once held conviction, wonder and wistfulness.

"He was a seeker of knowledge. Not the knowledge of the worldsea (her translator had labeled the word an "untranslatable utterance" but Sirra could feel the meaning) *but a forbidden knowledge—the knowledge of the past and of the Aboveplace.*

"He built strange devices and placed them as high as he could to listen for the sounds of the Abovefolk. He strove to reach higher and higher, but found his own fear limiting him. He told me he had often felt a pressure building in him as he rose, a pressure that threatened to take his reason away. I asked him if it was like the pressure

of the Rite of Adulthood we all face when we descend to the Holy Chasm and behold a tiny part of God. He said it was similar in many ways but inside-out. The pressure came not from outside, crushing him in holy splendor, but from inside, as if he himself were creating the divine pain."

Sirra caught her breath in sudden realization. Vogel's father-in-action had felt pressure because of his ascent—or more accurately, a distinct lack of pressure—from the surrounding seawater. The effect must have been unsettling.

"One day, his crude devices told him that there had been a disturbance Above. For quite some time, he had been detecting other strange noises that he could not understand, but this new sound was unique. Something had happened Above that had never happened before. My father called on one of his friends, a younger vix named Vicar.

Sirra knew the name was only her own mind's approximation for Vogel's sentiment. The name he had used was, obviously, a mere "untranslatable utterance" to her computer, but the sense of it was "he or she who speaks for the gods." Vicar seemed to fit.

"The two of them rose higher and higher, despite the mounting feeling of dread, until they had left the world of vixian experience. No creature had dared to rise so high. And still they rose. My father passed the uppermost of his listening devices and began to hear faint sounds of struggle above. There was a battle taking place.

"Vicar told my father that the sounds were of an infernal conflict that was not for vixian ears to hear.

"Then came the Song. My father could not, despite tellings and retellings, fully explain the rapture of the Song. He said it was like hearing a perfect note of music (Sirra was surprised the translation came so easily to her mind. Did the vix have music? She realized that even after thirty-five years, she and her fellow researchers knew very little about the natives) *sung by every creature that ever existed. The note sounded, and sounded again, and again, over and over, each time perfectly, each time the same duration, the same pitch. The note played and played.*

"My father and Vicar were enthralled. They continued the climb, heedless of the mounting danger to their bodies and perhaps their souls. Then they came to the Above. My father told me that it was a place of effortless movement, but also of suffocating evil. He could not remove his entire body to the Above, as if some force held him back. There was nothing there, save for a strange ledge, attached to nothing, with creatures resting on it. My father would not approach them, but Vicar did.

"Creatures like you, Speaker."

Sirra did not open her eyes. She completed the story to Vogel in a half-whisper. She did not need to tap the words out on her vixvox; the mental link she had with Vogel was stronger than it had ever been.

"And Vicar swam towards the creatures, and one of them touched him. And he asked the creature 'are you God?'"

Vogel took up the story smoothly. "*And as he asked the question, the Song ceased, in mid-note, and Vicar knew she had offended. When my father and Vicar descended again, neither was ever the same. My father could not swim very well after that. The* [doctor] *told us that my father had lost the winds within and would not live long. He was right—only four seasons later, my father-by-action was gone. His mind had gone, little by little, in the last season, and the* [doctor] *told us that the winds in his head had quieted as well. My father did not live in our world much after the encounter with the Above. But he always told the story the same way.*"

Sirra opened her eyes and stared at Vogel's head, aware that the vix' wide-set, unblinking eyes were much cruder than her own (but also much more complex than necessary for a creature that spent its entire lifetime in the darkness of deep ocean: another mystery the researchers had not been able to penetrate) but feeling the need to connect with Vogel in a *human* fashion. "I'm...sorry."

"*Why?*"

"Because I'm to blame. Your father went mad and died because of us. Because of me." The years floated away effortlessly, fog in sunlight, and she was again on the remains of the *Beagle* with her grandonly Yallia and Khadre. The sensation of touching the vix was fresh and just as electric as it had been those thirty-five years ago.

Vogel did not speak for a few moments. Sirra prepared herself for anger, sorrow, retribution—anything but the question he asked her.

Are you God?

Sirra was silent.

My father did not ask that those many seasons ago. Vicar did, but the answer she received is a closely guarded secret among the Crusaders. I now ask you: are you God? Or are you That-Which-Shall-Never-Be-Named?

Sirra felt a chill as her mind attempted to translate that last utterance. The sound for "That-Which-Shall-Never-Be-Named" was different—much lower in frequency according to her suit indicators, almost low enough for her ears to hear it if she had not been encumbered by her diving gear. And it had a feeling to it—a feeling Sirra associated with the infernal, the demonic.

Vogel was asking her if she was God or the Devil.

"I am neither. I and others like me are not from your world."

This much is certain. Where are you from?

"That's difficult to explain." Sirra sighed inwardly, trying to begin her answer. As she thought, something Vogel had said impinged itself on her consciousness. It had slipped past her then, but now she frowned at it. "Vogel, did you say the Crusaders guard Vicar's secret?"

Yes.

"Where is the answer recorded? The answer Vicar received from...Above?" She had almost said "from me," but decided not to press the point now.

I don't understand. Recorded?

"Yes. I know you have records—you pass along much of your history orally, I know, but I have seen some, well, writings your village has. You yourself even took me to them seasons ago."

Yes, Speaker, I know what records are. But there are none for Vicar. She keeps her own secrets.

"They died with her?"

She is yet living.

Another flash of insight. Vicar was alive—the vix Sirra had touched thirty-five years ago survived to this day. And Sirra knew the name she had chosen was accurate, but not exact.

Bishop.

* * *

Iede smiled slightly as she piloted the lifeboat down to her twelfth consecutive simulated landing. She turned expectantly to Aywon.

"All right. I think you're ready," he said softly.

Iede did not answer. She closed the holo program with a word and avoided Aywon's stare.

"What is it?"

"I will leave if it is your will," Iede said softly.

"It is. You know why it has to be done."

"The ruins."

"Of course. You must tell the rest of the colonists about them."

"My Lord," the honorific slipped out despite Aywon's admonitions, "I shall of course carry out your wishes, even if my limited human understanding does not comprehend the divine purpose behind them." She did not look at him as she spoke.

Aywon's voice was a growl. "I've told you, over and over, not to refer to me or anyone else in Ship like that. We are not gods, Iede!"

Iede kept her eyes focused on the deck.

"Look at me!"

Iede met his gaze, trying to hide her terror. She had angered him, but she was prepared to suffer his wrath. Her life was his—having saved her so long ago, she was prepared if he should want to take it now.

But his features softened slowly, and within half a minute he was looking at her not with anger but with pity. "You can't do it, can you?"

"My Lord?"

"I'm a god. We're all gods here." He faced her as he spoke, but something in his bearing suggested that he was not speaking to her. "No matter what I say, you'll think of me that way."

"Yes." Iede hoped this would not make him angry again, but what else could she say?

He continued to focus elsewhere, then abruptly shifted his attention back to her, his eyes focusing almost imperceptibly on hers. "That will change presently. In the meantime, you must return to the planet and tell them of the ruins."

"As you wish, my Lord."

"Listen, Iede," Aywon said, floating closer to her and grasping her by the shoulders, "I could simply order you to tell everyone down there, but I want you to fully understand why this is so important. These ruins are, as I said, about ten thousand years old—sixty-one hundred local years, that is. This is only an estimate based on...well, many factors—no need to go into that now. We think the estimate is fairly close, give or take a few hundred years. But what we don't know is who built them or where those beings went. Once that mystery is solved, a potential threat to the mission will have been identified and we can take steps to help you remove it."

"The mission, my Lord?"

"The colonization mission."

Iede stared at him for a moment, puzzled. "I do not understand, my Lord."

Aywon smiled slightly. "Sorry. We refer to the events on...your world as 'the mission.' An old habit. You see, as far as we are concerned, this mission is not over. It began over two hundred and twenty years ago but cannot yet be termed a complete success."

"When will that be, My Lord?"

"When you are fully self-sufficient and all outside threats to the colony's survival are eliminated."

Despite her reverence for Aywon, Iede found her planetary pride swelling. "My Lord, are we not now self-sufficient?"

"*You* ask me that, Iede?"

Iede stared at him, uncomprehending. Why should she have any special insight as to colony management?

Aywon shook his head. "It doesn't matter. One thing is undeniable. The ruins represent a mystery that may pose a threat to the colony. You must tell your world so that its scientists and explorers can investigate."

"Will you help us, My Lord?"

"I have helped all I can. But there may be...a sign, later, if you solve the mystery."

Iede shivered at the prophecy. Something about Aywon's bearing caused her great dread.

"But we must now focus on returning you to the surface. And for that, we must be cautious." He glanced at a spot on the wall that Iede was only dimly aware of as a timepiece and said, "In a few minutes Ship will be in shift-change. The third-shifters will be moving to their posts while the seconds leave. Once third shift is underway, we will make our move."

Iede nodded. She had learned from the holos that Ship followed the same day that Newerth did, and although Ship never fully slept, the third shift, which took place during the nominal sleeping hours, was the least populous. There would presumably be less chance of running into a wandering god during their escape.

Aywon swam to a wall console and performed a series of elaborate, intricate movements along its surface with his slender fingertips. The console slid open noiselessly to reveal a thin sliver of metal that glinted ominously in the chamber light.

Even the alien design did not hide the item's purpose: it was a weapon.

"I will not ask you to use this, Iede," Aywon said, not looking at her, his eyes fixed on the weapon, "since I know you could never hurt one of us." Now he looked at her, and his eyes were soft. "But I will. You must return to the surface at any cost."

"You would kill a god for me?"

"No, not only for you, Iede. For all of you. And I will do much more." For a moment, his gaze was no longer upon Iede, though his eyes did not flicker from their position. Iede saw them unfocus for an instant, as if Aywon was looking into another time.

A soft chime sounded. Aywon nodded, then said when it had ended, "Third shift has begun. We will leave in five minutes." He stared at Iede for a moment, then picked up the memory disc he had compiled for her. "As I told you, this disc contains everything you'll need to find the ruins below. You shouldn't have any problems using it on the colony's machinery." He handed the disc to her. Iede took it and stared at it reverentially for a moment, then secreted it in her tunic. She stared at Aywon, her mouth opening as if to speak, but she did not trust herself to make the request she had so desperately wanted to utter since she had arrived on Ship.

"Iede, you want to ask me something. I think I know what it is, and I have an answer for you. I cannot come with you to the surface. Even if somehow my body could survive the transition to gravity, I could never betray my principles to that degree. I—*we* must not interfere with the colony's development any longer. Do you understand?"

Iede felt a flush coming to her face. Aywon's answer was well-reasoned and firm, and utterly inappropriate. She had had a different question in mind, and now it shamed her even as it burned in her brain.

"My Lord, I...."

"What's the matter, Iede?" Aywon swam closer to her and lightly touched her cheek. She was startled to discover that she was crying.

"I...."

Realization seemed to dawn on Aywon. "You were going to ask me something else, weren't you?"

Iede did not answer. She could not.

"Even a god can be wrong, eh?" Iede did not react, and Aywon said gruffly, "Well, what is it?"

She looked at him longingly, hoping that such a god would not be offended by a mere mortal's offering of love. She did not trust herself to speak—she wanted the moment to convey her message.

Aywon stared at her for a long moment, then swam away hastily. "Iede, I don't understand. Are you...." For once, Aywon appeared flustered and embarrassed. "...Well, proposing something? Sex?"

The word exploded in the air between them. Iede recoiled at it and suddenly began to shake in mortification. He had understood her, and now she was more ashamed than she had ever been. "My Lord," she began, "I meant no offense. I...." She squeezed her eyes tightly shut.

Iede felt Aywon's smooth hands on her shoulders. "No, you haven't offended me, Iede. It's only...well, I'm sure you've noticed our anatomy." He paused for a moment to pick his words. "We're all hermaphrodites. When we are directed to reproduce, we do it ourselves. There is no sexual intercourse on Ship, and there hasn't been for about seventy years. A little over forty or so of your years. So I'm not offended by your offer, in fact, I am flattered, but it would be impossible. Literally—impossible." He smiled, taking away some of her mortification.

Iede sought refuge in a change of subject. "My Lord, why are you...the way you are?" As soon as she asked it, she realized how disrespectful she was being. But the need to change the subject, even slightly, away from her foolish mistake was paramount.

Luckily, Aywon did not seem to mind the question. "I'm not one of the Bloodweavers...the geneticists, but I have had the basic indoctrination on our history. I am told that in order to ensure changelessness, we strove for full hermaphrodism. Each offspring is the direct genetic duplicate of its parent. In a closed environment such as Ship, we can virtually guarantee sameness generation to generation. It's been this way for three generations, near enough."

"My Lord, I know that our science below could not hope to compare to yours, but it occurs to me that—"

"You're about to ask me about cloning, aren't you?"

Iede nodded.

"That was considered as an option. But I have not told you the whole truth about us. I use the term 'hermaphrodite' to describe myself, but that is not quite correct. Although I have a penis, it is incapable of impregnating anyone. Except myself."

Iede did not respond. She tried to keep the horror off her face.

"It's quite complex, and since I am not well versed in the field, I can give you only a simple explanation. My anatomy, and the anatomy of everyone in Ship, is such that the male sex organs, the testicles, are functional, but the penis is a, uh, a biological holdover. It serves no purpose save for urination. I remember being told that possession of a penis greatly reduces the risk of a urinary tract infection. Oh, and we have no prostate gland."

He spoke matter-of-factly despite Iede's mounting disgust. She knew her thoughts were unworthy, that she had no right to judge this god and his...could she even use the pronoun anymore? Could she even think of Aywon as "male" or "female?"

"I see I've upset you. I'm sorry." Aywon looked sincere. "I just wanted you to know how very different from you we've become. That's why we could never...have sex." Iede could hear the upset in his voice at the word.

"To answer your question about cloning, though, it was decided that even if we perfected cloning, there could be no guarantee that shipmates would not still impregnate each other, uh, *conventionally* and thus stir up the gene pool. The transformation to self-functional hermaphrodism, or a sort of asexual reproduction, was necessary to ensure genetic purity."

"It is not for me to judge the gods," Iede said, as much to herself as to Aywon.

He stared at her and said, with uncharacteristic irony in his voice, "No, it isn't." He waited a moment before adding, in a softer tone. "We are not admirable in many ways, Iede, but we have also made a great many sacrifices for the success of the mission. And we will make one more soon." Again, his eyes unfocused and he was elsewhere. When he returned, he swam toward the chamber door. "It's time to go. Follow me, stay quiet, and do as I say."

The two left Aywon's room and swam silently through the corridors on their way to the lifeboat bay. Iede knew the route almost as well as Aywon did—she had spent hours at his computer studying the twists and turns of the path they were now following. Despite the haste with which they traveled, she stole glances down access corridors she would never traverse, wondering what lay deep in the bowels of Ship. She had studied as much of Aywon's files as she had had time for, but much was still unknown to her. The temptation to break off from Aywon and investigate further was strong— only her twin desires to return home and tell her people her story kept her steadfast. That, and her almost unquestioning obedience to her god, despite his protestations against godhood.

They were nearing the final leg of their journey when another god emerged from a hatchway before them. There was no time to duck into a side tunnel; Aywon would be forced to deal with this situation.

The god's eyes widened as she (something indescribable about the god's bearing suggested femininity to Iede—after Aywon's revelations about the gods' sexuality, Iede found herself almost pathologically determined to assign gender to all she met in Ship) took in the pair before her. She opened her mouth to speak, but Aywon was quicker. He produced the thin rod of milky translucence from a flesh pocket on his wrist and in a smooth motion aimed it at the god.

There was no sound, no discharge of light, but the god crumpled into herself and began a lazy tumbling spin, her limbs motionless. Aywon slid the rod back into his flesh holster, and it disappeared from sight.

"What happened?" Iede whispered.

"It doesn't matter," Aywon said, and, anchoring himself against the bulkhead, shoved the unmoving body out of his way.

"Is she...dead?"

"I told you it doesn't matter," Aywon repeated, his voice flinty. He opened the hatch from which the god had emerged seconds before and gestured for Iede to follow. Iede could not resist another glance at the gently cartwheeling body of the unfortunate god—she wondered if she had seen something that would haunt her forever.

The rest of the trip was uneventful; the pair slid through metal-white tunnels with ease. At last they came to the lifeboat bay. Although it was as clean and gleaming as the rest of Ship had been, a faint air of disuse hung in the chamber. Aywon approached the lifeboat and played his fingers gently on its surface. Iede could not see a control pad, but presently the lifeboat's outer door raised open as it had done so many days ago on the surface.

"Get in, Iede," Aywon said gently.

"Yes, my Lord." Iede swam slowly to the portal, stopped with one hand on the jamb. "My Lord, I cannot repay you for what you have done for me, and for all of us. I will do your bidding to my people. I shall never forget what I have seen here."

"No, you won't. Good-bye, Iede. Continue to watch the sky for your final message after you have unlocked the secret of the ruins."

Iede looked at him quizzically. "Final message, my Lord? What—"

"Get in, now. Before others come," he said, and pushed her gently into the lifeboat.

Iede entered the craft and looked back out the doorway at Aywon. He stared back at her stolidly, then touched the hull, and the iris valve closed.

Iede hesitated only a moment before climbing into the control saddle in the front of the ship. Her hours of training came back to her and she pressed the proper surfaces to ready the lifeboat for its descent. Displays come to life in front of her and to each side, projected in three-dimensional representation. One display showed the bay doors slowly opening beneath her and Newurth hanging in space below. Iede released the lifeboat from its moorings and gave the superior jets a half-second burn. She fought back sudden sorrow as the lifeboat dropped rapidly out of the bay with the action of her thrusters. Iede swallowed hard and fought to keep her eyes clear of tears as she began the process of returning the craft to Newurth.

CHAPTER
25

Sirra fought to contain her emotions. Could Bishop know who she was? Could her capture by the crazed vix have been a kind of revenge for what Bishop had undergone all those years ago?

She calmed herself. Bishop had never spoken of the incident to her, even when they had been alone at the lava vent. And how could Bishop possibly recognize her after so many years? Bishop couldn't even have seen her when she surfaced, so unaccustomed to light as the vix were.

That raised another question. How did these creatures, presumably adapted to life at these depths, rise to the surface and survive? Yes, Vogel's father-by-action had died, but not immediately. Both vix ought to have suffered horrible nitrogen narcosis with pain so intense that neither would have continued to surface. Was it possible, however, that these creatures possessed some kind of internal system to compensate for the severe drop in pressure? Why would they have such an ability? The vix were fish, not mammals: they did not breathe oxygen from the air, but utilized the high amounts of dissolved oxygen in the water. They did not need to surface—in fact, they would not be able to breathe once out of the water.

"*Speaker?*"

Sirra shook herself within her suit. Maybe Vogel could help answer these questions.

"Vogel, you asked earlier if you would be Lifted if I touched you. What do you think it means to be Lifted?"

"*I am not certain, Speaker. But I have been taught that those who follow in the path proscribed to us from the time-before-water will one day reclaim their place in the holy depths. Those who do not will rise to oblivion.*"

Vogel's answer raised far more questions than it answered. Sirra had to take things one at a time. "Why did your father-by-action rise, then?"

Sirra felt the despair of deep mystery swell in her as Vogel's emotions surged through her suit gloves. "*I have asked that question of myself for many years. I thought to ask Bishop, but I have never had the courage. Then you came, and I have thought many times to ask you, but again, I am afraid."*

"What are you afraid of, Vogel?"

"Wrath. Bishop's, at first, but I now know that her wrath is that of a child's to yours. I have been taught that there are some questions one does not ask."

Sirra's scientific mind took great umbrage to that, and she bristled. "There are no questions forbidden to you, Vogel. The only way you can advance as an individual and as a race is to ask—ask everything, question all accepted modes of thought and investigate for yourself. That is the path you should follow."

"Who are you?"

Sirra blinked, then grinned sheepishly inside her mask. She should have seen that coming. For all her words about truth and science, here she was, deceiving this creature who may well represent the first tentative moves towards pure scientific inquiry his race had yet taken. Vogel wanted to know—and Sirra suddenly had an impulse to tell him all.

"All right. But I can't just tell you—I'll show you. You wait here; I have to get something that will take you to the answers. You are going to be Lifted, Vogel—but it is nothing like what you think it is." As she spoke, she felt curiously liberated, as if a crushing weight had been removed from her mind. She felt better than she had in years.

"I will wait, Speaker." Sirra felt dread mixed with eagerness in him, and she knew that he was at once terrified and elated at the prospect. She withdrew her hands and began her ascent. Her mind whirled as she mentally prepared the mission: she would need a scout sub and some way to fill it with seawater of the proper pressure so Vogel could rise and not be damaged. He would have to stay in some kind of holding tank so he could survive the trip and explanation.

She giggled when she thought of Fozzoli's response to what would surely be the strangest request she had ever made of him.

Fozzoli did not explode when Sirra had finished. Instead, he nodded slowly and said quietly, "Sirra, something has come up. We've received a directive from the Coordinator's office. All research concerning the vix is to be terminated immediately."

Sirra stared at him blankly. "What do you mean?"

Fozzoli sighed. "Just what I said. We're shut down."

"For how long?"

"Indefinitely."

Sirra stared at him, then looked helplessly at the rest of the lab, as if trying to wrest control of the laboratory from the Coordinator's unseen presence. She made vague gestures with her hands and heard herself mumbling incoherently for a few moments before she found her tongue and said, more clearly, "Did our Coordinator give a reason for this...decision?"

"Not really." Fozzoli shuffled to the communications panel and pressed a button. The text of the Coordinator's message filled the air between the two scientists.

Sirra's lips moved slightly as she read the order. When she had finished, she looked meditatively through the words at Fozzoli, then slashed her hand through the speech, closing the file. "Dangerous? They're not dangerous, if you know how to handle them." Her objection sounded hollow in her ears. She grew angrier at the prospect that perhaps the Coordinator might be right. "And how did he find out about what's going on?" she said, changing the target slightly. "We haven't sent in any reports lately, have we?"

"Of course not. We've got nothing to report, yet," Fozzoli said, matching her anger with calmness.

"Well, I'll be domed if I'm going to let him tell me to stop my research. Until he sends some goons out here to shut us down in force, we'll continue with the operation. I'll need a scout sub, pressurized to—"

Fozzoli's expression silenced her.

"What?" she said.

"Sirra, we've got to stop."

"The hell we do!"

Fozzoli's defeated countenance twisted in exasperation. "Listen to me for once, Sirra! It's very easy for you to dig your heels in and make proud noises about never quitting, but just think for a moment!" Fozzoli lowered his voice and continued. "The Coordinator won't tolerate anyone disobeying an emergency edict like this. You read the order—there's no wiggle room. If we don't stop, now, he'll not only send some goons out here, but he'll replace you, me, the whole domed staff with people he can trust. How long before the Coordinator notices we haven't reported in? And how long before he sends a squad out her to stop us? A few days? You really think you're so close to a breakthrough that a few days will make a difference?"

The question sounded rhetorical, Sirra knew—but for just a split second, she thought she could hear hope in Fozzoli's voice. He was giving her a way out—and she knew the man too well to think he would not remain here with her pursuing illegal research up until the moment some government thugs tore his hands off the consoles. But he'd do it only if she was sure that she was on to something big. If Vogel didn't come through for her, she would ruin not only her own career but Fozzoli's as well. Her work was approaching the twilight years, while Fozzoli was only beginning to make a name for himself. Did Sirra have the right to place all of his promise in jeopardy?

She made her decision. "I've got Vogel down there waiting for me. I need to tell him I won't be bringing him up just yet."

Fozzoli's face showed relief, and just a hint of disappointment. "This thing'll blow over, Sirra. The Coordinator's edict has the force of law only until the Assembly is convened. They'll overturn this as sure as we're sitting here. Let's use the time to correlate all of our data."

Sirra nodded. Yes, much work could be done with the data they had. Perhaps Fozzoli could come up with something they had missed. But Sirra couldn't shake the feeling that she had lost momentum at a crucial moment in her studies and was not sure if she could ever get it back.

Only two days had passed during their exile back to the mainland, and despite the considerable opulence of her mainland estate Sirra had grown angrier. The Assembly had indeed convened but had not instantly overturned the Coordinator's edict—they had instead decided to debate the issue. Sirra found to her chagrin that she was not very interested in the data Fozzoli brought to her in increasing postures of excitement. He was finding more and more subtle hints about vix language that Sirra had grasped instinctively with her unusual talent. Fozzoli had been shuttling between his mainland office and Sirra's home for the past two days while she sat in her apartment and sulked. She was not proud of herself—her attempts to hide behind aged cantankerousness did not work, at least not on herself.

Late in their second day of waiting, Fozzoli approached Sirra with a curious expression. "Sirra, you have a call."

"From whom?"

"She says she's your halfonlyaunt."

Sirra reeled, and for a moment did not grasp the meaning of the word: her grandonly's daughter—as it applied to herself, Sirra had all but forgotten its meaning. Her ha'lyaunt (the word still rung queerly in her mind) had left the Family perhaps twenty-one years ago to pursue her insane preoccupation with Ship. Despite her many attempts to keep her attention on her research and away from her ha'lyaunt, Sirra could not insulate herself from the knowledge that Iede had founded a growing quasi-religion. Why was she calling now? Had Iede somehow found out about the interdiction regarding the vix and was going to try and convert her sibling into her religion to fill the void?

She was being silly, she knew.

"Thanks, Foz," Sirra said faintly. Fozzoli opened his mouth, but Sirra turned to look at him and he understood. *Not now, my friend.*

When Fozzoli had left, Sirra activated the comm outlet in her sitting room. The screen lit up to reveal Iede's face, still youthful despite its thirty-six years. Iede was three years younger that Sirra, but Sirra knew her own face was far more aged.

"Ha'lyneice. It's good to see you again after all these years," Iede said, her voice a youthful melody. She was smiling broadly in what appeared to be sincere delight.

Sirra was determined not to return the emotion. "What do you want, Iede?"

"It's been…nineteen years since I last spoke to you."

Sirra was unimpressed. "Yes, it has. I won't lie to you and say I'm interested in what you have been up to, Iede. So why are you calling?"

The faintest hint of disappointment flickered over Iede's face, but then it was gone, replaced by her placid mask of composure. *My God,* Sirra thought, *she really does look happy. Brainwashed, but happy.*

"You want me to get to the facts, eh, ha'lyneice? You haven't changed. Ever the scientist. Just like Grandmother."

"Yes, and you're still just like…." Sirra couldn't finish the thought. The effort she had expended to remove Iede from her conscious life was nothing compared to the mental energy she had directed trying to eradicate her knowledge that Iede's father was the traitor that had nearly cost the fledgling Family their lives—Lawson. That Yallia was her Grandonly and Sirra herself had no genetic connection to him did not help in this instance—her ha'lyaunt carried his blood in her veins. Nothing could wash it out.

"Don't call me ha'lyneice. Call me Sirra. What did you want?"

"I've been on a journey to Ship."

Sirra resisted the impulse to sigh in exasperation. "Really, Iede, I'm a little busy here," she lied, "and I haven't got the time or the patience to hear about your visions, so—"

"No, no, Sirra. Not a spiritual journey, though the experience was certainly…enlightening. No, I was *there*. Physically."

"Up in Ship?" Sirra's eyebrows climbed.

"Yes. And I have learned something the gods wish me to impart to all of us."

"You're saying you are a prophet?" Sirra couldn't quite keep the disdain out of her voice. Was Iede telling her the truth or had she finally lost what tenuous grip on reality she possessed?

Iede cast her eyes downward. "I make no such claim. I am just a messenger from the gods."

"A prophet, then," Sirra snorted.

"If you want to use the term." Iede's voice was cool and even.

"All right, give it to me. The revelation."

"I have a memdisk the gods gave me with the data on it, but before I send it, I need your help. I came to you so that you might point me in the proper direction to investigate this data. I did not know where to go, and although your area of specialty is the sea, I thought that you might know of a reputable and open-minded person who could conduct an excavation on land. Discreetly."

"What are you talking about?" Sirra spread her hands helplessly in front of her. "Excavation?"

"You will understand when you see the contents of the disk. Are you ready to receive?"

Sirra's expression of annoyed puzzlement intensified, but something in Iede's manner made her curious. Her ha'lyaunt had never been forceful or focused on mundane affairs to this degree—Sirra's memory of her was that she had always seemed in a slight daze, as if she were in the grip of a narcotic. Iede was still gentle, soft, and mystical, but now had an added aura of *purpose* to her Sirra had not seen before. Against her better judgment, Sirra nodded and gave the appropriate instructions to her computer to record the data in Iede's memdisk. "Go ahead," Sirra said faintly, and she saw the panel indicator acknowledge the transmission and begin recording.

Half a minute later, the transfer was complete, and Iede's smile, which had remained faint on her placid face, intensified slightly. "Review this revelation carefully, Sirra, and please contact me when you have an idea for someone who could lead the expedition." And Iede's image winked out, leaving Sirra with an odd feeling of dread as she considered the contents of the transmission.

In twenty minutes, Sirra knew the data, if authentic, would overshadow even the discovery of the vix thirty-six years ago. She spent two more hours examining the contents carefully, looking for any alternate explanation for what she had seen. She could imagine no other. The formation was far too symmetrical and orderly to be merely the product of water and wind erosion on ordinary rock. There were but two possibilities, both almost equally shocking.

If the data was authentic, there seemed no other explanation but that a civilization had existed on land on Epsilon Eridani III some eight thousand years ago. If the data was a carefully designed forgery, then someone had gone to an incredible amount of trouble for…what? Could this all be merely a hoax designed to embarrass whomever was taken in by it? If that was so, was Iede in on the ploy? Sirra could not believe that. Iede was many things, but a prankster was not one of them. Therefore, Iede must have been taken in as well. Who would want to deceive someone like Iede—Iede, who had deceived herself with her 'religion' so well?

The thought struck her that Iede was not the target of the hoax—Sirra herself was; Iede was only being used as the conduit. But the question then remained, why would someone go through such an elaborate hoax just to embarrass Sirra if she chose to reveal the findings to the scientific community?

Sirra could think of no reason, but she could not shake the nagging feeling that someone was watching her, baiting her, tempting her to go public with the data and ruin whatever standing she had among her colleagues. She could imagine the derision when scholars all over the planet descended on the supposed site of the ruins to find nothing but chlorinated lichen and ordinary rock. Whatever clout she had wielded would be lost to her—she could forget about trying to buck the Coordinator's ban on vix research.

But if the data were authentic, she could hardly conceive of the sheer import of the discovery. Could she ignore what Iede brought to her merely because of the risk of professional embarrassment? But how could she ask other scientists to drop their work to pursue this if it turned out to be a false lead?

There was only one option. She would have to go herself. She was no archaeologist, but surely she could visit the site and learn if Iede's data represented a real find or a hoax. And by going alone, she did not risk embarrassment should it turn out to be nothing.

She opened her mouth to tell her house computer to call Iede, but heard herself say, "Call Doctor Khadre Seelith." She sat back, surprised at herself, as her computer completed the call. Then she leaned forward defiantly. Why shouldn't Khadre be in on this? And for that matter, why not Fozzoli, too?

It took little convincing to secure Khadre's participation ("You don't think I'll hold you back?" was the aged scientist's most serious objection, and Sirra had dismissed it with a wave of her hand) but Fozzoli was another matter.

"We'll need surveying equipment, which we don't have," he was saying over an hour into the discussion, "and none of us has the first domed clue how to run the sorts of tests that'll make the trip worthwhile."

"Foz, you're not understanding the point of this trip," Sirra said. She could sense his resolve against the trip weakening. "We're not going to make a detailed survey, we're going to see if there is anything to see. I'm sure we can do that much. If there is something, we'll come back and announce our findings. If not, well, no one's to know we went at all."

"And if there is something, then what? We announce that the gods told us about this place?"

Despite herself, Sirra found herself defending her halfonlyaunt. "Why not? It's the truth, or nearly. What does it matter how we came by the knowledge, anyway? If there is evidence of a pre-colony civilization here, that will shatter the entire field of epsilology."

Another half hour and Fozzoli was convinced. She had smiled at his final comment before he switched off: "I wasn't really that opposed to the idea until I discovered how much you wanted to go. Then I had to fight you."

Sirra sighed when Fozzoli's image blinked out. Only one call left to make.

"I've found you some scientists, Iede."

Sirra was the first to meet Iede at the departure location two days later. The four "conspirators" (as Fozzoli had persisted in calling the quartet) had agreed to meet well outside the outskirts of the city in an inconspicuous area that Iede had frequently used as a gathering point for her religious meetings. Iede liked the spot—to the north, the direction the expedition would be heading, was a vast flat plateau that most Epsilologists agreed was a dry salt lake. The area commanded the plain in such a way that Iede had frequently imagined thousands of followers standing on the dry lake, looking up at the crude pulpit some of the rocks created. Now, of course, the lake was empty, save for Sirra approaching on her landsail. She had told Iede that she had relegated most of the task of assembling the necessary survey materials to Fozzoli, who had grumbled at the impossibility of stuffing all the tools he wanted to bring into the tiny compartment on Iede's airfoil. In the limited contact Iede had had with the man, she had liked him, even with his complaining.

Sirra navigated the landsail to a stop near Iede's outcropping and walked the short distance up the crags. She carried only a small knapsack, which she unceremoniously unslung and dumped on the ground a few meters before Iede.

Iede stood next to the airfoil. She had chosen her vestal gown for the trip and indeed had brought no changes of clothing.

Sirra glanced pointedly at Iede's head. "Still keeping the baldness, eh?"

"As the gods command," Iede responded calmly, looking into the distance.

Sirra started at her head for a moment longer, then snorted. Iede made no comment.

"So, three days?"

Iede's voice was even as she replied, "At the recommended speed for this airfoil, the journey to the ruins will take three days, yes."

"Better find something to talk about, then, hadn't we?"

"If you wish. I am content to remain silent."

"Does that mean you don't have anything to say to me?"

Iede turned to look at Sirra. Her ha'lyneice was grinning, but there was no mirth in her eyes. "You do not approve of me," Iede said simply. "As you would have it, I have wasted not only my own life but the lives of countless followers who worship a dream, a fantasy, a—"

"No, no, no—not a dream. I'm aware that there is a ship up there somewhere—" Sirra gestured vaguely with her hands "—and I know what it was. It was the ship that carried us here about seventy years ago, or what's left of it. But that's all it is. It's empty. About thirty years ago, I think, we sent up a ship, at great expense, to investigate. There was nothing. No radiation, no openings, no response to communication attempts. The only reason we haven't gone up there to scrap it completely is that anything of value has already been shuttled down ages ago."

"And why do you believe that?"

Sirra blinked at the question. "Why? Because it's true."

Iede softened her voice to a near whisper. "How do you know? Have you been up there? You are a scientist, Sirra, and I would have thought, an empiricist. Do you have firsthand knowledge of conditions inside Ship?"

Sirra did not answer immediately, and when she did, her voice had lowered as well. "No, I don't. I also don't have firsthand knowledge about the interior of this planet, but I can deduce what must be there from surface features. Much of science is not empirical observational data but a chain of reasoning, of deduction, from observable features."

"And if I claim observational data that disproves a deduction, what then? If I were to go to the interior of this planet and find not molten rock but, let us say, a little old man squatting on a toadstool, what then? Do you still hang on to your deductions in the face of observations to the contrary?"

"When such observations are unreliable, of course," Sirra answered, her eyes locked on Iede's.

"And you believe that mine are unreliable? The product of a deranged mind?" Iede had not raised her voice during the conversation and did not now. She did not blink as her eyes absorbed her ha'lyneice's gaze and turned it back.

After a breathless interval, Sirra said, "Deranged? No. But I don't know that your observations weren't a vision, a dream, or a hallucination.

Can you honestly say that there is no chance that all of your experience wasn't a product of an overactive imagination?"

"Perhaps it was. In that same vein, can you absolutely confirm that you are not now experiencing a dream?"

"I hate philosophy," Sirra muttered. She raised her voice again. "Of course not," she said. Her voice softened and she shifted her weight a bit. Her posture became less confrontational and more sisterly. "But, look, Iede—can't you see that this 'experience' of yours is exactly what you have been wishing for, for years? Doesn't that make you doubt it just a little bit?"

"If you are saying that I have deluded myself into seeing exactly what I want to see from my gods, I concede that such a phenomenon is possible. But I have not created the topological data, have I? From where did this data that our expedition will examine come?"

Sirra gave up. "That's why I'm here. To see if there is anything to this."

"And if not? If somehow you are right and this is all a product of my fancy?"

"I don't what to hurt you, Iede. I don't like you, and I don't like your religion, but I won't take you to anyone for treatment if this all turns out to be a hoax." Iede could hear the pain in Sirra's voice.

"And if it is real?"

Sirra didn't answer. The silence stretched out for several seconds until a sound startled both of them.

"Hey! I could use a hand with some of this stuff!" Fozzoli called out from his small single-occupancy scooter, onto which he had stuffed an impressive array of scientific gear. He brought his scooter alongside the airfoil and powered down. He looked at the two women quizzically. "What's going on? We still going?"

"Of course," Sirra said, moving rapidly away from Iede to help him unpack. Iede observed where to move different items, then also assisted.

When the gear was stowed into the airfoil, Fozzoli turned to Iede and said, "We've met, but only on holo. I'm Abromo Fozzoli, but everyone calls me Foz. Well, not everyone, but your ha'lyneice does," he stopped and paled slightly. He opened his mouth to say something else, closed it, then opened it again. "So, er, is there anything else to do, or...?" he trailed off, his eyes darting quickly to Sirra, then to the airfoil, with an affected air of examination.

"Dr. Fozzoli. I'm very glad to meet you in person," Iede said softly. She could see that her words did not have the calming effect she had hoped. Fozzolijumped when she approached him and laid a hand on his arm. "My ha'lyneice has told me a little about you—not much, though. I gather that she has represented me to you as well."

Fozzoli had the grace to look embarrassed. "Well, not a lot. Just, well, a few things."

"I hope you can form your own impressions in the next three days."

Fozzoli squinted at her. "So you've really been up there?" he said suddenly.

"I have."

"What's it like?"

Now Sirra interrupted. "Dr. Seelith is here."

Fozzoli and Iede turned to see Khadre's one-person transport (an enclosed model, unlike Fozzoli's open-air scooter) approach from the south. The craft sighed to a stop close to the airfoil and unfolded elegantly. Khadre climbed out of the pilot's saddle and stretched luxuriously. "Hello, everyone. Am I late? The trip took longer than I had expected," Iede knew Khadre, of course, revering her only slightly less than her gods. The woman was wrinkled, but sturdy—her face carried implacable strength behind considerable age.

"Dr. Seelith. I am honored you agreed to come with us," Iede said, beginning a genuflection then thinking better of it.

"Iede, how are you?" Khadre asked, sincerity evident in her voice. "You are looking well."

"I am well."

Khadre's absent gaze drifted past Iede to Sirra and Fozzoli. "Hello, Doctors."

Fozzoli smiled and thrust out his hand. "Dr. Seelith, it's an honor. I've read everything you've published about the vix. Brilliant stuff."

"Thank you." Khadre acknowledged the complement gracefully, then turned her attention to Sirra. "Dr. Geniker?"

Sirra smiled. "I haven't used that name in years. It's just Sirra. How are you, Khadre?"

"As well as could be expected. I'm still fighting against the dying of the light, so far."

"Rage," Iede said suddenly. The others turned to look at her. "I'm sorry, Dr. Seelith, but the quote is 'rage against the dying of the light.'"

Khadre's lower lip thrust outward. "Hm. Thank you. I'll try to remember that." She turned toward Sirra again. "Are we ready to go?"

"Ask Iede. This is her expedition."

Khadre turned back toward her. "Are we?"

"I'd like to say a brief invocation before we depart," Iede said. She saw Sirra's eyes roll skyward but pressed on nonetheless. "If you would all please raise your eyes to the skies and repeat after me," she said, lifting her arms up. She paused briefly and intoned, "Those who watch over us protect and guide this holy endeavor." She paused to allow the others to repeat her words. They did not. Iede continued regardless. "We go at Your bidding to fulfill Your will. May Ship continue its great circle forever and ever." She lowered her arms and opened her eyes. The others had not repeated her words, nor, Iede suspected, had they even looked upwards. Remaining genial, she said, "If you'd like to take your seats, we may begin now."

The journey to the ruins was uneventful, if one discounted Sirra's occasional outbursts at Iede's explanations of her religion. Fozzoli's questions seemed, to Iede, to be devoid of spite and sarcasm—when he asked her about some of her doctrines, he did not seem to be trying to trap her in an inconsistency. Khadre did not comment on the discussions, and Iede did not dare appeal to her for an opinion.

Only once did Sirra's temper flare so badly that Iede seriously considered abandoning the project and finding new companions. On the evening of their second day out, Fozzoli resumed his questions about planet-bound life under the guidelines laid down in Costellan's verses.

"So you verify that your interpretation of the verses is correct through meditation and prayer?" he had asked quietly. Khadre and Sirra were sleeping the rear of the airfoil.

"Mostly, though we do use textual analysis and scholarly research. For example, we check the passage in question against the other verses He has written to find inconsistencies. If the interpretation matches other established verses, we consider it valid."

"But those original verses—how did you interpret them properly if you had nothing to base your decisions on?" Fozzoli's question, like all his others, seemed to Iede to be a genuine attempt to comprehend her religion.

"Some of the verses were quite simple to interpret. We consider those the 'base' verses, if you will. For example, here's one of the most basic tenets we have. It's from Costellan's Verse 223. 'Consider the sun/While it shines upon your head/You will always have life.'" She smiled at Fozzoli.

"That's a simple one?"

"Of course. The sun isn't Epsilon Eridani III, of course—it's the Ship itself. As long as it is there, we are safe and protected."

Fozzoli frowned. "I don't know. It seems to me that that verse admits to several meanings. How can you be sure that that one is correct?"

"As I said, we pray and meditate as well. No one has ever proposed an alternate meaning for that verse. It is one of our most basic beliefs."

"Pardon me for sounding rude, Iede, but how do you know that's not an example of *credo consolans*?"

"Of what?"

"A belief you cling to because it is comforting. It's very comforting to believe that Ship is watching over us, protecting us, ready to intervene to stop tragedy from...." He stopped. His eyes widened. "Of course! I see what you're saying!" Iede smiled and nodded as he continued, "You were saved by Ship those thirty some-odd years ago, weren't you? When the Dome flyer malfunctioned and flew away! And so was—" he began to turn in his seat to find Sirra's eyes watching him.

When Sirra spoke, her bitterness was almost palpable. "Yes, Foz. Everyone in this airfoil except yourself was saved by ship's actions that day. But not all aboard the vessel lived. Viktur Ljarbazz died. Ship didn't save him, did it, Iede?"

"No. But I am surprised that you admit Ship saved the rest of us."

"I accept the theory for now. I have no compelling proof of it, but I will accept your theory until more facts come to light."

Iede turned to face her completely. "Before we left you said that Ship was deserted, that it was a lifeless hulk floating around in orbit. Do you still think so? Did you ever think so? How can you, a scientist, deny facts that are right in front of you merely because they lead to a conclusion you do not wish to draw?"

"I don't know what happened that day. Maybe Ship didn't intervene. Maybe it did, but only on some automated system that we can't understand. But if there are gods on board, and they chose to save our lives but not Viktur's, then they are no gods of mine."

"It is presumptuous to try and understand the will of the gods. I do not fully understand why they sent me back to explore these ruins, but I go at their bidding. Can we condemn them for failing to save the life of one man when they saved three others?"

"If I believed in them, I would send them all to hell. You should be thankful that I don't," Sirra said, turning her back on Iede and Fozzoli and pulling the thin blanket snugly around her.

The party arrived midmorning at the coordinates Iede's map designated. Fozzoli, Iede, and Sirra clambered out of the vehicle and helped Khadre extricate herself. The old scientist seemed appreciably stiffer and more tired than the others but brushed off questions about her health with remarks regarding the upcoming survey.

Iede scanned the landscape, one hand shielding her eyes from the sun. She had not truly expected to find tall alien monuments reaching skyward in fantastic splendor but could not help but feel a twinge of disappointment at the bare horizon. The terrain seemed even more inhospitable than several of the places they had traveled through on their way. Rough-hewn rock formations broke up the hilly countryside, and gnarled Kentleigh trees twisted towards the sky like arthritic fingers.

Iede sighed quietly, lifted her face skyward, and intoned the prayer of guidance. She faltered in the middle of the prayer, imagining Aywon's disapproving face watching her from the observation room. She smiled at the sky and said quietly, "All right, Aywon. No more prayers. I suppose I should just help with the survey equipment." She turned back towards the airfoil and blinked in surprise. Sirra was standing not two meters behind her, staring at her in disgust.

"You were praying," Sirra said, her comment more a statement than a question.

"Not exactly. How can I help you?"

"You can't. This is scientific. You just watch."

"There is nothing I can do to help?" Iede spread her arms.

Sirra crossed hers. "No. If you really want to help, just stay out of the way. Let us do our work."

"It would seem, ha'lyneice, that your cult is more exclusive than mine."

Sirra scowled and stepped closer. "What do you want from me, Iede? I've come all the way out here to test your domed 'vision' against reality. I've even brought in two others, one of whom is still young enough to be impressionable, and by the way I don't really appreciate you brainwashing him—"

Iede's outstretched hands rotated, palms up, as if deflecting Sirra's ranting. "Sirra, please. You can't believe that a few days of casual conversation about my lifestyle—"

"Your religion. Call it what it is."

"—Religion, then, could fundamentally change his belief system? And even if it could, that would be his choice."

"Not when you fill his head with lies and distortions, half-truths and—"

"None of what I say is a lie."

Sirra's jaw twitched. She said softly, through clenched teeth, "No, I suppose not. Not when you yourself believe it so fully." Her voice rose again. "But just because you believe it doesn't make it true."

"Of course not."

Sirra's eyes widened at this. "What?"

Iede laughed gently. "You think I believe in my religion out of blind faith? I have arrived at this stage in my spiritual growth through dedicated study, prayer, meditation, and finally, in an incontrovertible, empirical experience aboard Ship. I know what I believe in is true through thought, prayer, and experience. That's why I believe in it—because it is true. Not the other way around."

Sirra's head shook slowly, softly, her eyes moving evenly in their sockets to stay fixed on Iede.

"I might add, ha'lyneice, that you should take your own advice. Just because you do not believe in something doesn't make it false."

"Hey! Ladies! You care to lend a hand over here?" Fozzoli's petulant voice sliced through the tension between the two old women, and they both walked back towards the airfoil to help the young scientist set up his survey equipment.

"You take a look, then," Fozzoli said, more than a little irritation in his voice. He withdrew from the eyepiece and let Sirra examine the data. Iede and Khadre watched, the former still serene despite the nine hours of work it had taken to arrive at their first dubious finding. Iede looked at Khadre, still not daring to speak.

Khadre must have felt Iede's gaze on her, for she turned and met her eyes. "I think they've found something."

"I see," Iede said. She had not been offered much information, but was content. She had learned all she needed to from Aywon.

Khadre seemed to interpret her remark as a request for explanation. "They've found some trace amounts of an alloy that should not occur naturally. At least, I think that's what they've found. None of us are really skilled in this field, so we can't be sure. But if it is an artificial alloy, someone must have created it. Which lends credence to your, uh, thoughts about the ruins."

Iede nodded. Khadre opened her mouth again, then closed it and turned to watch Sirra and Fozzoli.

Sirra leaned back from the eyepiece. "I don't see how we can tell. So you found something that registers on the mass spectrometer as an iron-carbon alloy. So? Maybe it is, maybe it isn't. And even if it is, how do we know it isn't a natural occurrence?"

"No way. No way this happens this close to the surface." Fozzoli was shaking his head violently.

"But we don't even know if we're reading the instruments properly."

Now Fozzoli looked at Sirra with contempt. "I know how to read a mass spectrometer, Doctor. Iron-carbon admixture. No doubt. In more than trace amounts."

Iede did not understand the science, but Fozzoli's voice was all she needed to hear to know that the devices he had planted in the ground had come up with something.

"Pardon my ignorance," Iede said, causing her halfonlyniece to turn to her and scowl, "but what is the significance of this find? What do you mean, an iron-carbon alloy?"

Sirra exchanged glances with Fozzoli and seemed to resign herself to the discovery. Iede noted without pleasure that her halfonlyniece appeared defeated even as she answered the question.

"Steel."

CHAPTER
26

The survey group changed position a dozen times before they found it.

Sirra could no longer pretend that Fozzoli was reading the instruments incorrectly, especially when Khadre had gently confirmed his results after the third site. Iede had not gloated, Sirra had to admit, but her ha'lyaunt's calm self-assurance was nonetheless grating.

After the sixth change in location, Fozzoli was no longer grumbling about the work involved in loading the survey equipment, shifting their position a few kilometers, and unloading again. He was far too excited about the discoveries. Even Khadre was energetic, helping Fozzoli calibrate the samplers with each shift. Sirra helped, but her mind was elsewhere.

"You don't seem excited, Sirra," Iede said, sidling up to her as the others took more readings of the deep soil. "Are you still skeptical?"

Sirra fought back anger. "No. But your explanation is still not the only one. Just because we have found what you said we would doesn't mean your religion is correct."

"I see that Occam's Razor needs some sharpening to cut through your ideology," Iede said, chuckling. "Yes: I could be a clairvoyant, gaining this knowledge through some supernatural, mystical source. Or I might simply be the luckiest person ever born, to have randomly picked a spot on this vast planet that happens to contain these artifacts. Or—"

"Don't be so smug, Iede. You could quite simply have been given this information by some other scientists. Planet-bound ones, I mean."

"But if that is so, what motivation would I have to drag all of you self-admitted non-experts out here to confirm something that is already known?"

"I don't know. Don't you always say that the gods work in mysterious ways?"

"Not at all. Their ways are not mysterious to those who watch."

Sirra sighed and shook her head. "You've got an answer to everything. That's why I am scared of your religion."

"Because it provides answers?"

"Because it provides *all* the answers. Doubt and uncertainty are what drive us to learn more. If I thought I knew everything there was to know, I wouldn't seek, I wouldn't grow. That's why religion is so dangerous."

Iede seemed to think about that for a moment, and Sirra felt a faint twinge of hope. She had not realized until she felt the hope swelling in her that she had been, not just haranguing her ha'lyaunt, but trying to convert her away from her religion.

"You may be correct, Sirra, but you still should be willing to admit that I have done what I said I would. You have found the evidence. Can you still deny that I have been to Ship to visit with those within her?"

"No."

"Then why do you still resist?"

"I'm angry at them."

"Why?"

Sirra glanced up, as if to show everyone in Ship (yes, she admitted, she believed. She would not be a scientist if she simply denied the evidence. In the absence of a simpler, more compelling conclusion, she had to admit that there was a Ship and most likely it was still staffed) that she defied them even while acknowledging them. "Because I wanted us to find this ourselves. We would have, eventually. Why do your gods want to interfere?"

"You would rather they had left us to our own devices."

"Of course. I don't want to owe them anything." Even as she said it, Sirra knew what Iede would say. Sirra turned away and looked pointedly at Fozzoli and Khadre, waiting the inevitable response.

"Anything *more*, you mean."

Sirra closed her eyes and saw Viktur's body being shredded by gunfire from the Dome flyer, heard his screams, the splashing of the waves, the relentless staccato sound of the drone's guns.

Iede walked halfway around Sirra and said, "Why are we here, Sirra?"

Sirra opened her eyes and the nightmare almost faded. "What?"

"Why are we still here? Surely, we have enough to go back and report our findings. What do we wait for?"

"I...don't know. There's something still here. I want to find it."

"How do you know?"

"The same way I know how to speak to the vix. I just know."

"Now who is the mystical one?" Iede chided, and Sirra could not help but grin.

"All right, Dome you, I get it. Let's see what the others have found."

At the twelfth site two days later, Khadre and Fozzoli were still glued to their instruments, talking excitedly in the language of science. Iede had raised the prospect of returning to the city to restock, and Sirra had to agree with her. The party had not bothered to forage, even if they could, and their supplies were running low. The trip back would take a minimum of three days, and the group had almost exhausted its field supplies.

"Let us stay here, then," Fozzoli said during their sparse dinner. "Khadre and I will keep working while you go back and get more food."

"That's six days, Foz," Sirra said. "You've barely got enough for three as it is. You're going to stay out here for three days without food or water?"

Fozzoli didn't answer.

"And it's more than the food and water. We need to find out what has been happening back home."

"I think she's right, Foz," Khadre said softly. "We have to go back. But I want to be on the return team," she said, looking at Sirra.

"Me, too," Fozzoli insisted.

Sirra spread her hands. "I don't make that decision. Besides, our place is in the water."

Fozzoli considered that. "Sirra, I think...." He stopped, looking at Khadre for help.

"Foz and I have been thinking about that. We want to postpone our marine studies for a while. We think that this discovery takes precedence."

Sirra fought to keep her face free from emotion. "We're not specialists, Khadre. We don't know much more than Iede here," she said. She looked at her ha'lyaunt and added awkwardly, "no offense."

Iede just nodded.

"Besides, I was on the verge of something with Vogel. I want to get back to that."

"The interdiction is still on," Fozzoli said.

Sirra snorted. "Not after this. You think the Coordinator will keep his ban on research after we bring back this data?"

Khadre shrugged. "Who knows? But Foz and I are agreed. We want to come back here."

Sirra looked at Fozzoli. "I won't stop you, Foz."

"Look, Sirra, it's just for a little while. I'll be back with you before you—"

"It's all right, Foz," she said, trying to conceal her pain. He wasn't really betraying her personally.

But she was not quite able to believe that.

Three hours before the four of them had agreed to leave the survey site and return to civilization, the core sampler sounded a tone it had not used before. Fozzoli and Khadre exchanged worried glances. "That better not be the 'I'm broken' sound." Fozzoli stopped the drill and examined the display. He fell silent.

"What?" Khadre said, moving towards him.

"I'm not sure," Fozzoli said slowly. "I think it's telling me there is a…pocket, or something."

"Like natural gas? Or water?"

Now Sirra and Iede moved closer.

"Uh…" Fozzoli manipulated the readout controls. "No. There's nothing. Just air."

Iede asked, "Do air pockets occur naturally underground?"

The three marine biologists looked helplessly at one another. Sirra chuckled under her breath. "We finally find something worthwhile and none of us knows enough to verify it." She glanced at the readout. "Ninety meters down, give or take. Anyone want to start digging?" She chuckled again. "Ninety meters. Might as well be on Ship itself, eh, Iede?"

"No. I've been to Ship."

"You don't think they can help us, do you?" Sirra asked, surprised at herself. She had meant the question to come out dripping with sarcasm, but she found herself waiting for an answer.

"They don't work that way," was Iede's brief reply.

"Wait a second. I think this thing has a camera feature. We might be able to get some pictures of what's down there," Fozzoli said, reading the technical file on the sampler's help program. He gingerly made some adjustments to the sampler settings. The holodata vanished, to be replaced by a blinking question mark cursor.

"I think the camera is just a flat pic. Not a holo. I'll display it here," Fozzoli said, pointing at the sampler's tiny video screen. The four crowded around as Fozzoli manipulated the low-resolution camera hub around, the dedicated floodlight casting a fuzzy white circle of light on jagged rock.

"Can you clean this up at all?" Sirra asked. Khadre examined the controls and made a few changes. The image instantly cleared but showed nothing discernible.

"The computer is recording all of this, I hope," Fozzoli said.

Khadre coughed. "Foz, I have a small amount of experience with these kinds of machines."

"Core drilling samplers?" Fozzoli said, not taking his eyes off the screen.

"No, but I do know how to operate a few remote cameras. Since my diving days are long over, that's about all I can do. If you don't mind…."

Fozzoli hastily moved out of the way. Khadre took over and after a moment's study, touched a single button. "I've set the camera on automatic sweep. The computer will build up a holo representation of the camera's findings as soon as it can, and we'll be able to see what's down there. I've also keyed in infrared, but I doubt that'll help."

Sirra shivered. Something had occurred to her, but she was not altogether sure she wanted to act on her instinct. She suppressed the thought, but it continued to gnaw at her.

The camera made short work of whatever it was scanning, and Khadre announced half an hour later, "Done. Here's what it found." A holo image sprang into view amongst the four surveyors.

The chamber was, as far as Sirra could tell, part of a tunnel. The walls were too smooth to be natural, and appeared to be reinforced by beams or pylons. A straight track, with regularly spaced plates of unidentifiable material, lay on the bottom of the chamber. All in all, the tunnel segment was roughly fifteen meters in diameter.

"It's a subway system," Khadre whispered.

Fozzoli nodded. "What kind of propulsion, do you think?"

"I've no idea. Maglev, maybe. Those plates."

Iede spoke. Although her voice was as soft as ever, her sudden involvement in the conversation make the others start. "Why would you assume that?"

"Well, those plates look a little like…." Khadre said, then laughed at herself. "I see what you mean. No, Iede, I should have kept to my original statement. I have no idea what the propulsion system is."

"Or even if it is a subway system."

"Correct. Thank you for being a pure scientist.".

Sirra ignored the exchange. Ordinarily, she would have snapped at Iede for imagining herself to be a scientist, but the same instinct she had felt earlier had risen in her again. She did not want to succumb to it, for fear of what she might discover. A picture was forming itself in her mind, and she did not understand how. She knew she was prone to flashes of intuition, but this was the strongest and most unsettling one yet.

"Sirra? Something wrong?" Iede had moved closer.

"No. But we've got to get back. Now. I've got to ask Vogel something."

"Vogel?" Fozzoli almost shouted. "Now? We've just found—"

"Dome it, Foz, I'll leave the three of you here to starve! Get in the airfoil!"

Fozzoli did not move. "What could you possibly want to ask Vogel that has anything to do with—"

"He knows about this place. So help me, they all do. Foz, please. I need your help in talking to him and getting him up to the lab. I can't ask any of the others to join me in violating the interdiction, and I'll need you there. You can come back here when we finish, I promise."

Fozzoli looked at her for a moment, then smiled his familiar half-smile. "*You* need *me*? You've never said that before. How can I refuse?"

The laboratory was cold when Khadre, Sirra, and Fozzoli entered it five days later. They had mutually agreed not to even try to contact the Coordinator and ask him for permission to reestablish contact with the vix. Iede had returned to Yallia City with an impressive letter of explanation from the three scientists, to round up more qualified surveyors and return to the survey site. Sirra still wondered at her halfonlyaunt's parting words: "May you find what you do not even know you are looking for." Metaphysical claptrap, she had decided, but the words still haunted her.

Fozzoli had spent the last thirty-six hours building a "lifting box" (as Sirra mentally called it) to bring Vogel to the surface. The result was a coffin-like rectangular container that would keep the internal pressure at twenty atmospheres and allow Fozzoli to hook up pumps once the box was brought back to the lab to increase the oxygen level of the water. He even had included a built-in vixvox.

"I'll get the heat up," Fozzoli said, striding to the lab's environmental controls. "It'll take a few minutes or so."

Sirra nodded absently. "I'll go and get Vogel, if he's still around. Or alive. I told him to wait for me, but it's been...about ten days, I think. He's probably given up."

"I'll go with you," Khadre said.

"On a dive?" Sirra knew the remark was foolish as soon as she made it.

"I can still handle myself in water," Khadre said. "Just show me the suits."

Sirra caught Fozzoli's look of concern, and walked to the suit rack. "Foz, can you handle things here while we go get Vogel?"

"Gimme some time to get the essential systems up again. Maybe half an hour."

"That'll give me enough time to get acquainted with Sirra's new theory," Khadre said, turning to face her.

"What?"

"You thought of something. Back at the survey site. That's why you suddenly wanted to come back here. What was it?"

Sirra did not speak. She looked away from Khadre, afraid of the old scientist. *What* she suspected was not the problem; it was *how* she came to her suspicions.

Khadre said, "I assume you wanted to keep something from Iede. Well, she's gone now."

Sirra took a breath before answering. "I...it's not a theory. Just a feeling. I get them sometimes."

"Yes, I remember," Khadre said. "I remember thirty-six years ago. You got a feeling then, when the vix came up to us. What feeling do you have now?"

"I'm not sure," Sirra said, looking pointedly at Fozzoli, who was making every effort to appear busy with the lab computer.

"Does it make you uncomfortable, this feeling?"

"No."

"Is that why you are so hard on your ha'lyaunt?"

Sirra swung her head around to stare at Khadre. "What? What does that have to do with anything?" The respect she felt towards the aged scientist held her back somewhat, as she had wanted to bluntly tell her to mind her own domed business.

"You hate her. You hate that she deals with feelings and prayer and other unscientific practices. But your own intuition is just that—it's like a religion with you." Khadre smiled softly. "Are you honestly telling me that you never considered the possibility that your intuition, your peculiar feelings of rightness, might be a genetic talent? And that Iede might share it?"

Sirra's eyes went wide. "Share it?"

"Of course. But she applied it to a religion. She created a religion out of nothing, Sirra, and a very successful one. I'm led to understand that fully fifteen percent of the population declares itself Shippies. That is the term used, yes?"

Sirra did not respond. Khadre's words struck her almost tangibly, made all the worse by her cursed intuition telling her that *Khadre was right.*

Khadre knew it, too. "Tell me what you thought of at the survey site."

Sirra opened her mouth once, then closed it again. When she opened it a second time, her lips stuck slightly, as if her body was trying to keep her silent. "Something told me to see Vogel. That he had the answers I...." she couldn't say it, but she had to. If she did not, she would continue to poison herself in her hatred of her ha'lyaunt. She straightened and said, loudly, "...the answers I didn't even know I was looking for. Vogel's connected to the ruins somehow. All the vix are."

Fozzoli gave up his charade of work to say, "You're saying the vix caused the ruins? How?"

"I don't know, domeit!" Sirra said, swinging around to face him. Her pent-up anger, stifled against Khadre, unable to unleash itself against Iede, found a target in Fozzoli. "That's why we're here, and that's why you're going to get your lazy ass working twice as fast on those domed systems!"

Her voice echoed through the lab, and Sirra glared at Fozzoli, hardly daring to look away from him.

The young man blinked once, then said, "My 'lazy ass' will certainly hurry up, Sirra, but if your equally reluctant posterior can find its way to a domed logic probe, I'd appreciate it." He turned again to the computer, then said, in a quiet voice but one which Sirra could hear perfectly, "That's it. I'm joining the Shippies after this. Just to piss you off."

Khadre laughed gently at first, then louder, until Sirra's blazing eyes crinkled slightly and the three scientists giggled like children who had farted in church.

Sirra watched Khadre surreptitiously as the two entered the dive pool. She had great respect for Khadre, but she could not forget that the scientist was *old*—fifty-three years old. Despite everything modern science could do, the human body was still subject to the ravages of such elemental forces as gravity and radiation. Khadre may still have eight, or even ten, years left to her, and Sirra was not going to let those years be taken away.

"How am I doing?" Khadre's voice sounded in Sirra's headphones. Sirra smiled ruefully and decided to play it straight.

"Just fine. Watch your suit pressure. And keep an eye on your blood color indicator. If it gets too green, then—"

"I think I can remember, Sirra," Khadre said, her ordinarily soft voice buzzing with the faint hint of irritation. Sirra shut up.

"All right, you two, I'm lowering the tank," Fozzoli said. Sirra watched as the specially prepared tank designed for bringing Vogel up to the lab was lowered into the water between Khadre and her. When it was submerged, Sirra unlatched the winch cable and said, "Got it. Keep an ear out for vix patrols, Foz. You see any large numbers of vix headed our way, you let us know."

"Sure. So you can tell me that you can handle it. I know the drill," Fozzoli said.

Sirra turned to Khadre. "Ready?"

"Yes."

"Let's go." The two adjusted the buoyancy controls on their suits. Sirra matched the settings on the tank and hung on.

"The descent ought to take only a few minutes, if Vogel is still where I left him."

"Why do you think he'll be gone?"

Sirra snorted. "It's been too long. Why would he stay there?"

"Because God told him to."

Sirra was about to ask Khadre "what God?" when she understood the comment. "He doesn't think I'm God."

"No?"

"No. I thought I told you—he's the one who has been using the most secular terms to describe me."

"I see." Khadre said, but her voice indicated otherwise.

"Look, domeit, I settled this with him. He asked me if I was God and I told him I wasn't."

"Oh, well then. That should clear it up for him."

Sirra turned to look at Khadre, annoyed. "What's the problem, Doctor? Do you disagree with my methods?"

"No, of course not. I just think for a brilliant scientist you have an amazing talent for missing the obvious."

"I suppose you're going to tell me what I'm missing."

"You are as much a God to Vogel as those in Ship are to Iede."

Sirra did not answer immediately but stared across the top of the tank at Khadre. "That sounds awfully poetic, but I'm afraid it just isn't true."

"I see."

Sirra bit off her reply and checked her proximity sonar. "We're coming up on where Vogel ought to be. Stay sharp."

The next few minutes were silent as the two watched their scopes and swung in lazy circles, scanning for the curious vix. Khadre was first to break the silence.

"I've got something at extreme range, bearing one-ten," she said.

Sirra swung around and turned her passive sonar to maximum gain. "Yeah, could be. Do you think we can risk shouting?"

"You tell me. This is your neighborhood. Or should I say parish?"

"Are you enjoying this?" Sirra barked.

"Oh, yes. I've not felt this good in years."

Sirra's anger melted away at that. It was worth taking the old woman's barbs if it meant she felt a little younger. She just wished there was some other way Khadre could recapture her youth without needling her about sensitive subjects.

"All right. Let's head over there. Slowly—keep your sonar on max."

The two changed the buoyancy of their suits and the tank to neutral and crept towards the source of the sonar emissions. It was slow going, as the tank encumbered their movements. Presently, they were close enough for their sonar to give a fuzzy image.

"It's a vix, all right. It's resting on that ledge. About nine meters down, thirty-nine…make it forty meters ahead."

"Can you tell who it is?" Khadre asked.

"Not unless we get much closer or he talks to us. The sonar images aren't clear enough to make out surface features. I think I'm going to have to call him. I just hope no other vix are around." She activated her vixvox, but before speaking into it, said to Khadre, "If this doesn't work and more vix start to appear, let go of the tank and get to the surface. Don't wait—go." She switched channels and said to the sleeping vix, "Vogel, wake up. It's the Speaker."

The creature stirred, kicking up a tiny patch of sand that Sirra's sonar dutifully registered. He swung his head towards the two. Sirra's earphones crackled to life.

"Speaker."

"Yes, Vogel. I'm back."

Vogel floated gently upwards, towards Sirra and Khadre. *"You did not forsake me."*

"Of course not," Sirra typed, glad that the vixvox did not transmit sheepishness. She resisted the urge to look at Khadre, who was no doubt grinning at Vogel's choice of words, or at the translation.

Vogel curled around Sirra, not touching her, but his intent was clearly friendly. He circled her two and a half times, then floated gently away, gracefully drifting towards Khadre.

"Speaker, whom did you bring? A [untranslatable utterance]?"

Khadre cocked her head and said, "What was that?"

"The computer can't always translate."

"But you can," Khadre stated.

"Yes. Sometimes. If I…." She approached Vogel. "Vogel, I need to touch you again. You will not be hurt—it will be like last time."

"I understand." Vogel hovered midwater. Sirra swam towards him and extended a gloved hand.

After a moment's rapport, she said, in a dreamy voice, "He wonders if you are a…well, the best translation we've got is 'holy warrior,' come to protect me from Bishop."

"From whom?"

"It's a bit complicated. Let's get him into the tank," Sirra said, Vogel's thoughts reminding her of the danger. "Vogel, has Bishop come back?" she typed, awkwardly, as she could only use one hand.

"*I don't know. I've been asleep for a while, I think. But while I was awake, I waited alone.*"

Sirra chuckled. "Ever the scientist, eh, Vogel?" She sobered immediately at the thought of the task ahead. "Vogel, my...friend and I want to bring you somewhere."

"*I remember. You spoke of Lifting me. I had worried that you had changed your mind. That I was...not blessed/damned enough.*"

The strange double-meaning of his words almost stunned Sirra enough to remove her hand. Even in her tight rapport with him, she could still not decipher the ambivalence he showed for what he called "Lifting."

"What's he saying? My translator's not getting much," Khadre asked.

"He knows what we're going to do, sort of," Sirra answered. She did not have time to explain fully—despite Vogel's report that Bishop had not been here, Sirra was still worried. "Vogel, can you see this box?" she said, tapping the outside of the tank.

"*Yes.*"

"We're going to Lift you in it. Can you please swim inside?"

Vogel's flank slid along her hand, and before she lost contact, Sirra could feel an emotion coming off him that was stronger than anything she had ever felt before. It was akin to the contradictory words he had used: blessed/damned.

Vogel was at once terrified and elated. He was not sure if he was going to heaven or hell, but his curiosity got the better of him. Sirra suspected that any other vix would have refused, preferring to suffer Sirra's wrath than risk a journey to what could be the most horrific, evil place they conceived of. But Sirra had met a vix for whom scientific curiosity—the need to *know*—overrode religious fear.

Barely.

Vogel swam around the tank a few times, then said, "*Speaker, I do not wish to offend, but why must I enter this...Lifting box?*"

"I can't really explain it, Vogel. If you don't go into the box and I try to Lift you...you may end up like Bishop. Or your father-by-action."

"*This box will prevent that?*"

"Yes," Sirra said. Again, she was glad the vixvox didn't transmit half-truths.

Vogel still hesitated but gradually nosed his way into the tank. Sirra swam up to the lip and placed her hand on his nose. "I will not speak to you again for a short time. When I do, you will be in a...strange place. You must do your best to remain calm. All will be explained to you when you are Lifted."

"*Yes, Speaker.*"

Sirra started to close the tank and cycle it, but she stopped the process midway and returned to the lip. "Vogel?"

"Yes, Speaker?"

"Thank you for waiting for me."

Vogel answered after a brief pause, *"You call me a scientist, but I still have faith. I knew you would return."*

The answer did not have the effect Sirra knew Vogel was hoping for. She started to tell him that she did not want him to exist on faith, but Khadre's voice interrupted before she could say anything of substance.

"Let it go, Sirra. You don't have to make atheists of the entire planet, humans and vix."

Sirra frowned, her face hidden from Khadre, who floated behind and below her. Wordlessly, she cycled the tank and set its buoyancy to maximum.

"Let's get back," Sirra said, and the three floated rapidly upwards.

Fozzoli was ready when they reached the lab. He positioned the winch above the tank and, with Sirra's and Khadre's help, hoisted it out of the water and onto the waiting exam table. He deftly attached the oxygenator hoses to the appropriate ports and began the pump.

"How long has he been in there?" Fozzoli asked, studying the readouts carefully.

"About nineteen minutes," Sirra said, climbing out of the diving pool.

"Eighteen minutes and forty-four seconds," Khadre added, waiting her turn at the ladder.

"I don't think he'll be hurt by that. The tank pressure held, mostly. I don't think he was in low oxygen for too long."

Sirra nodded inside her pressure suit and found the appropriate controls on the tank's exterior to activate the vixvox. "Vogel? Can you hear me?"

The tank supplied a voice for Vogel. It was gentle, hesitant, and somehow sad. *"I hear you. Where am I? Is this...am I Lifted?"*

"I still wish I knew what that really meant," Fozzoli muttered.

Khadre had come up behind the two of them and said, "How is he?"

"I think he's doing all right. Talk to him more, Sirra."

"Vogel, you are with some other Speakers. You are where some of the Speakers live."

The tank's computer voice said, stridently and artificially, "untranslatable utterance."

"Calm down, Vogel. You will be fine."

"May I see?"

Sirra exchanged a look with Fozzoli. "Can we?"

Fozzoli thought for a long moment, then shook his head. "I don't know how. We can't just open the tank up, and even if we could, his sonar wouldn't work in the air. And we can't show him a holo for the same reason."

Sirra took a deep breath. "I'm sorry, Vogel. Your...eyes aren't able to see this."

The voice did not change timbre, but Sirra could nevertheless imagine his disappointment. *"I understand, Speaker."*

"Vogel, I need you to tell me how you feel."

"I am limited in movement, and my senses tell me I am trapped, yet I can reason and think clearly. I am afraid, Speaker."

"Don't be. No harm will come to you." Sirra paused, then asked, "Do you feel anything pressing on you? Squeezing you from the outside or inside?"

"No."

Fozzoli nodded, his lower lip protruding. "That's good. Pressure's good. Domeit!" he said suddenly. He half-ran to a small cart and wheeled it over to the tank. "I should have been recording all of this!" He connected a contact microphone from the cart to the side of the tank and shook his head in anger.

"He'll talk plenty, Foz," Khadre said, her hand resting lightly on his shoulder. Then, to Sirra, she added, "Can you ask him about where he thinks he is?"

Sirra stared at the tank. "I'm almost afraid to. I don't want him getting too excited. Also, I'm not sure how the translation will hold up." She brooded for a moment, then tapped out, "Vogel, you say you have been Lifted. If you could see, what would you see?"

"I don't understand, Speaker."

"I want you to describe what you would be seeing if your eyes could...understand what was around you."

There was a considerable pause, during which time Fozzoli leaned over from his position of rapt attention near the recording cart to look at the tank's indicator dials before Vogel spoke.

"I would see much like what I would see in my town, but it would be different. I would see with [untranslatable utterance] *instead of* [untranslatable utterance]. *There would be something all around me, but it would not* [untranslatable utterance] *me. And I would not* [untranslatable utterance] *but I would* [untranslatable utterance] *instead, as if I were on the sea bottom."*

Sirra wanted to stomp her feet with frustration. Khadre looked deep in thought. Fozzoli held his earphones tightly to his skull as if that would help him understand. "Nothing. Not even possible from the computer. It's as if he's using a whole different language."

Vogel, try to explain it to me as if I were a child."

"Why, Speaker?"

Sirra tapped out angrily, "Because I command it!" She felt Khadre's head swivel to stare at her.

"Godhood has its uses, I see," Khadre said softly.

Vogel started to answer. *"I would not see like I do now. I would use...new parts of myself to see. Seeing would not take effort, even the tiny effort it now does. And I would use* [untranslatable utterance] *to see, and it would wash over me like a warm current, but it would not push me. I would not be at the mercy of the waves, but would decide where I want to go on my own. I would look up/down and not be afraid."*

Sirra cocked her head slightly at his answer. "Is he describing...sight?"

Fozzoli frowned. "You mean sonar?"

"No, no...sight. Eyesight."

Fozzoli's face contorted in a grimace. "How? When the vixvox translates 'eyes,' he means his sonar. How could he even have the concept of sight as we do?"

"Through legend," Khadre breathed.

Sirra nodded. "I think he's talking about sight. And something would wash over him like a warm current...that's got to be light. He said it would not push him. What else could it be?"

"What do you mean, what else? Who knows what it is? It could be anything!" Fozzoli spread his hands as if to encompass the broad spectrum of possibilities.

"Sight seems to fit the description, Foz," Khadre added.

"Did I do well, Speaker?" the tank's voice asked.

"Very well, Vogel. Rest, now."

"But I have a question, Speaker, if I may."

"Yes?"

"Why do you torture me?" The simple question coming out of the soft computer voice chilled Sirra.

"Torture you, Vogel?"

"You must be She-that-must-not-be-named. What have I done to deserve this torment?"

Sirra looked helplessly at Khadre, whose confused face revealed no insight. Sirra tapped out, "How are you being tormented, Vogel?"

"You have Lifted me, and although I would not have believed it, I am here, now. This place is [untranslatable utterance]."

Fozzoli gasped.

Sirra spun to face him. "What?"

- 344 -

"One of the possibilities for that last sound was 'hell.'"

"Why do you say that, Vogel?"

"Because you tantalize me with visions that I cannot have, then ask me to describe them to you. Why do you not simply give me the gift of [untranslatable utterance]? *I did not truly believe you existed, She-who-must-not-be-named. I believed in science, and reason, and experience. But now I know that Bishop was right. And I will pay the price for my heresy."* The tank voice fell silent.

"Vogel? Vogel!" Sirra tapped his name, adding exclamation marks so the vixvox would give her words added emphasis. There was no answer from the tank. Sirra glared at Fozzoli. "Can we do something to the tank?"

"What do you mean?" Fozzoli took the headphones off and stared at her.

"I don't know—send something through the oxygenator, anything. Something to get his attention, snap him out of it."

"What do you think that will do?" Khadre said gently.

Sirra whirled. "Get him to talk to me...to us." Sirra chafed at the correction but made it anyway. She glared at Khadre, daring her to comment upon her diction.

The old scientist smiled frostily and said, "You'd torture him more? Ask yourself what you'd do in his position. If you prod him, won't he look upon that as more torture? See this from his point of view."

"His point of view? He thinks I'm the devil! How can I pretend to understand what that's like?"

"You're the one with this intuition talent."

Sirra gritted her teeth, then relaxed enough to say, "I never claimed I have a psychic talent or anything. I am good with languages, that's true. But—"

"Good with languages?" Fozzoli said, half-laughing. "You can practically read the vix' minds, Sirra. You know you've got some innate sense of meaning. I don't know how you do it, but you do it."

"So what are the two of you saying? That I need to use my magic wand and read Vogel's mind? Well, I can't. No more than I can read Iede's mind." The sudden revelation shocked her. Was that true?

"You can't?" Khadre asked.

"No," Sirra answered, but she knew it was a lie. She knew why Iede's behavior had always been enigmatic to her, and why Vogel and Bishop were also closed books. For all her professed atheism, Sirra knew she was deeply afraid. Not of God's existence or nonexistence, but of her own strength of conviction. She was afraid that if she truly got to understand Iede, she too would start to believe in God. Or gods.

"What's funny?" Fozzoli asked. Sirra suddenly realized that she was smiling ruefully.

"Nothing. I just...." She could not voice her fears. How could she explain that she was afraid that she would not lose her faith in atheism (a contradiction in terms) but would, if she weakened, replace cold reason with wishful belief. She did not want to grasp the crutch of religion, for once it was in her hand, she would never walk without it.

But there seemed little other choice. Vogel was by far the most progressive and cosmopolitan of the vix Sirra had dealt with, yet even he had plummeted into the abyss of superstition and dogma. Sirra owed it to him to help him climb out, even if it meant a little risk that she, too, would come to understand and accept religion.

"All right." Sirra reactivated the vixvox and said softly to Vogel, "Vogel, it's the Speaker again. I am going to release you back to your town, but I am coming with you. I have to show you something—something that is as close as I can get to what you seek. You will just have to trust me."

Vogel did not answer, and after several seconds' wait, Sirra looked at Fozzoli. "We're going to have to get him back down there. I'll try to explain to him what we saw at the ruins and see if that jogs anything in him."

"And if not?"

"I'll have to go to Bishop with the same thing."

"That's crazy. They'll kill you."

Sirra shrugged. "We'll find out later. Meantime, hook the tank back up to the winch. I'm going down."

"I'm coming, too," Khadre said.

"No. You can't help me in this. You'll only get in the way. I'm sorry, Khadre."

For a brief moment, Khadre looked hurt, but she didn't fight. Without a signal between them, the three made preparations for Sirra and Vogel to descend once more.

"Vogel, you are safe now. You were always safe, though."

Vogel swam around Sirra in a significantly wider circle than before. *"Speaker, what are you? Is this more torture? Can I believe my senses?"*

"Yes, as much as you ever could."

"Ah. You seek to teach me the first lesson. That I can only ultimately prove my own existence. I am a mere vix, Speaker, but I know that much."

"Yes," Sirra said, impatient to impart her discovery. "Vogel, I'm going to tell you something, but I'm going to do it...differently. Please come here and be still."

Vogel hesitated, but complied. Sirra saw his smooth flank hover just a few centimeters from her hand, and she glanced at the suit gauntlet coupling. Fozzoli would have prevented her, using force if necessary, from doing what she was about to do, if he knew about it. Sirra had told neither Fozzoli or Khadre of her intentions. She knew the risks were great—in all likelihood, she would lose her hand to the pressure or the cold, and possibly damage the integrity of her suit and drown, but she had to help Vogel.

She adjusted the internal suit pressure to maximum and felt the tightening on her skin. Quickly, she released the coupling at her wrist and freed her hand from its armored gauntlet. The deep-suit was multilayered, and there were still two layers of tough elastic-like skin between her and the water, but the armor she had just removed did most of the work. A tremendous stream of bubbles shot out of the wrist where the suit's air supply rushed to try and equalize pressure. Her suit computer sounded in her helmet: "Warning! Loss of suit integrity! Return to safe depth immediately!" The warning continued, but Sirra ignored it as best she could, holding onto the suit gauntlet with her still-armored hand. She reached out and touched Vogel's flank; even through the two layers of elastic, the sensation was almost the same as touching with her bare hand. She carefully directed the air stream away from his body.

She could not immediately tell what she felt. At first, she thought the effects of the rapidly decompressing suit had played with her brain—strange sensations flooded her mind; feelings of gentle floating, of vaguely threatening danger on all sides, but a gnawing curiosity to explore those very dangers; and underneath all, a steady hum of dread at some unidentified but lurking terror.

She was reading Vogel—not just his thoughts, but his soul.

She did not stop to wonder why she would be so able to connect with this alien when she had only received gentle impressions from fellow humans, even during extremely intimate moments. She just concentrated and tried to send him the images, thoughts, and emotions that went into the discovery at the ruins.

She had no idea how long she had until her suit failed completely, nor any idea how long it would take to send her thoughts. What was the speed of telepathy? Or was it empathy? The words did not come. Sirra felt the sensations that she now loosely identified as Vogel's soul change in subtle but unmistakable ways.

She could interpret the changes, but not solely because of some mystical, magical force that only she herself and her sister possessed—her training in the vix language, her close association with the race for close to thirty years, Fozzoli's academic and keen mind, and, yes, Iede's discovery of the ruins all contributed to her interpretation.

She knew what had happened on this planet eight thousand years ago. The knowledge was there, in Vogel's mind, buried under layers of superstition. Only the questing nature of Vogel's scientific personality had uncovered the barest corner of the secret, and even then, the vix had not known what he had found. Unconsciously, he had reconstructed the truth from observations of his world, from discussions and interviews with countless others, including his father-by-action, and even from legends and myths he had undoubtedly been taught in his youth by his culture and its omnipresent religion.

He had done all of this alone, with no hard data. Sheer force of reason had led him to doubt, correctly, the stories he had been told and which all other vix believed as a matter of course. He had been prepared to test his theory even at the cost of his soul, if he had one at all.

Sirra knew she had to save him. Without intending to, she had shattered the delicate, fragile theory he had constructed, reinforcing the lurking religious dogma Vogel barely managed to keep at bay.

She let her hand slide off of Vogel's body and watched as the stream of bubbles from the opening at her wrist grew thinner. Somewhere in the back of her conscious mind, she knew what that meant: her air supply, which had drained itself in a frenzy to keep the suit pressurized against the deep, was running out. She had perhaps enough time to return to the lab and save herself, but she realized with sick horror that she had not yet told Vogel what she had promised him. Her message about the ruins was not what he needed to hear—he needed her to reestablish his trust in empirical science. Her Lifting of him had only served to shatter what fragile lattice of rationality he had built against the tempest of superstition, and the knowledge of the ruins would do nothing to rebuild what once was. He had become a worshipper where he had once been a scientist—his world's first. And Sirra had done that to him.

She had traveled into his mind and soul, but her journey had been one of discovery for herself only. If she left now, would not Vogel think he had been tortured yet again by his devil? How could she possibly regain his trust in the future? Sirra knew that if she did not repair the damage she had done, he would never open his mind to her in the same way again.

Logically, she did not need Vogel anymore—he had told her everything she needed to know, and she had a moral obligation to return to the lab and tell the others. If she died down here, no one would ever know what the ruins meant. Besides, she did not know if she would ever be able to convince Vogel that his scientific theories, conceived unconsciously and developed without his true knowledge, were essentially the correct ones. How could she justify staying here to spare the feelings of a barely sentient alien when she had information vital to the survival of her entire planet?

She could not. She slid the gauntlet back onto her hand and snapped the coupling into place, then set her buoyancy control to maximum rise.

"I'm sorry, Vogel," were her last words to the brave, visionary vix who would never understand what he had done to deserve such pain.

Sirra shot upward towards the lab, only barely managing to get word to Fozzoli of her predicament before she blacked out.

"You'll be getting my bill later," Fozzoli's disembodied voice said to her. "I've picked you up twice now, and that kind of roadside assistance doesn't come cheap, you know."

Sirra managed to smile and opened her eyes. She was in the lab's infirmary. She tasted plastic and raised an unsteady hand to her mouth. She was wearing an oxygen mask. Her eyes focused enough to reveal Fozzoli and Khadre standing over her.

"I think you'll make it. Mild anoxia. Gonna take more than that to kill a tough old bird like you," Fozzoli said.

Khadre leaned in closer and said quietly, "I'm not an expert, but I don't think you were suffocating long enough to give you permanent brain damage. We've called in a team from the mainland," Khadre patted her shoulder, forestalling Sirra's objection, "and they'll be here in a few hours to transport you back."

"We had to, Sirra," Fozzoli said. "We didn't know how bad you were." He sobered and added, "We know it means they'll shut us down, and we'll be censured and all that, but...."

Sirra started to speak, but her throat burned and she coughed. She regained her composure enough to croak through the mask, "We won't. I know about the ruins."

Fozzoli's eyes widened. "You spoke to Vogel?"

"He spoke to me. I understand it all. Don't worry," she added, and closed her eyes again. The simple act of speaking had drained her. She drifted back into sleep.

The next time she woke up, she was looking into the eyes of a familiar male. His skin was unusually baggy, especially under the eyes, which gave him a somewhat hang-dog appearance. He flashed a penlight at her with clinical precision, and Sirra blinked back water.

"She's awake," the man said, continuing his check of Sirra's pupils.

"Yes, she is, and would you mind not shining that domed light at me?"

The man's lip twitched, and Sirra recognized him. He was Doctor Franshen Gernallas, one of the people on the physicians' board who certified researchers as fit (or unfit) for field work. He had done Sirra's physical half a year before.

Gernallas moved aside and withdrew the penlight to reveal Coordinator Kiv standing some distance away, in the corridor outside the infirmary, talking with Khadre and Fozzoli. "Mr. Coordinator? She's awake," Gernallas said again. Kiv, Fozzoli, and Khadre all tried to enter the room simultaneously. Sirra tried not to smile at the situation—then the memory of what she had done to Vogel sobered her instantly.

Fozzoli muscled ahead of Kiv and Khadre and approached Sirra's bedside. "How are you feeling, Sirra?"

"Much better."

"The doc's confirmed what we told you—no permanent damage."

"But there just as well could have been," Gernallas' voice sounded over Fozzoli's shoulder. Fozzoli mouthed the word "asshole" (Gernallas could not see that from behind Fozzoli) and continued. "Kiv's here, and he wants to talk to you."

"I see. We'll talk later, Foz. Thank you for saving me. Again."

Fozzoli grinned. "It's becoming my life's work." He squeezed her hand affectionately, then stepped aside.

Kiv approached her, his expression cool. "I am pleased you are recovering," he said evenly.

Sirra nodded. She felt no obligation to make the interrogation easier on him.

"I think you know why I'm here."

"I broke the rules. Again."

Kiv's lips tightened slightly. "Yes, you did. A direct edict from my office. I don't issue them often, nor do I do so lightly. You may have brought the entire vix population down upon us. I have had to recall our entire mercantile and industrial fleet—"

"Oh, stop it, Kiv," Sirra said, tiring quickly of his rhetoric. She heard Gernallas gasp quietly at her disrespect. "If you think that, you haven't read one page of any scientific report on the vix. You know very well that the various vix communities are isolated from one another. Even if the settlement under us is going to wage some kind of holy war against humanity, there is no way the other settlements could even know about it, much less coordinate any attack."

"I have read your reports, the ones you publish," Kiv said. Sirra knew that he had grouped all scientists together with the generic 'you.' "But it seems you know quite a bit more than you bother to tell the public, or your government."

"That's enough, Kiv," Khadre said, pushing past Fozzoli to come up next to the Coordinator. "You can reprimand us for what we've done, but don't start on some vendetta against all science because of your relationship with me."

"Khadre, do I have to remove you?" Kiv said over his shoulder. Sirra's eyes widened slightly at the tone in his voice: he hated his mother.

Khadre started to speak, but Sirra cut her off hastily. "Look, Coordinator, you want me to reveal what I know about the vix? I'm ready to do so. Foz!"

"Yeah?"

"Can you project the data in here when I ask for it?"

Fozzoli sighed his well-practiced expression of exasperation. "Well, I'll have to move the portable holothrower into here, and then set up a link to the main computer and get the stuff you want when you want it...."

"All right, then. Go ahead." Sirra said, then sank back into her pillows. Fozzoli left, grumbling, and Sirra started relating the data of the ruins based on Iede's interview with the gods.

"You mean she has been up to the remains of the ship?" Kiv asked a few minutes later when Sirra had finished telling him the story.

"I said so."

Kiv did not answer, but stared at the floor for a moment.

"That's not really the important point here, Coordinator. The point is—"

Kiv's head snapped up. "I am afraid none of you know yet about what has happened. A few hours ago, before I arrived here but after Doctor Fozzoli placed his emergency call to the mainland, Milante Observatory detected what we thought was a meteor shower. Closer examination revealed that it was Ship, or what was left of it, breaking up and entering our atmosphere. The debris fell into the Wide Sea at what our maps show as the deepest point, near a trench called...," he paused, and Khadre said, "the Sisyphus Trench?"

"That's the one."

There was stunned silence. Then Fozzoli, who had returned with the equipment while Sirra had briefed the Coordinator, said, "So Ship is...gone?"

"Yes. We think most of it has either burned up or fallen into the trench."

Sirra turned her head to look at Khadre and Fozzoli. It was Khadre who finally spoke. "She told us...she knew this would happen."

"Who?" Kiv asked, finally turning to look at his mother.

"Iede. She said, in the airfoil, that the gods would be giving her one last sign if all went well with the survey."

Fozzoli cut in. "This is a sign?"

"What else could it be?" Sirra said. "You don't think their orbit decayed suddenly, without any warning, and just happened to send Ship into the deepest trench we've yet found, do you?"

"Maybe they knew their orbit was decaying and that's why they brought Iede up to them," Fozzoli said.

Sirra shook her head. "I can't believe that any group that could keep Ship running all this time would not be able to keep a simple orbit stable."

"Pardon me," Kiv said, "but are you telling me you knew this was going to happen?"

Khadre swatted away the question impatiently and said to Sirra, "But the sign was supposed to be if all went well with the survey. How does Ship know that it did?"

"They must've been watching us," Sirra said.

"Even so," Khadre continued, "they can't read our minds, can they?" A brief, terrifying silence filled the room before Khadre said, in a shakier voice, "No. Not possible. So how did they know the survey was a success?"

"Wait a moment. Coordinator, sir, when did you say Ship started to fall?"

"We received notice from the Observatory about an hour and a half after your distress call came in. But to return to the point—"

"Could they have been monitoring my transmission?" Fozzoli said.

"You mean they killed themselves when you called for a doctor for me?" Sirra frowned. This didn't make any sense. "What exactly did you say?"

"Uh…." Fozzoli's eyes looked ceilingward. "Oh, well, here. I'll play it back." He used the holothrower to call up the outgoing messages database and selected the appropriate one. Fozzoli's voice filled the air.

"This is Research Station Bitter One calling EMS. This is Research Station Bitter—"

Fozzoli's voice was interrupted by the EMS respondent. "EMS here. Go ahead, Bitter One."

"I've got a diver down with anoxia and possible pressure damage. We've placed her on oxygen, but we don't have a doctor at the station at this time. We need an emergency team here immediately."

"Hold it," the EMS operator's voice lost much of its formality and sounded skeptical. "You're Research Station Bitter One, and you say you've had a diving accident? But there's no doctor there?"

"Yes, we broke the law, all right? Send some cops, too, if you like, but send a team. Doctor Sirra went down to talk to the vix. She must have removed her glove to talk to them better, or something—" Fozzoli looked at Sirra with a strange mixture of admiration and disapproval as his voice continued, " —and her suit must have started to depressurize—"

"All right," the EMS respondent said, sounding more frustrated than concerned. "I'll scramble a team and get them out there. But I'll also have to notify the Coordinator's office about this."

"Tell any domed one you want," Fozzoli's voice had reached a crescendo of anger, "Get the domed Coordinator himself out here, if you can get his head out of his—' Fozzoli switched off the playback. "Uh, that's all that is relevant."

"What's the rest?" Sirra asked as innocently as she could.

"The rest is not germane to the question at hand," Kiv said calmly, looking pointedly at Fozzoli, who had the grace to blush. "I have heard the transmission once before."

"But what's in there that might tell Ship that the survey went well?"

"Vogel. It has to be," Sirra said. "Somehow, Ship knows that the ruins are tied up with the vix."

"Are they?" Kiv asked.

"Yes. And I know how." She took a deep breath. "My official report will be far more scientific, but here's what I've patched together from my sources."

"One moment. Before you begin, what are your sources?"

The question gave Sirra a slight, grudging admiration for Kiv. He was just as interested in the discovery as anyone else was, but he held his enthusiasm in check pending her credentials, as it were. "You would have made a good scientist, Coordinator."

"My interests were elsewhere. Now, your sources, if you please."

"Well, the ruins were one. Nothing in particular, just their existence. But mostly, I base my hypothesis on the thirty or so years of experience I have had with the vix—studying them, learning their ways and their language. Although Doctor Fozzoli is far more expert than I at linguistics."

Fozzoli, surprised at being thus complemented, stammered, "Thanks, Sirra."

"That's all?" Kiv said. Sirra knew he suspected her talent. She had long since been rumored to have some magic power of perception that would have, in an earlier age, have branded her a witch but that now merely meant she was the winner in some genetic intuition sweepstakes.

"No. I also feel that the answer is the right one. I can't explain it much better, Coordinator. You're just going to have to trust me on this, to be later confirmed by independent analysis, of course. Now, may I begin?"

"Please," Kiv said, leaning forward. Khadre and Fozzoli followed suit. Only Dr. Gernallas appeared uninterested.

"The vix are the descendants of genetically-engineered surface dwellers who lived on this planet approximately eight thousand years ago."

Khadre and Fozzoli did not react visibly. Their scientific minds were no doubt hard at work already, trying to find confirming and contradictory evidence. Kiv, however, reacted much more like a layperson.

"What?" he said, his voice neither incredulous nor awestruck. He spoke as if he had not heard Sirra properly.

"I don't know if I can make it any more plain," Sirra said.

"Try to," Kiv said.

"The vix are not native to the seas. They were altered, bioengineered, to live there." She turned to Khadre. "That's why there are no vestigial organs." She turned back to Kiv. "Originally, some eight thousand years ago, the land surface of this planet was home to an advanced race. This race bioengineered what we now know as the vix, and for some reason, the surface dwellers died out, leaving only ruins."

"Why, Sirra?" Fozzoli asked.

She looked at him with exasperation. "I don't know. Vogel knew only the history, not the motives. All of the vix know, in a way. The facts of their...experience gradually became legend, then myth, and finally religion. We will spend quite a while unraveling it, but now that we have a place to start—"

"I don't understand," Kiv said calmly. He did not seem amazed at the revelation. "If the vix are animals who have been bred or engineered for intelligence then why—"

"No, Coordinator. The vix aren't sea creatures who were tinkered with by the land-dwelling natives—these *are* those natives."

"But...why?" Khadre said. Her voice was so searching that Sirra imagined Khadre was trying to reach back into the past to demand an answer form the long-dead air-breathers. "Why would they do this?"

Sirra shook her head. "I don't know." She looked up and found Fozzoli staring at her curiously.

"Sirra," he said, in a tone that made her dread what was coming next, "do you know all of this just from deduction? How could you possibly piece this all together from Iede's vision, the ruins, and Vogel's mind? You said yourself that the data has become a mystical religion to the vix, so how could Vogel possibly have known this?"

Sirra started at him, at once cursing him for reading her so well and forcing the issue on her, now, when the Coordinator could hear—and blessing him for his insight. Fozzoli was a smart man, and he knew her very well. All right, she thought, maybe this is for the best.

She did not take her eyes off him, but she could nevertheless feel Kiv's and Khadre's on her.

"Vogel doesn't know this, not really." She paused, summoning the strength to utter the words she knew would send her world into a new age. In the back of her mind, deep inside where her ancestral memory dwelt, she felt other women. She felt her grandonly Yallia there, who had secured the dominance of the Family against the Domers (a dominance, Sirra noted with newfound respect, that men like Kiv had tempered into compassionate rule of the remaining Domers) and whose power and rage were held in check by her sense of justice; she found her great-grandmother Kuarta there, who had made a great sacrifice for the goodwill of her race and whose calm strength pulsed quietly in Sirra; and she felt her great-great-grandmother, Jene Halfner, who had acted while others had merely watched. These women were in her; their genes were in Sirra's tissues and brain matter. Sirra knew, as they had known, that nothing would come from ignoring truth. Fozzoli had known it too, in his way—he had given Sirra the last necessary push to reveal what she knew.

"The vix are not experiments, or colonists, or freaks. They are outcasts. Written into their genetic code, or as my ha'lyaunt might say, their very souls, is a constant reminder of their sin. Their ancestors committed the greatest sin their race had ever conceived: they had wanted peace. Peace through cooperation rather than competition, peace through communal life rather than hierarchical struggle. And because of their philosophy, they were...changed. The ancient land-vix were masters of biology, though they had not yet achieved even rudimentary space flight. They sent their heathen brothers and sisters to the sea with adaptations that would allow them to live near naturally occurring oxygen vents to pursue their heretical ideas of social equality."

"So all of them are being punished?" Khadre asked.

"Yes. The sea is their exile."

Fozzoli shook his head. "That still doesn't answer my question. It just makes it more important. Sirra, *how do you know this?*" he pounded his fist into his thigh to emphasize his question.

"Every vix has the knowledge of their transgression written into their minds. I suppose it was part of the punishment. No vix grows up without massive guilt for a crime they are only vaguely aware of, and vix like Bishop and her descendants created a religion to try to cope with it. You were much closer to the answer than you thought, Foz. When I said I would not have discovered this, despite my...talent, I meant it. You translated their language in such a way as to be very, very close to their past. It was through your efforts that I was finally able to understand their...." Sirra paused, searching for the words. When they came, they were the most perfect descriptors of her meaning she could have hoped for: "...Original sin."

Khadre stepped to her son and placed a hand on his shoulder. Kiv did not seem to notice at first, then leaned towards her. Sirra looked back at Fozzoli. He was crying.

"They're just like us," he said.

Months passed before Sirra saw Iede again. She had tried to convince herself that the pressures of working on Vixian studies (the name for the natives had undergone a silent but overwhelming change from lowercase to capital initial letter on all official paperwork) kept her from visiting, but the simple truth was that she did not want to see her ha'lyaunt. She did not want to thank her.

Iede had aged alarmingly in the months after the trip to the ruins. Sirra had never been struck with her youthful appearance until it was gone. The two stared at each other for a brief moment when Sirra arrived at Iede's residence, then Iede's characteristic smile appeared.

"Have you come to bask in the glory of your...victory?" she said, and Sirra frowned. Not at the barb, but at the sentiment behind it. Iede had not only grown old, she had become bitter.

"No. I wanted to talk to you."

"Oh? About what?" Iede's tone indicated that she was not curious. She turned away from Sirra and retreated further into her residence.

Sirra stepped into her house and shut the door behind her. "About religion."

Iede straightened perceptibly and snorted in a manner remarkably like Sirra. "Now you want to talk religion. Now that my whole world has quite literally fallen on me. Now that the religion I have built has collapsed utterly." She whirled to face Sirra. "And you say you are not here to gloat?"

"I'm not. I just wanted to ask you—"

"No!" Iede exploded. Sirra was shocked into silence. "You won't do this to me! You have everything you want. Why do you come here and do this to me? Go away, Sirra. Let me live out the rest of my miserable days in relative peace."

"Iede...." Sirra began, then took a step closer to her. "You taught me something."

The words had their intended effect. Iede softened and became a bit more like her former self. Sirra continued before the moment died. "I did something that I am not proud of. Something that only you would understand."

Iede looked at her in anticipation.

"I had to abandon the Vix. One particular Vix. His name is Vogel. I had to...deceive him. The same way you were deceived."

"What?" Iede's face narrowed.

"Maybe 'deceived' is the wrong word for you. Hurt. I had to hurt him, in the same way you were hurt. Or the opposite way."

"I don't understand." Iede paused, but Sirra made no answer. "How could you know what I am suffering? How can you compare what happened to me, to my movement, with what happened to a Vix? Sirra, our connection with our home has been severed. Ship represented not just a guardian force looking out for us but a link to a past none of us have ever known directly. We've lost both now."

"Yes. And I know you think this is a curse. But—" Sirra continued through Iede's rising objection, "—it is a blessing. It's the best gift your gods could ever have given us. They have released us."

Iede did not answer. She looked at a spot on the wall past Sirra's shoulder. "What aren't you proud of?"

"What?"

"You said before that—"

"Oh. I did the opposite of what your gods did. They sacrificed themselves to free us and allow us to finally grow and make this planet our home. I cursed the Vix in such a way...."

"What happened?"

"Their chief scientist, or heretic, had a notion that the guilt built into their race by the engineers of eight thousand years ago was not real. He was beginning to transcend his own limitations, a feat of no small order. He was beginning to defeat his programmed religion. And I set him back. Perhaps for the rest of his life. I confirmed his religion and crushed his curiosity."

"Is that so bad? You yourself said religion was programmed into the Vix. Why should you change that?"

"You didn't see what I saw. Iede, you know how I felt about your religion."

"You made your feelings plain enough."

"It was a crutch, Iede. You'll see that soon enough. Your own gods believed that. Why else sacrifice themselves? But even your religion was based on something—you made a choice to create and follow it. I might disagree with your choice, but I can accept that you were in control, at least a little. Vogel wasn't."

"Vogel?"

"The curious Vix."

"Leave them alone. Their gods will—"

"We're their gods, Iede!" Sirra seized her halfonlyaunt by her upper arms. "Everything you told me about what Groundwatcher Aywon told you is true for us. I understand what he was saying, perhaps even better than you do. I don't want to be a god. Especially to a race with such a history as the Vix." Sirra released Iede's arms.

"Then go back and fix it. Like you were before. But you may find that religion is not easy to shake." Iede looked at her with hollow eyes. "You seem to think that religion is just an opiate to the masses. But it is real, as real as any chart or graph you scientists can create. You know my religion was based on something, and you know the Vix's is also."

"It's based on a misinterpretation and, in the case of the Vix, a genetic disposition that is not their natural makeup."

"Who is to say what the Vix were destined to be? You?"

"Yes. Domeit, yes!" Sirra turned away. "It is up to me to fix it. In such a way that it will never happen again."

"How? How do you determine the future of a race without becoming the God you wish to deny?"

Sirra did not face her. But she knew the answer.

EPILOGUE

Eelywhee swam toward the rock again. She knew her mother didn't much like it when she spent so much time in the water, but Eelywhee was a strong swimmer, even by humix standards. Besides, she would not get a chance to swim like this for many months if the mission went according to plan.

She reached the rock and glided up on its smooth surface. Night had fallen some time ago, and Eelywhee wanted to see the stars. She hoisted herself onto the rock and looked up. There was something eerie but exhilarating in simply seeing the stars. Her sonar was obviously no use, and the stars burned quietly above her like little else did on her world.

What would it be like up there? The *Iede's Odyssey* was orbiting above her, barely visible to the naked eye, and Eelywhee knew a crew was even now on board her, making final preparations for the voyage to the neighboring planet, nominally designated EE4 but affectionately known as "the Iceball" to those preparing to explore it.

Much had been made of the voyage, and many historians compared the trip to the one four hundred and twenty years earlier, made by the simple humans. One of her shipmates told her that those who had made the crossing reckoned time differently; to them, almost seven hundred years had passed since their arrival. Eelywhee had been interested enough to investigate this oddity and was surprised to learn that one of the second colonists, a woman named Jene Halfner, (an appropriate name for a mere human, Eelywhee had thought) had been a distant ancestor of hers.

Eelywhee knew her mother would be getting angrier and angrier as she stayed on the rock, looking up at the stars, but she was a grown fullwoman, ten years of age. Her mother no longer had any legal sway over her. Still, she owed her respect. She reluctantly slid into the water and swam speedily back to shore, savoring the flow of water over her back.

What must it have been like three hundred years ago, before there were any humix? Eelywhee wondered if she could have lived exclusively on land, like the humans (although she knew some of them made brief forays into the water if only for minutes at a time) or dwelled underwater and never known wind, or soil, or any of the many pleasures land offered. To be a half person—the thought was almost inconceivable, yet there were many millions who lived such a life. Their numbers were dwindling, to be sure—she had heard that only about one in ten was still simple human now, as compared to one in five not sixty years ago. They were respected, protected, and given full citizenship, of course, but Eelywhee was not the only humix to pity them.

And what would they find on Iceball? Would it be a rock in space, inhospitable to human and humix alike? Would there be life on it? Eelywhee thrilled at the prospect of discovery, even as she felt apprehension at leaving her home, though only for a few months.

But, she knew, it was the next step.

The End

CPSIA information can be obtained at www.ICGtesting.com
Printed in the USA
LVOW130812230413

330470LV00003B/286/P